GUARDED

The Silverton Chronicles

CARMEN FOX

SMART HEART
PUBLISHING

To Nana
WYWH

ACKNOWLEDGEMENTS

This book was a labor of love, and many, many people have helped me make it happen.

No one matters more to me than you, my reader. I rely on you to tell your friends, post reviews, and send me feedback. Without you, my stories would remain locked inside my desk drawer. Thank you.

My thanks also go to Laura and Julie, who witnessed the book's early days, when Ivy was still a shy little thing.

Many fantastic authors have taken the time to offer their advice along the way, among them Anna Stewart, Amanda Bonilla, Saranna DeWylde, Jaye Wells, Sharon Ashwood, and the wonderful Mary Buckham. You rock.

My editor Zoe Markham, my illustrator Dorin Olaru, and my book designer Ana Grigoriu were an inspiration. Thank you for your hard work.

I've had the best beta readers a girl can want, among them Cher G., Renée P., Lynn J., Dorothy C., Michelle B.S., Kelli W., Kari M., Melanie W., Mary H., and Mara S. I appreciate your efforts more than you will know.

Wonderful, wonderful Shaz. Your willingness to proofread means the world to me.

Finally, thank you to my family. All of you. Most of all Mama, Papa and Walter, Britta, Rebana, Björn and Michelle. HEDGL.

CHAPTER ONE

SHOOTING THAT CHEATING SON OF a bitch gave me a satisfying thrill. The moon was out, and scraggy branches obscured my cross-hairs, but I still got the bastard dead to rights.

My calf muscles contracted in a spasm. Crouching for twenty minutes would do that, I guess. I pushed myself up and shook out my legs. Save for the whistling of the wind through the trees, the park was quiet at this time of the night. The perfect place for clandestine activities. My boss called these night jobs 'character building exercises,' whereas I called them plain depressing. Our filing cabinets were a veritable cemetery for marriages, and my victim's name would soon decorate the next tombstone. My father could have landed there if my mother were a less trusting type. I swallowed. Not the kind of thing I liked to be reminded of.

I adjusted the angle and once again pushed the trigger of my Nikon D90. However did Mr. Wenthorpe lure his mistresses? Not to be cruel, but with his squat build and hawkish nose, my money was on expensive gifts rather than looks.

A strong hand clamped my shoulder. "Why are you spying on me?"

I wheeled around. Parker Reeves. My neighbor's broad ribcage rose like a living, breathing mountain.

My heart thumped in my chest, flipping one way then the other with enough force to startle me into retreating a few inches. Here was a man who should have no trouble attracting the ladies. Big brown eyes. A hint of stubble on a slightly rounded chin. His figure filling his jeans and tee nicely, with arms built for wicked dreams. A rush of warmth flooded my flesh.

But I didn't want to go there. Not with him. "I wasn't spying."

"You took photos of me." His glare folded his features into something feral. "I call that spying."

"How? I didn't even know you were here." I packed confidence into my words, even though my body urged me to scram.

"Are you going to hand me that memory card voluntarily?"

"You got this all wrong. I'm here for that guy." I pointed into the darkness.

He peered across to the empty bench, where my camera's victim had minutes ago slathered his hands over his curvaceous date. My pulse jigged. The guy had disappeared. A snarl erupted from Parker's throat.

"I can prove it." I fumbled with my camera and forwarded through the close-ups of Mr. Wenthorpe mid-pucker. "Satisfied?" I held the display up.

He studied the picture then aimed his frown back at me. "Let me say this only once. If I ever catch you pointing that camera at me, you don't want to know what will happen to you. Understood?"

My lips trembled and I pursed them tight.

He spun around and vanished among the bushes with more grace than his hulk of a body should have allowed. I pushed my hands into my jeans pockets, brushing the cool smoothness of the metal plates that had become my constant companions. Their presence gave me a measure of comfort. Then again, what good were my guards, the most potent magical weapons I possessed, if I didn't think to use them in times of danger?

I lifted my chin and stalked to the car. On the bright side, this could have gone worse. If Parker ever discovered I was aware of his *real* identity, I'd be puppy chow.

Underfoot, the trampled grass formed something akin to a path, yet bumpy enough to antagonize my delicate stomach. I touched my clammy forehead. Yup. I was coming down with something. What a crappy day.

I slumped into the seat of my car, willing my hands to stop jittering, and took off. My stereo's funky beats didn't calm me as much as distract me. By song number five I was tapping along. Parker's presence aside, I got the pictures I wanted. All in all, a successful mission.

The distinctive smell of petroleum entered the car's interior. I pulled a face.

Not again.

A couple of seconds later, my not-yet geriatric, but no longer youthful Ford Mustang stuttered and wailed. The thumping sound of 'Bad Religion' heaved it into my driveway, but I knew I might not get it started again. Dammit. My third repair this year.

A shadow peeled off a dark corner and rushed across the road. My thoughts of the unfairness of life lifted, and I smiled. Dressed in his usual muted colors, Florian gave a mock salute. Not even the lack of a California tan detracted from the fact that he was, by all accounts, a handsome devil. But it was his inner qualities that made him my best friend.

I got out and slammed the door shut.

Flo shot me his trademark grin that half begged to be mothered, half promised a naughty night. "Happy birthday, Ivy!"

"Not so far. I think my car's kaput." I sent an eyeroll toward the steam escaping the hood.

"Oh?" His forehead puckered. "Let's see. Did it slug and thud into the drive?" His index finger in his ear, he shook his tilted head, as if to force out some lingering noise. "Check. Is it stinky?" He sniffed the noxious plume surrounding the vehicle. "Check. Broken side view mirror? Check. Well, I can confidently say I notice nothing out of the ordinary."

"You're a funny guy, mister. If you're not too busy doing standup tomorrow night, do you think you could chauffeur me?" I pouted. "I have a work thing, and getting the car fixed might take some time."

"Aww, come here. Of course I will." He yanked me into a firm mother-bear hug.

I held tight. His fresh, if powerful, cologne was a scent for sore noses, and I added another couple of gratuitous sniffs. "Thanks. I needed that."

"I'll let you get some rest, then. You don't seem in the mood for a birthday bash. But if you change your mind, you know where to find me." Despite his curious looks at my front door, he knew better than to invite himself in. With a wave, he turned and crossed the road to the large building he and his siblings called home.

I *never* let anyone enter my house without at least half an hour's notice. The metal guards on my walls would reveal my secret. And more than anything, my friendship with Florian was based on mutual subterfuge.

He didn't tell me he was a vampire. And I didn't tell him I already knew.

I picked up the mail from my welcome mat, then dropped it and my bag on the small table by the coat rack. The background hum from the guards on my walls, one on each side, reassured me they were charged, yet I couldn't help but touch their patterned surface to double-check. These magazine-sized power houses protecting my home dwarfed the tiny metal plates I carried in my pockets, not to mention those on my charm bracelet and on my belt. But like their miniature counterparts, grooves meandered and intersected across the surface, ready to collect and discharge magic energy with the right spell. The patterns appeared random, unless you knew their secrets. One day, my life might depend on that knowledge.

I closed the curtains covering the big glass doors to my backyard, and picked the one birthday present I'd received off the back of the armchair. A little black dress Julia, Florian's sister, had given me at the break of dawn. I held it against myself in front of my tall bedroom mirror, then hung it in the back of my wardrobe. As if I'd have the balls, or the occasion, to pull off a sexy number like that. Julia's other present, pricey mandarin-scented body soap, fared better and was put to use straight away.

My shower was as fragrant as it was quick. Balancing a towel on my wet hair, I clamped a bottle of soda under one arm while the other hand carried my celebratory ice cream. Full fat, of course. None of that frozen yogurt, twenty-calorie crap for me today. The disc was already in the Blu-ray player. I placed my goodies within arm's reach and went to fetch the remote from the top of the cabinet.

The corner of an envelope peeked out from a bunch of glossy leaflets that had come in the mail. My heart hopped. Last week, my attorneys promised an update on my trust fund money, and after the day I'd had, I needed some good news.

The paper was off-white and velvety to the touch. My full name was written on the front in all-too familiar calligraphy: Felicity Jocinda Ivy Bell. Postmark: Silverton.

It couldn't be. With shaking hands, I turned the envelope over and glimpsed the signature. My heart thumped in my chest now, trying to carve its way out.

Lathan.

The name I'd hoped never to hear again.

CHAPTER TWO

M Y PERSONAL BOGEYMAN IN DEMON form. As if signing his name hadn't been enough, Lathan's insignia was printed on the back. I inched my fingers up my right arm and found the same mark. My throat tightened. He'd branded me the way he'd branded his stationery, with three jet-black pyramids woven together in a geometric abstraction of a cage. Images too horrific to put into words tripped up my thoughts.

I fumbled to tear open the delicate paper.

> *My dearest Felicity,*
>
> *Happy 25th birthday!*
> *My castle is empty without you. I had your private quarters decorated in preparation for your return. You are going to be pleased.*
>
> > *In eager anticipation,*
> > *Lathan*

I stared at the letter as if reading it again would erase the words and leave behind a blank page.

One shallow breath followed another. I shuffled across the carpet to the fireplace, nearly toppling over my feet. My hand found the lighter even if my mind wasn't keeping up. Fire sprang to life, its heat too brief to warm me. The paper went up in flames, and I didn't turn away until every last scrap had crumbled to ash.

Reasoning came back at a snail's pace. That had always been my problem. Feelings exploded from nowhere, and my thoughts had trouble keeping up. But they'd now joined the party and lost no time reassuring me. The laws of magic prevented someone as powerful as Lathan from putting as much as his pinkie in the human realm, or 'Oldworld.' The Rim, the border between the worlds and a feat of magical engineering, would suck his powers right out of him.

So why didn't my muscles relax? He'd sounded so confident. But what reason could he have for coming after me four years after I'd gotten away?

The letter was an empty threat. Had to be. Something to mess with my head.

One blow after another had combined to make this into the worst birthday. I yanked a sheet of paper from my jacket pocket, crumpled and a little torn. A two-story house with a glazed front stood overlooking the beach, and with four bedrooms, a skylight in each. There'd be space for dogs, perhaps a horse. My shoulders fell, my neck lost some of its tightness. I ran my thumb over the paper.

If Lathan thought he could destroy my dream, he'd be in for a hell of a surprise, because once I got the money to buy a house like this, perhaps a new identity, I'd be gone, and he'd never find me.

I wilted into the couch and opened the tub of ice cream. It was cookie dough, but all I tasted was the cold on my tongue.

———— ·•· ————

I got off the bus and took a deep, drawn-out breath, trying to blow away my headache. Lathan's attempt to psyche me out was bad enough, but the more immediate threat came from Parker. I was on his shit list now. He or a member of his household could waylay me anywhere, and I knew he was dangerous. So the frequent glances over my shoulder weren't paranoia, but precaution.

Then again, he'd be keen to uphold his image as a successful computer mogul who'd become one of Silverton's success stories. His mansion spoke of his wealth, although not as much as the acres of woodland that came with it. But like so many in this wretched town, his clean image hid a dirty truth.

As per my usual routine, I popped into the coffee shop on my way to work. Nothing beat the scent of fresh, strong coffee in the morning. I placed my order and skimmed the clientele.

All five men in the line stared at me. I shifted on my feet and shot them a tentative smile. The tall dude at the end had a Colin Farrell thing going on. Yes, I could get into him. The guy in front of him should be in some Viking movie, with fur and weapons covering his massive bare chest. Perhaps the two would be amenable to an Ivy sandwich?

Okay. That was weird. And totally gross. I wasn't a romantic like Flo, but I wasn't quite that easy either. For a guy to be in with a shot, he'd have to prove he could hold his own in terms of wit and brain power. Looks alone had never been a deciding factor. Perhaps it was their interest in me that had connected to my libido. Come to think of it, the guys on the bus had gawked at me as well.

On second thought, maybe I'd got it wrong and their attention was nothing to do with attraction. I wasn't even that pretty. Crap, did I have something in my teeth? I closed my smile, paid the barista, and hightailed it out of there.

The fresh air carried somewhat of a bite. I took the shortcut to our office, which was housed on the third story of an apartment block. Fred, my boss, insisted the peculiar location kept the overheads down, and we had the added advantage of being surrounded by our own neighborhood watch brigade. I was no more than thirty minutes late by the time the office door slammed shut behind me.

I deposited my breakfast on my desk, shook the chill from my jacket and relaxed. Time to stop driving myself crazy.

The glow from fitted lamps gave the room a gritty atmosphere, not unlike the detective agencies in old black-and-white films. Normally, my boss would sit on his swivel chair behind a monstrous, old-fashioned oak desk. Not today. For the first time since I'd known him, he'd taken time off work. He'd survived one hell of a year, and no one deserved a break more than he.

According to the list Fred had left, most of my day would tie me to my desk. The only variety I'd see would be a quick trip to the 'burbs to pick up a statue for a client. I called Flo to let him know what time I'd be home, and got started. First things first. I saved the original photos of Wenthorpe onto a flash drive we kept hidden in the safe behind a large watercolor landscape, then went about cropping them. One set of the processed photos went into the client's file, and I saved the other set on another flash drive for our official records.

The morning passed quickly, and I dedicated the afternoon to filling in forms and sending payment reminders.

"You've got mail," a woman whispered in her most alluring voice.

I checked my cell. Florian's text consisted of garbled words and exclamation marks. Over the years I'd learned to decode his messages. It was after seven p.m., I was late, and he was getting impatient.

Since the garage had confirmed my car was in need of expensive and elaborate surgery, and would remain in ICU for another few days, I rode the bus home. Florian stood outside his house, his finger not-so-subtly tapping his watch. Sheesh. Really?

Although he preferred hushed grays and dark greens, tonight he was dressed in black, from his expensive shoes up to his tailored shirt. Only the orange backpack he'd slung over his shoulder ruined the ninja apparel. A dark leather belt wrapped around his narrow waist. The guard etched into the buckle was a necessary fashion statement for any vamp who preferred not to shrivel up like dried apples during the day.

Many kin, from vampire to demon, relied on and used guards, but few could weave them. Florian's was of decent enough quality, produced by a capable weaver, but its copper base had long lost its reddish gleam. Still, I couldn't exactly make him a better one.

"What's with the bag?" I pointed at his colorful accessory.

He unlocked his new black Mercedes with a beep. "Supplies. Hop in."

The earthy smell of the car's creaky leather seats made me want to snuggle up and go to sleep. A stark contrast to my Mustang, which needed monthly refills of air fresheners to drown out the many pints of energy drink I'd spilled over the years.

Florian tossed the backpack on the seat behind him and faced me, awaiting my instructions. I dug out the file to check the address. He pulled out of his drive and joined the sparse traffic on the roads skirting the town center.

"It won't take long." I stuffed the file back into the bag. "Pick up a statue, and we're done. What are we watching tonight?"

"I don't mind, as long as it's funny and has smooching."

I grinned. "Smooching? What are you? Charlie Brown? Say kissing. Or sex." A shudder ran through me, perhaps from a draft.

He gave a suffering sigh. "Let's watch that movie about the British President."

I was pretty sure he meant the Prime Minister portrayed by Hugh Grant in 'Love, Actually.' "Yeah, okay."

Twenty minutes later, we reached the first signs of suburbia. Gone was the hodge-podge blend of mansions and in-the-sticks farmland of our Custer Fields.

"Welcome to the dark heart of Silverton." Flo sounded serious.

Here, the fashion *du jour* was to not stand out. The cars belonged to the same price bracket, the houses were built from the same blueprint, and most likely the people who lived here lacked any individuality.

I fumbled with the shoulder strap of my P.I. bag. "Thanks again for helping out."

He shrugged aside my gratitude. "It's not like I had a date. Besides, Julia's on my ass about where my life's going, and that it's not about getting laid." He snorted. "As if that's all I do."

I tapped the fingers of one hand to count off. "There's also daytime television, sci-fi books, celebrity magazines." I did a mock wave. "Pah, she doesn't know what she's talking about."

He shot me an oh-no-you-don't look. "And whose side are you on?"

"Why, yours, of course." I fluttered my eyelashes while curbing the grin that wanted out. "Wasn't that clear from what I said?"

"Could have fooled me." He shifted down a gear. "It wouldn't be too bad if my brother hadn't gotten a job. Traitor. Now it's, Eli this and Eli that, and why can't you be more like Eli. Glad she's out of town. I needed the break."

A sad smile crept onto my lips. I'd been friends with Flo's family since Dad had handed me the keys to my house, located opposite the Dupree's home, for my eighteenth birthday. In its former life it had served as a guard house for the mansion where Parker Reeves lived, but it had since been converted into a small family home. My neck muscles tensed, hot and painful. Leaving my friends would be hard. But Lathan's letter had only intensified the need to disappear from my current life.

"Anyway," Florian said, piercing my thought bubble, "I've now been reduced to least-wanted status at home and keep to my rooms. So, coming out here with you is the most excitement I've had in a week. Even if—" His finger surged forward in the direction of a street sign. "I think we're here."

He parked the car. Side-by-side, we strolled along the quiet road in search of number nineteen. The American cliché of happy families was evident in every white picket fence and manicured lawn.

Flo nudged me. "What do you know about the statue?"

"Fred said it's expensive." I kicked a tiny stone that tarnished the otherwise neat-as-a-pin sidewalk. "The guy who hired us told him it used to belong to his family a long time ago. The current owners, Melissa and Stephen Carter, inherited it from an uncle."

"There's nineteen." He jutted his chin at a large house with no remarkable features.

The lights were on downstairs, although thick curtains prevented anyone from looking in. The lack of toys and gimmicky window hangings indicated the Carters had no kids that might be woken by the sound of visitors.

I lifted my hand to ring the bell. Florian stopped me with a snap of his fingers. He pointed at the door. It was ajar. My heart lurched. I knocked three times, and the door swung open. With curled fists, I stepped into the entryway and made my way along the corridor. The smooth mosaic floor gave a clean, spacious appearance, emphasized by a large mirror on the wall and a small table with a crisp white table cloth. Patches of light illuminated the space from the room to our right.

"Hello?" I called into the silence.

A growl from behind made my skin crawl. I whipped around. Florian's face was grim, his posture unnatural and stiff.

The hairs on my arms stood on end, and I suppressed a shudder. "Are you all right?"

"Can't." He propped his hand against the wall. "Not feeling well."

My gaze followed the direction of his stare. Large crimson stains pooled on the immaculate living room carpet. Oh shit. Blood.

I turned back. Florian's pupils dilated to form two black marbles. His canines lengthened, coming to sharp and lethal points. The pounding of my heart overrode my motor skills, and for a second, I stood rooted to the spot.

This wasn't how I'd envisioned his secret being revealed to me. I'd pictured cupcakes, not a full-out blood frenzy.

At last, the switch labeled 'common sense' flipped and triggered me into action. I fingered the guards in my pockets. The small plates were my only chance.

"Harra-deferdi." The incantation to charge them reeled off my lips in a bare whisper. With every syllable, magic prickled along my skin, flowing into the grooves in the metal surface.

His muscles tightened. Like a hellhound on PCP, he pounced, teeth gleaming in the dim light.

My skin went cold. *"Fintero,"* I mumbled.

The guards expelled a blue and orange flood of crackling energy that slammed Florian into the wall. Its opposing force spun me into a coat rack. Pain exploded in my skull. I scrambled up and felt my temple. It was wet and sore.

He dove at me. At the last moment, I stumbled up and out of his way. His head whacked into the mirror, which shattered into a thousand sparkling pieces.

With fast, shallow breaths I slinked back against the wall. My thigh bumped into the corner of a set of drawers. *Crap, that hurt.*

I'd run out of space to move. "Please, Flo. Stop this."

He came at me again, his face gaunt and dead. Once more I activated my guards, stuffing in every scrap of energy I could scrounge together. The jet pulsed past his ear.

The smell of singed hair hung in the air. The heat drained from my body, leaving me with shaking limbs and a tired mind. One way or another, this confrontation had to end.

Skin magic was my last shot, no matter the cost.

CHAPTER THREE

I DUCKED UNDER FLORIAN'S ARMS AND rattled off the new spell. No more pulsating jets. A continuous stream of light hissed from my guards. Flo twitched under its electric field and strained against it, face contorted, but the magic wouldn't let him escape. Every second, the spell drained more life force out of me. My arms shook, and I ground my teeth.

I inched the heavy beam, with Flo in its focus, toward the open door. Perspiration ran down my temples. This had to work. One deep breath, one final push. Bright sparks flew off into the corridor's darkness. The force exploding from my guards smashed into his chest. He plowed past the threshold into the breezy night and collapsed in a heap on the grass.

I said a thank-you to whoever might be listening and threw shut the door between us.

Sweat burned my eyes, and I mopped it up with my jacket sleeves. My surroundings shifted from focused to blurry and back, and a giggle bubbled up from inside. For one wonderful moment, my muscles throbbed with power. My first use of the guards in a real-life situation had been a success. *Take that, kinfolk.*

After a few more breathtaking seconds, the high crashed. Bone-dragging fatigue and a bitch of a headache trailed the giddiness. I pressed my palm against my thumping forehead. Instead of *skin magic*, kinfolk should be calling it *ninja* magic. You think it's cool, until it kills ya. With my eyes shut, I leaned against the door and wiped my brows.

Although I'd been told about blood frenzies, Florian's change from best friend to psycho had taken me unawares. His human façade had lulled me into believing myself safe.

Even now I couldn't wrap my brain around it. Knowing he lay bruised on the other side of the door made my chest ache. I swiped my hand across the smooth paintjob of the door, twitching to open it. But he should be his old cheery self when he came to. All he needed was to stay out of the house, away from the smell of blood.

My nerves still in a jumble, I glanced toward the living room. With considerable delay, the private investigator in me jumped into action. First things first. Where was the blood's owner? Not inside, because the ruckus would have alerted them to my presence. Had he, she or they managed to call an ambulance?

I stepped inside the room. While my home was minimalist for a lack of time to shop, the Carters' choice to forego original features seemed deliberate: white carpet, white sofa, white pillows, and white curtains. Even the TV set was housed in a unit of the same deathly shade. Or used to be, anyway. Now, two merging pools and the matching splatter on the walls, furniture, and ceiling added a touch of color. Like a sick piece of art. Whatever happened here hadn't been pleasant, yet by my reckoning it had been quick.

I bit my tongue against the metallic smell, and with self-imposed detachment searched the room for a phone to call the police, while alert for clues. Since my detective experience of handling murder scenes was pretty much zero, nothing useful jumped out at me.

I tripped. *Well, lookie here.* The very item we'd been hired to retrieve. I picked up the statue and grimaced. The owners had had a reason for tucking it away on the ground near the sideboard. The statue was a tiny little thing, no bigger than my hand. In terms of shape, it resembled a flattened cat, or a deformed lizard. Maybe the rock had been too hard to carve into something pretty, although they'd buffed and polished it to a high shine.

Should I take it? Our client had already paid for it, so by law it was his. On the other hand, this *was* a murder scene.

My ears pricked. A whisper came from somewhere.

Slam.

I jerked round toward the rear of the house.

Dammit. My fight with Florian had made a right old rumpus, but since nobody had asked us to keep the noise down, it hadn't occurred to me the assailants, or indeed killers, might still be here.

Loud voices announced the presence of two men headed my way. There was no time to run outside, at least not without being spotted. I jumped behind the long drapes nestled in the corner of the window. For good measure, I shifted a large potted plant in front of me.

"Is no right, Max. If we bury instead of dump in backyard, it takes cops longer to find."

"Idiot. You think a bloody mess in the livin' room don't look suspicious? Course they'll look in the yard. Don't know why we tried hidin'em. Did a right job on 'em, didn't ya? Shoulda brought Jeff instead." The man groaned. "This was meant to be a quiet gig."

"Ah, it is done. Do not worry your head." The other guy gave a hearty belly laugh.

Max sniffed. "Well, you coulda waited till they said where they put the damn thing."

"If statue's here, we find it."

My fingers tightened around the cold, polished form in my hand.

Doors slammed, chairs thudded, feet clomped, and pillows ripped. Max and his partner rained down chaos on the house. I nosed the curtain ajar and stole a glimpse to assess my situation.

"Shit," the one with the strong accent said. "I don't find it."

My stomach somersaulted. Okay, situation assessed. If my internal kin-radar was to be believed, the two rough but otherwise normal looking dudes were in fact demons. I closed my eyes, forcing my galloping pulse to slow. If I stayed here, I'd be found. No way would they let me walk away, even if I handed over the statue like a good girl.

"I ain't taking the heat for your mess." Max sounded determined.

Careful not to shift too much, I stashed the statue in the back pocket of my jeans and slid my hand toward the front. My house keys jangled. Shit. I clasped my fist around them.

"Hang on," Max said. "Hear that?"

The tearing and shuffling stopped. I stiffened, my breath caught in my throat.

"I hear nothing. Maybe they have cat?"

I swallowed past the fist in my throat. I had to risk it. Inch by inch, I slid my guards out of my pockets until I held one in each freezing-cold hand. The incantation to charge them rolled from my lips. At least one thing was working for me.

"If there was a cat, I'd know. I'm allergic."

Footsteps drew closer, and I braced myself.

"Think it came from the window here."

One was so close I smelled his musky aftershave. Going by the grunts, the other demon trailed right behind him. The nausea in my guts pushed its way up. Since my power reserves were drained, I had one shot at overpowering them.

Afterward, I'd run like hell and take my chances with the crazy, blood-thirsty vampire outside.

My options totally sucked.

"Okay. Not cat. Maybe is Jeff?" the one who wasn't Max said.

"Nah, Jeff was told to wait outside. He does as he's told."

One moved the plant aside while the other stepped up and whisked the curtain back. They looked at me, eyebrows raised high.

I smiled the smile of a brave little toaster. "Hi guys."

Max's scarred face twisted into a spiteful grin, and his hand shot out. "Gotcha."

My lungs rattled, and I raised my guards to release the energy. Glistening magic spilled into the men. They crashed back the length of the room like they were attached to an elastic band. A tall lamp wobbled and collapsed on top of them. I didn't take the time to be impressed by my handiwork, and made a beeline for the door. The mirror shards nearly became my downfall. *Don't fall. Do not fall.* They slipped under my feet, and it took both arms to regain my balance.

I was outside, halfway to the sidewalk, when the house door slammed. A thump and a moan slowed my steps, followed by the sound of bone on bone. I wheeled around and sneaked into the shadow of an oak.

Florian was up.

With frightening speed he punched the first demon in the face and kicked the other in the stomach. Auburn hair that fell in waves to just below his ears swayed with each brutal move. A crunch. I winced. He'd broken Max's neck. The body fell to the ground and landed at an odd angle.

The other guy brandished a knife. Flo was a lot faster and ripped it from his hand before the demon had taken half a step. Demons could lift boulders and punch holes through brick walls, yet Florian wafted this one aside as if he was an annoying fly. Strength didn't count for much without the speed to connect with your opponent, apparently.

Florian brought the dazed demon's neck to his mouth and sank his fangs into the guy's throat. His shoulders moved up and down as he drank deep.

Cold sweat burned the skin on my back. Vampires didn't kill for blood. At least that's what I'd been told. The demon snack slid to the ground. Florian rolled his head. His fangs retracted, and his tongue flicked around his mouth and teeth, like a cat's after a meal.

I retreated further into the low-hanging branches, rustling their leaves. My heart banged inside my chest. *Quiet.*

"Don't run, Ivy." His voice coaxed. "I'm not hungry anymore."

At least he recognized me. I didn't move, but held my guards at the ready.

He advanced. His intense brown eyes, the kind seen in novels of the bodice-ripper genre, shone like two wells of oil. Was the dark figure gliding toward me *my* Florian, or still a creature in the throes of a blood frenzy?

His fluid and deliberate steps made no noise. My gaze was glued to his mouth. If those fangs made another appearance, I'd be out of there. For now, I'd stand my ground, hoping my thumping heart wouldn't set off another fit of violence.

If only he'd show me that impish grin of his, or the customary twinkle in his eyes, I'd be sure everything was fine. He stopped less than two feet from me and leaned forward. My breath stilled.

CHAPTER FOUR

THE GASH IN MY FOREHEAD pulsed hot under Florian's breath. He planted a kiss on my cheek. "Better wipe our prints off the door handles before the cops get here."

Startled by the contact, I snapped out of my stupor. "Are you better?"

His irises were back to their usual deep brown. "I've sated my hunger. Still, better not stay here for too long." Sparing no glance for the massacre he'd created, he headed toward the car.

I let out the mother of all sighs, lifting the back of my T-shirt a couple of inches to air out the sweat. A cucumber scent hit me, a sure sign my deodorant had been working overtime. I stepped over the bodies and the puddle of blood, on the lookout for witnesses. Nothing moved. Still, I wasn't going to stick around.

I nudged open the door and stopped. My neck tensed. What was that noise? I glanced around. "Florian?"

No reply. The breeze had gained strength, ruffling branches and swishing grass helms across the drive. I swallowed my unease, gathered myself, and went inside.

Uncertain as to what objects I'd handled, I wiped along the surfaces I assumed people would touch in a situation like this. My gaze skimmed over the red-sodden carpet to make sure I hadn't stepped in the blood. Without locking the door behind me, I hurried out toward the car, wary of the lingering shadows. Each streetlight cast a different shape onto the sidewalk, like hooded figures waving their fists.

The Carters were dead, and we'd killed two more people. Why wasn't I screaming my head off? Perhaps the breakdown would come later.

I picked up the pace and didn't stop until the door handle of Florian's Mercedes was in my palm. I swung open the passenger door, but didn't get in. Not yet.

"You definitely all right now?" I asked across the roof, limbs tensed, fight-or-flight response on standby.

"Yes, I'm fine." He gave me a sheepish look. "I guess we have a lot to talk about, don't we?"

"I guess we do."

He sat and patted the passenger seat. "Come on, hop in. I won't bite. Not unless you ask me to."

He seemed to have flicked the experience aside like it was all in a day's work. And maybe it was for him. Nervously, despite his assurances, I removed the statue from my jeans and climbed in.

A wail of sirens whooshed by. We shifted low in our seats. Two more police response units, light bars flashing, blew past us. Up and down the street, houses came to life. Heavy curtains were whisked aside everywhere. Seems the exchange hadn't been as quiet as I thought.

Flo started the ignition. "Home?"

"Hell, yeah."

We were locked in silence, although I didn't miss his confused glances. Perhaps it was time to say something. I shifted and was about to open my mouth, when high beams shone into Flo's rearview mirror.

He blinked and ducked. "Idiot." He pulled into his driveway, and the other car bulleted past, too fast to see my hand gesture.

"Good talk, Ivy." The corner of his mouth twitched.

The engine idled, the heater on max, but the warmth streaming in didn't thaw my icy bones. I took a deep breath. "Okay, I'll go first then. As you've guessed, I've got a measure of familiarity with guards and, you know, things that go bump in the night."

"You mean things like me?"

"It's a long story."

He snorted. "Okay, then. Take all the time you need."

I bowed my head, unable to shake my stiff, almost painful posture. "I was kidnapped when I was nineteen, brought to Alethia to work as a slave, creating guards so that Lathan could sell them."

"*The* Lathan?" Flo's eyes widened.

I nodded. "Humans make perfect slaves. No magic whatsoever, as far as I know, and easy to break. Something broke in me too, I think, because one day I no longer needed his running commentary to understand what species another person was. I'd developed kind of a sixth sense for that." I scoffed. "After nearly two years, Lathan was certain I'd never leave him. He talked about our great destiny and how we'd rule Alethia one day. Even reduced the number of watchmen that followed me around."

"But you got away?"

"His advances got increasingly urgent, and I wasn't sure how long he'd accept my 'no' as 'no.' So I took a chance and overpowered a merchant preparing to travel to Oldworld."

"A fae, I assume?"

"Of course." I gave a brief smile. The fae's feeble magic was the subject of many jokes among the kin. "The Rim only allows beings of little or no magic through its portals. Good thing, too. Anyway, I took his place to hop through the gate and, well, that's how I got home."

Florian flared his nostrils and inhaled. He gazed to the front of the car, onto the high brick wall shrouded in shadows. "Why would Lathan get someone to teach you how to wield guards? It's a downright stupid idea to give your prisoners the means to defend themselves."

"Think of it like inmates making license plates, except these license plates can be weapons. Anyways, I was trained to *weave* guards, not wield them as weapons."

"Could've fooled me." He rubbed his chest.

"Can we leave it, Flo? It's not so much that I don't want you to know, but talking about it brings it back. I'd rather not dwell."

"Okay. I get it." He nodded. "By the way, you're welcome. You know, for saving your life."

"Thanks," I mumbled. "Of course you also tried to end it. Unless it's normal for a best friend to whip out a pair of fangs, but I don't recall Cosmo mentioning it."

His shoulders jerked down. "That's who I am."

"Guess so."

"Are we okay then? Me a vampire and you Xena Warrior Princess?" The twinkle returned to his eyes.

He moved forward and we hugged. His lack of a pulse didn't bother me, and under the car's blower, his skin had heated up nicely. In fact, I found it hard to let go.

I rested my hands on his shoulders, and the hammering behind my eyes ceased. "If you're okay with this, I'm good, too."

He leaned back and ran a finger along his chin. "I hate that you were alone through your dark time."

"Yeah. Well, except for your sister."

He stiffened. "You told *her*?"

"Only because she weaseled it out of me." I lifted my palms. "She taught me more about kin life in Oldworld than I knew from my time in Alethia." My teeth plucked my bottom lip. "It's not like I can ignore them, you know. Kin, I mean. I can sniff you guys out. One look, and I know what you are. Guess you can appreciate the nerve it takes to leave the house."

He gripped my hand. "It explains why your social life is deader than three-week-old road kill."

A smirk rolled over my face. "Well, if your first long-term suitor had been a crazy-ass demon who put on a show of torture to sweet-talk you, you'd find it difficult to trust, too."

Amazing how easy it was to make light of my year in hell, but it was the only way I knew how to cope. Denial also played a huge part. What choice did I have? Hiding under the bed wasn't my style.

Florian switched off the engine and frowned. "You look pretty banged up there."

I accepted a tissue from his mysterious bag and swiveled the rearview mirror to eye the gash on my temple. Blood had trickled down my cheek and was already in the early stages of drying. Although a little spit helped the caked blood come off, it couldn't hide the wound itself. "Does this bother you?"

"A few drops won't send me into a blood frenzy, if that's what you mean, but seeing you like this... Of course it bothers me. And it was my fault. I'm so sorry." He rummaged in the first-aid kit he'd taken from the back seat. He produced two hideous adhesive bandages with the Superman logo in bright colors. He pressed one into my hand for later, and he stuck the other on my forehead. As a final touch, he planted a kiss right on top of it. "There, there. All better now." He readjusted the mirror. "So those guys back there. Could you tell what they were? They didn't taste human."

I bunched my mouth. "Demons. Small fish, thank God. If they'd been mid-level or higher, we'd be the ones without a heartbeat now."

"No heartbeat either." He prodded his chest. "Don't be speciest."

"Sorry."

"Any idea what they were doing there?"

"I think they were after this." I held up the statue.

"Okay, it's hideous." Florian said it like it was a clue of vital importance, and grabbed it. "It's our statue, right? The one we were supposed to pick up?"

"Looks like."

"Might be a magical artifact." He rotated it between his hands and looked at it more closely. "Whatever it is, it's probably dangerous."

"Four people are dead." I lowered my voice. "Something tells me it's not a lucky charm."

He laughed. "But demons don't make friends with other demons. Not even those scraping the bottom of the barrel."

I snatched the statue back from him. "Either they were after a huge payout for this thing," I wiggled it, "and this new spirit of cooperation is temporary, or there's a real bad-ass out there who's got enough magical muscle to get them organized." The more I thought about it, the more the idea of keeping the statue close made me jittery.

"So maybe it's best if we hang on to it for the time being." Florian gave the polished rock a cold stare, but made no move to take it off me.

I let myself out of the car. "I guess."

We interlocked arms and headed toward my house. After tonight's adventure, I appreciated the company, even if it was only a short hop across the road.

"I've been thinking." Florian sounded tense. "Since becoming a vampire, I haven't found my place in this new world. Maybe Julia's right and I should get a job." He tilted his head. "Especially since she threatened to stake me if I didn't get my act together."

Yes, that sounded like his sister.

He peered to his house before returning his attention to me. "My guard keeps me safe from the sun, although I'm of limited use around noon on a sunny day."

"About that. The guard on your belt is decent enough, I guess. But if you like, I can make you a better one. One that should let you survive the sunniest day without hiding."

"Thank you." His focus shifted past me. "It's an heirloom. I got it from my sire. You know, the guy who made me."

"Oh, okay." Wow. This was the first time Flo had confided something personal in me. My heart contracted. Guess we'd broken through the last of our barriers. I smiled and placed my hand on his arm to encourage him to expand.

His gaze landed back on my face. "Anyway. A midday slack period isn't a problem in your line of work, is it?"

I narrowed my eyes. "Hang on. Are you angling for a job?"

"Why not?"

"Are you serious? I think tonight's given you the wrong impression. A P.I.'s job's usually a lot more sedate. Mainly paperwork. On a good day, talking to a handful of people. All dull. And you won't get to bed them or eat them afterward either."

Florian pulled a face, somewhere between profound hurt and a pissed-off cocker spaniel. "Okay, let's get this straight. Food and people—two completely different categories. I'm still the same old human me. Believe me, feeding's tough enough on the soul, even if I don't socialize with my...meal." He stopped in front of my door and turned me toward him by my shoulders. "So, assuming there's no pool of blood around to awaken the frenzy, I'm perfectly capable of talking to people without eating them."

Ooh, touchy. Somehow I'd violated an unknown code of conduct.

Right. Accusing someone of random acts of violence, no matter how justified, was taboo. Check.

I wedged the toe of my sneaker into the gap between two slabs. "You're right. I'm sorry."

Who was I kidding? The chance to spend more time with my best friend before I left for good wasn't something I'd deny myself. "I'll square it with Fred when he gets back. Only as an assistant, though. Don't go getting any big ideas."

"You won't regret it."

"Pick me up on Wednesday, and we'll see." I unlocked the door and stepped inside. A vampire as a private investigator was a wacky idea, and today's events didn't fill me with too much confidence. But maybe, just maybe, he'd work out.

CHAPTER FIVE

I TOSSED AND TURNED MYSELF INTO a semi-dream state, but it held no peace. Not surprising, given who my nightmare caller was.

"There you are, my love." Lathan's familiar voice cut through my already confusing images.

The tension drained from my limbs like liquid butter. His hushed singsong slid deep into my mind, like sticky fingers poking and prodding my skull. Yanking on threads of not-yet-formed thoughts and molding them into ideas of his design. I stood in his private chamber looking out through the glassless window.

Without a sun or a moon, Alethia's sky shimmered in a perpetual gray-orange hue which reflected dark red in the Maroon Lake. It was a place of stunning beauty. Most kin here couldn't conceive living anywhere else. And yet, all I dreamed about was to one day return to my four walls, staring at the yellowed grass in my backyard.

My hands pressed tight against the window sill. My body ready to fling itself out, to escape my prison. In the distance, a dusky pink bird with long bony legs soared across the lake just above the water level, and with a brief flutter of its truncated wings it landed in a barren tree to settle in for a nap.

I'd been here many times before, by this window in Lathan's room, watching the same bird. My body shuddered in anticipation of what came next. On cue, Lathan's large hands slipped around my waist. He pressed me close against him, his breath warming my neck when he bit my earlobe.

"We belong together."

His words flowed into my body, drenching my mind with his will. Even though a tiny part of me wanted to shake off his embrace, a moan fought its way through to my lips and I basked in the truth of his words. Lathan was the most powerful of Alethia's seven kinlords. He was forever. And I belonged by his side.

"Come to me, my love. I am yours, as you are mine. I'm... still... standing, better than you. Looking better day by day..."

What?

My eyes blinked open to the radio alarm clock which blasted out a rocky tune. My pulse rattled out of sync with the song. Light teased the curtains, but didn't quite dare enter my bedroom. With a frown I pushed myself onto my elbows and sorted through my thoughts. This was what it must be like to get acid flashbacks.

Sweat drenched the fabric of my Hello Kitty jammies and left a taste of salt on my lips. I wiped away a few involuntary tears and counted my heartbeat until I was calm. The nightmare was a familiar visitor, but somehow my revulsion for the demon had lacked fervor this time.

The terrors of the night lost their ferocity when confronted with my morning routine of a quick workout, breakfast, and a shower. I lounged about the house until noon, drinking more coffee than was good for me. Once more I phoned the lawyers dealing with my dad's estate and my trust money, who assured me they were doing their best to cut through the red tape, but I should expect not to see a penny for another few months. Their feet-dragging didn't surprise me. After all, they were paid by the hour.

More time with Florian. There were worse fates.

The flip side was a few more months at risk from Lathan, having to put up with Parker and Co., and ignoring the kinfolk that Silverton attracted like honey attracted Pooh Bear. After a quick lunch of cereal and an apple, I needed a rest from the strenuous relaxation. Armed with a magazine, I kicked back on the bench in my backyard.

The grass out there had the parched look it got when you didn't own a sprinkler system. I cast an envious glance over at the large house next door. The drive that wound past my house widened into a parking lot of sorts, framed by the mansion's immaculate lawns. Immaculate, because Parker Reeves wanted them that way.

The honking of a car's horn out front caught my attention. I jogged through the house to the peephole to check who it was. My shoulders slumped. My mother. I fought the instinct to hide in my closet and opened the door instead.

Her gaze flicked up to the adhesive bandage with the Superman logo on my temple, and her eyebrows lifted a fraction.

Standing at five foot four, Mom and I were of more or less equal height. This was where our resemblance ended. On the inside, we were even more at odds. I was my father's daughter, from my willful dark-reddish hair to the tiny round nose I'd love to exchange. My heart pinged with pain. Despite our differences, I missed my mother, at least our bouts of silliness, our card games, and most of all, her hugs. But these wonderful memories stemmed from a time when Dad was still around. Since she married Alan, we hadn't seen eye-to-eye on many things. Maybe our relationship would be different between us if she knew about my ordeal at Lathan's hands, but any mention of magic or demons, and she'd surely ship me off to a highly secure, albeit top-of-the-line mental facility.

"Hi." I tried to quench the rising nostalgia that made me want to throw myself into her arms.

She fixed me with her gaze. "Hello, Felicity."

I hated that name. "What are you doing here?" I swallowed. "I mean, what brings you here?"

She frowned. "Civilized people wait until the guest enters the house before they start an interrogation."

Oh crap. If she tried to get in now, she'd run into my guard's invisible shield. That would be tough to explain. On the other hand, once invited, my guards would recognize her and allow her unhindered passage any time she wanted.

It was a tough choice.

I lowered my head and stepped aside. "Come on in."

Not a moment too soon. She breezed past me toward the living room. It was her second visit since I got back from Alethia four years ago, and last time, I'd had plenty of advance warning to stash the guards under my bed and behind my sofa.

She peered at the wall behind me, and her nose wrinkled. Complicated shapes and grooves meandered through the copper plates, each line with a specific purpose. She walked up to a guard and studied the pattern for a moment.

Crap. Don't touch them.

"It's art," I said, for want of a better explanation, and steered her away. Even though I'd designed them for functionality rather than esthetics, I liked to think of my guards as art.

"Is the artist a friend of yours?" My mother sounded concerned. The idea of *her daughter* being friends with artsy folk must terrify her.

"Yes. Absolutely." I maneuvered her through the French doors into the yard.

"Have you had a chance to mingle with your neighbors yet?" Her chin pointed toward the mansion. "They've lived here for a while, haven't they?"

"Only about a year, and they're not that sociable." I motioned to my garden bench. "Look, Mom, not that I'm not happy to see you, but was there a reason you came?"

She turned to me and lifted her chin. "I was on my way to an exhibition of Indian art and pottery. The mayor is going to be there. Anyway, your house was on our way, so I thought we'd drop off your birthday present. Alan's getting gas."

She handed me a gift bag decorated with pink flowers. A faint warmth covered my heart and brought forth a smile. The card read, *To Felicity, from your Mother and Alan.*

My smile faltered. We weren't what one would call an affectionate family.

I peeked inside the bag.

"I would have brought it over yesterday," she said, "but first an emergency with the maid, then a Rotarian function. You know how it is."

"Sure I do." I kept the sarcasm to a minimum.

The tight dress I pulled out was a bright red, although it wasn't the color I minded so much as the length, or rather lack thereof, which bordered on slutty. If I didn't know better, I'd assume she and Julia were competing to see who'd get me to wear the least amount of clothing.

I shot Mom a big, toothy grin. "Thank you. I love it."

My superb acting earned me a smile from my mother. If these rare signs of warmth were a regular feature, I'd feel crappier about leaving Silverton at the first whiff of my trust fund. But in our relationship, less was more. Countless times I'd called and tried to reconnect, but her life since Alan was about him, his work, and her charities. She probably wouldn't even notice I was gone.

My heart contracted. She didn't the last time.

A cough to our right rippled the air. Parker stood stone-faced at my yard's perimeter. The six-foot-plus broad-chested power house of danger appeared like a bronze statue molded and cast by a perfectionist.

Heat rose into my cheeks and I shoved the dress into its bag. Arms crossed tight in front of me, I got to my feet.

"You must be the neighbor." My mother beamed at him. "Why don't you come on over?"

"Mom." My voice was too quiet.

He stepped over the shin-high fence.

Mother rushed up to greet him. "Where are my manners? I'm Maggie Smith. I assume you know my daughter Felicity?" With this, she grabbed me by the elbow and pretty much yanked me in his direction.

Despite my growing panic, I accepted his outstretched hand, while keeping my eyes low, too confused to form any coherent thought that went beyond *shit, shit, shit.*

"You'll have to excuse my daughter. She's shy." My mother gave a but-what-can-I-do shrug.

"No problem." His rumbling inflection resonated deep in my body. The guards I carried offered protection against many kinds of mind magic, but something about him nudged my senses. Like a ghost hand prodding the inside of my chest.

"I'm Parker Reeves. Nice to meet you both." His gaze shifted over the dorky Superman logo on my forehead. "I should have popped in sooner, Felicity. My schedule's been difficult. I wanted to apologize to you about the other night in the park. I was wrong to accuse you."

Surprise tugged at my eyebrows. "Thank you," I whispered. "I appreciate it."

"Please don't worry." Mom's smile was all honey. "I'm sure it wasn't as bad as that. Still, it's terribly nice of you to come over to apologize, isn't it?" She prodded my ribs.

I pressed my lips together. There's nothing like my mother to bring out my petulant side.

"So, Parker." She moved next to him and hooked her arm into his. Her voice had taken on a conspiratorial tone. "This is a big house to live in by yourself." She fluttered her eyelashes. "Or do you live here with your wife?"

My throat dried. Not even my repeated coughs steered her off-topic.

"No, ma'am." He shook his head. "I'm not married."

I let my shoulders droop. She was acting like he was just a man. And right now, he even looked like that was all he was.

GUARDED

His gaze darted from left to right, perhaps seeking a way out of my mother's tight grip. *Oh, Parker. If you knew what's good for you, you'd run right now.*

Mother versus werewolf. This was *Thunderdome* all over again.

CHAPTER SIX

M OM PATTED PARKER'S ARM AND steered him away from the corner of my yard that had once been a flower oasis and now was a pile of dirt. "Look, I've had a marvelous thought. You two are neighbors, but Felicity tells me she doesn't know anything about you. How about you and her get to know each other a little better?"

Ground, open. Swallow me. Please. I peered at him, an apologetic smile on my lips.

The poor guy's features showed a jumble of emotions. His gaze pivoted between me and my mother. "Well, I mean…"

"Felicity has an open schedule." Her face made sure I didn't contradict. "So maybe you two could grab a coffee sometime?"

Why was he nodding? He was supposed to be stronger than that. Stronger than a short woman with a slight build and a skewed sense of romance. He was an alpha werewolf, for crying out loud, and bossiness was in his genes.

"That's marvelous." My mother didn't give him a chance to change his mind and returned him to the fence, his cue to leave.

"Nice…to meet you." One last puppy-dog glance at me, and he stalked off.

She dragged me along with her toward the house.

My cheeks were on fire, and I felt like a harem girl who'd been sold to the highest bidder. "You shouldn't have done that."

"Well, are you seeing anyone?"

I glanced at my feet. We'd covered this ground many times. But a werewolf? Oh, Parker and his pack made for convincing humans. They paid their taxes and were by all accounts law-abiding citizens, leaving the rest of humanity unaware of their presence among us. But not me. I sniffed out his kind a mile away.

"I thought so." Once again her tone reeked of absolute conviction. "You'd better find someone soon, Felicity, or you'll end up an old maid. Mark my words. Your looks won't last forever."

I was twenty-five. Nice to know I was on the downward slope already.

"Besides." She nudged me. "I can tell when people are meant for each other. Just wait."

The doorbell rang. I ran to open it, relieved to put distance between me and the source of my humiliation.

My stepfather stood in the doorway, his mouth twisted in an awkward smile. "Hello, Felicity. Sorry, I'm late."

I invited him in and thanked him too for the birthday present. If I hadn't been looking for it, I'd have missed the slight tightening around his eyes when he noticed my *art*.

Alan and I had our issues, but it wasn't like Mom consulted me about falling in love with him. By the time I'd returned from Alethia, they were already engaged. She didn't talk much about him to me, perhaps to spare my feelings, but she once let slip they'd both lost their partners. I dug deeper. Imelda Chesterton, Silverton's premier gossip queen, confirmed Mom's story and added Amanda, his fiancée, had run off with one of his business partners.

In the beginning, we'd gotten along. Not well, but well enough. But his attempts to replace my dad bugged the crap out of me. He gave advice when none was requested, and tried to impose a curfew, even though I didn't live with them. How crazy was that?

Lucky for me he got the message in the end. I liked my independence. If he couldn't deal, tough. Never again would I let anyone take away my right to do as I pleased.

"Guess what happened, dear." My mother's tone was almost chirpy. "Our Felicity got herself a date with the handsome young man who lives next door."

He wrinkled his brows. "That's nice. I'm sure you'll have a good time."

Yeah, once more with feeling, Alan.

He excused himself to go to the bathroom, which provided Mom with the opportunity to heap on the dating advice.

"When you go out, be sure to put on something sexy. You're a pretty enough girl, but men are dim and won't take notice unless you dangle your charms in front of their face. So, tight dress and plenty of makeup."

I squirmed. Not the talk other girls got from their mothers. Besides, neither Parker nor I had agreed to this alleged date. Still, if it made her giddy to believe we were headed for a happily ever after, why burst her bubble?

I put on a brave smile. "I will, Mom. Thanks."

"Are you ready to leave, hon?" Alan marched back in.

"In a minute. Did you bring the box for Felicity?"

He shook his head. "It's still on the landing. I'll come by and drop it off another time."

"I wanted her to have it today. I told you right before we left to put it in the car." She let out an exasperated sigh and patted her strawberry-blond hair.

I raised my hand like a schoolgirl. "Hello, standing right here. What box?"

"Some of your things from when you were younger." Mom seemed excited, but then she'd been grinning from one ear to the other since her success with Parker.

Alan touched my mother's arm. "Honey. The exhibition?"

"Yes, yes, of course." She placed a kiss on each of my cheeks. "Happy Birthday, dear. Enjoy yourself with Neighbor Parker."

I covered my slipping smile with a cough. She turned her head just before reaching the door and mouthed *"Tight dress."*

The early rays of the sun fought their way through my curtains, dancing across the walls of my bedroom. This was going to be a good day. How could it not be? With Fred painting the city of Paris or Washington or Moscow red—I should have inquired about his destination—I was the senior investigator. As my protégé, Flo would be doing coffee runs and filing records, which left me free to concentrate on the big decisions. Like what to order for lunch.

I stretched, contented for once. Whatever had led me to believe Flo couldn't handle the truth about me? Were there more kin like him and his sister, who'd be able to accept me, a mere human? If so, perhaps I should come clean with their brother Eli.

As long as Parker didn't find out. He'd freak, which might end up fatal for me. Werewolves had more reason to be cautious than any other kin, because if trouble came knocking on their door, they couldn't move to Alethia. They needed Oldworld's sun and moon the way I needed oxygen and caffeine.

But this was too nice a day to waste thinking about werewolves.

After breakfast, I kicked back on the softest couch in the world and opened the paper. The slanted arm rests held my head at the perfect reading angle. So far, no news on the massacre at the Carters' place. The only murder in the Silverton Gazette was that of a young woman, raped and stabbed in some alley.

I exhaled sharply. When had our town become such a cesspool of crime?

A noise yanked me from my thoughts. A whisper from… somewhere. I shot a glance through the window. Clouds were pulling in from the east and the branches of the humongous oak rustled in the breeze.

I sat up and removed the statue from my backpack. What did two demons want with an ugly heirloom? No carvings or symbols adorned the surface, although the texture under the gloss finish appeared porous. A flicker of something familiar touched my senses. Energy, like a charged guard.

There. I tilted my head, listening. The object whispered to me. In an instant, the sound was gone. Most likely, I'd misidentified the hum from my fridge. Still creepy. Noises or not, I tucked the statue away under my sofa, out of sight.

A tap on the living room window startled me. Florian beamed at me with his white, human-looking teeth on display. Each of his hands held a large cup of steaming Starbucks.

This time I didn't hesitate to invite him into my sanctum. "You could have come in through the front door, you know."

"That's for visitors. Besides, I know you spend half your time in your backyard anyway."

"Yeah, but not this early in the day. And not in October."

His gaze moved first over the guards on my walls, then over my shapeless T-shirt down to my tight-fit denims. "Nice of you to get all dressed up for me."

"Sarcasm doesn't become you."

He pouted. "*Everything* becomes me."

I took the cup off him and bustled him toward the sofa. "Yeah, right." I dragged the statue out from under the sofa again. "Here." I held it in front of his nose. "You wanna be an investigator? Investigate."

He squinted at it. "It's made of some rock material with crystals in it. It's gray. Quite ugly."

"That's it?"

"It's useful for clobbering you over the head with if you don't leave me alone."

I scrunched my face to suppress a smile. "Spoilsport."

No matter how much time we spent staring at it, tilting it this way and that, it didn't give up its secrets. I hadn't expected it to, of course, but perhaps I'd hoped that Florian, with his superhuman senses, would notice something I hadn't.

"So," Flo said at last, "what's the plan?"

"Turn it over to the police?"

He let out a grim chuckle. "As far as they're concerned, we were never at the Carters' place. Besides, if this thing does have a hex on it, the police wouldn't know what to do."

"Yeah, I guess magic isn't taught in cop school. Demons, fae, vamps. The girls and boys in blue would dirty their panties if they knew what was out there." And who could blame them? If I had the choice, I'd live in ignorance, too.

"Guardians, on the other hand." Florian lifted his hand. "If they were around, they'd take care of this business like *that*." He snapped his fingers.

"Guardians. Really?" I narrowed my eyes. "Poor deluded Flo."

Julia's books referred to the Guardians as a bunch of demons in charge of watching over Alethia and Oldworld. A bogeyman to stop baby kin from stealing or lying.

"Heathen." He picked up his cup. "Ready?"

I wrapped the figure up and flung it back under the sofa. "You're driving."

The journey was quick, and the passage of time was helped along by Flo telling tall tales of Guardian miracles. He parked in the basement parking garage, and we took the elevator up.

At the office, I raised the key to the door and stopped cold. A narrow gap gave me a glimpse inside the room. Someone had cracked the lock. I held up a hand to warn Flo to stay back, and slid open the door.

Florian came up from behind. "What's up?"

"It's open." I stepped inside. No burglar, no mess. Thank God.

He followed in and squinted. "Is anything missing?"

My quick scan of the office revealed nothing out of place. Although they'd hardly be interested in taking the potted plants. "I can't tell. I'll have to check our files."

"Do you want to call the police?"

I shook my head. "Let me do an inventory first. Maybe it was just a drunk neighbor getting the doors mixed up."

Wouldn't be the first time. Far from it. In fact, if I had to bet, my money would be on Mr. Higgins from upstairs. Twice now I'd caught him jigging his keys in our lock, then kicking the door, calling out for Elsa to let him in.

I shuffled to the desk and called a locksmith. Then I got to work on the cabinets, but a thorough inspection exposed no signs of foul play. "Everything seems undisturbed."

This was looking more and more like neighborly mischief. Of course, I couldn't rule out that somebody had come in and taken a photo of whatever they needed. A few months ago, a former mark of Fred's had broken in and set fire to his file. A futile endeavor, since his wife had already found out about his affair and initiated divorce proceedings. Fred hadn't pressed charges, as the damage to the office was minimal and he felt a certain sense of moral responsibility for the man's predicament.

Not sure I would've been as lenient. My distaste for cheaters brought me close to throwing stones inside a glass house, sure, what with my silence about Dad's mistresses. Or one-night-stands. I never asked him about them, because it was so much easier to pretend I didn't know, but I smelled the perfume on him, spotted the lipstick after a night out with friends. I balled my hands. Too late to call him out on it now, of course.

I slammed the cabinet drawer shut. "Hang on." I moved over to the wall. "Nope. The safe is uncracked. No reason to involve the police." Fred wasn't a fan of the cops anyway.

"Okay." Flo shook his head. "First day, and already my first crime. How exciting."

"A rare event." I waved him off and reached for the employee questionnaire. "We might as well get on with it. Okay, name. Florian Dupree. Age?"

He moved his head, mouth open, as if only now remembering where he was. "Age. Twenty-seven, no, twenty-eight, according to my papers."

"And in real life?" I fluttered my eyelashes at him to coax him into answering my burning question.

He winked. "Somewhere between my fake age and the age of our beautiful town. Let's say I look good for my years."

Ah, yes. To be an immortal vampire in an ever-young shell. I bet if I were a vamp and looked twenty-five forever, my mother wouldn't hassle me about finding a boyfriend.

After we'd completed the employment document, I moved on to the cogs that kept the P.I. machine turning, starting with the phone system and our databases. While I was talking my mouth sore, Florian busied himself folding the multi-colored printer paper into origami hats.

I ground my teeth against the rising frustration. This was getting us nowhere.

Twice I dispatched him on a coffee run. He returned far too quickly.

At two o'clock, I changed tack. "These photos are for a Mrs. Wenthorpe, who hired us to see if her husband is cheating on her." I handed him an envelope. "As it happens, he is, so be careful when you deliver the evidence. Some wives get trigger happy when confronted by messengers of bad news. Should you make it out alive, see if she can give you a check right away."

He grinned. "I think I can convince her, don't you worry."

"Oh yeah?"

"I have a way with the ladies." He held up a hand as a goodbye.

Having a vampire collecting our fees would be quite an asset. With their glamour, by which they took control of others' minds, they could bamboozle anyone into anything. Fred would be amazed if he came back and our accounts were up-to-date.

An hour later, the locksmith arrived to install a new lock. I palmed two sets of keys and placed another in Fred's desk.

I dedicated the rest of the afternoon to the statue. What possible reason would two demons have to work together in order to get their mitts on it? The file Fred had gathered on it was thin on details. Albert Bertrams, the guy who'd hired us, had given us enough to go on to track the statue down, but not a smidgen more. My fingers crossed, I called his number.

"I'm terribly sorry," his housekeeper said, voice wavering. "Mister Bertrams was killed in an accident two days ago. So tragic."

My heart lurched. The poor man. "I'm sorry to hear that." What now? Hang up? I coughed. Not until I knew if his death was more deliberate than she suspected. "If this isn't too forward, would you mind telling me how?"

She sniffled. "He was run over. Would you believe, the driver never stopped to check if Mister Bertrams was okay. It's a terrible world."

Could this be a coincidence? "That's horrible." I bit my lip. "Did you work for him long?"

"Oh, twenty years. He was such a nice man."

"Well, I'm sorry to intrude. Thank you so much for your help." I hung up. Her tears had moved me, but I couldn't overlook the timing of his demise. A quick search in the online Gazette gave me more information. The driver, a drunk teenager, was apprehended not far from the scene, slumped and sobbing behind the wheel.

I leaned back. Nothing to indicate Bertrams' death was anything other than an accident. Whether that was good or bad for my investigation, I couldn't say.

My gaze fell on Flo's assigned desk. Perhaps our assumption was wrong. Just because Max and his partner were demons didn't mean the statue had preternatural associations. In this realm, demons were people too. Maybe they were after a big payday. Bronzes by Rodin and other big-name artists were worth millions, of course. This stone blob wasn't my taste, but neither was Picasso's early work. It would also explain why Bertrams had offered us a mighty buck or two for its retrieval.

To find out more, I contacted the other previous owners whose names Fred had listed. Only one of them had anything to say on the topic.

"Yes, I remember the thing." The man's voice was hesitant. "Tony Carter, my neighbor, bought it off me. At the time I was glad to get the money for it. I mean, who couldn't do with extra cash, right? With this recent interest I'm thinking maybe I let it go too cheap, though. What do you think? Is it worth something?"

I consulted my notes. Tony Carter was listed as Stephen Carter's uncle. "No, probably not. So I take it someone else contacted you regarding the object?"

"Two guys. One was a private detective like you."

"Fred Abner?"

"Rings a bell. Can't remember the other guy's name, sorry."

I hung up and gave my bottom drawer a deft kick. Without a name for the mysterious second caller, I was stuck again. Damn.

An Internet search for *statue* would yield a gazillion hits. I ransacked my brain for a way to narrow down the search criteria, but the only descriptive word that sprang to mind was *creepy*. The problem was, the statue didn't stand out in any way. It looked like a flat blob made of rock material. No artist's name, no nothing. How the hell would I search the Internet for that?

Perhaps an expert would shed light on my puzzle. I dug a business card out of a file from a previous case. On the front it read:

Reliable

Peter Henderton

Henderton Antiquities

1-555-555-1897

The word *Reliable* had been written in the top right corner in Fred's precise hand. If Henderson confirmed the statue was a well-known artwork or thousands of years old, I'd rule out a nefarious intent for the demons' actions. If, on the other hand, Mr. Henderton told me the thing was worth nothing, I'd have reason to suspect a preternatural connection.

"Yes, Miss Bell? Let me check, yes?" He left me hanging for a good eight minutes. "Miss Bell? I've checked my files. It is indeed possible I know the statue you're talking about? What an exciting find if you're right, yes? I'll have to have to take a look at it to be sure?" The man's sentences lilted up at the end, as if the power of speech surprised him. I pictured him as an elderly, almost frail man with small spectacles and an *aw, shucks* face.

I agreed to drop by the next day. Finally, some sort of progress. If nothing else, Henderton's words halfway confirmed my suspicions. The demons had killed the Carters to pick up a little goldmine. Nothing more to it.

I deserved a treat. And nothing less than a creamy latte would do. I grabbed some change and my jacket, and headed out.

Clouds blocked the sun's rays, giving downtown a depressed feel. I rubbed my arms warm and hurried down the alley between two adjacent apartment complexes. The statue had been a nice distraction, but exposed among people, my Lathan paranoia took hold again. Twice I checked behind me for steps, twice I found no one following me. The sigh of relief at reaching the coffee shop unharmed came from the depths of my gut.

The *Java Joint* was like a second home to me. The cute guy behind the counter knew my order by heart, from the milk-laden latte right down to the lemon cupcake. He threw in a few glances at my chest for free. Perv.

Most days, I had no trouble blanking strangers' unwelcome attention, but today, I smiled at him. He may only be fifteen, but, hell, I wanted to ruin him for all other women.

Christ. Why would I think like that? What was wrong with me? Now even kids weren't safe from my jigging hormones. Perhaps I needed to get laid. I muttered my thanks and walked off. Keeping my gaze glued to the floor, I ran into a solid body.

So not the day to mess with me. "Watch out," I snapped.

"You too."

I peered up and froze.

CHAPTER SEVEN

My COFFEE HAD SOAKED INTO a tailored white shirt, ruining a whole lot of buck per square inch of the finest cotton. I swallowed. "I'm so sorry."

The owner of the shirt smiled down at me, which added to my guilt. His twitching lips made him look amused rather than annoyed.

Chin-length blond hair, blue eyes.

Ping. Before I knew it, my hormones were boogying again. My mind had become some Playgirl mansion, and everyone was invited.

Jeez.

I wet my lips and reached for a handful of napkins from the holder on the counter. "…too hot…" I toweled them over the brown-splattered fabric. "…klutz that I am. I'm sorry." I rubbed against his torso with more vigor than could be attributed to a simple desire to clean up.

The man curled his palm around my hand. "Everything's okay, miss. It was just an accident."

Why did he have to be so nice about it? I'd done a horrible thing. This place served their coffee super-hot and I could have scalded him. I scrunched up my face. "I'll pay for the cleaning. Here, I'll give you my address."

"There's no need." He patted my shoulder. "Go get yourself another coffee. Honestly, no big deal."

With a bruised ego I watched him walk away. No one sunk her chances with the opposite sex with as much finality as I. Every time. I balled my fist. Granted, immersing a man in half a cup of caffeine wasn't the ideal way to catch his interest, but the way he'd rejected the exchange of personal information veered my frail ego way past disappointment toward humiliation.

I stared at the puddle on the floor.

"Don't worry." The barista rushed to my side with a mop. He cleaned up as if he served a hundred klutzes like me, and returned to his spot behind the counter.

"I'm sorry." I checked my pocket for more change, but found none. Of course I'd left my wallet in the office.

"This one's on the house." He steamed fresh milk into the cup and handed me my latte.

"Thank you." I gave the kid a grateful glance.

"Hey, you look like you needed one."

With slow steps I shuffled back to the office. Mr. Weinstein from number thirty held the door for me. I poked the button of the elevator with two fingers until the doors slid open. Why did I care about the coffee shop guy's abrupt rejection? Sooner or later my mother would succeed in setting me up with someone, *before my looks deserted me*. The cabin jerked to a halt, and I stepped out.

In the hall, I balanced my nearly empty cup of latte between my thigh and the office wall. My circus trick was even more impressive since I simultaneously fumbled for the key. Steps echoed behind me, giving me a sense of safety. In a complex this size, people were in and out all the time, always more than happy to chat. No one more so than Mrs. Milton in number sixteen, the mother of a disaffected emo who spent all day attached to his earphones as if they somehow provided nutritional support. But I wasn't in a chatty mood and kept my gaze glued to the lock.

A force smacked into me. My body slammed against the door frame, sending a searing pain across my ribs. A large hand over my mouth muffled my yelp. I twisted my head around.

A prick in my flesh, and the blood in my veins ran cold.

"Nearly over, Felicity." The figure speaking had two eyes, a nose and a mouth, yet his features didn't melt together. Some kind of magic pixelated his face.

I sent my hands toward my pockets, but my nerves failed to pass on the message. My pulse rattled in my ears and slowed. *No. Oh God.* The injection, my inability to identify a face—the same MO as the night I was kidnapped.

I focused. I squeezed. But my muscles didn't comply. Mind and body disconnected from each other, and my guards remained untouched. The stranger spoke words I didn't understand, and my legs followed him like those of a robot along the corridor and back into the elevator.

My pulse should have been racing, but it beat a calm rhythm. My distress lived only in my brain. Could anything or anyone save me? I'd dropped my drink and my keys outside the office. Would that be enough to make Flo come looking for me?

The elevator mirror showed my face, pale and lifeless. My

chest lifted and fell the way it should. So why did it feel like I was suffocating?

The doors slid open. We stepped into the dim underground parking garage. The smell of fuel nudged my stomach, but not even my gag reflex was under my control. A man and a woman passed us, their arms interlinked in comfortable togetherness. My mind yelled at them, my eyes pleaded for help. They paid us no attention. If they had, would they've seen his real face or a fuzzy one, like I did? My abductor steered me toward a far corner.

With every step my guards poked into my thighs, reminding me of their existence. I held my breath and instructed my hand once again to move up to my pocket. It didn't obey.

We approached a long, black sedan with a license plate that, like my kidnapper's face, refused to fall into focus. Another spell. I'd heard of magic that hid elephants in plain sight, blocking a face and a license plate from active sight would be easy for anyone who knew the right words. And my kidnapper hummed with skin magic, the addictive kind.

I peeked at the man from the corner of my eye. A fine grey suit hinted at a well-heeled lifestyle. No distinctive markers. Had he been following me for long? Despite the sameness of his clothes, something about him seemed familiar. Was this the guy who'd kidnapped me nearly six years ago?

Sweat dripped into my eyes. I closed them against the sting. *Move, Ivy, goddammit!* Yet my body waited for the man to open the trunk, then followed his mocking invitation to climb in. He chuckled, and my blood ran hot enough it burned. Finally. A twitch of my fingers. The lid came down and my world turned dark.

With darkness came the fear. The roiling of my stomach. The cold sweat that drenched my top. Deprived of distractions, I was left with thoughts of Lathan. He'd warned me, of course, but I'd been confident he'd fail. Thought I could fight my way out of any situation, when at the moment of truth I hadn't managed a simple *'no'* in protest.

My mind flashed back to the time I'd first met the demon kinlord. The vortex of the gate deposited me in a cavernous, icy hall. Large windows let in a few rays of light, shrouding everything in dirty grayness. Lathan appeared like a shining vision in the darkness. His long coat billowed with each hurried step, and his pale, symmetrical features were as delicate as those of an angel.

The sound of a commotion interrupted my nightmare recollection. Two men argued outside my cramped cell. A grunt. Glass shattered. The car shook as if from an impact, rocking up and down like a boat in rough sea. A second, more forceful bang. Another voice, a woman this time. Then everything went quiet.

The trunk door lifted, and gray light from the parking garage's grimy lamps blinded me. My blurry gaze fell onto an unfamiliar figure. Different clothes. He wasn't my abductor, although I didn't discount the possibility the two were partners. He was alone, though, which perhaps bode well for me.

But trust didn't come easy for me. The new stranger spoke a few words in another language. Another prick in my neck, and a prickle came over my skin. Was this a second spell to knock me out, or one to counteract the first one?

Pins and needles in my arms and legs heralded the return of my motor functions, but I was still a far way off being able to defend myself. The man helped me out of the trunk.

"Wait here," he said.

Funny guy. As if I was in a position to go anywhere. He jimmied the car door of the sedan with a burst of magic and leaned in to search the glove compartment. When he extracted his torso from the driver's cabin, one hand held a folded sheet of paper while the other fumbled in his pocket.

My vision cleared. Oh crap. A demon. I inched my hands toward my pocket, which in my current state still wasn't easy. With his back to me, he punched buttons on his phone.

"Director Vanguard," he said in a hoarse, breathy pitch. The kind of voice that made a woman's knees go weak.

Other women's knees, that is. Christ!

He tapped his fingers on the roof of the car. "I don't give a shit. Pull him from the meeting." Another pause. "It's Waylon Carmine. Tell him if he's not on the phone in two minutes, I'll come over to HQ in person. I got a feeling he's gonna change his mind real fast."

The demon opened the piece of paper without paying me any attention, and I relaxed my stance. My body was back under my control. Kind of. The initial movements were jerky, but nimble enough to pull the guards from my jeans. The cool metal against my skin cleansed my synapses. It was good to be back. Better still to charge my guards.

As long as his back was turned, I might as well get out of here.

"Director Vanguard... I never said you were my flunky." He sighed. "Yeah, now you're getting close to pissing me off... Okay then. Listen, I need information on a man who rented a silver Honda Civic under the name Angus Jones. Probably an alias... Yeah, get me everything you can dig up on him." He read out the information from the rental agreement, including the car's license plate, which came into focus as soon as I heard it. Without a goodbye, he parked the phone in his pocket.

I discharged my guards at him and ran. Four car lengths later I lay spread-eagled on the floor. One guard glistened a few yards away. But I had one left. I tightened my fingers around it and—

A hefty leather boot pressed on my hand, not enough to hurt me, but it pinned me in place. The demon crouched and took the guard off me, and picked up the other before helping me up.

Intense demon-green eyes appraised me. They were set in a face guaranteed to have women do a double-take, to spike our heartbeats and make us forget we were really looking for a sense of humor in a man.

Oh yes, he was dangerous all right.

His plain white T-shirt followed the curves of his chest, and a leather jacket hung over his broad shoulders. With his eight-o-clock shadow, he was the ultimate bad boy. Early thirties. Lazy smile. A small but deep scar over his right brow. And a mouth perfect for exploring bits of me that rarely saw the light of day.

And yet his exterior hid how *bad* this boy really was. I ran my tongue over my dry lips, reveling in my tightening nerves. Power oozed from every inch of his sinful body. A high-level demon, not the riffraff usually encountered in Oldworld.

Demon or not, he was perfect for all sorts of nighttime activities.

I gave myself a good talking to. This obsession with getting laid had to stop. I was not that desperate. Besides, even if he wasn't in league with Lathan, he couldn't be trusted. *Now stop drooling.*

He motioned for me to take a seat on the hood of a battered hatchback. I followed his suggestion and frowned. Ordering me around was so not the way to get on my good side.

"I'm Waylon Carmine," he said. "Ivy, right? If memory serves, you don't like the name Felicity."

I blinked.

He adjusted his jacket. "I knew your parents."

"My parents?"

"I'm sorry about your father's death."

My tongue refused to obey. I knew not all demons were bad. More powerful, yes. Manipulative, sure. But evil? Except for Lathan, the few others I'd met in Alethia hadn't struck me as devil-like. That wasn't to say I should let my attraction to the specimen before me override my caution.

A knowing grin spread over his face. Okay, so the first impression I'd made was that of a total nincompoop.

I pulled my shoulders back and replaced the dim-witted expression with a suspicious squint. "That's quite the coincidence, you being here," I said, glad my voice had received the memo to sound normal. "Are you going to tell me what happened while I was locked away like a sardine?"

He stuffed the rental agreement into the inside pocket of his jacket and leaned against the Honda, his reflection drawn along the curves of the bodywork. "I don't usually explain myself. But since we just met, I'll make an exception. I was on my way up to your office when you came out the elevator. The magic practically rolled off your friend like sweat. I didn't want to start anything with you in the way, so I waited for my chance. The guy put you in the trunk, and I questioned him."

"Right." I made a point of glancing around. "Where is he?"

He wrinkled his nose. "Well, if that nosy woman hadn't come over to check we weren't fighting, he'd now be trussed up in my trunk, ready for interrogation. I mean, I could hardly beat him up with her around, could I?"

My hands curled into fists. "Do you fight people often?"

"Matter of fact I do. You're safe from me, though. So why don't I return your guards, you'll stow them out of the way, and we'll go talk somewhere more private?"

Perhaps a narrow, dark broom closet? I expelled a deep breath. This was what it must be like to be a guy, thinking about sex every five seconds. How the hell did they get any work done?

"Let's have a drink." Waylon slapped his thighs and pushed off the Honda. "My hotel isn't too far from here."

I glared at him, the full force of my doubt expressed in one glance. Perhaps he was on the level. Perhaps not. No way to tell.

"Hey, it's not like I'm taking you there to fuck you."

I recoiled. Did he eat candy with that mouth?

He leaned to one side and produced a wallet from his pocket. "Here. There's proof I knew your family." He handed me a photo. Waylon had one arm around a woman, who cradled a baby to her chest. His other arm draped over a handsome man in his twenties. Even though the photo was creased and the colors faded, my lungs tightened. I knew my dad instantly.

By a process of elimination, the woman and the baby had to be Waylon's family. I handed the picture back. What would my father have made of his *friend* if he'd known he was a demon?

"So?" Waylon asked. "Ready to come?"

What was his angle? Demons always had one. Was he going to use his friendship with my dad to ask for a loan? Dad's generosity used to attract freeloaders like rich people attracted 'friends.' Or had Waylon come to pay his respects? Whatever his reasoning, if I passed up the opportunity to talk to someone who'd known my father, I might kick myself later. Who knew what tales and anecdotes lay hidden in Dad's past?

"Ivy? Still with me?"

"Yeah." I squinted at him once more then set my jaw. "Yeah, I'll go with you."

In Waylon's rental we drove to the Bankside Hotel. In all likelihood, his meaningless chitchat was meant to de-stress me. Damn him, he succeeded. I snuggled into the seat and unlooped my spine.

Soon, the Bankside loomed like a soulless high rise in the distance. Waylon stopped outside and handed the key to a helpful valet. At least he hadn't taken me to a seedy motel. In fact, everything about him so far had been on the up and up.

Waylon stepped into the elevator. I followed, trying hard not to let my gaze linger on his butt. Who was this guy? And how well had he known my dad?

His room was spartan, with few personal belongings, but the personal touches—a potted plant, well cared for and in full bloom on the mantelpiece; personalized stationery, ready printed with the guest's name and the hotel's address—gave it a welcoming feel.

I took a seat on the bright red sofa, my hands tucked between my knees to stop them from tapping on my legs. After the guest service brought up a bottle, Waylon placed the do-not-disturb sign on the outside door handle. I wet my lips and crossed my ankles. Alone. With him.

If my klutz came out again, I'd hate myself.

Waylon took his leather jacket off, revealing well-defined biceps under his T-shirt, and threw it on the large stately-looking desk.

Somehow I'd entered Upsidedown World. He came across as a person who'd hole up in a garage and swig beer. Yet here he was, booked into the most exclusive hotel in town, plying me with wine.

His phone rang. He sent a mere nod in my direction by way of apology and answered. "Director, what have you…? So, it's as we thought. And there's no way to track the guy? … Okay, never mind. Thanks."

"Was that about my attacker?" I asked.

He placed his phone on the desk. "That was the director of the IEA. No news. Any idea why somebody would wanna abduct you?"

I didn't need to ask about the IEA. The Interracial Enforcement Agency had been founded by representatives of The Big Seven, as the seven kinlords of Alethia were collectively known. They basically governed the lives of kin living in Oldworld.

If Waylon was miffed at my lack of a reply, he didn't show it. "The guy must have consumed shitloads of energy. A human doing skin magic. He'll need to recharge, so you should be okay for a few days."

He placed his phone back into his jacket pocket and came over to grab the bottle off the table. If he took off his T-shirt, too, would his abs be a collection of tiny Legos or one solid plate? Perhaps he wasn't married. He didn't wear a ring. I licked the wine from my lips.

"More?" He was preparing to top up my glass.

"Just a little."

He poured and walked back to his desk where he produced a handful of photos from a briefcase. Him? A briefcase? Every minute the guy became more of a puzzle. And dammit if I didn't want to crack it.

I flicked through the pictures. The same three people—the woman, Waylon and my dad—in various poses against different backgrounds.

Waylon's maybe-wife was a stunner. I hated her on sight.

He stared at me with his deep green eyes. "You look like your mother, you know?"

"I look nothing like her."

"Not your stepmother. Your real mother."

I jerked against the pillows, nearly spilling the wine over the upholstery. My heartbeat shot up to about one hundred and eighty miles per hour. "M-my real mother?"

"Figured you knew. The woman in the photos?"

My real mother. The words echoed in my mind. I placed my fingers against my forehead and pressed. Was he making this up? I checked for any telltale twitches in his face. Nada. Not a wink.

Another mother. A 'real one.' As if the mother I knew was made of wood and operated by strings. My chest tensed. I bit my lip, trying to form a three-dimensional image from the photo. It didn't work. The idea was too abstract, too unreal.

"Feeling all right?" Waylon sat next to me, his hand on my knee.

His spicy cologne tickled my senses, causing my body to align with him like a magnet. He leaned forward and tilted my chin with his finger. I swallowed. A smile, then he lowered his mouth onto mine.

CHAPTER EIGHT

WAYLON'S LIPS KNEW WHAT THEY were doing. His taste covered my tongue, his hands gripped my butt. Everywhere he touched, my nerve endings fired, sending spark after spark into my pelvis.

Why didn't I pull back?

I pressed against him, and the burning need that had teased me for days faded. Like a parched throat getting water after days of drought.

He jerked back and shot to his feet. "Shit." He wiped the back of his hand over his mouth. "That shouldn't have happened."

Oh my God, how embarrassing. I pinched the bridge of my nose and swallowed hard. "I'm—"

"Hang on." He disappeared inside another room.

I slumped, and rubbed my palms across my face. Why did *I* feel embarrassed? He was the one who'd kissed *me*. The only reason I forgot to shove him off me was that he'd taken me by surprise. My shoulders fell, because my logic was far-fetched, even for me.

He returned with a sparkly necklace and placed it around my neck. "That's me thinking clearly again. I s'ppose I got carried away there for a sec, didn't I?"

I touched the necklace. "What the hell happened?"

"We kissed. What, too subtle?"

I frowned. Did he think that was funny? "You had no right."

His eyebrows went up. "Hell. You seemed to enjoy it as much as I did. And if I hadn't stopped when I did, we'd be in the bedroom now. I'm a fucking hero."

A shiver tiptoed down my spine. I certainly wouldn't have made him stop.

He shrugged. "If it helps, it wasn't your fault. You can't control yourself."

What a jackass. I jutted my chin out. "You have a high opinion of yourself, don't you?"

"That's not what I meant. I mean, biologically you can't help yourself."

"Great." I flung out my arms. "Now you're God's gift to *all* women?"

"Shit, you're difficult." He tousled his hair. "Okay. From the beginning. A long time ago, a group of demons sliced space out of the skies, right here, above Silverton. The new world became Alethia, a place filled with the purest magic you could imagine. It was made to allow kin to move beyond the Rim. And if they're powerful and possess too much juju, they're not coming back, not even through the few permanent portals that exist. It worked, and entire families and kin left for Alethia. Even whole races emigrated."

Alethia? My pulse picked up. This conversation had taken an unexpected turn. I forced my face into a nonchalant expression. "Been there. Done that. So what?"

He raised an eyebrow. "You've been there? How?"

"I was kidnapped." I gulped down the lump in my throat. "By Lathan."

He sat up straight. "*The* Lathan? Kinlord of the demons? Fucking hell. How did *that* happen?"

I peered up from under my eyelashes. His gaze was locked on me, any glint of humor gone. "Why should I tell you?" My voice crackled.

His see-how-I-care attitude returned in the form of a shrug. "Listen. This is tit-for-tat. You want to find out why you're horny, you'd better give me the what's-what on your time with Lathan."

So my rampant randiness wasn't something I'd imagined? My guts spiraled. But perhaps this was a good thing. If it was a medical condition, I could get it treated. Take pills or whatever.

I'd already told him more about myself than I was comfortable with. But I wanted to know more. Needed to know more.

Guess he got himself a deal. "After one of my mother's dinner evenings…" I faltered. No, I couldn't say 'stepmother.' No way. "I walked to the bus stop. On the way, some guy stepped behind me, injected me with something, and took me away to Alethia. Lathan put me to work, building guards he later sold." I took a jerky breath. "Anyway, I was there almost two years, when Lathan was busy with some catastrophe or other. I got a chance, and hopped through an open portal." My vision blurred for a second. If my plan had failed, who knew what Lathan would have done?

Waylon bobbed his head. "All the kinlords own one permanent portal to let them import Oldworld, non-magical goods. Nothing dangerous. Anything passes through with too much juice, and the whole thing would collapse." He raked a hand through his hair. "At least you got away. I should have come back sooner. Fuck. I'm sorry, babe."

Shoulda woulda coulda. It was too late for good intentions. "Don't call me babe, and we're good. In any case, today's kidnap attempt was definitely also Lathan-related. Why the hell is he after me again?"

"Why wouldn't he want you? He knows who your parents were, and with you having satyr traits, well…" He smirked. "Come on, you must know you're sexy as all hell."

The warmth in my head turned into a scorching fire. "Don't say stuff like that." My stomach plummeted. "Wait. Satyr? What are you talking about?"

"On your father's side?"

"Are you crazy?" I set my glower to stun. "Dad was human."

Wasn't he? Or perhaps those permanent tiny lumps on Dad's head, where he'd *banged his noggin,'* had been satyr horns.

"No, he was definitely a satyr." Waylon's tone didn't waver. Not even a little. "Satyr royalty even. Graeme, King of the Mountain Springs, was his proper title. One of the most powerful of his race, which means he was horny as hell. Seriously, babe. Up for it all the time." He chuckled, but a glance from me cut him off. "It's the satyr in you that's sexing-up your thoughts. On their twenty-fifth birthday, a satyr reaches maturity. That thing you're feeling, where you wanna fuck the hell out of every living being? We call that *motive*. Not easy to control at first, and perfect for Lathan's plans."

My veins turned to ice. The meaning behind Lathan's *birthday wishes* now stared me in the face. The bastard demon had known all along. This would explain…everything.

I gave a grim chuckle. "He's always been a little stalkerish. Would you believe he proposed to me a few minutes after we met?" I twirled my finger next to my temple. "Even though I said no, he wanted to know where I was all the time, needed constant access to me. He used this." I rolled up the short sleeve of my T-shirt, which covered Lathan's mark.

Waylon gripped my arm, studying the shape with a grim expression. "That djinn-ridden son of a bitch!" His face softened. "I'm so sorry."

I ripped my arm from his grasp. Pity was the last thing I needed.

My mind flashed back to that fateful night. Lathan had come in with a large, shiny ring in hand. It bore his mark, and I thought he was going to offer me another betrothal ring. Instead, he turned its surface into a glowing disk. I knew then something was going to change. Something that I might never get over. He grabbed me and pressed me onto the bed, face down.

That's when the pain started. Lathan pushed the hot seal of his ring onto my arm and released the magic. No shoving and pleading made any difference. The mark's one use was to give him complete control of my body and mind. Its power rushed into me, spreading its oily tentacles to stamp me as his, outside and in. By magically connecting to his mark, Lathan would know what I knew, feel what I felt, and could march me to whatever location he chose.

"Ivy?"

I blinked hard to get Waylon back into focus. "What?"

"Did he…you know?"

"Rape me? No." Small mercies. I cleared my throat, trying to sound like normal me. "Right after the branding, he took my nervous system for a test drive. Using just his mind, he had my body bucking with joy, replaced by searing pain, and then another swoop into rapture. But no sex."

His shoulders relaxed. "I s'ppose he wanted to wait till you're twenty-five."

I closed my eyes for a second. We were way past the guessing stage. But I wouldn't let myself wallow. The minute I stayed still, my past got a chance to catch up with me.

"If I'm half satyr, what's the other half?" I shuddered. "Demon?"

His gaze dropped. A sad smile played on his lips. "No. Jocinda, your mother, was a leanan sidhe. She was trained by her father who also trained me. To be a Guardian." He stretched out long legs that ended in a pair of hardcore leather boots. "Her father was a brather demon, and your mom got the Guardian gene from him. So did you. It's up to us to police magical activity and deal with the most dangerous kin."

His words slammed into me and stole my breath. Me, a Guardian. Okaay. Quite a tale this Waylon had spun in that pretty head of his.

"I know it's a lot to take in," he said.

I put on my "duh" face.

His lips didn't twitch, his face devoid of humor or trickery. But with my past, it paid to doubt anything a demon said.

"We were the last Guardians," he said. "When your father joined us, we had a party, the three of us. Barely enough of us to police a city, of course, let alone two worlds, but we righted some serious shit in our time." He wet his lips. "Now they're dead."

Dead. Only rarely did I say the word to describe my dad's departure. It sounded so final. The image of the woman Waylon claimed was my mother beamed up at me from a photo. Would I push the dreaded word into a drawer when thinking of her, too? I ran my thumb over her face. Swallowing hurt, and I struggled to hold back my tears. This was messed up. The revelation of her passing shouldn't affect me so much. I never met the woman.

Waylon sipped his wine, taking his time, although I wasn't sure he tasted it. His gaze was fixed on some far-away point. "At your mom's funeral, Graeme made a plan. A crazy plan, but hey, the dude *was* crazy. Before you became a Guardian, he wanted you to have a safe childhood. We bound your magic till your twenty-first birthday and hid you in a pool of humans. Here, in Silverton."

And what a memorable birthday my twenty-first had been. Lathan had thrown a party in my honor, invited people I'd never heard of and made them offer me expensive gifts, when all I wanted was my freedom.

Did Waylon say 'my magic?' "Erm. To my knowledge, no magical talents have yet manifested." I glanced to the side then smirked. "Although I can make a bar of chocolate disappear pretty fast."

"As I suspected, you're gifted." He echoed my smirk. "You already know how to use guards. General spells and potions might need some prodding before we can break them free from your genes. Oh, you can also read auras."

"Like colors that surround people?"

He chuckled. "That's human ignorance. Auras happen when a person's soul oozes out. They tell you the race and how much power whoever you're looking at has. Humans are born without magic. But all kin races give off an aura at their own frequency. Fae recognize their fae frequency, and so on. Fae do not recognize werewolves, though. But you and me have Guardian genes, which gives us an all-access pass. As I said, you should have gotten that around your twenty-first year."

So my ability to distinguish between kin didn't come from what Lathan had done to me. A small load lifted. He hadn't broken me after all. Instead, my gift, or curse, was rooted in *Guardian genes*. Talk about information overload.

I fingered my new necklace. "What's this thing for?"

"You've inherited your father's *allure*. His come-fuck-me call. Yours is *very* strong."

My pulse raced, as it did each time his language got crude. It throbbed in my neck, in my ears, in my wrists like it was powered by a steam engine.

But I was a good girl. A normal girl. I pulled back my shoulders. My body might betray me, but my upbringing wouldn't, so I shot him a deliberate and outraged look.

He licked his lips. "The more time you spend with a guy, the more he'll wanna fuck you."

"Can you not use that word?"

"What word?" His teeth flashed in a broad smile, too sexy and provocative to ignore.

I lowered my gaze and studied the carpet loops instead. "Never mind. So does any guy want to…have sex with me?"

"That depends on how you feel about him. Unless you've dismissed him as unworthy, yeah, pretty much. The guard I've sliced into your necklace will reduce your allure, but it can't get rid of all of it."

I traced the lines on the pendant with my fingertips. "And what do I do about this other thing? The motive? Will the guard take care of that, too?" Because so far, it wasn't doing a good job. My libido was still interested in ravaging him right here and now.

He tilted his head. "It won't. But as I said before, it should ease with time. I heard fucking like rabbits helps."

A shudder somersaulted down my spine. His smuttiness, my confusion. If he kissed me again… The evening was headed toward an ending I didn't want. I leaped to my feet and marched to the door. "Well, it's been nice chatting, and thanks for saving me and all, but I'm going to go see if I can wake up from this crazy dream now."

He arched his brows. "Is it my swearing? 'cos if it bothers you, tough tit."

I left the room, cutting off his laughter by slamming the door. The elevator crept down level by level, but I was past caring. My head swam, my insides churned. A Guardian. A real-life Guardian? This seemed like something Dad should have given me a heads-up about. Perhaps he'd meant to before Lathan came for me, but death interfered in his plans.

Down in the lobby, I stopped, uncertain. My cell and my money were in the office. If I went back up to borrow cash, how pathetic would that look?

Not an option.

The guy behind the reception desk let me use his phone, but Florian didn't pick up. I ground my teeth. The renewed onset of a tension headache was no surprise. Guess I'd have to walk it. With a hard slap against the glass, I swung open the hotel's door, teetered between walking out and staying inside, and nearly ran into a man. He jumped aside.

"Sorry." I squeezed past.

"No problem," he said. "Hey, don't I know you?"

I spun around. Foot half inside the hotel, half out, stood the guy from the coffee shop. His black beanie and black scarf were designer articles, but his smile was one of a kind.

He touched my shoulder. "Are you okay?"

I gave a sound resembling a scoff. My whole life had come crashing down on me, and I was *not* okay. A deep breath helped keep my imminent breakdown under wraps. "I didn't bring my purse and I can't reach my friend to come pick me up. So I've had better days. And here I am, ruining your day for a second time. Are you hurt?"

"Not at all. I'd be prepared to share a cab with you, even without insisting on bullet-proof separation between us. What do you say?"

I didn't know him, but declining his offer would surely sound ungrateful. I pressed my toes into the sidewalk slab as if drilling for an excuse.

"I'm sorry." He slid off his soft leather glove and held out his hand. "I haven't introduced myself. Greg Davies."

"Ivy Bell." We shook.

"Since we're not strangers anymore, how ' bout that cab? As an extra guarantee, I should mention we'd be chaperoned by an escort licensed by the State of California."

"The what now?"

He pointed over his shoulder. "The cab driver. You wouldn't be alone with me in case you're worried I'm an axe murderer."

Was that thing on my lips a smile? How the hell had he wheedled that out of me? I tilted my head. "You don't look like an axe murderer."

"Well, that settles it. Let's find ourselves a cab."

One by one, the knots in my shoulder disappeared. A few hours ago, I'd cursed him for rebuffing me. His offer to share a ride went a long way to restoring my confidence. Heck, if I were a guy, I'd be balling my hand into a fist, shouting, "Score!"

We walked to where the cabs waited, and he held the door for me. I got in and gave the driver my address. Greg joined me, and immediately started talking.

There was more to him than a lovely smile. To my surprise and utter delight, he also proved to be a fantastic distraction. I hadn't chuckled this hard since I was twenty-four. Through my laughter, blood pumped extra hard through my body. Was this my motive putting a saucy spin on an innocent cab ride?

"Sometimes, bartenders blend into the background." He flicked his hand. "You have no idea how many people bare their souls to their buddies without even trying to be discreet."

"Any juicy gossip?"

"They might not excel at keeping secrets, but I do. They wouldn't come back otherwise."

"Good for you. Although," I beamed an innocent smile, "I can keep secrets, too."

His laugh was pleasant. Melodious and regular like water running over rocks. "Nice try."

Too soon, the cab pulled up outside my house. My mood sank. The distraction had lowered my blood pressure. Ten minutes without the fear my head was going to crack from an overload of information, from the kidnap attempt, from the jumble of emotions.

"Let me run in and get you a check." My hand gripped the door handle, but I couldn't make myself open the door.

"Don't be ridiculous." His tone was firm. "What kind of gentleman would I be if I allowed you to pay for the cab I would have gotten anyway?"

"I can't *not* pay."

"Well, you could invite me in for coffee." He shrugged. "My evening ended abruptly and it's too early to go home."

My eyes twitched, and I didn't know why. Was it the thought of allowing a stranger into my house? Or the thought of not allowing *this* stranger in? The blond hair poking out from under his hat and his open smirk gave him a roguish-but-nice look, like a guy you could take home to Mom, but who'd have a trick or two saved for bedroom fun.

"No, really, just a coffee." His lips quirked. "I don't make out on a first date." His gaze held mine. "You don't mind, do you?"

Blue eyes were so hard to resist. I smiled and turned to the cabbie. "Could you pick him up in half an hour? Thanks."

Greg grinned and shooed me out of the car.

Getting involved mere months before I was about to move away may be pointless. But today, more than ever, I needed human company. "Come on, then."

We walked up the short drive. Key in hand, I froze. I glanced at him, and back to the door. Oh yeah. I'd just made a big mistake.

CHAPTER NINE

WHAT A CONUNDRUM. IF I opened my front door and let Greg in, he might soon hightail out of here without a word. The guards on the wall might look like art, but if he touched one, he'd get zapped by the energy nestling inside. If nothing else, my mother's visit had proven once again they were too much of a talking point.

He studied me. "What's wrong?"

Everything. "Nothing. I didn't expect company. Could you give me, say, two minutes so I can go in and pick up my bras and stuff?"

He let out that warm laugh of his. "I don't think I'd mind seeing your *bras and stuff*."

My stomach gave a happy jig. "Funny." I cocked my hand like a gun and hurried inside.

In two minutes flat, I'd removed the guards from the corridor, living room, kitchen, bathroom and bedroom, and stashed them in the back of my closet. Letting a stranger into my home was a risk, but the buzz in my tummy, egging me on to give this guy a chance, was too hard to ignore.

Wind, meet caution. Tonight, I *wanted* to be reckless.

I ushered him inside. Oh, shoot. I'd been so busy hiding the guards, I hadn't given a second thought to any underwear which might lay strewn about.

I took a half-twirl. Bedroom door closed? Check. Living room tidy? Check. Good. I exhaled and loosened my fists. I was in the clear.

While he had a look around, I rummaged through the kitchen cupboard, then the pantry in the back for the expensive coffee. I poured the water and soaked in the aroma. Pure bliss. I placed the spoon aside and handed him a cup.

"Tell me about the neighborhood." He put the steaming drink to his lips.

I motioned for him to sit. "Quiet. No nosy neighbors to speak of. Pretty much heaven." I took a sip and reveled in the bitter-sweet taste. My coffee contained enough sugar to sink a small ship. 'Food to settle your nerves,' my dad used to call it. "So, Greg. What were you doing at the Bankside in my hour of need?"

He settled back and gave an audible '*Aah.*' "I was shooting the breeze in their bar with a couple of friends, and they both hit the road early. To think, if they didn't have diapers to change, I wouldn't have run into you tonight." The intense look in his eyes was hard to miss.

I swallowed. "That would have been a bad thing?"

"A very bad thing."

My insides purred like a happy kitten. I fingered the pendant to make sure it was still around my neck. "I thought after my clumsiness you'd steer well clear of me. Who knows how safe you are around me?"

He gave a soft chuckle. "Well, we don't always want what's good for us, do we? Besides, and I can't believe I'm admitting this, I went back to the coffee shop in the hope of running into you again."

Be still, my stomach. "You did?"

He shrugged. "I never should have let you walk away like that, but I would have found you one way or the other." A car horn sounded. He checked his watch. "Damn, it hasn't been thirty minutes."

I rose. "Hang on, let me get you a check. Please."

"No way." He took two slow, considered steps toward me and placed his hand on my waist. His mouth had the art of the sexy half-smile down pat. "Maybe we could meet up tomorrow? I'll let you buy me lunch, if you're so insistent."

A date. I had a date! Something clutched my throat. Instead of a clever response, I pressed out a vague humming noise then nodded.

We walked down the hallway, his hand warm against my body. At the door, Greg stopped. His free hand caressed my cheek. My heart galloped, while I stood frozen. No motion or word of mine would scare him away now. He bent forward, and his mouth found its target. Soft lips brushed against mine. The delicate contact tweaked the nerves along my spine, and I wanted to lose myself in his taste forever. From the way he held me to the way he used his tongue, everything about him was gentle, as if I were precious to him.

The car horn sounded again and we separated.

"About tomorrow…," I said, voice hoarse.

"New Deli at half past one?" Another knee-buckling kiss to say goodbye.

My grin hurt my cheeks. "'kay."

He slid his hand off my waist and walked out to the waiting cab. I stared after the headlamps long after they'd disappeared around the corner.

Back on my sofa, I scrunched my polka dot pillow between my hands. Was this what I'd been looking for? What my mother had been so keen to procure for me? If so, fate was a real bitch to dangle a relationship in front of my face so soon before I'd be leaving.

But the fire in me burned too hot to not take the chance. Which raised another problem. How much of me was I ready to give? Holding hands? Making out? Sex? For a second, the walls danced before my eyes.

The moment I met Lathan, trust and I parted ways. It was no accident my best friend hadn't been allowed into my house for fear he might uncover my secret. Besides, it had been years since I'd been with a man. Things had changed since then. Not the mechanics of the act, perhaps, but my worldview.

The doorbell rang. I checked the clock. The longest day of my life, and it wasn't even ten. I opened the door, and my shoulders sagged. My stepdad wiped his feet on the welcome mat.

I frowned at my late-night visitor. "Alan."

He wiggled a large cardboard box in front of him. "Your stuff."

I let him past and closed the door behind him. Best to get it over with. I bustled him into the living room where he balanced the box on top of the chair. His gaze roamed my walls. A hint of a smile tugged at the corner of his mouth. I bet he couldn't wait to tell my mother my *art* had disappeared.

"What do you want me to do with this?" He tapped the lid.

"I'll take it." I dropped the box off in my bedroom and took a peek.

Cool. I lifted my dad's favorite college T-shirt and stroked over the soft maroon fabric. Although it was faint, Dad's scent still lingered underneath the musky smell of dust.

Alan appeared in the door frame. "He was a good man, your father."

I took a sharp breath. "You knew him?"

His lip twitched. "Yes. A long time ago."

Perhaps if I'd taken the time to talk to Alan on occasion, I'd know these things about him. I chewed my lip. What would Dad make of Alan as my stepfather? I'd like to think he'd be pissed, but in all honesty, he'd probably be happy for my mother.

Maybe that was my cue to give Alan a break. I smiled.

He raised a hand. "I'll be off then. Good night."

I replaced the lid and shuffled after him. "Good night. And thank you."

"Not at all."

As soon as the door fell shut, I went back to rifle through the rest of the box. Yearbooks, pompoms, old school playbills. At the bottom sat a framed picture of Dad, Mom and me, on my fourteenth birthday. My chest tightened as if it had caved into my lungs.

I threw my hairbrush and pens into the drawer of my oak dresser and replaced them with the photo. *Stupid, sentimental Ivy.*

I hung my guards back where they belonged, and reactivated them with an incantation. Half past ten. The clocks ran slow today. Back in the living room, I tried Flo's cell again. He'd freak out when he found out what he missed.

"Ivy? Where the hell are you? Are you okay? I've been looking everywhere for you but—"

"Calm down, I—"

"Don't tell me to calm down. Nobody's seen you. You weren't at work or at home. A pool of spilled coffee outside the office, and I found your keys by the door. What was I supposed to make of that?"

"I tried to phone you."

"No, you didn't." His voice was firm, perhaps a little teacher-like. "I kept the line free so I wouldn't miss your call."

Okay, I saw what had gone wrong. "You didn't answer any calls that didn't come from my number?"

"No, I told you."

Yeah, that figured. "Well, one of those was from me. My cell's in the office and I tried getting hold of you from a different phone, you monkey."

"Oh."

I rubbed the heel of my palm over my eyes. "I'm okay. But I could do with a friend."

"Okay." He hung up. A few beats later, the phone rang. "Me again," Flo said. "You do mean me, right?"

"Who else?"

"I'll be right over."

I rolled my eyes and smiled. *Dork.*

He knocked within seconds. I opened the door, ready for a hug. In one lightning-fast movement, he pulled me into his arms, squeezing me so tight I thought I was going to pass out.

"Can't breathe." My words came as a wheeze.

His embrace warmed the corners in me that Waylon's words had chilled to subarctic temperatures.

Flo loosened his grip and led me to the couch. "Now." He arranged me between the pillows. "Tell me everything."

I clawed my hair, sorting through the day's events. "God, where to start." Feet tucked underneath my butt, I pulled Flo into the seat next to me.

The condensed version of my afternoon spilled out of me. No dithering. Strange how things became more real when said out loud. And a little more frightening for it.

His arm snapped up, his finger extended. "I told you so. I said Guardians were real, didn't I?"

I arched my brows, a little hurt. "That's what you want to focus on?"

He gave me a peck on the forehead. "No. Sorry… In truth, this kidnap attempt has me worried for your safety. Would you like to stay with us? I can use my vampire powers on anyone who tries to mess with you again."

I laughed and patted his hand. "No, that won't be necessary. I appreciate the offer though. What I needed was a hug."

And hug me he did. Then he made me hot chocolate, put on a movie, and cuddled up with me on the sofa. "Better?" he asked.

I glanced over, my heart swelling with warmth. "Much."

He didn't let go of me until the credits rolled.

I sat up. "That was good. Thanks, Flo."

He grinned. "Am I the best friend, or what?"

I chuckled. "You are. Remind me to get you a mug that confirms that."

"Another one? Yeah, all right."

I stretched and yawned. "I'm wiped. Totally, absolutely wiped."

"Then let me not keep you any longer. Till tomorrow, fair maiden." He got up and bowed low at the waist.

"Get out of here, you goof." I threw a pillow after him.

"Oh, all right." He left, and his steps clacked against my hall tiles.

I tracked them with my ears, picturing his bouncing gait. As soon as the lock clicked shut, I slouched into the couch and emptied my brain. An urgent whisper, on the edge of audibility, interrupted my lack of thoughts. I straightened. Did it come from under me?

I slid onto my knees and placed my hands on the floor to get a look under the sofa. Yuck, was that a dead rat? My brain kicked in. The statue. The damn thing had slipped my mind.

I tugged it out, and the whisper became louder, almost forming words. My breaths sped up, but I was too curious to be afraid. The absence of symbols or marks bothered me. It made no sense. What was the point of making a statue if not for decorative purposes? I massaged my forehead and looked again. Huh. How did I miss that? The grain was regular, like one of those 3D posters which morphed into an image if one had the patience to stare at it.

I relaxed my posture and allowed my vision to blur. The world retreated. My eyes and ears tuned into the object in my hands and, one by one, shapes emerged. With the sharpening of the image, the sounds from its core whirled into the noise of a crowd.

A chill coursed through my blood, like frost-flakes on a window. High-pitched cries drilled through my marrow, ripping the air from my chest. Faces on the statue's surface contorted in pain, gripped by the throes of death. My hands clamped tight around the stone. The faces' screams drove tears into my eyes. They *wanted* to be heard. I knew it as I knew the horrors they felt.

My muscles tensed, paralyzing me. Wails roared in my eardrums. Deafening. A dark sentience coated my tongue, my neck, until my lungs shouted out their anguish, adding my voice to theirs.

The stone object fell from my hands.

CHAPTER TEN

THE STATUE DROPPED ONTO THE carpet with a solid *thud*. I ripped open the front door and fled the house. What was wrong with the world all of a sudden? Why wasn't anything in my life, I don't know, normal? I crouched on the step by my driveway and embraced my shaking body, trying to retain its warmth. Tears poured down my cheeks. Tears for the voices, and for myself. I'd never, ever thought it possible for your entire soul to be on fire.

"Ivy?" A tissue dangled in front of my face. "You okay?"

I blew my nose and wiped my eyes to look up at the pale figure. In an instant, the world was back in focus. "Why are you still here?" I asked. "Are you watching over me?"

Florian's eyes shone. "Let's say I take my new profession seriously. But obviously I'm not doing that great a job, because my client just blasted out of her house like spray from a hillbilly's shotgun." He grasped my arm. "Is someone in there?"

"No, no one's in there. At least I don't think so." How could I make him understand? I couldn't wrap my head around it. "The statue. It screams. I mean, it's in pain. *They're* in pain."

He raised an eyebrow. "Oh. That's... What?"

I pointed at the house with a shaking finger. "See for yourself."

"Right." He marched into the house. A moment later he came back, statue in hand.

My gut spun deep inside, as if trying to drill its way out of me. I scooched to the edge of the step. "Stay away with that thing."

"Hey, it's okay. See?" He waved the object around. "Not a peep."

I tilted my head and listened. "You're right."

He held the misshapen rock under my nose. I dodged aside.

He ramped up his frown to a scowl. "Ivy, quit horsing around. You're scaring me."

"I'm serious." I gulped, my throat still sore. "A moment ago it was screaming. Hundreds of voices. I felt their pain."

"O-kaay." Florian sat beside me. "Well, it's quiet now."

I listened again. Still nothing. I leaned closer to my friend, my hands glued to my thighs. The noise was gone, and the faces had disappeared from the stone surface. "I'm not making this up." I rubbed my arms. "It did scream."

His mouth formed a thin line. "It's not that I don't believe you," which I assumed meant he didn't, "but as you can see," he shook the blasted thing, "it's fine now."

"I wasn't imagining it." Tough not to sound like a five-year-old if you're treated like one. I sighed. No point taking it out on him. With deliberation I set about relaxing the coiled tension from my muscles.

Flo patted my arm. "Honey, you have an excuse to be jittery tonight. You've been through a lot. How are you feeling now?"

I didn't have the energy to come up with a retort for the *jittery*. "Like the universe is messing with me."

We sat in silence for a few minutes. The breeze whispered in the trees, air heavy with impending rain.

"It's getting late," I said at last, "and I'm absolutely wiped."

He pulled me to my feet for another hug. For once, his cologne didn't lift my mood.

I stepped back. "Good night. And thanks."

"Hang on. You forgot your doodad." He pressed the statue into my hand. "Get some sleep."

I watched him walk to his post across the street, then stared at the thing I was holding. The knotted mess that was my stomach unfurled somewhat, although I hadn't forgotten the earlier turmoil. Who knew if I'd ever forget?

Back in the living room, I stuffed the statue under my sofa. At least I could take comfort in having a vampire watch over me tonight.

"Tell me, Felicity. Do you think of me often?"

My muscles lacked control. I couldn't shake my head or sneer.

"I shouldn't have tried to pick you before you were ripe. I fear I tipped my hand too soon."

A cloud clogged my brain. My thoughts meandered, refusing to stay focused. I whimpered.

"Shh. Everything is going to be all right. You're ready now. All grown up. To hold you in my arms again, bathe you in such sweet pain. Not long now."

Lathan's hands trailed down my shoulders, nerve endings quivering under his skillful manipulation. I needed to flinch, to move. Instead, I gave a rapturous moan. My stomach churned. Oh God, I didn't mean to.

"I've had many nights to dream up new games, my darling. I will make you crave me, thirst for my touch. Very soon, sweet Felicity. Very soon."

I awoke with a start. Light streamed in through the curtains, bright enough to add to the splitting headache pogo-ing in my skull. My eyes took a few seconds to focus. Never before had my nightmares deviated. I had a rotation of maybe three or four scenarios, all based on actual events. This wasn't one of them.

Bile had forced its way up during my sleep, not surprising given the subject of my nightmare. Christ, why would I dream of Lathan like this? I swallowed, but the bitterness on my tongue remained. His touch had been so real. I'd felt him doing things, yucky things, to my mind. Did this latest nightmare mirror a subconscious desire?

My arms locked around my body. No way. Motive or not, I couldn't be so depraved. His letter and the kidnap attempt must have rattled me more than I'd admitted to myself.

The family photo I discovered in my box last night drew my gaze.

Yup. Dreams aside, my reality held its own mysteries. Was Waylon's crazy tale true? Why had my mother never told me I wasn't her real daughter? Looking back, perhaps not being biologically related explained our disconnect. My dad had made her raise me as her own, then abandoned her in his death. Perhaps that had left her with a sense of resentment.

I peeked out the hall window to find Florian's post empty. Probably getting some rest. With the distance of a few hours' sleep, his reluctance to believe me now seemed logical. I'd been a victim of my nerves coupled with a bad case of imagination. But Waylon's story… Shit, I had to know how much of it was true.

My parents' house sat on a rolling hill beyond a line of trees. Despite the short twenty minute ride, I rarely visited my mother, and each time I did, my emotions ran riot. The carefree memories of running into Dad's arms were tainted by the knowledge I would never do so again.

It was nine thirty by the time I stepped onto the drive and paid the cabby. Alan's car wasn't in its usual spot under the large yew tree. Good. My resolve to be nicer to him hadn't yet faded, but the conversation I had in mind was between Mom and me.

I unlocked the door and stepped inside. Light flowed through large windows into the drawing room and bathed the walls in a vivid orange. My mother wasn't here, and she wasn't in the spacious lounge either, so I continued through the house to the patio. She sat in a chair on the lawn, where she sipped iced tea under a large striped parasol that offered protection from the midmorning sun. A prudent precaution in summer, but in fall, a mere affectation. I sighed. This conversation was going to be a blast.

The vista gave a good idea of the size of the estate. Part of the lake where I'd learned to swim glittered through a patch of sparsely foliated trees. The sight was so familiar it hurt. At least my family's wealth made sense, what with my dad being royalty.

"Hi." I lifted a hand.

My mother, dressed in a white suit, blended seamlessly with the chair she sat on. While her greeting was friendly, it lacked any noticeable enthusiasm for my unannounced visit. With an authoritative wave, she instructed the maid to bring another cup and a pot of coffee for me.

"Where's Alan?" My fingers danced over the scones and pastry, and my stomach gurgled, reminding me I'd skipped breakfast.

"Away on business. He left first thing this morning." She blew a strand of short hair from her face and turned her head toward the wide open space beyond the house. "He works so hard. Sometimes I worry about him. He's competing with your father, bless his soul. I reassure him all the time, but you know what men are like."

Even though she knew I didn't, she'd never allow fact to get in the way of a good stereotype. "Speaking of Dad, I ran into an old friend of his the other day. Waylon Carmine?" I raised my shoulders a little as if ducking to await her answer.

She frowned in labored concentration, even though the name was so unusual that, once heard, it stuck to your mind like a glob of bubblegum.

Her eyebrows shot up. "Yes, yes, I believe I know who you mean. A terrible mouth on him." And she went about describing Waylon to a T. "Of course, he'd be a lot older now. Hopefully more civilized."

Hardly. As for his age, no point telling her Waylon was a demon, and that when it came to kinfolk, the concept of growing old took on a relative dimension. Instead, I studied her face. She revealed no hint of suspicion that I might have uncovered her secret.

I sipped the fresh coffee, its aroma making my eyes roll. Damn, she had the best stuff. "Speaking to Waylon made me realize how little I know about our family history. Like, where did you and Dad actually meet?" My gaze fixed on her face so I wouldn't miss a single telltale blink.

She picked a scone and cut it with the precision of a surgeon before putting a piece in her mouth. "We met in an antiques shop in Redwood. It was a whirlwind romance, and you were born almost before we had time to say our vows." She laughed, then her face lost its cheer. "It was a bit scandalous at the time, of course. My parents were outraged. Oh, we were so in love. This Waylon, he was your dad's best man."

My mother was a straight shooter, so her flat-out lies lit a fuse in me.

"What happened to Waylon?" I asked. "Why didn't he stick around if he and Dad were so tight?"

"I don't know, Felicity. Why the questions all of a sudden? One day he was there, next he was gone. I'd forgotten about him until you asked, you know."

"Interested, is all. What about you? Have you always wanted to be a housewife and a mother? Or was this Dad's idea?"

"I had plans to become an architect when I was younger, but sometimes life happens. I met your dad, and a career didn't seem important anymore."

Inside my head, I screamed. In the real world, my interrogation proceeded with deliberation. And yet, no matter the question, all I got were vague answers.

You were a quiet baby, good as gold. Your birth? It was over in a flash, dear, without complications. Yes, your father's parents did make it to the wedding, of course they did. Well, it was so long ago, I don't recall what they looked like.

My mother had never been a good liar, and she wasn't lying now. In fact, over the course of our conversation, her answers convinced me of one thing. As far as this woman was concerned, I was her daughter. Period. But if this was true, someone had messed with her mind. Her existence was a constructed lie, and she didn't know it.

My stomach boiled, my temper barely held in check by my curled fists. Besides baby-me, Dad was the only one who'd gained from this web of deceit. His wife was dead and his baby needed a new mother. My lips trembled.

Hang on. Calm down. I didn't know for sure.

The maid popped out for a refill, and my mother asked her to call a taxi for me. Her tennis lesson couldn't be postponed, she assured me, otherwise she would have loved to spend the day with me. "Have you talked to your neighbor yet?" she asked.

"No. And I wouldn't hold my breath. He's a busy guy, you know."

She shook her head. "Well, have you made any effort?"

To stay out of his way? Plenty. "It doesn't matter. But I may have met someone else."

"How exciting. Listen, we should do this again. Then you can tell me everything about him, okay?"

I nodded, my heart contracting. Deep down, she still cared for me, without a clue her affection was rooted in a lie.

How would Dad have managed this level of mental re-write? To invoke such strong magic, he would have needed help. Waylon would be his obvious partner-in-crime. Bending my mother's will wouldn't have cost the demon a single doubt.

I drew her into a spontaneous hug.

For a fleeting second she returned my embrace. "What's up, dear?" She extricated herself. A smile touched her lips. Was this genuine tenderness in her eyes?

"Nothing, Mom. I had a good time. Thank you."

She walked with me through the house to the already waiting cab, my arm through the crook of her elbow. I didn't care what Waylon said. This gentle woman by my side was my mother.

A long ride home and two cups of strong coffee later, I was in the garden venting my frustration on the weeds.

Round about the time I'd pulled my sixtieth plant invader, a throat cleared behind me. I turned. Parker stood outside the fence. What did he want?

"Er. Hi." I raised myself to a standing position and placed a palm on the small of my back.

"Hi. Listen. About that coffee. Are you free now?" His hands hid deep in the pockets of his casual slacks.

If I hadn't known better, I'd have thought him a regular guy, maybe in his late twenties or early thirties, asking a girl out on a date.

Except he wasn't a regular guy. Something about him made him stand out from the crowd. And this wasn't a date.

My gaze dropped to the patch of lawn under my feet. "*Right* now?"

"Yes."

I swallowed. Only one way to find out his true intentions. "Okay."

"Okay then." He lingered.

Were we meant to shake hands?

He shrugged and turned. "Pick you up in thirty minutes."

He hurried back to his mansion, and I wiped my clammy hands on my jeans. My heart pumped hard. Was agreeing so fast, or at all, a good idea? Without knowing what scheme he was cooking up, I was more at risk from him than ever. Then again, werewolves hadn't stayed undetected by normal humans for so long by killing off their neighbors.

After a hot shower and a thorough scrub, I rifled through my closet for something to wear. Coffee with a werewolf was new territory for me. How did one dress for the occasion? Combat pants and a machete, together with a laced, raw twelve-ounce steak, in case he had an attack of the nibbles, perhaps?

I put on my jacket. A rustle from within drew my focus to the paper, more crinkled than ever, with the picture of the property. *My* property.

I folded it up and stowed it back in my pocket. Whatever Waylon had told me, in that house or one like it, away from Silverton and the bad memories, I'd be human again. Soon. Lathan's only way of getting to me here was through his minions. Once I was out of their reach, I'd be out of his, too. But until the day I waved bye-bye to this sorry town, I'd take the blows as they struck me. Including a non-date with Parker.

I checked the clock at half past eleven, and then waited on the bench in my yard. No words could capture how stupid I felt. Even in those lonely moments, when I'd wrestled with my desire to get a date, a werewolf, or any kin, had been at the bottom of my list of dream candidates, right behind Austin Powers and 'The Blob.'

As if on cue, Parker's large frame appeared on the path behind my house. His almost amber hair was cut short at the sides and a little longer on top. He'd opted for a fitted brown sweater and black pants, which hinted at long, strong legs. All the better for chasing his prey.

It was simple enough attire, yet it packed a punch. A pressure in my chest made me ache to touch him, to draw him close. I pressed two fingers against my temple. Yeah, a crush on a killing machine wasn't what I'd hoped for. To mask my embarrassment, I put on a relaxed, almost bored expression. "I'm so sorry about this." I got to my feet and stepped over the fence to stand opposite him.

Wow. That cologne of his did odd things to my head. My thoughts dissolved, replaced with ones of me and him cuddled up before a fireplace. As if.

I angled away from him. "You don't actually have to go, you know. My mother, she can be, well, a force of nature. She means well, though." I twisted on my heels. "I think."

He waved it off, as if dealing with unreasonable mothers was his part-time job. "We should discuss a few things, shouldn't we?"

Should we? At least this vague suggestion blew my cozy thoughts away.

"We *are* neighbors." His gaze remained firm.

"I guess." I followed him to his car, telling my heartbeat to shut up for once.

His choice of coffee shop was a local café I hadn't been to before. The scent of roasted Columbian beans softened my tension. The cakes had a home-made look to them, and the coffee machine that dominated the area behind the counter was a feat of engineering in gleaming steel.

Parker pointed toward the back. "Go find a table for us. I'll get the coffee."

Although I preferred to pay my way, I had a feeling this would be a no-go with him.

A discreet booth in the back offered privacy, and I used the brief respite to settle my nerves. Parker took the tray from the counter and glanced around, searching. I waved to catch his eye.

"Afraid somebody might spot us together?" He set down the tray with a bemused smile.

On a plate between the two coffees sat a white chocolate chip muffin, a slice of chocolate gateau and mini chocolate cupcakes. I was warming to him already. "After everything, the least I could do was make sure you don't have to be seen with me." At his invitation, I picked a mini cupcake.

"So, do you often take pictures of people after dark, Felicity?"

I gulped down the cupcake in a few swallows. "I'm a private

investigator. That's what we do. And my name's Ivy. In the part of the world where my mother isn't in charge, I go by my middle name."

Parker placed both elbows on the table, rested his chin on one hand and regarded me for a moment. "So, Ivy. A P.I., eh?" He smacked his lips. "Don't take this the wrong way, but you don't exactly look like Philip Marlowe."

"Your point being?" I narrowed my eyes, while my mouth pulled into an unbidden smile.

"You're tiny. I mean, I'm sure you can take care of yourself. What if you need to overpower a 200-pound man, though? Do you at least know how to shoot your gun?" His eyes glinted.

"Shoot?" I scrunched my nose. "Yes. Aim and hit the target? Not so much. The last guy who made fun of my size still walks with a limp."

"See, you hit one target right."

I lifted my gaze. "I was aiming for his groin." I squished my cupcake. "No, I don't carry a gun. And believe it or not, my size is an advantage. If you were an unfaithful husband and I followed you to a bar, trust me, I'd go unnoticed among the usual throng of people."

Parker's grin turned mischievous. "Well, Veronica Mars, I hate to be the bearer of bad news." His voice reverberated through my nervous system. "I'd notice you." He sipped his coffee. "If I was an unfaithful husband, that is."

Heat rushed to my head. Was he flirting with me? "My attempt to blend would only fail if I were too distracted. If you were the unfaithful husband." Cripes, was I flirting with him?

His grin deepened, and I, too, beamed at the latte in front of me. Who'd have thought a werewolf could be so playful?

He fumbled with his cup. "From your mother's matchmaking attempts I'm guessing you don't have a boyfriend?"

More blood poured into my face, egged on by my racing heart. "So, you're in computers, aren't you?"

"Yeah, that's right." He might be too polite to chuckle at my inelegant segue, but his lips twitched as if it was hard work.

His open posture was a far cry from the threatening air he'd put on in the park. His hands lay flat on the table. Almost touching my own. Anyone observing us would have thought we'd been dating for months.

Soon the coffee shop's lunchtime business picked up and the "Mom-Mom-Mom" of the four-year-old twins in the booth next to ours got too much.

"I think that's our cue. Ready?" Parker flicked his head and got to his feet.

Five minutes later, I leaned back in the blue BMW sedan's molded seat. "Do you write the software yourself?"

He joined the flow of traffic. "In the beginning I was hands-on. Hacking into people's computers, virtual holidays, I offered all sorts of services and products to fringe elements of society. The wackier the better. Sadly, the customers with the big bucks lacked my sense of adventure. So I went mainstream, and the company took off."

"I'm no expert, but I'm pretty sure hacking's illegal."

His glance was all tease. "Only if you get caught." His cell beeped. "Excuse me." He reached for his Bluetooth ear set and pushed a button. "Reeves."

Outside, the clusters of buildings thinned. Trees swayed in the breeze, launching red and yellow leaves into the air.

"She did *what?*" Parker's voice spiked, adding a layer of tension over the otherwise pleasant afternoon.

My focus shifted, like a veil being draped over my eyes. A warmth displaced my unease. What was going on? Was he glamouring me? But werewolves didn't have those powers. Did they?

"Don't do anything until I get home." His words rolled like gravel down his throat. He took his earpiece out and slammed his hand on the steering wheel.

I tried to drag my fading apprehension back, reached for it with my mind, as if yanking a chain. But I didn't have the strength. A sea of serenity lapped over my troubled thoughts, soothing the ripples.

"Sorry." He shot me a quick glance. "There's some stuff brewing on the, uh, family front. It's hard to explain."

I brushed the back of my hand over his arm, feeling his small hairs come to attention under my touch. "I understand. I guess handling a large pack is quite the responsibility."

"A what?" Parker's grip tightened around the steering wheel, his knuckles turning pale. He swerved to a halt at the side of the road near the entrance to a hiking trail.

Why wasn't I scared? I'd given away my secret to a werewolf. But Parker wasn't who I thought he was. Perhaps my Guardian genes gave me a deeper insight into the real him.

He leaped out of the car, sprinted around and ripped open the door.

His forcefulness brought a smile to my lips. "Where are we going?"

He carted me out by the elbow and pulled me deeper into the woods. "How did you know?" A cavernous rumble underpinned his words.

The pitch of his voice didn't tally with the vibe I got off him. I stumbled, not sure how to read him. Was he angry with me?

"I said, how did you know?" He gave me a shake.

"What do you mean?" The sound of my weakness was like a slap in the face. What the hell was wrong with me?

Parker's face twisted, his brows furrowed. A dull ache from where he gripped my arm traveled along my pain receptors. Dear God. A tremor rumbled in my limbs. Had I ignored the warning signs? Even felt safe? What kind of a sicko was I? Or was it something *he'd* done to me?

I delivered a swift kick in the shins.

"Hey." Parker loosened his grip.

I ran as if a hellhound was after me, because right now, there was.

CHAPTER ELEVEN

THE SWIRL IN MY MIND had me so bewildered, I hadn't thought to use my guards. I tried to pull them out now, but couldn't get to them without slowing my pace. Behind me, a twig cracked. Either that, or Parker was literally snapping at my heels.

The speed guards on my belt didn't require my touch. How could I've forgotten? My lips moved and—

The white-as-cotton-wool creature was by my side, then under my feet. Of course he had supernatural speed. I flailed my arms, forcing me to divert my focus from the spell. No good. I fell sprawling down the hill and landed on my stomach. The impact killed my scream, and the sudden pain in my chest drove tears to my eyes.

I pushed myself up. Something heavy came down on my back, pressing me flat on the ground.

I'd been stupid, so stupid.

My mass of trembling limbs jerked to throw him off. My only thought was to get away. To not die. My arms lashed out, elbows back, to punch the wolf. My bone connected. A yelp. But there was no give. No promise of escape. He was too damn strong.

A rumbling growl grew from a place above my head, reverberating down my neck and spine, shaking my muscles into limp surrender. Warm breath blew against my ear. A long, rough tongue slid over my cheek. I clenched my teeth. The rest of me played dead.

The furry load on my back shifted, spread along my body, and human hands pinned my wrists.

"Shh. It's okay. Never run from a werewolf, especially not if he's upset. Ever." Parker took a deep breath. "I'm going to turn you over now, okay? Stay calm."

He pushed himself up on one hand and rolled me over with the other. Supported by his elbows, he lay face to face with me. Whatever weird werewolf mojo he'd used to muddle my mind earlier, it was gone. My thoughts were clear. Relatively speaking.

My breathing refused to slow down. Specks of gold sparkled in his eyes, and the muscles in his shoulders undulated with the tiniest motion. God help me. He was naked. I peered at his bare chest, smooth and sculpted like a model's, and blood pooled in my cheeks.

I made myself lay still, focused on the cold seeping into my back from the forest floor.

He hadn't killed me yet. I was still intact. I'd call this a draw in my favor.

"Hey. It's over, okay?" His hand cupped my trembling chin. "Why did you run?"

"You hauled me into the woods." I controlled my tone, eager not to annoy him.

"Hey, I got upset. That's understandable, isn't it?"

I glowered.

"Oh, God," he said. "You actually thought I was going to hurt you? Werewolves are nothing like you see in the movies."

"I know about your kind. I once had a run-in with a pack of lycae."

His forehead furrowed. "Not the same! We're sentient. They're animals." His chin jerked. "What aren't you telling me? You say you've seen lycae, which to my knowledge don't exist in Oldworld. Are you fae? What?"

I strained to breathe under his weight and made a wheezing sound. He placed his elbows further up by my shoulders and eased the pressure, but didn't release me.

"It's none of your business what I am." If my voice could kill, he'd be facing rigor mortis soon.

His eyes narrowed. "It is now. You'd better talk, or this is going to be a cold, wet, and highly intimate night for both of us. Because I'm not budging."

Inside my body, a puckering far south warred with the desire to punch him. "What the hell." I lolled my head to the side to avoid his gaze. "I'm not as human as I thought I was. I just found out I'm part sidhe and part satyr. Lucky me."

"Okay. Doesn't explain how you could have run into lycae."

"I once spent some time in Alethia as Lathan's guest. Yes, *that* Lathan. It wasn't voluntary. And I don't like talking about it." I peered at him from the corner of my eyes.

He raised his eyebrows. The rest of him was still, unthreatening, and my body relaxed. Even my mind calmed. Then again, I'd learned that around him, my feelings couldn't be trusted.

He got to his feet. "Come on." He led me back the way we came, his hand clasped around mine.

I stumbled after him. My diaphragm twitched, further antagonizing my queasy stomach.

His clothes formed a small pile at the base of a tree, almost as if he'd taken the time to fold everything up before he'd come tearing after me. While he got dressed, I focused my attention on a small clearing just ahead. For the most part. Every peek I stole at his bronze body and his cannon-ball butt cheeks sent another heat wave through me. In the end, I turned around to escape temptation. The spicy fragrance of the sun-drenched lilac shrubs, now past full bloom, flooded my lungs.

"It's beautiful here, isn't it?" He stood behind me.

His warm, regular exhalations fell like sunshine on the top of my head. He was so close, I could no longer distinguish between the scents of the forest and the biting aroma of coffee on his breath.

"Still alive in there?" he whispered. "I can't smell any fear on you now."

"I'm absorbing everything. So much has happened, it's a wonder my brain hasn't imploded."

He turned me to face him. "Sorry I didn't catch on earlier, but I get that being torn out of the human world and thrown into one of magic must be frightening. Even after all you've been through, or especially because of it." He bunched his mouth. "If you're willing to learn, I'll show you it doesn't have to be scary. I can help you. Books on kinfolk, self-defense; we'll find a way to beef you up."

I frowned. "I know plenty about kin." After all, I owned a copy of *The History of Preternatural Races in the Oldworld*. It held buckets-full of info on the blood-thirsty and downright terrifying elements of society. "Plus, I can wield guards. Don't go getting any ideas about saving the damsel. I can look after myself."

"Clearly." He chuckled.

Snorting, I turned my back on him and marched toward the spot where he'd left his car.

"Show me your guards, then." He caught up with me.

Keeping my chin high, I produced them. "They'd knock you out flat."

He palmed them and slid them into his pocket.

I shoved him into a tree. "Hey, they're mine."

He recovered and nudged me, with a lot less force than I'd used. "Just to make sure *you* don't go getting any ideas."

At the edge of the woods, the bright sun was out for once and blinded me. Its rays highlighted the indigo blue paintjob of his car. If there'd been a dent in it, it would have shown, but its bodywork was flawless. Like its owner's.

Heat filled my ears and cheeks again. This was unreal. Was there no way to stop dirty thoughts before they entered my head?

Parker held the passenger side door until I was *safely* tucked away inside.

The engine started with a smooth purr. Now the adrenalin had subsided, a dull ache flared up in my chest, likely from my close encounter with the hard ground. I rubbed small circles over the area, but kept my pain to myself. Intuition told me he'd pick up on any cracks in my armor and use it to further flaunt his dominance.

Parker focused on the road ahead, his face inscrutable. My time with him so far had been quite the rollercoaster ride. Hanging out with a werewolf was trickier than with a vampire. At least Flo had an even temperament, with the exception of a slight sensitivity to blood. I wiggled my nose to combat an itch. "You never told me what you were doing in the park the other night."

"I'm not sure that's any of your business."

"Really? I can't imagine it's any worse than what I already know about you." I drummed my fingers on the arm rest, studying him.

"True. Okay. I bought some weed for one of my pack. Pregnancy is hard on our females, and the stuff helps."

"Ok." I glanced out the window. "Thank you for telling me."

"Sure thing. And now we're friends and all, can I give you some advice?"

I bunched my mouth, expecting nothing good. "Sure."

"Quit letting it slip to folk that you know they aren't human. That's only gonna get you killed sooner."

"It was your wolf mumbo jumbo that made me do that."

He looked at me sideways. "My what? If you think I have mumbo jumbo, you need those lessons on kinfolk more than I thought. I meant you should be less careless." He tilted his head. "And we should teach you how not to fight like a girl."

I was saved from having to think of a witty comeback when he pulled into the driveway. His BMW came to a halt and the engine's hum died. Once again he motioned me to wait inside and sprinted around the car to hold the door for me. Instead of a thank you, I glowered. His bright smile indicated he didn't get the message.

He walked me to my backyard, by all accounts unaffected by my silent treatment. I slid the key in the lock of the glass door leading to my living room and eased it open. "Thanks."

Parker didn't move away. Why wasn't he leaving? Our coffee-slash-attack date was over.

Whatever. See how he likes not getting his way. I stomped into the kitchen, his entry into my house blocked by the humming metal plates my mother thought were art.

He knocked on the glass door. "Don't you want your guards?"

Good point. I marched back and extended my hand, beckoning with my fingers.

"Wanna invite me in?" He dangled the small plates from his fingers and rolled his eyes toward their large cousins on my wall.

What was the use? He hadn't killed me so far. "Come in. Don't break anything."

He handed me my possessions and headed straight for the carved copper plate above the sofa while I stood, uncertain, in the center of the room. My mother's upbringing urged me to offer him a drink. As if.

His cell rang. He retrieved it from his pocket and spoke in short sentences. "I'm coming now." He hung up and glanced at me. "Sorry, I need to go. But I did have a good time." He stepped close and fixed those big, brown eyes on me. "You know, before we started assaulting each other."

I stared up, transfixed, and smiled. "See ya."

Truth was, I'd enjoyed myself, too.

At one thirty, I was on my way to a *real* date with Greg. Rumor had it dates didn't have to end with being chased by a hairy animal. Greg was perfect to test the theory. I walked into the New Deli, a mere twelve minutes late, rolling my hands into fists to warm my fingertips.

Greg sat at a corner table, from where he greeted me with an exuberant wave, followed by a peck on the cheek.

"Nice to see you, too." I beamed. "What can I get you?"

"Surprise me."

I bought a couple of sandwiches at the counter, one for each of us, and fell into my seat, confidence wavering. "So, tell me about your day."

He shot me a bashful smile. "I found a large diamond, won the lottery and ran into Angelina Jolie. Still, seeing you's been the highlight."

A sheet of warmth unfolded under my skin. "Flatterer."

"Is it working?"

Oh, it so was. Somehow I couldn't wipe that smile off my face. "Maybe. Keep going and I'll let you know."

He did. Within minutes that feeling of year-long familiarity had returned. I could so easily sink into his uncomplicated personality. His voice soothed, while the blue of his eyes whipped up quite the frenzy in me. A heady cocktail that wouldn't let go.

Many of the diner' visitors appeared to be regulars, because hardly anyone studied the menu before ordering. Was Greg a regular, too? He sat with an arm up on the backrest of his bench and looked more than comfortable in the surroundings. He chatted about work, about his coworkers, and after I mentioned my ailing Mustang, about his Corvette.

Yet so far, he'd given me very little about himself, a sure-fire way to pique my curiosity.

"So. Who are you?" I placed my elbow on the table, chin in hand. "Any skeletons I should know about?"

He shifted forward, but not as if in discomfort. More as if reaching a decision. "I was raised in the South by my mother and a cat named Blinky." His gaze dropped. "When I was sixteen, I fell in with the wrong crowd. Add to that the rebellious phase teens go through, and it's no wonder I earned me some trouble with the police." He placed his hands on his table like a man with nothing to hide. "I was never officially charged with anything, though."

I leaned back from him. Nothing about him screamed danger or bad boy. If anything, he had a gift for taking my mind off the elephantine hiccups in my life. Guess he'd turned himself around.

I placed my palm in his. "It's okay. Thanks for being honest with me. That couldn't have been easy."

"Some things are worth the risk, you know?" His thumb traced the ridges between my knuckles.

"I guess they are." I underpinned my words with a meaningful gaze at our hands. "So what brought you to Silverton?"

Three women carrying about a hundred shopping bags filed into the table behind me. They were loud, not just in voice but in attitude and actions. We waited for them to settle, exchanging coy smiles in the meantime.

"Where were we? Oh yes. The reason I moved to Silverton." Greg's full eyebrows jiggled. "The call of fame and fortune." He shook his head. "No. A buddy had a business proposal. It sounded good, so I packed up and landed here."

The woman sitting with her back to me struggled up from her bench and kicked my foot, which I'd angled away from my seat. She waddled off to the bathroom, and I sent her a nasty glance.

"Would you like to go for a walk?" Greg asked.

I glanced at the wall behind him. The dark-framed clock opposite me showed the time. "Oh." I double-checked on my watch. Damn. How could it be three already? "I'm sorry. I'd love to, but duty calls, or at least paperwork and phone calls do."

He folded his fingers around my hand. "When can I see you again?"

My heart thumped in my throat. "The weekend?"

"That's a long time to wait." Greg pulled me closer across the table. He leaned in. A mouth softer than whipped cream grazed my lips. My insides swirled and skipped, more content than they'd been in a while. He pulled back and glanced up. I smiled. He brushed a strand of hair aside and kissed me again, deeper, lighting a fire in my pit. He parted my lips for a brief caress with his tongue. Too brief.

He withdrew, but held on to my chin. "Maybe we could take the afternoon off and go back to your place?"

Sure enough, my body responded to his words with a powerful urging to blow off work and satisfy the raging desire in me. Behind him, a middle-aged man sent a disapproving glare.

I shifted away from Greg's touch. Something niggled at me. Why was he so keen on me? My allure would affect any guy I believed worthy, Waylon had said. Had I bamboozled Greg? Or was his interest genuine? Jeez, what I needed was a Handbook for Satyrs.

"Everything all right?" He frowned. "I've been going too fast, haven't I? I'm sorry. I'm not usually so forward."

"No. *I'm* sorry." I gave a long sigh. "You have no idea how sorry." Part of me didn't want to leave. Wanted to ignore my doubts.

"That's okay. I didn't mean to pressure you." He sat up and removed his hand from mine. "Besides, work comes first. So, the weekend?"

"The weekend." Encouraged by his grin, I gave the man behind him a challenging smile and stole one last kiss.

Then we went our separate ways.

I stopped back home to pick up the statue from under my sofa. By the time the office building popped into view through the cab window, it was nearly four. I was still high on Greg-ness. Our date had been so easy. No complications. No fear he might turn furry at a second's notice, or attack me in a frenzy if I got as much as a paper cut. Perfect, if it hadn't been for my suspicions about whether his attraction was real.

I entered the office. Florian looked up from a newspaper and smiled. His tailored smoky green jacket gave him a perfect male model figure, which, if I knew him at all, was the result of a calculated purchasing decision.

"What time do you call this?" he said.

Typical. The one thing Flo wasn't laid back about was time-keeping.

I waved him off. "Keep your pants on. Have you checked for news about the Carters? The papers should have the story by now."

He waved the newspaper in the air. "Nothing."

The phone on my desk rang. I answered, making it a point to ignore Florian who held up his wrist and tapped his watch.

"Ivy? It's me. Fred."

I pointed at the phone and mouthed *Fred*, then twisted the invisible mouth key so Flo would stay quiet. My boss would find out about my new hire in person, not during his break. "Hey, you. Having a great time?"

"Listen. I should have told you earlier. I cut my vacation short, because I got a lead on Heather, a possible eyewitness to her disappearance." His voice cracked.

Six months ago, his daughter Heather vanished. One day she'd brought him his lunch, the next she was gone. Hardly a trace.

"That's great." I frowned. "But four-month-old information? Is that going to be reliable?"

"I'll take what I can find."

Who could blame him? Since her disappearance, Fred's wrinkles had deepened trying to figure out what happened. Smiles had become a rare treat. "Need my help?" I asked.

He laughed so quietly I had to strain to hear it. "That won't be necessary. Could you just check something for me? It's in her file."

"Yeah. Hang on." I put the phone down and opened the drawer to my, or rather Fred's, desk.

The yellow folder was well thumbed and frayed at the edges. I spread out the large photos and documents it contained in front of me. Most of the pictures I'd seen many times. One of Heather. Another of the clothes she was likely to have worn on the day of her last sighting. An alley where the cops found a purse that Fred identified as hers, even though it lacked any distinguishing features or sure-fire proof she'd owned it. The remaining pages were copies of the police report Fred had received from a contact within the police department.

I picked up the phone. "Got it. What is it?"

Silence.

"Fred?" I glanced at Florian, who raised his eyebrows. I shook my head. "Fred? Still there?"

The line was dead.

CHAPTER TWELVE

I SLOWLY HUNG UP, HAND TREMBLING. Patchy reception wasn't anything new, and we'd been cut off before, but something in his voice set off alarm bells.

"What happened?" Flo sounded worried.

"He… I don't know. We got disconnected. Hang on." I tried to rouse my boss on his cell, which went straight to his answering machine. "No. Maybe he had to turn off his phone."

"Or maybe the people at the pool told him to keep the noise down."

I stared at my friend. "What pool?"

Flo sat on the edge of my desk. "Well, he's on vacation, right?"

"That's what I thought. Turns out, he's investigating his daughter's disappearance. And he didn't tell me." In a way, I wasn't surprised he'd turned up a clue on his daughter the cops had missed. Behind his deeply-etched smile lines lurked shrewd investigative skills. I rubbed my temples. "I don't like him going off by himself."

Florian placed a hand on my shoulder. "Did you know her?"

"She and I hadn't been friends exactly, but I liked her. *Like* her, I mean. Present tense." I sniffed.

Heather going AWOL had hit too close to home for me. I'd convinced myself everything would turn out all right for her. She had eloped with a secret boyfriend. Or gone traveling. But maybe I should have known better. She could be in trouble, and only her dad was searching. Or she could be dead.

"Ivy?"

I blinked. "What?"

"It's getting late." Mr. Tactless was at it with his watch again.

Even without being clairvoyant I foresaw some nasty encounter with the sole of my sneaker in its future.

"Stop doing that." I made sure my glare packed a whopping big punch.

"You can try his cell again later," Flo said. "He's fine. If he was in trouble he'd have said something, right?"

Yeah, Flo and Fred hadn't met. My boss wasn't the type to bother anyone. Still, Flo had a point. With Fred, age was on the outside. Inside, he was as sprightly and active as a forty-year-old.

"Okay, let's go." I took my bag and traipsed out of the office. He locked the door and overtook me as I got to the elevator, and then ushered me in with a flourish of his hand. Polite *and* efficient. Come to think of it, he might be my mother's ideal man. If he wasn't being nicer to me, I'd introduce them.

We drove to see Peter Henderton's antiques warehouse.

Henderton's place was situated at the far end of the old industrial estate. Florian pulled into Redbrick Road. Since Silverton had become a major hub for computer technology, many more traditional companies had been forced to shut down, leaving warehouses unattended and in disrepair. Isolation and abandonment as far as the eye could see. Yet against the backdrop of the bright pink dusk, the area had a somehow romantic feel. Go figure.

We parked in the concrete yard in front of the building. I slung one strap of the backpack over my shoulder, leaving the other dangling.

My gaze swept over the building. No main door, only a faded sign with Henderton's name above an open gate. Inside the warehouse, empty crates lined the wall and patches of packing wool littered the pocked cement floor.

"Hello," I shouted. "Mr. Henderton?"

A tall, bulky man with a thin, fraying moustache strode toward us. Henderton didn't look anything like I'd imagined him. As if his green eyes and his aura hadn't already convinced me he was a demon, his walk practically screamed 'I want to crush you with my bare hands and plug the holes in my house's foundation with wads of your still warm flesh.'

"Ah, Ivy Bell. Good. Peter Henderton. Is my name, I mean. Let's see the statue you were talking about."

I tightened my fist around my backpack's strap. "I brought a picture. The actual statue's not in my possession."

"Not good enough. I'll need to look at the real thing."

I took a step back, my pulse hammering in my head. No way was this the real Henderton. His intonation was all wrong.

Florian tensed, but didn't make a sound. We were such a good team. Like Batman and Robin. Or Cagney and Lacey. With me being the tough, bitchy one, of course. He simply lacked the attitude.

I lowered my hands to my pockets. "There was an accident at the owner's house and the police have the statue now. So the picture is all I can show you."

A snap came from the dark belly of the warehouse.

"You're lying," fake Henderton said. "I know you took it from the Carters. Show me your bag, Miss Bell."

The Carters? "Yeah, I don't think so." A flash of insight. That night when I'd found the statue, the demons had mentioned another guy waiting outside. "Say, you wouldn't happen to be called Jeff, would you?"

A small, stocky demon stepped out of the shadows. He stared at us like he'd study the menu for his favorite restaurant. Yes, we were definitely the appetizer. He cracked a grin. "How does she know your name?"

So my shot in the dark had hit the bull's eye. "You mentioned the Carters. Henderton never knew that name." The sharp edges of my guards cut into my palms. I glanced at the tall man. "You followed us home that night, didn't you?"

The shorter of the two demons slapped his partner's head. "You idiot. You were seen."

Jeff shrugged. "What does it matter? They're here, and they probably have the statue in that bag."

Shorty wiggled his head and laughed. "Let's see." He swaggered toward us.

Jeff followed at his heel. "Be a good girl now. It'll be over in a second."

The quick double toe loop of my heart faded against my single-minded focus. The good news was that, somehow, Jeff had missed Flo's performance outside the Carter house. Plus, they didn't know about my guards.

I peered across to Flo, whose sanguine smile sent a shiver down my spine. His serenity didn't bode well for the demons.

To give the magic time to pool inside the metal plates, I retreated until I'd reached the concreted area outside the warehouse, where the pink of the sky had been replaced by navy blue, dotted with hundreds of tiny, yellow stars. Skin magic would be overkill at this stage. Use guards, avoid physical contact. Simple, really.

Jeff swaggered after me and came within striking distance just when my plates vibrated with maximum power.

I aimed my hand at his chest, the guard hidden in my palm. "*Fintero.*" My whisper was barely audible.

A stream of sparks painted the night a pale blue. The flare of energy ripped him off his feet. He collapsed on the ground, skull striking solid cement. His eyelids twitched once, twice, and he lay still.

Hell. What kind of sissy-assed demon was this?

Florian, who'd finished his exchange without creasing his shirt, watched me with a glint of appreciation in his eyes. "Good deduction on the Jeff thing," he said. "How'd they know we'd be here, though? Do you think Henderton is working with them?"

"What am I? Madame Zarutha, clairvoyant extraordinaire?" The adrenaline pushed my voice up an octave. I took a few measured breaths to diffuse my panic. I was safe. We both were.

Flo placed his fists against his waist. "Well, why don't you check and see if he's hiding out back?"

"Sending me into the lion's den? What about you?"

He rubbed his tummy. "All this exercise has made me hungry." His smile was one of innocence.

My stomach contracted. "You're not going to kill them, are you?"

"This one," his finger shot to the demon by his feet, "is already dead. Broken neck. Very tragic. Yours," he pointed at Jeff, "will be shortly. Waste not, want not, right? Besides, they won't tell us anything. It's not up for discussion, so get! Unless you want to watch, that is."

"But, you can't go around killing people." My tone dipped low. "It's…wrong."

It *was* wrong. Totally wrong. Morality wasn't the only reason for my concern, though. While he claimed not to 'enjoy' violence, he certainly partook in it with a certain casual acceptance. What if all this killing was the first stepping stone on his way into the darkness?

"What do you think they were trying to do to us?" Florian shook his head. "And better the cops find a couple of dead bodies than two alive and pissed demons. The poor humans wouldn't stand a chance." His gentle voice stood in stark contrast to his coal-black eyes.

I gulped my reply. It was scary how eloquently he justified murder. And damn him if he didn't have a point. Besides, I hadn't spoken out when he killed the other two demons.

I wheeled around, tuning out his feasting with a mental rendition of Gloria Gaynor's 'I Will Survive.'

Inside the warehouse, at the far back, the remains of the person I assumed had been the real Peter Henderton lay sprawled on the ground, limbs angled as if trying to fit into a cartoonish body chalk line. *Probably not working with the demons, then.* The broken office lock from the other day offered an alternative explanation. Had they planted a bug? If Jeff had followed us home from suburbia, he could have easily found the office, too.

I sashayed around Henderton's body. My stomach lurched with each step.

A couple of tissues from a box on his desk helped avoid

fingerprints. Henderton, it seemed, had an almost religious aversion to tidiness. His desk heaved under a jumble of papers, and week-old coffee crusted the insides of four mugs.

I thumbed through the stack of documents. Tucked under a half-eaten candy bar was a page with a crude drawing of a statue like the one in my possession. According to Henderton's doctor-like scribble, the stone blob had a name. *Collective.*

Sheet of paper stuffed in my backpack, gaze leveled straight ahead, I walked past the three bodies to rejoin Florian. His rosy cheeks and clear, sparkling eyes spoke volumes about the restorative effect of his snack.

"Felicity, my darling. Come to me." Lathan's peculiar, ephemeral voice floated through my head.

"Leave me alone."

"Why do you fight me?" He sounded genuinely puzzled. *"Haven't I been good to you?"*

I tried to tear myself loose, to push him out of my head. Our conversation became a tug of wills. The more I refused him, the more he persisted. Gradually, though, his mind took over mine, enclosing it from all sides until he extinguished every spark of independent thought.

"Let me show you real happiness." Lathan's resolve became a haven of comfort. *"We are meant for each other. Alethia will kneel before us one day, so powerful is our union."*

The alarm clock shouted a rock song into my ear and woke me.

I sat up and wrapped my arms around my knees. Lathan couldn't leave Alethia. No way, Jose. Julia's books had been adamant, and my early research extensive. He. Could. Not. Leave.

Every bone in my body urged me to let the world revolve without me for a day. But that wasn't me. You idle, you think. In my current state, thinking wasn't a good idea. And yet... My brows furrowed. I slowly got to my feet. What if the statue was responsible for my nightmares? Or what if my satyr or sidhe or guardian heritage was to blame? I knew nothing about my parents' real backgrounds, and how their genes would influence me. Perhaps it was time to learn who I was and where I came from.

I punched a number into my cell phone. The concierge connected me to Waylon's room. "Waylon? It's Ivy."

"Glad to hear from you, babe. I've been worried."

Yeah. Mr. Cool worried? Good one. "I owe you an apology. I charged out of the room like a bull, without even saying thank you."

"No worries. I'd taken you by surprise. In my head the whole scene had played out differently." I wanted to be angry at him for what he'd done to my mother, but his voice sent a tingle racing across my skin.

I swallowed. "You practiced our conversation?"

"Well, yeah. Last thing I wanted to do was upset you. Then I saw you and, boy, I started thinking with my cock."

God, this guy was laying it on. And I was lapping it up. "It's genetic, I've been told."

A brief chuckle. "Add to that the guy trying to abduct you, and I s'ppose I was less than suave."

Heat rose up into my face. At least he couldn't see the red on my cheeks. Small mercies. "Anyway, I'm calling because I need to know more about my parents."

"Like what?"

"For example, how did my mother die?"

"Oh shit. That kind of talk."

"Yes." I firmed up my voice. "And how someone ruined my human mother's life."

The deep breath on the other end lasted forever. "I'd rather talk in person, babe."

"Don't call me babe. I mean it."

"Sure, babe. When can we meet?"

I scratched my neck. Unless he'd suddenly become ugly, a face-to-face wasn't a prospect I relished. Sure, my belly filled with a titillating buzz just hearing his constantly hoarse voice, but why place myself in temptation's way? If anyone was going to feel the effect of my allure again, it should be Greg.

"Still there?" Waylon's voice slid like smoky barbecue sauce through the phone. "You pick the place."

"How about Kelley's, at the corner of Viewpoint Cross and Long Lane? Say, nine o'clock?"

"I'll be there."

I hung up. A crowded bar, with its thumping music and abundance of alcohol, was the worst place to be thrown together with the man who turned me into a drooling mess at the crack of a smile. But perhaps that was the price to pay for the answers I'd been waiting for.

Three hours later, I was back at work. Flo had already bought coffee and cake, and I was ready once more to dive into the mystery of the statue.

"We still don't know what a Collective is. The Internet's proven useless." I shooed Florian out of my way and unpacked the box with our case material. "It is curious, though. To get demons to work together, well, that takes power. They don't usually like playing nice and they never share."

"And we've now encountered two different demon pairings. Since Jeff showed up in both locations, we know all four were connected." Florian re-dunked the bug he'd found in the phone in a glass of water. Once we deduced the presence of a listening device, it hadn't taken long to discover a screw on the receiver was missing. A hatchet job, which made my failure to spot it even more embarrassing. A slip of anger wormed its way into my gut. We were P.I.s and hadn't noticed we were under surveillance.

I tucked my pen's cap end into my cheek. "To get to the big bad, we should start at the beginning. Let's find out the names of the guys you…"

Flo grinned, but made no move to finish the sentence for me.

"…of the demons that killed the Carters." I sent him a bruising stare. "You know. Max and his friend. Their habits, contacts, and friends might lead us to whoever's paying their salaries."

"And how do we get their names, boss? Dead people tend not to be talkative."

"Can't you bamboozle a cop?"

"I could, but how do we find out who's worth glamouring?" Florian wrinkled his forehead. I would have laughed if I hadn't been so tired. After a minute of chewing his lip and scratching his head, he pointed at the computer. "Can't you use that machine to find out?"

"They won't publish this kind of information on a public website. And since neither of us can hack into their system… Oh. Hang on." Why did the craziest ideas always come wrapped in logic?

"What?"

"I think I might know someone who could help us with that."

CHAPTER THIRTEEN

As soon as my house came into view, doubts crawled into my brain. Was this a mistake? Just because a decision was logical and convenient didn't mean it was necessarily the right one.

Florian pulled into his driveway and turned off the ignition. "Ready?"

I twisted my fingers, not sure how to put into words what I had to say next. My sour lemon face probably wouldn't soften the blow. "Maybe you shouldn't come with me."

He shifted in his seat, his gaze probing me. "Why? Is this guy your new best friend? Afraid I'll get jealous?"

"What? That's ridiculous. It's just, well, Parker doesn't know you. I'd have more success if I went by myself, is all." I poked him playfully to lighten his mood. "You know, he might be a tad reluctant to commit a felony in front of a stranger."

Florian's chin jutted enough so his bottom lip stuck out. "Well, what if you run into another duo of demons? Who's going to protect you then?"

"I'm fine." I gripped the door handle. "Why don't you pop home and I'll be over when I'm done?"

"Whatever. But if you're not back in fifteen minutes, I'm coming over."

Even though I wasn't an expert, I was sure hacking wasn't a give-me-a-minute kind of endeavor. Not to mention the time it would take me to convince Parker. "It may take longer than that. Quit worrying. It's our neighbor, Flo. Plus, demons wouldn't be able to get past this guy's security system. Trust me. They have cameras everywhere. Sometimes I wonder if any are pointed at my bedroom."

"Oh, that makes me feel better. You're going into a house full of pervs."

I laughed. "Talk about calling the kettle black." I opened the door and stepped out, then leaned my head back in. "Okay, here goes nothing. Wish me luck." I turned, and my hair caught in the seatbelt pulley of the car. "Ouch!"

"See, you're a mess without me." Florian smirked.

I untangled myself and primmed my lips against the pain. "Okay, I'm definitely going."

I crossed the road and strode up the walkway. Convincing Parker to help me wouldn't be easy, but he was a guy and therefore he could be manipulated. My mother's success at getting him to take me out for a coffee had proven that. If I showed confidence in his ability to get into the files without getting caught, his ego might feel compelled to live up to my expectations.

There were five cars in the parking area outside Parker's house, including his BMW. I strode up to the entrance. The hefty double doors did their best to look impregnable. Everything was designed to not look inviting. Deep breath. I rang the bell.

A tall, broad-shouldered werewolf in flip-flops and board shorts answered the door. Blond wispy hair topped a cherubic face, and by appearance alone, he wasn't more than seventeen or eighteen years of age. He frowned and placed his body in the space between door and frame. With guys with shoulders this broad, why bother investing in doors?

"Hi." I raised a hand. "Can I speak to Parker?"

"I'll check if he's in." The beach boy disappeared up the stairs.

As soon as he was out of sight, I swung open the door and entered the hall.

Nice. I was about to give a low whistle in appreciation of the pristine interior, when Parker and his flip-flopped friend clomped down the stairs.

"Thanks, Rollo." Parker nodded at the Surfer Dude who shuffled off in a huff.

If Parker was surprised to see me, he didn't show it. He greeted me with a firm hand on the shoulder like we were old friends and invited me upstairs into his office. A long stained-wood display cabinet with clear glass doors extended along one wall, and windows on two adjacent sides of the office let in plenty of light. A pile of paper stood neatly stacked on the corner of his desk. Not a speck out of place.

I sat on one of two rolling chairs arranged side-by-side. Parker perched on the edge of his desk and crossed his arms.

Stick to the plan. I cleared my throat. "The other day you mentioned you regretted the lack of excitement in your life. Is that still true?"

His brown eyes looked at me through narrowed lids. "What kind of excitement did you have in mind?"

I swallowed. Where did that dark and broody voice come from?

My prepared speech trickled from my memory. "Nothing. I

mean." Inhale. Concentrate. "I was wondering if you could do a little bit of computer, erm, research for me."

"You want me to search the Internet for you?"

I averted my eyes and directed them to his outstretched legs. Long, muscular legs, covered by dark jeans, which were tight enough to showcase their contents. A wave of muggy heat rose along my spine.

I plucked on the collar of my T-shirt and inhaled sharply. Apparently, my motive only needed a nice pair of legs to make an appearance, and off it went, along valleys of fantasized debauchery and mountains of longed-for ecstasy. With a werewolf, of all creatures.

I forced my attention back up to his face, fumbling to pick up the thread of our conversation. "No. I was thinking along the lines of hacking. You know, into computers?"

His eyes widened, revealing his sparkling brown pupils in full glory. I shifted on my chair, trying to recall the words that were meant to flatter his pride into doing me this favor.

He placed a hand on each of my armrests and rolled my chair toward him. My knees dug into his legs. The fabric of our clothes didn't suppress the jolt that flashed through me. His face inches from mine, I sat rooted between his arms. Breathing him in. Uncertain of what would happen if I stirred.

He moved his lips to my ears. His soft, hurried breath caressed my skin. A series of shivers cascaded down my spine, stroking my back straight in one quavering motion.

"If it's adventure you're after," he said, "I'm sure the two of us can come up with something better than that." He playfully bit my earlobe.

With a push of my legs I jerked the chair, and myself, out of his grasp. "What are you doing?" My words came out more huskily than I wanted. I pitter-pattered my feet to propel the chair backward.

He slunk purposefully after me, his lips parted as if he enjoyed the slow chase.

I reached for my necklace. It wasn't there.

Shit. My mind sifted through the past couple of hours at warp speed. I'd put it on after my shower, had it on at the office, the car… The car! It must have come off when I'd snagged my hair.

The air around me hung heavy with pheromones and promises, and the further away I moved from him, the more I wanted to turn back and jump into his arms.

The wall stopped my retreat. Trapped. I side-stepped up from the chair toward the door.

He caught my arm and spun me around. "No more running." Without warning or fuss, he pressed his mouth onto mine.

Passion slid through my lips, down my throat, setting my body alight. Oh my goodness. How could anyone taste this good? The hands I'd raised to shove him now circled around his neck. Closer, until our tongues knotted into a single unit. Clamped between his hard shape and the wall, I fed hungrily from him, filling the greedy emptiness inside.

A door swung open. "I couldn't stop him, boss."

A hand yanked Parker's arms. He lurched away from me and stumbled. The sudden shift snapped me out of the spell. I blinked at Florian, focusing on him as if waking after anesthesia.

"Ivy?" His words came from far away.

I wobbled. He held me up, his keys dangling from his hand. "It's okay." He deposited me in the chair, then wheeled around and punched Parker in the face. "What did you do to her?" His breath came fast.

Parker's growl ordered the hairs on my arms to stand to attention. In a pleasant way. Too pleasant. I shook my head to throw off the effects. Something was still messing with me. I had to get away. Get my necklace.

I snatched Flo's keys and launched past the young surfer wolf, out of the room. The stairs were too smooth for me to confidently leap down, but somehow I got to the door in record time. Across the road. To the car. With distance from Parker, my heart grew heavy and my legs weak. But I didn't stop until I'd fumbled open the door of the Mercedes. Where was that stupid necklace? I slapped under the front seat, scrabbled inside the map holder, bent to check underneath the car. My pulse zapped in my ears, whispering worst case scenarios. What if I didn't find it?

There. Between the rocker panel and the door, the delicate chain glistened under the on-board lights. The clasp proved stubborn, but I was stubborner. At last, the guard was back around my neck. *Breathe, Ivy, breathe.*

How could I've been so careless? More to the point, how could I've kissed Parker? I hadn't initiated our makeout session, but I'd damn sure joined in with vigor. Oh, what a sneaky little game these two satyr traits had played with me. But I was on to them now. One was as dangerous as the other, and I'd never again be alone with a man without double-checking the necklace was in its place.

Although…the kiss had been quite something. My insides melted just from the memory. How was he still single? Heat pushed into my cheeks. Perhaps I shouldn't think about our tongue wrestling match.

As stoked and confused as I was about our lips' encounter, he was likely to be frantic. Werewolves didn't do *anything* casually.

Oh no. I'd left Florian alone with him. A vamp and a wolf locked in a fight wouldn't end well for either of them. I was back to pounding the gravel before the car door slammed shut. Back across the driveway, through the door, then up the stairs. Parker's and Florian's voices carried down the corridor. I crashed into the room, just as Florian made a swoop for Parker.

Flo skirted Parker's outstretched arm in one quick motion. He twisted to place his fist into Parker's gut. Parker *oofed* then clipped Flo's leg.

"Hey," I shouted. My helpless glance at Surfer Dude elicited a mere shrug.

Why didn't he intervene?

Parker and Flo danced on quick feet, both as nimble as the other. Flo with the floating grace of a hummingbird, Parker with the agility of a fighter jet.

This was getting silly. I stepped into the mix. Surfer Dude caught the fabric of my T-shirt and yanked me back. There was a lot more oomph to him than his lean physique suggested. I thrashed around and fell flat on my ass.

Florian rushed to my side without taking his eyes off the other two. "Are you hurt?"

Parker growled. As it had done before in the woods, my vision blurred. A veil filtered out all negative thoughts, leaving me to focus on a strong and capable Parker.

Luckily, his wolf mojo stopped as quickly as it had started.

"Rollo, leave us." Parker dispatched Surfer Dude out the room and banged the door shut.

A belated flame of pain licked the bottom of my spine as if the impact had disintegrated my coccyx into sawdust.

Flo placed his hand on my shoulder. "Are you injured?"

"I don't think so." I pushed back the wetness pooling in the corners of my eyes. "I'm fine."

"Great. Then you won't mind telling me what's going on." He straightened and placed one hand against his waist. With his other, he pointed a long finger at Parker. "There's no way this guy's human."

"Yeah, well, neither are you." Parker's head was turned down, but his gaze trained on Flo.

I pushed back my shoulders and prepared to channel Martin Luther King, Jr. He wasn't the only one who could unite the races. "Vampire," my hand touched Flo's arm, "meet werewolf." Then

I stepped back, because everyone knew what Dr. King's good intentions earned him.

Neither Parker nor Florian spoke. They glared at each other, necks tight, without blinking. Ten, twenty seconds of peace.

Great. I for one was ready to move on. "Now, back to our conversation."

Parker turned his back on Flo and led me by the arm to a chair. Eager to stretch the harmony a while longer, I let him.

"I'm so sorry for earlier." He crouched before me and took my hand between his. He immediately dropped it as if it were covered with razor blades. "I don't know why I suddenly…I mean, I would never…"

I waved him off, but my guts tensed. He would never? As in, would never…with me? *Asshole.* "Forget it." My tone drew a thick, fat line under that event.

It wasn't as if I fancied him either. My motive had made me succumb to his kiss. It certainly hadn't been *my fault.* I stood and circled his still crouching form.

Parker exhaled sharply. "Ivy, I mean it."

"She said to forget it, dimwit." Florian wrapped an arm around me.

Back at full height, Parker gave me a withering glance. "So why did you come over again?"

Business talk. I could do that. Beat by beat, my pulse slowed. "As I said. We'd like to hire you."

"That so?" He muttered, and his gaze darted back to Florian. "What for?"

"Florian and I are working on a case."

Parker frowned. "Hang on, you work together?"

I tilted my head. "Didn't I say?"

He rubbed the bridge of his nose between index finger and thumb as if to assuage a torrent migraine. "No, I thought you two were… Never mind. So you need work advice?"

"As I was about to ask before things got weird, I'd like you to hack into the police's internal files. Can you do that?"

He let out a low whistle and flopped his butt on his desk. His brows shot up. "Sure, I can." They shot down. "But I won't."

"What? Why?" I glanced between him and Flo, who looked puzzled too.

Parker gestured for Flo and me to take a seat. "You're not a wolf, although you certainly have the temper of one." He acknowledged my lethal squint with a twitch of his mouth. "What I'm saying is that I shouldn't care what you do. But I can't deny a little neighborly concern, and I won't go out of my way to get you into trouble."

"That day when I told you about me, you promised to help." My subtle reminder of our moment in the woods pushed my blood a little bit faster through my veins. "Was that a lie?"

His jaw muscles rippled. A tiny spark of panic punched my gut, before a lightness of mind washed over me and purged me of worries. As an alpha, he was used to analyzing situations for the best outcome. It was my duty to trust him, to abide by his decisions without question.

"I said I'd help you to protect yourself from creatures like him." He pointed at Florian. "I've met his kind before."

I nodded, my thoughts swimming. "He *has* tried to kill me once." I beamed at Parker. "But he didn't mean to hurt me." My gaze zigzagged through the room, then settled back on a shifting Florian. "It's what vampires do sometimes."

Flo scratched his forehead. "Ivy? What's with the swaying? Are you all right?"

With a jolt, I was back. And so was that familiar warmth in my cheeks. Parker's mojo had done it again. He sure knew how to mess with my sanity.

CHAPTER FOURTEEN

THE TWO MEN STARED AT me, Parker leaning against his desk, Flo from my right. Their mouths were drawn tight, but at least they were united in their confusion. And even though I shared it, my odd turns around Parker weren't going to be the subject of conversation.

"I'm good. Sorry." I laughed my time-out off so we'd change topics. "Something I ate, I think."

Even though Florian's frown remained, he knew me well enough to leave it at that.

"Bullshit. What's wrong?" So werewolves smelled lies. Not a rumor then. Best to make a note.

My fingers busied themselves with the hem of my top, and my mind with a wild search for an appropriate response. Perhaps to someone with my ancestry, an alpha's aura was like a piece of chocolate laced with Prozac. But I'd be damned before I told Parker about my Guardian genes. He'd rub his hands in glee if he heard his temper made me go all gooey.

"Things have been kind of hectic recently." With luck, tiptoeing around the edge of the truth wouldn't set off his lie detector. "Both of you finding out my secret, work pressures, you know. I'm tired."

Parker pulled a face. "And you want to add to that by getting me to hack into police computers?"

"Actually, this is what I'm here for." Florian didn't acknowledge my grateful smile. "I'm the one asking for this info. Ivy won't get hurt. I wouldn't allow it."

I sneaked a peek. Did he honestly think he was in with a shot where I'd failed? Parker didn't know him.

The alpha rolled his shoulders, walked around the desk, and lowered himself into his chair. He tapped the end of a pencil on the desk, studying my best friend. "Do you want to tell me what this is about?"

"Not really." Florian flicked his hands in a take-it-or-leave-it fashion. I'd half expected an elaborate yarn of stupendous proportions, but for once, the bubbles that usually seemed to power him were flat.

"I'll find the information for you, if you leave her out of it." Parker's tone left no room for misinterpretation. "So, fang boy, what is it you're looking for?"

Go figure. Not half an hour ago his tongue had done amazing things in my mouth, and here he was helping out Flo while ignoring me like a chewed-up apple core. Men were so flaky.

Flo crossed his legs and locked his hands behind his neck. "I'm looking for information on a crime that happed to a couple called Melissa and Stephen Carter."

Parker had a few follow-up questions. For all I knew, I'd become invisible. I stepped across the room to the cabinet, then moved to the window overlooking my backyard, and finally flopped onto the sofa, very unladylike. My body sank into the soft pillow-hug. The far-too-common puckering behind my eyes was gone, my stomach for once calm. I studied the two men, now engaged in a conversation like adults.

Shudders of bliss still lurked under the surface, ready to emerge every time I thought of Parker's kiss. For a second, his lips and big, brown eyes had sucked me into a different world. A world where my motive ran rampant and passion burned like fire. A glorious world.

But also a world of make-believe, because none of those feelings had been real. My satyr magic had bamboozled both of us. On a conscious level, I understood that. So why couldn't I get past that damn kiss?

"Ivy said you could do it. Now that she's put you under pressure, are you feeling a little impotent there?" Florian's voice matched his challenge. He stood behind Parker, his gaze locked on the computer screen.

"Give me a minute here, pretty boy." Parker waved at him like he'd swat at a fly.

"Dog breath." Florian grinned at me over the edge of the computer. Two fingers came up behind Parker's head. He was giving him bunny ears? What was this, second grade?

"Okay, I'm in." Parker gave a satisfied hum. "What are we looking for again?"

I got to my feet and took a step to join them. His wolfish growl stopped me in my tracks.

"Those the names you wanted?" He pointed at the screen.

Florian fished a pad and a pen from his blazer pocket. The consummate professional investigator.

I laughed. "When you told me you were always prepared, I didn't expect this."

Florian copied down the information. "I'm like the Scouts that way. And if you're a good girl, I'll do some exploring later." His eyes twinkled.

Red so wasn't my color, and yet I felt it descending on my cheeks once again.

"You're such a pig." Parker.

"Fart head." Florian.

"Oh, puh-lease." I rushed over and gripped Florian's sleeve. "Say 'thank you, Parker.'"

"Thank you, Parker." Flo stowed his pad back inside his pocket.

"Thanks. I owe you." I raised a goodbye hand and dragged my friend with me out the room as fast as my little legs could carry me.

Five minutes later, I stood in my kitchen and watched the kettle boil. A task they said was impossible. My shaking hands picked two mugs from the cupboard and placed them on the counter.

"So, what happened earlier? You nearly blacked out there and were saying stupid things." Florian flitted around me like mother hen. "*It's what vampires do sometimes.*" His voice was distorted, as if to mimic me. Badly.

"I don't sound like that." I shrugged him off. "And I don't want to talk about it, okay?" I took a deep breath. "But I'm sorry. I shouldn't have said that."

The coffee granules bubbled on contact with the water and left flakes floating on top. No one makes coffee like the 7-Eleven's no-frills range. Probably because it barely qualified as coffee. It had been a late-night purchase and I didn't like wastefulness. Florian accepted his cup and followed me into the living room, where I kicked off my trainers and took a seat on the couch.

Five minutes later, Julia's head peeked in through the open living room door.

"Hey there. Come on in." I waved her in with a broad smile. "You're back."

Also known as Lisa McMahon, bestselling author of the urban fantasy series *Nightstalkers*, Julia was always at the ready for the stray fan pic or interview. Her makeup was perfect and her eyebrows plucked to give her face an open and approachable look.

"It's been a long trip." Julia disappeared into my kitchen to pour herself a cup, and then sat in the armchair opposite me. She crossed her legs, bouncing the upper one up and down so her spike-heeled shoe was in constant danger of falling off.

"So, Ivy has finally let you in on her secret?" She tilted her head at Florian.

"We *are* best friends. Of course she told me."

"I kind of found out by her reaction."

"What happened?" He glanced at me.

I giggled. "After I escaped from Alethia, I went to Julia unprepared, expecting to find nothing more than a human shoulder to lean on."

"Ah, I get it." He stretched his legs out in front of him, crossing them at his ankles.

"Not sure you can." I scratched my cheek, waiting for the painful rock in my throat to disappear. Odd how memories can evoke emotions as strong as at the original event. "I mean, no one can. Anyway, there I was, a normal human after months in Bizarroland, right? The moment I stepped through your door and spotted Julia, a voice shouted in my head. Vampire! Vampire! Like a DEFCON siren. So I was stammering and stumbling, trying to get away from the kin who'd *stolen* my friend's face."

"It was comical." Julia sipped her coffee and grimaced. "I put her out of her misery and glamoured her into telling me everything about the kidnapping."

"For weeks after that I avoided her and weaved guards to protect me from everything." I softened my expression. "She didn't beg. Instead, she left books by my door. Not just her *Nightstalkers* series, with important points highlighted in neon pink. For example, that you lot can't enter a house without invitation? Total nonsense. Unless the owners have guards, of course."

"I think that's probably how the rumor got started." Flo chewed his bottom lip.

"Could be, yeah." I smiled. "She also surprised me with rare and old books about all kin. My trusted and well-thumbed copy of *The History of Preternatural Races* to mention just one."

He touched his nose. "Ah, I wondered where that had gone."

"And the more I learned about vampires, the more I understood I had no reason to be scared. I now regard you lot as humans with a blood disorder and a hypersensitivity to sun."

"Flattering. Just like that," he snapped his fingers, "you got over it?"

Truthfully I wasn't sure I was over it now, but I was on the road to recovery for sure. I nodded. "Hey, Julia could have killed me. Instead she helped me. I might be neurotic, but I'm not stupid."

He gave a doubting hum. "Let's not rush to conclusions."

I slapped the back of his skull.

He flinched. "Hey, Sis. You know that neighbor of ours, Parker? He's a werewolf!"

She stroked a hand along her bare calf. "I had a feeling he was." Her eyes rolled up. "That body of his is to die for. You know Damian in *Nightstalkers*? I based the description on him. Shame he's a furball. I could have had a lot of fun with him."

That my grin was as fake as the spirited nod I gave her bothered me. Her insatiable appetites hadn't been lost on me, although the thought of her and Parker together made me uneasy.

"Yeah, a real hottie." Flo frowned. "You know what? Let's not talk about him, okay? He's not that interesting."

Julia tucked a strand of hair behind her ear. "Werewolves and vampires have always been at odds with each other. We've had a number of skirmishes with their kind in the twenties and thirties. You should be careful around him, Ivy. It takes a lot for them to shed their humanity and let out the wolf, but once it's done, an angry werewolf can quite easily kill you."

Just my luck then that in those moments when I should be scared of him, his aura mojo comes out and I merely want to cuddle or giggle.

A whisper fought its way into my head. I sat straight.

The soft rustle came from my sofa. My heart rate went up. Why didn't Flo and Julia hear it? Their ears picked up sounds even a dog's couldn't.

Crap. There *was* something wrong with me, then.

"Hey, Earth to Ivy." Julia waved.

Where were my manners? I could practically hear my mother's voice admonishing me. *It's inexcusable to ignore your guests, Felicity, even if you're in the midst of battling insanity.*

Decibel by decibel, the voices dimmed and vanished. An apologetic smile spread over my lips, although I knew it didn't reach my eyes. "Sorry."

Florian tutted. "You're not with it today, are you? I was explaining to Julia why we can't do the shopping for her. I mean, *I* would love to." He placed his hand flat against his chest. "But work comes first. We should case out the demons' home." He looked earnestly at his sister. "We in the business call that a stakeout, Sis. Now, the cops will have tossed it already, but maybe we'll find something human eyes have overlooked."

Good thinking on his part. One hitch. "Actually, I have plans tonight. I'm meeting with Waylon again." His face fell, and I mouthed "*sorry.*" "We'll do it tomorrow, okay?"

"Wonderful." Julia clapped her hands. "My little brother's all mine tonight then. And we have so much to prepare." She scowled at my blank face. "You didn't forget my book launch for *Diner for Lost Souls*, did you?"

Her parties were a surreal treat. I stole a glance at Flo and grinned. "We'll be there." I playfully kicked a leg in his direction. "Anyway, time to go now, Flo. I need Julia's advice."

His expression was one of outrage. "About your meeting with that Waylon dude? Why can't I help?"

"You just can't." I rubbed my warm neck.

"You heard her." Julia lifted her perfectly manicured hands. When he didn't budge, she got up and bustled him out my house. "Girl talk."

His protests were cut off by the door slamming shut. Julia returned. "So what's the story with you and this Waylon? Tell me about him."

Oh, if only there were words. Instead, there was that heart-melting, pulse-spiking sensation that messed with my head at the mere thought of him. I swallowed. "It's not what you think. He was a friend of my dad's."

She smirked. "A *hot* friend of your dad's?"

"So hot." I buried my face in a pillow. "Don't judge."

"I'm the last person in the world to judge. Come on. Let's get to work then."

She beckoned and I followed her into my bedroom. I placed my hands against my hips, surveying the outside of the wardrobe, perhaps expecting instructions. "So, what the hell does one wear on non-dates with one's father's coworker?"

She giggled. "It's not an issue my women's magazines have covered recently, but we can probably put together an outfit without their help, right?"

We spread out my clothes on my bed. Julia stalked from one end of the room to the other, dismissing one combination after the next. She eyed the tiny patch of fabric currently draped over the arm of my chair.

Time to step in. "Okay, I know what you're thinking. That's not a good idea. I was serious when I said this wasn't a date."

She raised her eyebrows and tapped the tips of her fingers against her chest. "What, and you can't look good? It wouldn't hurt to dress up a little, just once in your life. You'll feel more confident, too."

"Like my mother," I mumbled.

"No, honey. Like a friend. You like this man, right?"

Hell yeah. "He worked with my dad. It would be weird. Plus, I'm kind of dating that other guy, Greg."

"Have I been gone that long?" She sat on the corner of my bed.

"I met him, Greg, a few days ago."

"Then it's too early for you to be exclusive." She waved me off. "As for Waylon, I can see how his relationship with your dad might be awkward for *him*, but that shouldn't stand in *your* way."

My brain already shouted every excuse in the world at me to throw myself at him. I'd hoped my friend would talk me out of it, not give me the final shove. "The guy isn't the type to think anything's awkward. You should hear how he speaks. Everything's effing this and effing that. I'm not a prude, but..."

"Turns you on that, doesn't it?"

I wilted under her smirk.

She pursed her lips for a knowing whistle. "I knew it. Okay, so why don't you use tonight to get to know him? And let him see who you are. Not some coworker's daughter, but a person who can stand on her own two feet. And if he accepts you for the amazing person you are, and you can think of him as a good man, then Greg will have to work a little harder to win you over, that's all."

I shot her a beaming smile. She was the best. Always knew what to say when I needed it most.

Or perhaps I was angling for her permission to dress up. Why? Because Waylon had a pull on me I couldn't explain. I touched my lip. My kiss with him had been so different from my kiss with Parker. And my kiss with Greg.

My breath stilled. Oh my God. Was this who I'd become? Miss Promiscuity?

Nothing was going to happen with Waylon. Greg didn't deserve that. He'd been so nice to me. Plus, he was one hundred percent human. A quality I'd come to appreciate lately.

My feeble protests didn't stop her from dressing me in the too-tight black dress, the one she'd gotten me for my birthday, too-spiky heels, and too little of anything else. She applied the makeup she always carried with her to my face and made me twirl for her twice so she could admire her work.

"Go on then." She shooed me out the house. "The makeup stays right here, so use it. And don't worry about the mess. I'll tidy up. Have a great time."

Before I'd mentally prepared myself, I sat in a musky cab on my way to meet Waylon, trying to rub away the headache that simply refused to go away.

At nine o'clock sharp I opened the door to Kelley's. Nestled between two colorful buildings that seemed asleep after dark, the bar was a well-frequented watering hole this side of the town center.

Inside, a wall of air slammed into me, and I took a second to orient myself. Among the crowd, my dress didn't stand out, which, as Julia had predicted, gave me a measure of confidence.

Waylon waited by the bar, tall and smiling. He wore a pair of faded jeans and an open striped shirt layered over a simple white tee.

"Hey," I whispered. My mouth was far too dry to say anything witty.

"Hey back at ya." His voice was as gravelly and sweet as a dollop of whipped cream with chocolate chips. "Quite the outfit, babe. Is the pretty dress just for me?"

Jerk. He knew how I felt about his come-ons. I stared at my feet. "You can borrow it later, if you want, but I'm not sure it's going to fit."

He chuckled. "Well played." He raised a hand at the barmaid, and the blonde darted over as if attracted by a magnet. Who could blame her? If anything, he was more gorgeous in this casual setting than he'd been at the hotel. I twisted away from him, directing my gaze elsewhere.

It had been a long time since I'd been to Kelley's. Silverton's kinfolk gathered here in droves, although most of them might assume they were surrounded by humans. That's how far their deceptions ran. But would they seriously believe the satyrs and incubi grinding and groping in the sparsely lit corners were Joe and Jane Normals? A slight tremor ran through me, the pleasant but unwanted kind. I briefly shut my eyes. Better. Slightly.

Waylon picked a seat by the wall at the last free table. For once I didn't mind sitting with my back facing the room.

"Getting tips?" He raised an eyebrow.

"Don't need them." Despite my bravado, I dropped my gaze.

As if he knew about my struggle between reason and carnal lust, he pushed the soda toward me.

I gulped half of it in one tilt and then pressed the outside against my forehead. Ice cubes clunked inside the glass while the cool condensation kick-started my brain cells. "I'm good."

"Okay then." He regarded me like an indulgent teacher. "So, you have questions."

I shrugged, still doubtful my voice would hold out. Another couple of swigs of soda, and I was as ready as I could be in the current situation. "Who put the mojo on my mother? My human mother, I mean." *Well done holding your nerve.* So why did my hands tremble like crazy?

His jaw clenched a few times. "I did, with your dad."

His unfeeling answer needled my insides. "That's it? Well, yeah, sure. Apology accepted."

"I'm not gonna apologize for any wrongs you made up in that pretty head of yours. He wanted to keep his daughter safe. That's all there is to it, babe."

"Don't call me that." But my voice perhaps showed only partial outrage. I had bigger things to worry about.

Would Dad have been so quick to scramble Mom's head if he'd known that, years later, Lathan would have no qualms about doing something similar to me? I should be livid right now. So why did Waylon's pathetic excuse sound so reasonable? Of course my dad would have wanted to keep me safe. It's what dads do. I'd spent too much time with Lathan and other kin to pretend the world, even Oldworld, wasn't a dangerous place.

In any event, going by Waylon's face, he considered the matter closed. And without a good counter-argument, anything else I said would sound petty.

I bowed my head. "What about my other mother? What happened to her?"

Even though he must have known it was coming, the question

made him wince all the same. "We fought powerful, dangerous people. Your mother found one messing around here in Oldworld. Slave trade, illegal magic, murder. She went undercover, and he fell in love with her." His shoulders sagged. "She banished him to Alethia. Before we knew it, he used the same tactics that made him top dog here to climb up over there. We don't kill when we can avoid it, but she should have made an exception in his case." He looked me straight in the eyes. "He became the new demon kinlord."

"Lathan?" I drew in a short, aching breath.

"You got it." His gaze grew distant. "Anyway, once relative calm had returned, Josie became pregnant. When your parents found out, they were happy. Thought they'd sit it out for a while. Let me carry the load. They got in touch and, hey, I got it, you know? That's what you do for kids. I was okay with it."

"Got in touch? You weren't fighting together?"

"We were buddies, but I'm no good being the fifth wheel. Besides, wasn't like I got bored. Plenty of baddies to keep me busy, you know? Anyway, at least you got to have a normal, happy childhood."

I scoffed. "Well, that obviously went according to plan." Not!

His face betrayed no sign of emotion. "Lathan never got over Josie. No matter she'd betrayed him, he wanted her back. Fucking psycho. So he sent his guys after her. Incompetent hacks ambushed her by a cliff side." He lowered his volume. "That's what got her killed."

Another thing Lathan had taken from me. Another reason he was so obsessed with me. But why didn't my mother's death feel real to me? As if I experienced my grief through a wall of bubble wrap. A smidgen of heaviness trickled through, perhaps the loss of what-could-have-been. Without any clear picture of her in my mind or happy memories, the pain simply had nothing to latch on to.

I lifted my chin to Waylon. His jaw was all angles, and I'd always been into math. If he kissed me right now, I wouldn't object. A wave of annoyance ripped through me. Was it me, or was my motive getting worse?

I sipped my soda, hands encircling the cool glass, and stared at the table until I was able to speak again. "Tell me more about my Guardian ancestry." My voice was croaky, although at least the heat in my face had subsided.

Waylon's hands caressed the rim of his glass. "It's complicated. Your grandfather was a brather demon. The original race chosen as Guardians. He fucked a leanan sidhe. Now pay attention, babe. The *son* of a leanan is the same race as his father. But daughters are always leanan sidhe. It's a quirk you only get with the leanans. So, in truth you're not satyr, but leanan from your kiss-me mouth to your sexy little toes. Just like your mother was. Clear?"

Blanking the sharp contraction of my pelvis, I pointed at myself. "Not satyr, but leanan. Got it."

He leaned in closer. "Here's the thing, though. Leanans take on the traits, or powers, of their father and grandfathers and so on. Nothing to do with human science, so we're clear. Look at it as magical genes."

"Still with you."

"Good." He smiled. "So, you have brather powers from your grandfather, plus your satyr charms from your father, and I think there's also two other types of demon and possibly an elf from way back mixed in that steaming body of yours. How much you inherited from each, I can't say."

How much longer would I ignore his sexy talk? "Well, lucky me, so far my satyr traits seem to dominate. No pun intended."

He chortled. "You're making too big a deal of this. There is much more to a satyr than sex. They put people at ease, attract confidence, and make people smile. So what if you wanna fuck? Hell, do it, I say. Doesn't make you a bad person."

I glowered. Easy for him to make light. His demon morals were skewed by nature. "And we, those with Guardian genes I mean, are particularly sensitive to magic, like, we can read auras, which is why I can identify the races of kin. Right?"

His thumb traced a drop of condensation down his glass. "Yes."

"My allure doesn't affect my friend. Not really. And we spend a lot of time together."

"There's your answer. If he's your friend, you don't think of him as a lover. But don't take it for granted. If the lust gets too much, you never know who you'll be wanting to fuck. Perhaps even me." His grin reached between my legs and did more damage than any man had done before.

"Stop flirting with me. Staying cool is hard enough." I sipped my soda and let his revelations run through my head. If I was open to magic, and the statue was magical, as we suspected, perhaps this was why I heard voices. I rubbed my knuckles against my forehead, as if it would shake loose the strands of information and store them in neat order. "So, what does a Guardian do? I mean, what's your day-to-day like?"

"Right now, I'm on the heels of The Circle. They're an interracial ring of badness, who've banded together to become one collective pain in the ass. The Circle's a business joint, made up of demons, vamps, humans, you name it. They pretty much cornered the market in winegrass and flackwood.”

“Sounds nasty.” I’d never heard of winegrass or flackwood.

“You better believe it.” His kissable mouth turned grim but determined. “They’re into slavery, contract killings and fuck knows what else, backed up by bad-ass magic and a lot of Oldworld cash. To top it off, they’re in league with djinn.”

I bunched my face. “Djinn? I didn’t think they were real.”

“Oh, they’re real all right.” He leaned back and stretched his legs out under the table, one boot on either side of my feet.

I kept the shudder forcing its way down my spine to myself.

He watched me like a hawk. “If a host lets a djinn into his body, he’ll get access to some pretty powerful shit. Mind magic, I mean. The problem’s with what the djinn get out of it. They have a claim on their host’s body and soul. They consume both in five to ten years, and then the host dies.”

“So, who’d take the risk? It’s stupid.”

He rubbed his chin. “Actually, it was quite common for humans and weaker kin to play host, back in the olden days. If a family of fae had a djinn among their midst, they’d stand a chance against more powerful kinfolk. After Alethia was created, the djinn disappeared to whatever shithole dimension they came from. Which is why my training in that respect was short. Now they’re back.”

“How are they different from other kin?”

“They ain’t kin, babe.”

I frowned, which he didn’t even acknowledge.

He licked his lips. “They’re a whole other species. I can’t read their auras or know them by sight. If I strike lucky and find one, best I’ve been able to do is banish host and djinn to Alethia. I mean, you can kill the hosts all right, but the djinn inside are tough bastards. They’ll live inside the corpse until they can hop to another body. Hard to keep up, you know.” He narrowed his eyes. “There’s only so much a single Guardian can do.”

I fidgeted in my seat, aware of his legs flanking mine. Each time he pressed against my calf or I inadvertently pushed against his, my breath slowed. “What about the Interracial Enforcement Agency? Shouldn’t they be all over the case?”

“Babe, if I can’t do anything, the IEA sure as fuck can’t. They’ve put half a dozen agents on The Circle and, well, let’s just say three of them are still alive, and that’s ’cos they were lucky. This isn’t one super powerful guy. It’s a bunch of ringleaders with a loose alliance. Get rid of one, another two take their place. And I don’t even know how many djinn are involved.”

So this was what Dad, and my mom, had done with themselves before I'd come into the picture. Their courage put my life to shame. Investigating the mystery of the statue was as much excitement as I could handle, and I only did that because I had to.

"You look like you need a break from all of this. How about a game of pool?" A confident grin accompanied his challenge.

I cocked my head. He looked like he was conceived in some dark pool hall. "I'm not very good."

"I'm in with a chance, then."

I tossed back the rest of my soda and we ambled over to the pool table. Waylon used spells to cheat mercilessly, and then promised to forfeit the game if I spotted them. I lost three times.

Between shots he filled me in about his day-to-day life as a Guardian. His tales sounded exotic and a little bit kick-ass. What struck me most, though, was the loneliness. Every action had to be checked and double checked from all angles, because without backup, mistakes might cost him his life. My heart went out to him, and with him, to my dad and to the mother I never knew.

Without my parents, he had no one to talk to, nobody to reassure him his actions were justified, to appease his mind or praise him, or simply to distract him from his responsibility even for a moment.

"I'm sorry," I whispered.

He glanced up. "What for?"

"That you're alone."

His gaze shot to the side. "It's not so bad."

But it was. His sagging shoulders, his grinding jaw, everything about him told of too much pain.

"It would be easier to talk about guards and Guardians in my hotel room." He gazed at me matter-of-factly.

Over the past couple of hours, the music had transitioned from poppy to soft jazz, and the conversations had morphed from loud banter to hushed discussions. Chat about Guardian stuff, if overheard, would definitely raise eyebrows.

Did I have more questions? Heck yes. But was I prepared to put myself in temptation's way any more than I already had?

Waylon hung his pool cue back into its holder on the wall. "I wanna teach you how to move Lathan's mark to someone else."

My pulse quickened. The idea of being free of the mark was enough to snag my interest. "I can do that?"

"Of course. But not here."

If I went with him, I might give in to my attraction. What kind of person would that make me? Julia had insisted that until someone promised me commitment, I was a free agent. It's not like Greg put a ring on my finger. More than anything, I needed to learn the spell. If that meant throwing myself into the unknown, it was totally worth it.

"Okay." The warmth that rose in me was due to more than the temperature inside the bar.

The crisp breeze outside was all the more a slap in the face. We walked side by side, apart like mere friends, yet bonded by something bigger. He knew more about me than I knew. How much I'd give to learn everything he had to teach.

My hand touched the handle of Waylon's passenger door, when my gaze zeroed in on a dumpster in the alley ahead of us. It stood at an odd angle to the wall and was dinged up like a NASCAR entrant. I squinted into the shadows. Unless I was hallucinating, I'd seen the alley before.

CHAPTER FIFTEEN

THE BLUE TRASH CONTAINERS, THE cobbled ground, the graffiti on the walls. Everything fit. This was the location where Heather's purse had been found. Well, potentially her purse. The photo in her file had been taken roughly from my current position. If I'd been a cop on this case, I would have shaken the bar's clientele until something fell out, yet the report on her disappearance didn't mention Kelley's.

"Ivy?" Waylon was in the driver's seat already.

Heather could wait until later. Had to wait. The bar was about to shut, and it was too late to question people. I hopped into the car and was treated to an anecdote of Waylon on the trail of a particularly mischievous bunch of gnomes.

The drive to the hotel passed in a flash. The concierge didn't bat an eyelid at my late-night visit. Guests got first class service, and discretion presumably came as a package deal. The elevator ride up was quiet. We positioned ourselves at opposite corners and made polite chitchat about the windy fall. The way friends might.

The thud of the penthouse door falling into the latch exposed our "friendship" as a flimsy charade. Waylon's gaze communicated dirty promises I knew he'd keep. But he didn't kiss me. Didn't even make the attempt.

"Drink?" He selected two bottles of cola from the mini-bar.

"Thanks."

He handed me the drink, and his finger not-so-accidentally brushed mine. My breath stuck in my throat, and I dipped my gaze to the blue label, reading the letters but failing to connect them into words.

"Come here," Waylon said. I obeyed. "Moving the mark to another person is a piece of cake. Just need to know how."

"Wouldn't I make the other guy Lathan's slave?"

"I'm not saying you saddle some poor human with it. But you never know when you'll get a chance to shift it to someone who deserves to be Lathan's bitch."

I crossed my arms. "Skin magic?"

"Yes, but don't worry." His patient tone put me at ease. "We're not talking about *your* skin. The mark uses the target's power. That's why you can only shift it to another living being."

I didn't protest. The reason for meeting with Waylon had been to gain knowledge, and this was more than I could have hoped for. So much more. The possibility of a future without the mark seemed too good to be true.

I nodded. "Go on, then."

Waylon stepped behind me. The room's atmosphere turned static. His torso pressed against my back, solid and hot. His hands slid along my exposed arms, and goosebumps traced the trail of his fingers. Our hands locked. He whispered an incantation and guided my arms through the air, mimicking the lines that were to shape the magic. This time, the air was my canvas. Instead of deep grooves cutting into metal plates, our magic stained the room with insubstantial blue ribbons. My lips moved in synch with Waylon's, repeating his words until I'd internalized the spell.

"Got it?" Warm air blew against my ear.

I giggled. "I got it."

He spun me in his arms. Face to face, our breath mingled, our gazes focused on each other. His finger curled under my jaw, and he lowered his head. Warmth paved the way for the softest lips, followed by the sharp edge of his teeth against my tongue. This wasn't a wait-and-see kiss. He meant business.

"I thought I'd never get to taste you again." He cupped my breast, weighing it in his hand. His other traveled toward my waist.

My pulse picked up, coursing through my veins like a jet ski. He hitched up my dress, grazed the skin underneath. Despite the boiling heat inside willing me on, I stiffened. Would the satyr in me take over? Would I lose all reason?

He kissed me with increasing urgency. Under his attention, my muscles quivered. With a contented sigh he continued his journey to the swell of my buttocks.

"I need to fuck you right now." His fingers dug into my soft flesh and applied firm strokes toward the nexus of my legs.

I arched my back. Everything about him added to the whirling inside my head and my belly. His manner, his looks, his words. That sexy voice. This man could drive me to the edge of sanity and I wouldn't object.

While he massaged my butt, his erection pressed against my stomach, a full, plump promise of a night I wouldn't forget. My body came alive with the thumping of a hundred drums, tapping a beat which sent one delicious ripple after another to my toes. How did he find my take-me-now spots so quickly? He fumbled with the zipper nestling between my shoulder blades. A knot formed in my pelvis, begging me to let him untie it. But another knot, further up, focused my thoughts.

"Hang on." My words sounded wispy.

His body stopped moving. Deep inside, the satyr's hunger burned hot, but it made no effort to take charge. Merely purred at the attention. I waited for the fear of intimacy to overwhelm me, to turn me into a nervous virgin again. It didn't come. The only question now was what I was really after. Part of me longed for a stable relationship, and nothing about him assured me he was the type. But perhaps stable was overrated. Why couldn't I do something reckless, have fun for once?

His hands remained in place, his breath raspy. How was he so still when my body was in such turmoil? I wanted him. Wanted his heat. His touch. Eyes closed, I inhaled him deep into my lungs.

"Come on, baby." He gathered me closer.

A slight nod was all the encouragement he needed. He slowly twirled me around. I kicked off my shoes, and, with unsteady hands, lifted my hair out the way. He rolled the slider of the zip over my spine, turning every inch into a seduction.

My dress brushed along my body and pooled at my feet. He spun me. A gentle kiss, deepening into a demand. One adroit motion later, the clasps of my bra snapped open. The barely-there fabric swept along my breasts. I shivered, and he chuckled.

He dropped the bra and stepped back. My hands prickled with excitement. I stood before him, covered by a tiny patch of silk around my bottom.

"Perfect." His word escaped in a single, throaty puff of air.

My bones liquefied. *Do not pass out!*

He closed the distance, his kiss rough again, fierce. If ever there was a moment I wanted to freeze in time, this was it. Those soft, soft lips of his nuzzled a line from the corner of my mouth to my neck, leaving moist heat in their wake.

One hand glued to my waist, Waylon used the other to cast off his shirt. He ripped the tucked-in tee from his jeans. Too slow. I slapped away his hand and forced the fabric over his head. Our skin touched. His muscles undulated against my flesh like ocean waves.

"Still with me?" he whispered.

I tangled my fingers in his hair, guiding his head toward my shoulder.

He lifted my chin with the crook of one finger. "Want me to stop?" His voice laden with the effort of his restraint.

My gaze flitted between his face and the space past his shoulder. Would he make me say it out loud?

"You're making me crazy here, babe. Talk to me."

I slid my hands reverently over his silky chest, to the line of hair that disappeared into the rim of his jeans. "You don't know what it's like," I said, "feeling like this. This is scary as hell."

"What are you scared of?" He dotted my cheek and jaw with kisses, each forcing another tremor into my flesh.

"Will I respect myself in the morning? But most of all I fear letting go. I could so easily lose myself in you."

His hands floated back to my butt. He lifted me and wrapped my legs tight around his waist. "I'll find you." He strode into the bedroom, his grasp around me firm. "I promise."

His words burst the last of my barriers and I relaxed into his arms.

The soft, crisp bedding cushioned me like a deep cover of snow. Waylon retreated long enough to take off his pants. Perhaps I should have helped him. Instead I was enraptured by his movements that so smoothly uncovered strong, shapely legs. My silky briefs came next.

"What about protection?" My words disguised a happy sigh. From his determined jaw to his powerhouse muscles, there was nothing boyish about him.

"Aren't you on the pill?"

I snorted. Typical guy. "Actually, I am. But that's not the only worry, is it?"

"We're not human. Human diseases don't bother us. Besides, I wanna fuck *you*, not a bag." He rolled down his boxers and I gasped. *Oh my*. My clit immediately jumped to attention.

In a second, his long, firm body covered all of me. His kisses brought moisture to my parched lips, his hands warmed my chilled skin. It wasn't enough. While my breasts loved the attention his capable fingers lavished on them, my loins screamed out for their share. Finding purchase on his flexed shoulders, I bucked my waist.

He chuckled. "Patience, babe."

Rather than waste my breath on a huff, I slid my hands down his back onto his ass. His buttocks curved like plump melons, with just a little give when I squeezed. He wiggled his hip, his penis rubbing against my inner thigh. God, this guy was going to be my undoing.

"Hey." His breath blew over my mouth.

I opened my eyes. A halo of yellowish ceiling light framed his flushed head. I ran my finger along his puffy lips. "Hey." The word little more than a breath.

"Last chance. You can still say no." He lifted his butt, letting the tip of his erection tickle my entrance.

A flame licked my thighs and burst through my body. My eyes fell shut and I pressed my hips toward him. He stopped moving.

I squinted a warning. "Don't toy with me."

He laughed, eyes twinkling. "Then say it."

"Say what?"

"That you want me to fuck you."

I was already so close. The need between my legs became unbearable. "I want you."

"That's not what I wanna hear. Say you want me to fuck you."

Oh God. I pushed against him, but it wasn't enough. "Yes. Yes, I want you to fuck me, jackass."

He bore down on me, into my slick opening. A long, never-ending stroke until he collided with the very end of me. I cried out, my fingertips digging into his ass. He was big, stretching my walls to their limit. He lifted a smidgen and plunged back in, deeper still. A delicious ache ripped through me, and I screamed.

My voice startled me. I'd never made a peep during sex before, but—

He dove in again, grunting. My eyes rolled under closed lids. I lifted my hips, receiving as much of him as I could take. Christ, this was good.

One hand on his waist, I moved the other to his back, slick with sweat. With better leverage, I lifted my legs. He rose to his knees, repositioned his weight onto his hands, and lunged back in. Pumping forcefully. In and out. Each release tore a gasp from my throat, each descent a "yes."

Blood rushed through my veins, puckering near the surface.

"Fuck, you're snug." He rocked his pelvis like a piston. Hard. Fast. My hips vaulted up to connect. The pressure against my clit built into a sphere, swelling until my gasps became one with his grunts. His mouth sought my nipples, sucking vigorously. A flick, a thrust. The pressure ball erupted and tore through my body. I screamed. For a few seconds, only my orgasm mattered.

One wave, two waves, and my senses recovered their basic functions.

Supporting his weight on his elbows, he remained inside, my aftershocks around his length making him twitch.

I dropped my arms to my side, sweat running down my temples, gluing the once crisp bedding to my skin. He unsheathed, forcing another contraction from me. My body was satisfied, yet already longed for him to return.

Lying on his back, he placed both hands on his rapidly moving chest. A black abstract tattoo on his arm glistened. "That was intense."

I rolled my head to the side, caring little that my hair stuck to my cheek. "Hell, yeah."

His light, happy chuckle traveled into my heart and spread like a blanket. Yes. Intense was one word for it.

After two more rounds, one passionate, the other extremely tender, I fell asleep, presumably with a fat grin on my face.

The diffused glow of the sun peeking around the edges of the drawn shades woke me. Waylon's elbow cradled my head while his free hand held a book aloft in front of his face.

I'd done it. Sex on a first date. I was now one of thousands of women who'd taken her sexuality into her own hands. Did I still respect myself? Since casual sex was no longer the domain of men, but also of the twenty-first century woman, I would have probably lost respect for myself if I *hadn't* given in to Waylon's seduction.

His unique scent curled up inside my nostrils, evoking at once a blend of familiarity and newness. In an instant, my body relived every goose-bumpy stroke by his fingers, every mind-blowing thrust. My legs and his were still intertwined, the sensation of skin on skin so profound it tested my lucidity.

But I was no longer afraid of my hormones. My ideas about an evil, sexually charged entity lurking inside my body had been well and truly debunked. The satyr and I were one and the same. Although part of me would always nudge me to take more risks, I had the strength to say 'no' if I needed to. In the end it had been *I* who'd agreed to spend the night with Waylon. And now, on the morning after, there was no vomit-inducing claustrophobia, only satisfaction and…triumph. All things considered, I was a happy bunny.

Once I'd reassured myself I hadn't sleep-dribbled over his chest, I stirred, hoping he'd initiate the post-coital proceedings.

"Morning, sleepyhead." He kissed the crown of my skull.

Well, someone was chipper. A good sign.

Since I wasn't yet ready to let him see the full glory that was my morning hair, I tilted up my head only a little. "Morning."

He placed the book onto the nightstand and shifted so his arms enveloped me completely. He planted a kiss on my forehead. "You sleep well?"

"I did, thanks."

"Regrets?" he said, his tone suddenly neutral.

"No." I cleared my throat. "You?"

He expelled a gasp of air as if he'd held his breath. "Well, it's a shame you wasted half the night on sleep. Other than your piss-poor stamina, no, babe, no regrets at all."

"Sorry." My body relaxed. "And you put so much effort into it, too. Did you plan the seduction or were you just hoping to get lucky?"

"A little of both." He drew me in tighter, his breath blowing over my hair. "After I'd fucked up our first meet, I thought I'd missed my chance. But then you walked in, wearing *that* dress, and I figured I might as well go for it. Besides, I hoped the sexually potent atmosphere in the bar might rub off on you."

I tsked. "Sad you have to rely on others to turn on the girls for you. Have you no game of your own?"

He laughed out loud and rolled on top of me. "That's for you to decide. Just in case, why don't you let me practice some?"

What could I say? I was in a charitable mood.

***

Around noon, Waylon dropped me off at the office. Since I was already late I didn't have time to go home and change. The afterglow of my night with Waylon surrounded me like a puff of eau de toilette; as sweet and heady as the scent of rose and lavender, and equally irritating to everyone I came in contact with. And by everyone I meant Florian. After a few highly inappropriate comments concerning my perma-grin and the clinginess of my dress, he perched on the edge of the desk.

I dug the Heather folder from the box and leafed through it for the photo of the alley.

"Here." I thrust it at Florian. "This is where they found what may have been Heather's purse. It didn't have her ID in it, only her phone number written onto the inside seam. Someone handed it in to the police, and Fred later identified it as hers. Anyway, I was there last night. This is right next to Kelley's Bar." I coughed. "Unfortunately I didn't get a chance to investigate at the time."

"Obviously." He pointed at my dress and wagged his eyebrows.

I threw a paper clip at him. "Maybe I wanted to doll up for work. Have you thought of that?"

"Yeah, if it was my birthday, you might."

I hit him with another paper clip.

"I am confused though." He didn't look it. The glint in his eyes gave more the impression of serious mischief being his play. "This was a quick meet-up with your dad's buddy, right? I thought your date wasn't until this weekend? Or are you double-dipping? If so, where do I get in line?"

As if I didn't feel bad enough about Greg already. "Yes, I was supposed to meet Greg this weekend." I crossed my arms. "I guess I'd better call it off, though. It wouldn't be fair to him."

"It depends on what kind of person you want to be." He nudged my shoulder.

I picked up the receiver, hung up, lifted it again, and finally dialed Greg's number. He'd been sweet and fun to be around, and best of all without baggage, but Waylon was a once in a lifetime guy. Not only did he already know everything about me, he couldn't care less about any of it. Plus, he was the bad boy every woman dreams about. So what if he wasn't human? Neither was I these days.

After a few rings, the answering machine switched on. "Um, hi Greg. It's Ivy here. Ivy Bell." Stupid. If he didn't remember me, my surname wasn't going to help. "Something's come up, and I need to cancel our date. I'm sorry. Um. Bye."

I punched the *end call* button and exhaled. "Awkward."

Flo scrunched his mouth. "That was awkward all right. And I must have missed the part where you told him you're no longer interested."

He was doing it again. Aiming his words where guilt had already had a good ol' nibble. "Not the kind of thing I should do via the answering machine, is it?"

"Yeah, or maybe you should have your cake and eat it, too."

I busied myself with miscellaneous paper to hide my red face from his smirk. Was I hedging my bets? There'd been no commitment between Greg and me, no promises of any kind. Basically, I hadn't done anything wrong. So why wouldn't the nagging feeling in my gut go away?

I moved my thumb across my lips, trying to recreate the sensation of Waylon's kiss. For a short while, his strong embrace had removed me from the world and its problems, and rather than feel recharged, I hungered for his shelter. Perhaps Waylon would come away with me. He had no ties to Silverton, and we fitted so well together.

Clearly my attitude needed readjustment. What was with all this making plans for the future?

Concentrate. Okay, back to Fred, who still hadn't called.

I sat and slipped my feet out of those painful shoes. "If Fred wasn't such a private person, he may have talked to me about Heather's case. He knew I'd have been there for him. But no, he didn't want to trouble anyone, never accepted any help, and now his obstinacy might have come back to bite him in the ass." I punched my fists onto the folder before me full-force.

Florian jumped off the desk, then frowned. "Easy there."

"Sorry," I said, my bile still simmering. It didn't take psychiatric insight to tell me it was born out of helplessness and frustration. "So where is he?"

"He'll call when he has time." Flo's voice soothed me. "Until then, we'll poke around a bit. Okay? We could check out the bar later. Perhaps her trail is also his trail."

I nodded. Doing something might stop me from worrying about nothing. If my concerns revealed themselves as unfounded, he'd still be ecstatic I'd found a clue that could help him find Heather.

While Flo went out to collect still outstanding payments, Fred's hand-written schedule for the week guided me through my remaining chores. Although the Collective should be my priority, running a business involved many variables, all of which took up time and resources. I'd promised Fred to look after his agency while he was away, and by God, I would. It was the least I could do.

I met with an attorney in town, visited a client's soon-to-be ex-husband for his divorce signature, and stopped by the town planning office for some blueprints before returning home by cab. All that in a getup I'd normally not be seen dead in. Perhaps I was already biased, but the men's looks no longer bothered me. If they fantasized about what they saw, well, for once in my life I related.

By the time I got home, the soles of my feet were killing me. I chucked my key into a bowl on the table by the door, slung my heels across the room, and placed a lasagna into the nuker. On my way to the bathroom, I opened the French windows. The balmy fall afternoon blew in a mild breeze, rustling some old newspapers on my coffee table.

"Ivy?" Waylon's voice drifted in from the backyard like smoke.

I wheeled around. "Hey you. Come on in."

He walked in with purposeful strides and kissed my cheek. My heart stuttered and goosebumps crept across my skin. What did this guy see in me?

I immediately gagged my doubting inner voice with a cliché. Why look a gift horse in the mouth? "Did you miss me already?"

He gathered me close, his thumb brushing over my bottom lip. "Fuck yeah."

My insides liquefied. So maybe he shared my hopes about our relationship's long-term potential.

I placed my hands on his chest. "It's nice to see you, but how'd you find me? I don't remember telling you where I live."

He placed his mouth on mine, a fierce kiss that claimed me as his. Did he know what effect his touch had? How his breath warmed a spot in me I'd never known was made of ice? When we parted, his lips were swollen, his eyes glazed. Satisfied with my work, I mussed up his hair.

"If I know where you work, I can find out where you live." His hand curled around my waist. "Being a Guardian, I have to be a good investigator, too. Speaking of."

I let him kiss me again. God, his kisses could set seaweed alight. We parted, and I placed my index finger against his lips. "Before you say anything else, I need a shower. It's been a long day and I desperately want to get out of these clothes."

He tightened his grip. "Need help? It's been so long since I had my cock in you." His gaze challenged me.

Damn that puckering that urged me to let him have his wicked way.

I rolled my necklace's guard pendant between my fingers. "I have to get changed first. Sorry."

The green eyes, his most breathtaking demon trait, reflected the lights from my living room ceiling, and his gaze lingered with dilated pupils on my face.

I sighed. "You have no idea *how* sorry."

He blinked, as if regaining focus. "Okay. Do me a favor, babe. Leave your necklace with me. Think it's run out of juice."

I did as he asked and jumped into the shower. In record time I was soaped, shampooed and rinsed clean. Without drying my hair, I pulled on my good jeans and a never-before-worn green top with a 'V' so daring I should get a medal. With Waylon around, anything less would make me look like the ugly duckling. In my current state of physical exhaustion, however, this was as far as my desire to keep up with him went.

Without the torture devices the salesman had optimistically sold me as shoes, my steps were much lighter, and I reentered the living room with more grace than I'd hoped. Waylon stood by the windows, looking out into the shaded yard. I picked up my necklace from the table.

He turned. "Let me help you." He clasped the chain at the back of my neck and kissed my hair. "Now let's take it off again."

For a second I was tempted to let him rip it off, together with a few choice items of clothing. But I wasn't going to make it that easy. As long as my hormones were under my control, I'd make him earn me. "One step at a time. Your head clear?"

"Yeah. Not that I'm happy about it." He explained how to

recharge the guard on my necklace. "Do that about once a day to be on the safe side."

"Okay. Now, how about some coffee?" If he didn't want me to fall asleep on him, a caffeine hit was mandatory.

He shrugged and followed me into the kitchen. Then we settled down on the sofa, where I let the warm bitter aroma of the finest Columbian roast surround me.

"Your guards are strong." He rolled his gaze over my walls. "That's a good sign."

I kinked my head. "A sign of what?"

"I want you to start training with me. You're a Guardian, and it's time you learned the ins and outs."

"Me?" I put my mug down and frowned. "Perhaps we got our wires crossed. I don't want to be a Guardian. In case you missed it, I already have a job."

"Being a Guardian isn't like having a job." He nudged forward on his seat so his face was close to mine. He stroked my cheek and my chin, tracing the line of my lips and sending waves of pleasure along my spine. "Don't you like me?"

If only he knew about my melting insides, about the warmth his touch brought forth. I swallowed hard. "Of course I do."

"Then trust me. Let me train you."

He bent over to kiss me, and the reasons to refuse his offer disappeared. The world narrowed to him and me. When I came up for air, his gaze softened.

"Now, about your apprenticeship." He burrowed his face in my neck, caressing the area beneath my ear with his nose.

"Not now." My voice was rough.

He nipped at my lobe. "Yes, now."

Withdrawing, I gave a little pout. "Why is this so urgent all of a sudden?"

"It was just an idea. Forget I said anything." But the hurt in his tone was raw. He took a long breath and stepped back. "Okay, this is going to sound bad now, but I have to leave. Tonight."

His words wiped the smile off my face, like someone had punched me in the gut. I shoved him away. "Are you serious?" How could he leave me so soon after we spent the night together? I didn't sleep with just anyone. Or maybe I did now?

"I have new info on The Circle." He lowered his head. "And I have to take care of it soon, so I gotta go tonight."

A dark cloud descended onto the tiny light flickering inside me. Had I fallen for a bad boy who was, in truth, nothing more than a bad boy? Albeit a bad boy who does good things?

He raised his hands. "If you became a Guardian, we could leave together." His face was inscrutable. "*Be* together. We could fuck every night. Not be alone. Wouldn't you want that, babe?"

Having sex? Was that what he thought I was all about? He wasn't that far off the mark, but things weren't that simple. Not for me.

I got to my feet, my gaze meeting his defiantly. "Are you kidding?" So this was the real reason for his interest in me. To turn me into a Guardian. And he'd used my satyr weakness against me. My skin went numb, my limbs tensed as if ready to flee.

"Just a suggestion." He rose and crossed his arm, suddenly looking uncertain. "I meant nothing by it."

"Well, I'm not going anywhere." My shoulders fell.

He took my hands. "Listen. I'll be back soon. We'll talk about it then. Here." He handed me a stone and a piece of paper from his jacket pocket. "This is a touchstone, a kind of telephone, for emergencies. It can reach me no matter where I am. Touch it and read the spell on this note, and we'll be able to talk."

A piece of rock—the *thoughtful* leaving present. This was what our brief fling boiled down to.

"Keep the touchstone with you. It'll hum when I call." He bent his head to within my line of blurred sight. "Did you hear what I said?"

"It'll hum." My voice sounded foreign.

He wrapped his arms around me, breathed in deeply, and kissed my forehead. The warmth I'd expected to feel, the tingle, didn't materialize. Everything was clear to me now. This was my future as a satyr. Me using men, and men using me. Passion without commitment. I don't know why I thought Waylon's interest was different. Perhaps because I wished it so. Because I wanted something special. To be understood. God, was I really that naïve?

Waylon released me from his embrace. The deep V between his eyes might have been from genuine worry about my mental state. After all, what good was a lunatic Guardian? Chances were about equal his air of concern was just for show.

I drew my spine up. This whole mess could have been avoided if I'd used my head. I walked into his trap with my eyes wide open. My eyes wide open, but not my brain. He'd merely done what demons did. They looked out for number one, and damn the rest of us. Wasn't this exactly what Lathan was trying to do? Use my hormones against me to bind me to him?

Instead of learning my lesson, I'd humanized Waylon. Dressed him up in vulnerable emotions and considerate behavior like my perfect little boyfriend doll.

My bad. My own fucking bad.

"As I said, I'll be back soon." He swayed a little, shoulders raised.

I lifted the rock up in a vague motion. "I'll call you." *The moment hell freezes over.*

He lingered for a moment, then walked out into the backyard. Although I was half dead on my feet, his sudden departure had my brain buzzing again. How had I so completely misjudged him? He'd turned my head with a pretty face and stories of loneliness, and gullible as I was, I'd allowed him into my house and into my heart.

Next day, I took my mind off Waylon with some retail therapy. Ice cream, potato chips, the usual essentials. Yet my mood didn't lift until Flo picked me up in the early evening.

"Men are bastards." Florian released the seatbelt and let it slide up into its housing.

I raised my eyebrows. "O-kaay."

"I'm playing the supporting friend role. And I believe this statement is a secret handshake to be let into the jilted lover's club." He beamed.

"I'm not a jilted lover." Even if I felt like it. "Waylon and I had a night, and now he's gone. That's fine. I have plenty of other things to do anyway."

"Like Greg?" He opened the door and got out of the car.

I followed suit, huddling deeper into my jacket against the chill. "Like work. I'm not even thinking about men right now."

"Of course not. But I bet you're glad you never had the opportunity to put a definite end to your blossoming relationship with him, aren't you?"

His eyes twinkled under the light from the crass neon sign, but he raised an interesting point. What an idiot I'd been. One of Greg's attractive qualities was that he was human. No magic. No drama. I lifted a shoulder to my ear and grinned. "Let's say it's nice to have options."

Inside Kelley's Bar, Florian all but rubbed his hands together. "I suggest we split up to cover more ground."

His intentions were transparent. A bar, alcohol, girls. A place where horny vampires got lost for hours. At least Kelley's wasn't half as busy or stimulating as it had been the night before.

I approached the über-tall blonde behind the gleaming bar and showed her Heather's picture. She cast a heavily mascara'd eye over it and shrugged before turning her attention back to wiping the counter clean.

My nails dug into my palms, and I blew out air. "What does that mean? Have you seen her or not?"

She glared at me. "Why should I tell you?"

Seriously? She was going to mess with me *today*? "Because otherwise I'll kick your ass so hard sitting down will soon be a distant memory to you." The tightness in my chest came close to bursting, putting pressure on my vocal chords.

Her eyes bulged and she took a step back.

Huh. Look at li'l bad-ass me. I rolled my shoulders and inhaled deeply. "It's important. Please?"

She picked up the photo and studied it more closely this time. In the end she shook her head. "Sorry."

I hadn't expected to be lucky at first try, but as I notched up more and more negative responses, a hollowness took up space in my chest. Perhaps the cops had been right, and the purse they found wasn't Heather's.

A small group of werewolves huddled over some papers and some beer. Feeling brave, I showed Heather's photo. They had no information, and neither had the human couple in the back. Heather had disappeared months ago. Even if she'd been here, who'd remember a face after all this time?

My next target's stare had been following me for a while. I'd been keeping him for last, because he was a satyr. The guy's aura shouted at me, and from his allure I knew chatting was the last thing he had in mind.

The satyr was medium height and carried himself with the confidence of someone much taller. His dark skin set off his brilliant blue shirt, and white teeth sparkled at me. And my motive sat up on its hind legs and begged to be let out to play.

At least someone was interested in me. This dude didn't know me, and his reason for flirting with me was a genetic one. Why shouldn't I take advantage to boost my ego?

I broke into a calculating smile and swaggered up. "Hi there."

"I was wondering when it would be my turn." His allure twisted around me like warmth on a summer day, his grin self-assured.

I fumbled my necklace. If I'd stopped Waylon's seduction in its tracks, I could stay in control around this guy. No sweat. "Oh, I always save the best for dessert." I gave him my best seductive look. "I was hoping you could help me out. I'm looking for this woman. Have you seen her?" I held up the photo.

He moved in to look at the face in the picture. "By the way, I'm Ewan." His voice was casual. "You?"

"Ivy." Clearly the wish to be seductive wasn't enough to wow him. I, on the other hand, found myself enraptured by Ewan's dark gaze. A gaze to make me forget the pair of green eyes. A gaze I wanted for myself. "It's nice to meet you." My words came in a purr, carried by my rising excitement.

"Tell me, my beautiful satyr." He leaned in. "How is it I've never seen you here before? More importantly, how soon can we make love?"

Wow. Guess my allure was running at full throttle now. "Ooh, straight for the brass ring." I placed a hand on his arm and laughed. "Let's see how much help you can give me first, okay?" At my touch, his allure tugged on my libido and took my satyr motive to the next level.

His eyes creased from a wide grin. "You're playing coy. That's good. But know I've called dibs on you for tonight."

His statement evoked a flush of excitement in the pit of my stomach. A subtle hair flick covered my burning cheeks, I hoped, and I applied light pressure against his bicep. "You've called dibs on me? Quite the romantic, aren't you?" *Focus him back on Heather.* I lifted the picture up. "So have you seen her?"

He studied the photo with a squint. "Yeah, I think I've seen her here before. She was talking to one of those guys." He pointed to the small group of werewolves by the pool table. "They were arguing about something."

I blew air up into my flushed face. The werewolves had mentioned nothing of the sort. "Is the guy she was arguing with here tonight?"

Ewan shook his head. "The fight was with a girl, and no, she isn't here. I've seen her around a few times though, always with that bunch over there."

He was so near, I practically felt his skin under my fingers. The pressure in my pelvis increased, a fiery pull that opened and closed as if drawing in air. The seminal moment in Waylon's arms had taught me I wasn't controlled by my lust, but it was time to dial back my allure. With luck, my motive would follow suit.

"Thanks. I appreciate it." I shot him a smile which I hoped would convey my apologies for turning him down.

"Wait. Where are you going?" His eyes were large, confused. "I thought we had a deal."

I had used him a little. Led him on. But it wasn't exactly as if he was looking for anything meaningful. He'd get over me in a heartbeat. No reason for that churning guilt inside my stomach.

I breathed deep. "I'll take a rain check. Thanks again." I gave a wave over my shoulder.

The lead Ewan had given me might pay off. More than that, his interest had done me good. If Waylon didn't want me, well, too bad for him. There were others out here that did. Still, a minute longer in Ewan's company, and I'd have been ready to go places I didn't want to go. I made a beeline for the door.

A cool breeze hit me outside. I turned into the alley where Heather's purse had been found. To my right, a couple of empty burger wrappers had wafted out of the trash containers and littered the ground. Assuming the purse was hers, it looked like Fred had been right all along. But what had Heather been doing in this deserted alley? Had she met with a secret lover? Come out for fresh air?

Maybe Florian would have an idea. Where was he anyway? Even if he'd been too busy to notice my exit, he should have caught on to my absence by now.

A hand yanked me into the shadows between the containers.

CHAPTER SIXTEEN

Amongst the grays of the alley and the hushed yellow glow from the street lights, Ewan's seductive smile radiated and instantly connected to my motive. "I knew you'd be waiting for me." He raised his eyebrows. "*Rain check*. Funniest thing I've heard all week."

My laugh sounded carefree, which turned my stomach. Flirting time was over. "It wasn't meant to be funny." I twisted out of his grasp.

"Come now. No more playing games."

I lifted my arm between us to buffer his proximity. "I'm serious. You seem like a nice guy, but I'm not interested." I stepped aside. Perhaps my bubbling desire would vanish with distance.

He blocked my path. "I can sense your need." He bustled my back to the wall, pressing up close. "The sweet music of your allure is calling to me, begging me to please you."

"I-I don't want that." A tremor had worked itself into my voice, yet my skin came alive, demanding his touch.

He pinned my wrists beside my head, the coarse bricks digging into the backs of my hands. His breath skimmed my cheek. "We're built this way, little satyr. We were built to come together, today, for one moment of bliss." His erection dug into me, twitching as if beckoning. "You can't deny nature's will."

Why wasn't I repulsed? Scared? I should be running away, screaming murder so he'd leave me alone. Instead, his touch lit my nerves on fire, mirroring the torrent raging in my veins. I wanted everything he promised. To feel his hard, dark body on top of me, under me, and most of all inside me. I wanted our sweat to glue us together, join us in a single rhythm, until I climaxed.

I ran my fingers through his hair. The protrusions, the tiny satyr horns, on his skull were covered in cashmere-soft fur. He grunted. I intensified my strokes along their lengths, and his breathing sped up. His lips left moist traces on my neck. A shiver washed over me down to my toes. Large hands trailed from my shoulder to my breasts as wave after wave of desire smacked through me, squeezing moans from my throat.

He hitched up my top. The jolt of cold fingers against my skin shook reason back into my brain. The grimy wall opposite me fell into focus. This wasn't right. Not in a back alley. I wouldn't be that person.

"No." I shoved. "Get off."

He wiggled past my defenses with a chuckle. "If that's your game, I'll go along."

"Stop." I arched my back to twist from his hold. Again I failed.

With a guttural sound he nuzzled the nape of my neck, no sign he'd heard me. He unbuttoned his pants and forced my hand toward his zipper. I yanked back, slamming my skull against his nose. A happy accident.

He jumped back with a yowl. I slapped his face. Definitely *not* an accident.

My brain was at sixty miles per hour within a fraction of a second. What now? Charging my defensive guards would take too long. I removed my shoe. *Whack.* The impact from my sneaker snapped Ewan's head to the side.

He ducked, hands raised to shield himself. "What the hell is wrong with you?" He backed away.

My motive had nearly disappeared. I hobbled after him, shoe at the ready. With a curse he whisked around and ran off.

I re-arranged my clothes just as a roiling sickness caught up with me. My stomach gurgled, and my eyes fluttered. Oh God. If I hadn't found a way to defend myself, how far would he have pushed me? Blood drained from my head, my neck, my arms, and took my body heat with it.

I'd resisted his advances, but for the first time I understood how powerful a satyr's allure was. And how devastating our motive.

My shoe back in place, I shuffled to the main road. The area felt more deserted than before. Where was Flo? I slid down along the cold stone wall near the bar entrance until my butt hit the ground. The fresh air in my lungs cleared my thoughts. Maybe the near-miss hadn't been entirely Ewan's fault. The way I'd reacted to him, the extent to which his allure had affected me, jeez, I'd never felt anything so intense. And I wasn't even a full-blood satyr.

Perhaps Ewan hadn't had a choice in the way he'd behaved either.

Footsteps approached.

Flo sat beside me and nudged me with his shoulder. "Everything okay?"

"Not really." I placed my head on my knees. "I don't understand.

How can I be normal one day, and have sex on the brain the next because I turned twenty-five? It doesn't make sense, and it's not fair."

"I guess not." He positioned his arm around me and drew me to his chest. "Magic isn't fair and makes no sense. You have to use it where you can, and as for the rest, you need to outsmart it."

"That easy?" I twisted my head to look at him. "And how exactly do you outsmart magic?"

"Hey, even my wisdom has limits."

I snorted. "Never mind." I rubbed the bridge of my nose between the tips of my fingers. Everything was too damn much. All I wanted was to turn back the time, or at least switch off. "Did you get anything?"

"Two phone numbers. But nothing about Heather. Sorry."

It looked like Parker would be seeing us again sooner than he'd thought.

"Come on, grasshopper." Flo patted my head and got up. "The night's still young."

I accepted his extended hand with a grateful smile. As soon as my full weight pressed on my soles, I winced, even though my sneakers were usually ultra-comfortable. "The night might still be in its infancy, but I'm not. I need to get home. My feet are still killing me, would you believe it. Plus, I need a break. You know?"

He glanced at his watch. "I'd rather push on. And we'll be doing little legwork from now on anyway."

"I'm serious." I took a deep breath. Why was my satyr anxiety so hard to admit? "If I don't get a break of at least twenty-four hours, I'll go mental."

"A break from me?" The hurt in his voice cut deep.

"No. Yes. I mean from all men. I want to go a day without giving off seductive vibes or getting turned on."

"Oh. Is that something I should have seen coming?" His eyes grew into the big, round eyes of a puppy. "Is there something I should have done? I mean, am I being a bad friend?"

I hugged him, pressing the area between my nose and my eyes against his neck, and reveled in his cologne. So familiar. "You're practically perfect. Don't worry about it."

"Practically meaning almost?" He squeezed me tight. "I can live with that. How about I take you home then?"

I craned my neck. "Getting more perfect by the second."

He dragged me with him to his Benz.

"So what do you want me to do tomorrow while you're having your scheduled breakdown?"

I shut my eyes. "With your compassion, how are you still single?"

"By choice, dear Ivy." His voice was all matter of fact.

I smirked. "The women's choice, you mean."

He slapped my knee. "I could have a girlfriend if I wanted to. In fact, I could have any woman I want."

I nestled into the familiarity of our banter. "Sure. By brute vampire force or glamour?"

"Shut up." Mr. Sulky-Lip was out again. Poor Flo.

The buzzing in my head stopped, lulled into a trance by the gentle whirring of the engine. I watched the fields and trees through the window, without thought, until he pulled into his parking spot outside his home.

"Are you sure about this?" His voice tightened. "You don't *have* to be alone, you know."

"I do. One day. No men. No confusion. Please."

He dropped his head. "Okay, I'll man the office without you. I mean, how hard can it be, right?"

Images of utter chaos, broken furniture and blazing fire sprung to mind. No. He'd manage. He'd proven quite the asset over the last few days.

I didn't wait for him to lock the car, and hobbled across the road and up my driveway. A casual wave over my shoulder served as my goodbye. A few steps from the entrance, I stopped. A sliver of color leaked through a gap between the door and frame. Had I forgotten to lock up? With my paranoia, this level of carelessness seemed unlikely.

The guards should keep my home safe, but with all that demon activity, I wasn't taking chances. I filled the guards in my pockets with magic. Then I eased open the door.

The sound of muffled conversation drifted through the corridor. My teeth clenched. Someone had broken into my sanctuary. I pressed a trembling fist to my mouth to stop myself from yelling out. Whoever it was, they'd pay for this invasion. I'd dish out so much hurt it would make their eyes water for years to come just thinking about it. Guards clutched against my chest, I crept along the corridor until I caught a glimpse of the living room.

I exhaled loudly through my teeth. A steaming cup in one hand, the remote in the other, Parker was watching a kung-fu movie in *my* house.

"Out." I yelled the word. "Now."

He looked up at me, unfazed. "Where have you been?"

"None of your frigging business. You think you can just break in here?"

A smile touched his lips. "I didn't."

My insides screamed. He'd gone too far, taken liberties with my friendship.

"Hey." He raised his palms. "Honestly, I didn't break in. Sit here, go on." He hustled me to the sofa. "Someone did try to break in, but not me." He disappeared into the kitchen to fetch a glass of water. "By the time I got over here, they'd already left. I only came in to wait for you."

My quick breaths hissed through my nose. His voice, his aura swirled around me. Soothing. Calming. I rolled my shoulders. "And you couldn't have told me this when I came in?" I cleared my throat. "I guess I should apologize, huh?"

He gave a curt bow of the head. "That would be appropriate."

"Sorry." I bunched my lips. "So, if they were gone by the time you got here, how did you find out?"

"Didn't I say? My security cameras cover the entrance to your driveway."

I knew it!

He held up his hand. "I'm not spying on you. It's simply the way the camera is angled, okay? Anyway, two guys were working on your door. When I came over to confront them, they ran."

The guards on my walls would, of course, recognize Parker as a welcome guest after my initial invitation, although I hadn't for a second thought he'd make himself at home. I massaged the pressure point on my forehead. "Why would anyone want to break in here?"

"Whatever they were after, they didn't expect your safety measures." He pointed at my guards. "I'm sure it was random thieves looking for loot. Unless you think it's personal?"

The whispering statue. The two guys had probably been demons.

Parker's face was back to a full frown. "You know who it was, don't you?"

"No idea." With his temper, a flat-out denial seemed the safest answer. Obviously, I'd overlooked the part where he literally smelled lies.

"Damn it, girl. I said to stay out of trouble." He leaped to his feet and started pacing.

My vision swam. "Calm down." *Don't lose it, Ivy. Concentrate.* "Please."

Parker's wolf mojo was messing with me again, while I was still defenseless. Tranquility whirled around my head in multicolored strands of light. Why worry about burglars or statues? Why worry about anything? With Parker living across the backyard, nothing was going to happen to me. He was my alpha and he'd take care of me.

A cavernous rumble shot through me and came out as a happy purr. My muscles unknotted, my mood lifted, and I dropped down on all fours. This was how we honored those ranked above us, and none ranked higher than Parker. I crawled to his feet and tapped his leg with my nose.

He retreated. Why wasn't he patting my head? Rubbing my ears? Wasn't I being submissive enough? I lowered my body and pawed at him.

He took another step back. "Ivy?"

I understood now. There was another way to please him. The animal way. Desire poured into me, transforming my awareness of him into a silent call-out for his touch. I circled him then offered him my hindquarters with a low whimper. My alpha would get what he desired, and I'd be glad to give it.

Almost immediately my mind cleared and my vision improved. In clear outlines, Parker crouched in front of me. I jerked back. What had I done?

His dark eyes held me in his spell. "Are you all right?"

A dry sob cut through my throat. I inched down the hem of my top and scrambled up, away from him, back onto the sofa. Heat stormed into my cheeks. The pressure behind my eyes increased. Torn between the need to bawl and scream my heart out, I sat unmoving. What could I possibly say? Never before had I so humiliated myself.

Parker handed me my glass of water and fell into the seat across from me. "What the hell were you doing down there?"

My reply was no more than a throaty mumble.

"You looked like...like one of my wolves." He leaned forward. "Were you making fun of me and my kind?"

"Believe me. None of that was fun." A deep breath. I pulled my hair over my face and cradled my forehead in my fingers. "Okay then. Short version. Basically, I have a mishmash of races in my ancestry, and because of this, I can read auras. Your aura is different from most I've encountered." I massaged my eyebrows. "When you lose your temper, it's like my mind thinks I'm one of your wolves. Crazy, I know."

Parker placed his hands behind his head, brows pulled forward into pleats. "Wow. I don't know how to respond."

"You and me both. Add to that my satyr heritage, and you can see where this is going."

"Still not entirely clear how that works. How does it feel to you when I get angry?"

My mind raced to search for a non-committal reply, but found none. "Around you, I go Zen most of the time. That's fine. But when you're worked up, the crazies come out. You could attack me and I wouldn't raise a hand in defense. Instead, I want you to look out for me, and, you know, other things which don't make sense."

"I see." He bit his bottom lip. "So, if I get pissed, you end up lying there like a doll, hoping I'd take care of you? Or maybe sleep with you? That's…rather inconvenient for you, isn't it?"

I squinted at the poorly hidden twitch of his mouth. "Are you making fun of me?"

His shoulders bobbed up and down, and choppy laughter burst from his lips.

"Come on!" I crossed my arms in front of me and shot him my best badass glare. "Trust me, being part werewolf fan-girl and part satyr isn't funny."

"Okay. Okay." His hands fluttered through the air. "The more I get to know you, the more certain I am that…" He grabbed at his ribs, struggling for composure. "Spirits, help me. If ever there was someone in worse shape to convince as a satyr," the pitch of his voice rose to non-human heights, "it'd be you. Let's say you lack the satyrs' worldliness." Another chuckle. "And the thought of you as one of my wolves? Yeah, I dig it."

"Stop it."

"Is it possible there may have been werewolf in your lineage?"

I knotted my eyebrows. "With my luck I wouldn't be surprised. When I was made, my parents picked out those traits which would mess up my life the most."

"Beautiful." He raised his hand then let it flop back into his lap.

I shook my head, willing this nightmare to end. "Please go. I-I need to be alone. I don't want to see or talk to anyone for twenty-four hours." I braced myself for his objection.

"That sounds reasonable. I'm just glad you're safe." He rose. "But we do need to talk about this. What about tomorrow evening?"

Yeah, Florian would skin me alive if I postponed the trip to the dead demons' house again. "I'm working late tomorrow. I can come by the morning after?"

"Say, ten o'clock?"

"I'll be there. And thank you, Parker." My voice broke a little. "For looking out for…my house. I mean it."

He shot me a quick nod. "You're welcome."

I locked the door behind him. In my new house, I'd have fresh flowers every day. An artificial fireplace would flicker happily, and a fluffy rug in front of it would invite me to lay on it and read. But here, in this house that had once meant so much to me, these cheerful items wouldn't feel right. Everything here had been contaminated by my father's and mother's past. They were to blame for Lathan's interest, my shameful behavior around men, this raging heat that only sex quelled. Both traced directly to my parents' relationship.

Without them, Waylon wouldn't have felt it necessary to toy with my heart. I wished I'd never met him. Wished I'd never let him into my house.

In fact, too many people had been traipsing through my home. My life had been so much easier before I'd generously given out all-access passes to Chez Ivy. And safer.

My nightstand housed not only emergency chocolate for when I couldn't sleep, it also contained my weaving supplies. From among the metal disks I picked eight large copper ones and placed them side-by-side on the worktops in my kitchen. For the next couple of hours, I designed new, stronger guards to replace the ones that currently hung on the walls. The old ones were stained. Unclean. Through my fault, my home was no longer mine alone.

I snorted quietly. The dreaded word: alone. I'd thought Waylon wanted to be with me. Now I saw it for the childish dream it had been. There were no knights in shining armor rescuing the princess from the windowless tower. Oh, he'd probably give it another shot the next time he rode through town, but I'd be much wiser then. I was done handing out invitations into my life like they were Halloween candy.

By the time my guards were ready, sweat poured down my back. I removed the old plates and hung the new ones in their place. The familiar incantation activated the network and magic sprung to life around me. And with it, safety.

***

My dreams had been fitful, but thankfully Lathan only featured in a cameo. I sat in my bed, cradling my throbbing skull. Usually on my days off, I'd putter about, read a little, and generally do nothing. That was a fine plan for when my thoughts weren't going at tornado speed.

Right now, my lack of activity focused my mind on my humiliating behavior. My wolf-out with Parker had been the last, and weirdest, straw.

No. Today was a time-out. A testosterone null field. A man-break was *so* what the head doctor ordered. Yet after reading for a few hours, restlessness crept into my limbs.

My necklace's recharge took a few minutes. Then my mind went back into neutral. I inhaled. Sniffed my T-shirt. Was this Waylon's scent?

Yup. Definitely losing it. He'd never been in the same room as my T-shirt. God, why couldn't I forget about him? We'd had one night of sex. My craving for him had been building steadily, but my occupation now bordered on obsession.

Twenty minutes later, I switched on the TV. Green numbers on a black computer-type background ran up the screen. Keanu Reeves' long, Hollywood-type face appeared. His lips moved the way Waylon's did when he spoke. The same smile. Even their voices were similar.

Christ. No thinking. Period.

I turned over to the History Channel. War. Bloodshed.

Much better.

The hours on my black-and-white checkered wall clock ticked by at a snail's pace. The weak shadow it cast moved even more slowly. I popped an aspirin for the headache and returned to watch World War II in color. How did pensioners spend all day cooped up inside their house? Perhaps this was how games like pinochle and bridge got invented.

Lunch time came. Hunger didn't. My stomach was acting up, getting worse when I shifted. Weren't kin supposed to be more robust than humans?

The phone rang. "Hello?" Crap. I wasn't supposed to answer it on my man-free day.

"Ivy? It's Greg."

Guess I could make an exception. "Hey. Great to hear from you."

"I'm sorry I didn't get in touch earlier. Shame we couldn't meet up."

My stomach shattered like it had been struck by a wrecking ball. "Yes. Sorry about that."

"Are you free this weekend?"

I exhaled. This was my chance at a normal relationship with a sweet guy who wanted to be with me. And right now, I needed normal. "Yes, definitely."

"Wonderful." The smile was evident in his voice. "Tell you the truth, I'm relieved. I thought you were giving me the run-around."

So he was smart, too. "Not at all. Of course not."

"Good. What have you been doing?"

Other men? My belly cramped again. Was this guilt? "Nothing exciting. Work and stuff."

"You never really told me about your job. Private detective sounds fascinating."

I gave a dry cough. He had no idea. "It's called private investigator, because we rarely detect. Not like the police. Seventy percent of the job is research."

"You get paid to find out people's birth dates?"

I laughed, despite the nagging weight on my shoulders. "We do a little more. We check into our clients' past, to see what they *didn't* tell us, then we check into those they want to know about."

"Cheating spouses, you mean."

He made it sound so humdrum. "Yeah, but also finding missing relatives, tracking down heirlooms or unsuspecting heirs to fortunes."

He laughed.

I shifted. "What?"

"You like your job. It's in your voice. You make it appear so unimportant, but you love it."

Yup. Definitely a smart cookie. The way he saw right through me filled me with optimism. "Okay, maybe I love it a little."

"Good. I like learning more about you." He sounded pleased with himself.

My neck warmed. "Seems you're having a pretty good idea of what makes me tick."

"Promise you'll let me find out what makes you tock on Saturday?" His voice was butter-smooth.

I tightened my grip. "Promise."

"See you then."

My thoughts lingered longer on him than they should have. He'd not been exposed to my allure, and he was still interested. Keen, even. A good sign. A very good sign.

Still, this was supposed to be my man-break. I scratched my forehead, finding it warm and moist. Crap. This was getting serious. I test-sniffled. My nose was free of gross fluey stuff. Not a cold then, but perhaps a tummy bug. Although nothing dubious had crossed my lips recently. Except for Waylon's tongue.

I dropped to the side and buried my head in the pillow. When was this craziness going to end?

Actually, Waylon's tongue had been quite the revelation. The man sure knew how to kiss. And kissing wasn't his only talent. My experience in the bedroom wasn't as vast as his, but it was sufficient to declare him an expert. I bit my lip. The way he'd always found precisely the right spot was a wonderful mystery. I rolled onto my back and stroked my ribcage. He'd been gentle, his fingertips barely touching my skin. Right about now, he'd added a teasing move, along the cup of my breasts, followed by an almost accidental brush of my nipple.

I squirmed. As if prompted by Waylon, I traced his languid strokes along the swell of my breast to the center. Then a quick flick.

I stopped. Did I just do that?

His intense voice, figment or not, urged me to carry on. Every spot he made me touch trembled. Despite the fabric barrier, warmth rose in my pit. He'd known what to massage. And how to massage it. I closed my eyes, and the smoothness of his skin came alive under my hands. His abs had the right definition, with curves to drive me senseless.

I sought the bottom of my top and snuck my hand underneath. He'd twirled my nipples, proficiently. My attempts were clumsier, like a radio operator through the silk of my bra, but no less effective. I rubbed my thighs together, keeping the rising need down. But his fictional weight pressed against my crotch, parting my legs easily, before shifting into position. His ghost blurred into the present, his breath covering my shoulder. The flutter inside my clit became unbearable. His mouth, my hand, closed around my nipple. I threw my head back and suppressed a yelp.

The ticks of my clock grew into his groans. My fingers found my entrance. Oh God, yes. My lungs pumped harder, blood rushed into my groin. Once again I was unable to stop the quiet calls of his name, begging him to finish. Where two fingers failed to mimic his girth or length, my imagination filled in. The heel of my hand stroked my clit, steadily, while Waylon thrust inside me. My other hand caressed my breast. I rolled my nipple between my fingers to imitate his sucking. The pressure increased, my wetness pouring into my panties. I felt him in me, striking my insides. He whispered my name, his tone hoarse and barely restrained. I panted for air while he rode me hard and fast, grunting each time he forced apart my walls. Oh God. It was coming. *I* was coming. His speed built, making me ache for release. A tightness missiled from my pelvis to my brain. The climax engulfed me, and I threw back my head and let out a cry.

For a second I lay motionless, willing my heart to slow. Breath after breath after breath, my room flashed back into reality.

Okay, this was new. Not the act, of course, but an early afternoon hand-job wasn't an everyday occurrence. I wiped my palm against the fabric of my panties and zipped up my jeans, letting the last contractions within subside.

The phone rang. I sat up, but didn't answer it. Not again. Especially not now. Why had I allowed Waylon to creep back into my subconscious? Just my luck I'd met the one man who could seduce me in his absence.

I rearranged the pillow, but didn't lie back down. Sweat clung to my back. I got up, woozy from dehydration, and made my way into the kitchen. Cool water from the faucet woke me up, but didn't settle my nausea.

Of course my health had been of little concern a few minutes ago, when Not-Really-Waylon had made my brain explode.

Huh. I turned the water off. Perhaps he'd done something to me. Given me some demon infection that made me lust for him. I rubbed my burning forehead. My vision swam, and Greg's crooked smile whipped my insides into a frenzy. His blue eyes morphed into brown ones with golden specks. Parker's full lips, open and moist, invited me. One kiss was all I wanted. One kiss, the way he'd held me that day in his office, careful yet firm.

When had my life turned into a movie reel of porn and chick flicks? My eyes focused, and Parker's image melted away. Immediately my stomach did a back-flip.

Okay. Not a demon STD. Just your garden-variety satyr curse where I was attracted to men across the board. Something heavy sat on my chest, clamped it tight as if to suffocate me. More than ever I wished for my dad to be here. He'd talk me through this. All the times I'd thought him promiscuous, he'd had no choice. Except where *he'd* taken enjoyment from his excesses, I hadn't been raised that way. As insistent as my mother was that I should find a man through my looks, she'd never advocated sleeping around. If anything, she'd been a bit on the coy side when it came to sex.

This wasn't fair. Why was this happening to me? And why hadn't anyone prepared me for a future in which I'd be a slave to my hormones? With a dry sob, I fell to my knees, clutching my stomach. The universe was screaming at me, and I finally got the message. For better or worse, I'd been decreed a card-carrying member of the kin races. No longer human.

My eyes burned, but I balled my fists. I was better than this. Being kin might drive me bat-shit crazy, but I would. Not. Cry.

I sat in that position maybe five, ten minutes. Breath by breath, my thought processes blanked out the upset stomach and the banging inside the skull. The headaches had started on or around my birthday, but they hadn't been twenty-four seven. In fact, they'd stopped for a while after…after I'd slept with Waylon.

Of course. Perhaps sex was like crack to a satyr. Without, we'd go into withdrawal. But why hadn't my hand-job done the trick? It stood to reason the sort-of-sex I'd indulged in half an hour ago should have satisfied my motive.

If anything, it had made the situation worse.

Shit. Whatever was happening, I couldn't work this out by myself.

CHAPTER SEVENTEEN

FLORIAN'S FLAWLESS HANDSOMENESS SET MY motive off the second I opened the door. But transferring my raging desires onto him wasn't what I was after.

"You got it?" I eyed the book in his hand.

"Here you go." He handed it over and marched into the living room. "Have you had enough of your no-man time?"

The humor in his voice cleared my head a little. "Uh. I don't know. I need to research something."

"You don't look good. Are you ill?" He lifted his arm to feel my head.

I ducked away. Involving him in my insanity attack had been a risk, but Flo had always been my first port of call. No one and nothing would change that. It didn't hurt that the Duprees owned an extensive library. When he told me on the phone that they possessed a book on the sidhes, I nearly sobbed in relief. It had to contain the answer, *had* to, because if it didn't...

Still, until my hormones had decided on what to do with Flo, it might be best to not get too cozy with him. Even the most innocuous touch could set me off.

"Ivy?" His voice hummed with concern.

"I'm really not looking for pity, okay?" I leafed through the pages, although my ice-cold fingertips didn't make this an easy task.

He lifted his hand. "Easy."

"Sorry." I closed my eyes and concentrated on my breathing. "Still a little bit upset from yesterday. And this no-man idea backfired."

"How?" He took my hand.

I recoiled, but almost immediately, my thoughts tore themselves free from the molasses of my hormones for the first time in many hours. The urge to find sexual gratification any which way faded.

Could touch be the answer? Was this what a satyr's motive and allure were about? Physical contact? One by one the pixels in my brain switched color until a picture formed. If a touch from a friend could calm me, no wonder intercourse, the ultimate kind of contact, was the feel-good peak for a satyr.

"Earth to Ivy." Flo slanted forward into my line of sight.

"Hang on. I'm thinking." I held on to him, let his warmth flow into me. My need for sex disappeared back to a soft background music.

I closed my eyes, filled my lungs with oxygen. Yup. I was myself again. For now.

I shut the book. "This is amazing. My mind's been screaming at me to find a man, and you come along, and my sex drive all but vanishes."

"What every man wants to hear." His lips pursed.

"Sorry. That came out wrong." I smirked. "I've been going crazy. Waylon kept going through my head, then Greg and Parker. I was in withdrawal, complete with nausea and a migraine. There seemed to be no way out of this insanity. Then you came along, and I'm better."

He looked at me with uncertainty.

I hugged him. "You might say you have the magic touch." I kissed his cheek. "Thank you."

He grinned. "Well, you're not the first woman to say that."

I nudged him.

"I'm sorry you're having such a hard time with being kin." His eyes lost their glint. "It sucks. But if physical contact makes your life more bearable, I have all the hugs you need right here."

I placed my head on his shoulder and reveled in his presence. Each second, the load on my lungs lifted. And so did my mood. Just minutes ago, I'd reached my darkest hour. Without this epiphany, who knew where I'd ended up? The hospital, or even an asylum?

"Okay, I'm ready." I got to my feet. "Work calls, right?" If nothing else, keeping busy with Flo by my side was the perfect way to stop me from overthinking this.

"Erm. Sure. If you think you're up to it." He gave me a sideways glance, but followed me out to his car.

We let his varied CD collection replace conversation. My mind still whirled. The solution had been so simple. A touch calmed raging hormones and quieted headaches. I should definitely write that down somewhere. Flo had once again rescued me. I peered at him, a tender smile on my lips. No matter how crappy my life got, he was always there for me.

Flo's nav system knew the way. Not that he would believe its directions. "Turn right? Where exactly do you want me to turn right?" He slapped the display. "Stupid machine."

By a miracle, we found the correct address.

"So far, our investigation hasn't been successful." He turned off the lights and parked. "Let's hope we score with our dead demons."

I frowned. "You wanna rephrase that?"

He pushed me away and grinned. "You have a dirty mind. You know exactly what I mean."

I grabbed the door handle. My first intentional foray into the dodgy past-time of crime. My life had really, really changed.

"Saddle up." Florian got out of the Mercedes.

I followed him. The steady breeze ruffled my hair and blew straight through my jacket. We filed along the narrow pathway and sidled up to the house.

The now-dead demons had shared a side-by-side duplex, framed by a well-maintained fence. The brickwork showed traces of a recent paint job. It went to show once again that even demon thugs blended in with soccer moms and workaholic dads. Only the yellow police tape on the door stood out.

"I got the door," Flo whispered. One push, and he'd shouldered his way through. The impact cracked the frame, but at least we had a way in.

His action hadn't been quiet, and I stopped to check if anyone had heard us.

My heart dropped in my chest. Two women in their retirement years shuffled up the street. One wore a flowery dress much too summery for the season, with a churchy hat balanced on top of graying hair. The other had compressed her volume into a zippered velour jacket and matching pants, like Sporty Spice might look in her sixties.

"Your face reminds me of a Girl Scout I ran over with my car last week," Flo said. "Bam, her wagon full of cookies flew up over my hood."

"What?" I blinked, half distracted by the women, who were chatting and hadn't yet noticed us or the splintered door.

I pressed my back into the shadow of a tree and held my breath, so as not to attract attention.

My life of crime was still in its infancy, but the signs spelled an early grave for me. If not by grisly murder, then surely from a heart attack. The women passed without sparing us a second glance and left suburban silence in their wake.

Florian slid the door wide open and listened intently. "Coast is clear." He disappeared from view.

I followed him in, my pulse still chasing its tail around my veins.

Opaque drapes enveloped the room in thickest black. Vampire

eyes apparently saw well enough, though. "I'll be back in a sec." Flo's voice trailed off in the darkness.

Like a bat I, too, had the uncanny ability to seek out obstacles in my way, only my version of sonar made me bump into them.

Stale cabbage stink hung in the air, not helped by the month-old cigarette smoke ingrained in the furniture.

Wham. Crap. I'd stumbled over the carpet and run into a chair. I bowed at the hip and rubbed my tender skin.

Flo reappeared. "You're noisy. Has anyone told you that?"

I pushed him. "No, but thanks."

"Just saying. Oh, and there's nothing upstairs. Here. I found this." He pressed something cool into my hand.

A flashlight, bless him. I switched it on and turned to my friend to thank him when the cone from the lamp reflected off something shiny on the wall. Above a worn wooden cabinet, a guard hung higher than eye level, the first indication that something other than humans had inhabited this space. *Well, well, well.* Maybe the police had left something for us to find, after all.

Once Florian had searched through and dismissed the cabinet, I subjected the metal plate to a closer inspection. Two parallel lines on opposite sides curved into a hook at the top, so the main function of the guard was to influence the observer's mind. Without being certain as to the plate's exact purpose, however, I was reluctant to touch it. Squinting at it from the side would hopefully tell me what I needed to know.

I'd always been kind of immune to the most common varieties of mind-interference, such as a vampire's glamour, and my guards helped protect against others, but different kin had different tricks up their sleeves. So it paid to be cautious with magic I hadn't seen before.

"What are these grooves for?" Flo picked up the chair and slid it over. "Can you tell?"

I handed him the flashlight and used his outstretched arm for leverage to climb up. "Imagine opening up a computer. Seeing the cables alone won't tell you what the computer's capable of. Shine up here, please."

He adjusted the light.

"There are specific markers that... Oh, here's one." I bent my knees to catch the bright beam without blinding myself. "This tiny dot, no bigger than an indentation left by a prong of a fork, reveals the guard's purpose. The important thing is where it's placed. See, it's interesting. When magic was first—"

"Ivy." He wiggled the light. "This sounds fascinating, but may I remind you of the following: it's the dead of night, we're in a house that isn't ours, looking for proof of nefarious activities by demons carried out in the name of what we assume is a real badass, and on top of everything, I haven't eaten in a while."

I hopped off the chair and pressed my hands against my waist. "What's your point?"

He was too smart to answer a rhetorical question when I was in a strop. "Just tell me. What does the darn thing do?"

"I'll show you." My right hand traced along a hooked line to the bottom. A quick incantation, and blue energy fizzed through the room and dissipated, revealing an extra drawer in the cabinet underneath the guard.

Flo pulled out its content, a wallet-sized booklet in the style of a journal. He opened it. "Aha. A ledger." He grinned at me as if he'd done the hard work and I'd spent the past ten minutes knitting him a scarf as a reward for his brilliance.

I narrowed my eyes. "What does it say?"

"Later." He dragged me out the house.

Was he kidding? I shook him off and built myself up in front of him. "What? Why?"

"Food first," he said with a toothy smile. "I'm starving."

• • •

Flo pulled the Mercedes into his driveway. All I wanted now was a hot bath, even if I had to crawl on hands and knees to the bathroom. His company had settled my urges, and sleep would reenergize me. Or so I hoped. "What's with the cars?"

"Remember? The book launch?"

I'd completely forgotten.

He jumped out and held the door for me. "You promised to show up at Julia's party." His voice made it clear attendance was an obligation, not a choice.

"But I'm beat." I glanced over to where my Mustang was back in its place outside my house, just across the road. The mechanic had promised to push the keys through the letterbox.

"Nonsense. Eli will be there, and it's time you two made up."

Eli, Florian's brother, had once asked me out. Sadly, I'd just discovered he was a vampire and, I admit, my rejection may have been a little more vehement than was customary in these situations. The discomfort between us was a predictable and constant source of amusement for Florian.

"Come on." He patted his tummy. "There's bound to be plenty of food in attendance." He absorbed my scowl. "Yes, even for you."

I poked his arm. "I thought you didn't socialize with your food."

"*I'm* not." He grinned. "My sister's socializing with my food."

At first glance, the Duprees' mansion was similar to the one occupied by the werewolf pack. Similar, but with unique quirks. Blood red Virginia creeper almost entirely covered the building's brick walls, its beautiful foliage giving it a "spooky" feel. It was an earthy, slightly eccentric and altogether appropriate home for Julia and her brothers.

The interior décor reflected the unconventional outside. While lights were an unnecessary luxury for the undead, Flo couldn't live without his soaps, or Eli without his documentaries, so the Duprees continued to use electricity in their private quarters and in the large ballroom. But down here on the first floor, eerie shadows, cast by flickering candles and torches on the walls, wrapped around the corridor which led us into the bowel of the mansion. What a fantastic talking point for visitors of Lisa McMahon, author of fang fiction.

Florian disappeared around the corner without saying a word. Luckily, I knew my way around the house well enough. The string quartet Julia had hired for the occasion played a beautiful tune which crescendoed into a heartrending finale just as I arrived at the entrance of the lavishly decorated hall.

The attendees, illustrious and beautiful, if not all human, were familiar faces from news and television. I was underdressed, but by no means skuzzy. My clothes were clean, my top and jacket presentable, and my sneakers gave me an artsy look. Despite that, I felt like a gazelle among lions.

Julia's stunning long red dress exposed her elegant shoulders. The fabric split from her slim ankles all the way up to her thigh. One hand held a glass of wine, the other rested on the arm of a man in denim and a white, casual shirt. Her gaze caught mine and she waved me over. I shook my head. I was tired, cranky, and the thought of having to be polite to strangers didn't rate highly on my can-cope-with list. I'd poked my head in, and that was all I was prepared to do tonight.

My sweeping glance came to rest on the blond mop of Florian's brother Eli. More than six feet tall, lean rather than muscle-packed, he wasn't handsome by Hollywood standards. Not the kind that would photograph well, anyway. His attraction stemmed from his personality. The animation in his face when he talked, the way he'd focus his attention on you, the little dimple in his right cheek when he smiled.

Christ, was my motive, this ever present hormonal burden, rearing its head again? Eli was talking to a pretty human girl who laughed and giggled at his every word. His peculiar sense of humor used to tickle me, too.

That was way back when, and things had changed. Three months ago, he'd almost ended up as a hood ornament for a BMW after darting into the street to avoid me.

I resumed my search for Florian. Strangers beamed at me, probably thinking I was some big-shot friend of Julia's. My squint made sure they didn't try to make my acquaintance. Five feet from me, Florian's auburn hair caught the light. He'd never looked more handsome or elegant. His dark eyes shimmered, and his smooth, pale skin begged to be caressed. While my motive wasn't swayed, I felt a silly sort of pride that he was my best friend. What he got out of the company of a shallow person like me, I couldn't fathom.

His attention focused on a middle-aged lady. His hand on her arm, he whispered something, and she laughed. His mouth moved again, and her smile slackened, her eyes glazed over.

Vampires weren't predators in the precise sense of the term. Rather, they were opportunistic feeders, undetected by society. It was entirely conceivable that practically every human out there had either been fed from or knew someone who'd been fed from. Vampires here in Oldworld left behind neither corpses nor memories as evidence of their eating habits.

Florian's glamour coiled around the woman. She was lost in his aura, and her mind was putty to do with as he pleased. A wink in my direction, and he steered her through the hall out into a small darkened room. I inched forward and peered around the corner, fascinated despite myself. He drew one arm around the woman in a close embrace. His free hand swept back her long, dyed hair. In one plunge, his fangs disappeared in the pale neck she freely offered. She gave a soft groan before her hands encircled his waist, lost to the outpour of endorphins the chemical secretion from his teeth compelled.

His black eyes looked up from under his lashes, as if daring me to turn away in disgust. A shiver ran through my body, more from excitement than repulsion. He bared everything that made him a vampire. The fact I was willing to share this moment with him was my promise to him, my acceptance of what he was.

By the look in his eyes he understood my gesture. Finally, his back straightened. Black eyes moved from me back to the woman in his arms, and he licked along the wound to close it up with his saliva, steadying his woozy meal with his hand.

By the time they'd rejoined the bustle in the entrance to the ballroom, the woman had recovered. She laughed out for no apparent reason, throwing her long curls back in girlish fashion. "Well, this was pleasant, my dear, but my husband will already be wondering if I've run away with you." She giggled again and was off.

Florian walked up to me with slow, deliberate strides. "Your turn."

I raised my eyebrows.

"Food." He hustled me into the large room toward the buffet table.

Boy, for a vampire, Julia sure knew how to cater for those who weren't partial to the red stuff. Tiny delicacies whose size certainly belied their true calorie content balanced in uneven, delicious piles on my plate. Once he was satisfied I wouldn't starve on his watch, he led me back out of the room and up to his quarters.

This wasn't my first visit. His living room and the huge LCD screen on the wall had welcomed me many times and with open arms, and his sofa was the object of my greenest envy. The other doors in this wing of the house, however, were a mystery to me because they were usually closed. Only Florian lived up here. Eli and Julia occupied different sections of the building.

"Be right back." He disappeared into one of these rooms.

The wide gap between door and frame revealed his bedroom. I stifled a gasp. Oil paintings of naked women and men in various poses donned his walls. A heavy metal chain with broad leather cuffs dangled off a hook from above his headboard, and a huge round mirror on the ceiling reflected the red satin sheets and leather straps lining his bed.

"You can wait in the living room," Flo said from behind the door.

His comment yanked me out of my stupefaction. This brief glimpse into my friend's private life had put an entirely new spin on his personality. While I'd always suspected Julia of having a tendency toward bondage, he hadn't struck me as the type.

I spun on my heels and fled to the living room, where I worked on bringing my pulse down to normal and squeezing the blood back out of my face.

Two minutes later he popped out, now wearing comfy jeans and a thick cotton shirt. He fell ungracefully into the round, frilly pillows of his brown leather sofa and invited me to do the same.

I toed off my shoes and sat.

"What's wrong?" Florian produced the small book we'd found earlier from his jacket. "I doubt you'll be able to see the ledger from over there."

"Why should anything be wrong? I'm good. Everything's... good." I moved an inch or two closer to prove my point.

"O-kaay." He squinted. "Maybe you should get food into you to up your sugar levels before we deal with this. You seem a little tense."

Frankly, there was no reason for me to behave like a coy schoolgirl only because he liked his sex kinky. He was unlikely to pounce on me, tie me up and have his wicked way with me. With both of us ending up naked on the bed. Leather straps tied around my wrists and ankles so I was completely at his mercy.

Sheesh. My thoughts had made a U turn somewhere along the way there, hadn't they? With a shake of my head I tucked into my food. Florian opened the ledger. Brows furrowed, he skimmed the content as if it were a Japanese instruction manual for a HiFi system.

"Here." He pointed at the last page of entries. "I can't believe how anal this guy was. What's he keeping this for, his tax return?"

In perfect longhand, the demon had written:

$10		STATE LOTTERY
$350	car service	BRIGHTSHEEN GARAGE
$5	donation	AMERICAN WILDLIFE FOUNDATION
$4,000	wet job (Carter)	GOD
$68.22	shopping	WALMART

"Wet job, as in murder." He rubbed his forehead. "Apparently ordered by God. There you go. God moves in mysterious ways, but I can't see why He'd want the statue."

"It's probably a nickname. Maybe for a priest or a leader of a sect?"

"Okay, and how do we find God?"

"Through faith, Florian. And repentance." I chuckled. "Crap. This is going to lead to all sorts of word play and bad jokes, isn't it? A church maybe?" I munched on a square of coffee gateau, glad to have my mind back on business. After a few minutes of silence, I pushed the plate away and slumped back with a loud sigh. "Honestly, I'm too tired to think clearly. I should go home."

Neither of us stirred. It was a quarter to ten and I was beat. How the hell had Dad managed to stay out all night at *his* age?

"Get moving then," Flo said after another minute, his body spread-eagled in a limp mass across the sofa.

I arched my eyebrows.

"Still digesting my food." He gifted me with an impish smirk.

I heaved myself up on my elbows and poked around on the floor with my foot for my sneakers, sliding forward on the smooth leather surface. "Fine. Don't see me out then."

With an exaggerated sigh, Florian rose and shuffled to the door, his arm held at half-mast instead of his usual bow. Had I done the impossible and worn him out?

By the time we'd reached the front door, he was his old bouncing self again. "See you tomorrow." He kissed my cheek and watched until I'd safely crossed the road. One last wave, and he disappeared inside, possibly to find a playmate for the night among Julia's guests.

None of my business.

CHAPTER EIGHTEEN

B REATHING RESEMBLED DRAWING AIR THROUGH a tiny straw. Feral lycae tore my limbs from their sockets and sliced my skin to expose blood-soaked tendons underneath. Their emaciated bodies packed more muscle than flesh, the stench from their matted fur almost evaporated under the pain burning my brain.

"Enough." Lathan raised a hand, and the lycae stepped back.

I lay motionless, blinking through the tears. Agony had forced beads of sweat onto my skin, but I was too exhausted to wipe it off.

Lathan leaned over, his green eyes glinting with a cold kindness. His proficient touch on my neck quelled the fire in me, his intimate attention ample reward for my suffering. His rough hands roamed over my nakedness. Why bother resisting? I was his possession. Light-colored hairs gave his chest a manly feel, a stark contrast to his angelic face. He spread my legs and entered me. No foreplay for me, and he'd already had his. Still, my body was ready for him. Pleasure warred with revulsion, and I groaned.

A breeze cooled our flushed bodies. Feathery grass on soft ground cradled my skin while a primitive need urged me upward, each thrust begging him to go deeper. His long blond hair fell onto my breast, nudging me nearer to completion. Lathan was with me in my mind, celebrating each new sensation, his laughter icy and triumphant. Wave after wave of rapture swept through my flesh, caressing the nerve endings connected to my brain. So close. So close.

Dull thumping in the air disturbed our rhythm, out of sync with our efforts. The illusion shattered and my eyes jerked open. The pink lampshade above my bed formed a startling contrast to the darkness from which I was emerging.

As understanding came to me, a deep shudder ripped through my veins. This hadn't just been a disgusting sex dream. No, Lathan had got into my head and taken control of my mind, as he'd done countless times in Alethia.

But even back then he'd never gone this far. He'd never let our relationship become sexual. Why hadn't I stopped him? Somehow he'd turned me into a willing participant in his sick games. My chest twisted into loops. I ran a hand up along my arm, scratching at his mark. If a knife could cut deeply enough, I'd shred my skin without a moment's pause. Scrape out Lathan's hold over me with my fingers bit by bit.

Each breath cleared my head a little more. No, it couldn't be true. Even if the kinlord drew on every strand of demon power in his possession, his mind could no more pierce the border separating the two worlds than his body could. He himself had once told me this when he'd considered me his safe possession.

But despite all self-assurance, despite all common sense, I sensed his presence, like a disease under my skin.

An insistent banging from my living room jarred my quiet misery. I scrambled out of bed and struggled into a coat from the rack to drape over my pajamas. Whoever was responsible for this racket deserved my gratitude.

Daylight put distance between me and my nightmare. And brought me one day closer to my planned move. At no point had my leaving Silverton seemed more urgent. Of course I needed someone for that daily touch to keep my motive in check, but once I was safe, finding a casual lover might not be too difficult.

Outside, Parker stomped past the windows to my yard, his eyebrows pulled deep into his face. "Ivy, open up!" That much I got from the movement of his mouth. The double-glazing blocked the rest of his words.

I'd just woken. What had I done wrong now?

Dealing with his confusing effect on me could wait. Perhaps a few minutes more would help him calm down. I went into the kitchen to make coffee. Parker followed along the outside of the house, motioning through the window for me to open the doors.

With slow deliberation, I poured the water into the mug and returned to the living room. He built himself up, shoulders back, arms crossed. His eyes promised a verbal lashing, but at least he'd accepted reality.

I opened the door. "Needed to get something off your chest, Sparky?" Smug? Me? Hell yeah. I'd diffused a difficult situation without bloodshed or wolfish cowering on my part.

He lifted his leg to move forward. Electricity sparked, and he bounded off my invisible shield. "Shit." He took a balancing step back and rubbed his arm.

"Yeah, sorry about that," I lied, sipping my coffee. Not quite the defenseless waif he believed me to be, was I?

"What's going on?" His voice crackled, his face grim.

"I renewed my guards. Keeping myself safe." A twinge in my head forced a sharp intake of breath, and I rubbed my temples to alleviate the ache.

"We had an appointment." His voice drummed in my skull. "You promised you'd come over at ten."

I looked at the clock. It was noon already. Time does fly when you're haunted by disgusting nightmares.

Another sharp pain behind my eyes. Like a pin drilling into my skull, mixed with a stench of tar that pervaded my senses. So familiar. So real.

Oh no. My guts clenched and nausea rode into my throat. It was a side-effect I'd endured before, a remnant of Lathan's mind magic. The truth unfolded like a red cloth in the snow of my ignorance. He'd done it. Lathan had found a way. Some magic, a guard or an artifact perhaps, had to be located nearby, giving him access to the mark on my shoulder. And with it, to my head. My legs crumbled, and I dropped to my knees. The cup fell from my hand, brown liquid soaked into the carpet.

The nerve endings in my body fired. A burst of acid shooting through each one. If I could only find—

Bright light flashed before my eyes. The world tunneled, and my skull hit the ground.

"You've found me out." Lathan's low chuckle swam in the oily smoothness of his timbre. *"You always were too clever for your own good. I told you I'd come for you."*

"Go away," I screamed, slapping my skull with the palm of my hand, trying to shake him loose.

"Never, my love. Do not fret, soon you'll sing a different tune."

My narrow gaze fell on Parker. "In...me in!" Although his mouth opened and closed, his words barely reached my ears.

Air. I needed air. I pawed on my top, desperate for oxygen.

"Now, where were we?" Lathan's mind was back in charge, forcing me to re-live my nightmare of pleasure. The soft grass, his body jerking on top of me and inside me. My deepest desires floated to the surface, lured by his slippery promises. One half of me felt like an onlooker, the other half was wrapped in the moment, bucking under his touch. My breathing turned into panting, culminating in a scream torn from my throat by desperation and release. Sobs erupted in my chest, my flesh trembling, frantic for a reprieve from the painful climax he'd induced.

I needed to find whatever he'd used to control me.

"Parker." I flailed my arm, pointing at the guards on my wall. "Lathan...inside."

Lathan's victorious laughter foreshadowed what both of us knew. I was losing the fight. My head lolled to the side where hopeless eyes registered a fuzzy Parker rattling the door frame.

"Come in," I mouthed. Then I sank into blackness.

I lay curled up in a California King bed, tucked underneath a thick quilted cover. Lathan was gone. The desire to get up and explore my surroundings needled me, while the louder part of me wanted to hang on to the feeling of refuge.

Except there was no refuge. My life lay in shatters. I was once a decent girl. Had morals the same as anyone else. At least I used to. Not anymore. If I wasn't already jonesing for sex during the day, Lathan had the power to make me crave it at night.

The end of the road. No escape.

I rolled around under the blanket, drawing it over my head for warmth.

My dreams of a new house? A new start? Why bother? My way out of Lathan's grasp was Waylon and his Guardian knowledge. But where did that leave me? Waylon had not used mind magic on me yet, but if he didn't get his way, who knew?

If one demon didn't own me, another would.

The emptiness inside grew from a husk into a cavern, filling my chest, squeezing the air from my lungs. Florian couldn't help me. No one could. I was the rope in a tug-o-war between a Guardian and a kinlord.

Now, didn't I feel special?

I bit my fist. *Don't cry.* They might get my body, but I'd not let them have my tears.

The door opened, and I flipped back the cover.

Parker extended a cup in my direction. "Figured you could use this."

The bitter coffee scent clawed into my nose. A lovely scent, but it was Parker's aura that proved the perfect haven for my battered mind. He sat beside me on the bed and reached for something on the bedside table.

"After your cryptic clue about 'Lathan inside,' I searched your house and found two things that didn't belong," he said without ceremony. "First, this." He waved the statue at me. "This doesn't seem to be your style and, well, I found it under your sofa. Seen it before?"

I sipped my latte and closed my eyes to drink in the pleasures of the sweet, frothy roast. "Fred, my boss, asked me to pick it up a few days ago for a client. I think it's called *Collective*."

Revealing how I'd come by the statue was not likely to be conducive to my continued feeling of comfort. At some point he'd undoubtedly wheedle the information out of me. For now, though, I wanted to avoid drama. And bask in his calm, even if it was only for a few minutes.

"So you think this interesting little piece of art has nothing to do with whatever happened to you?" He squinted, as if judging whether I was on the level. As if his lie-detector nose didn't give him enough of an advantage.

I raised my arms in a helpless gesture. A coincidence of this magnitude seemed improbable. The possibility that Lathan had had it planted at the Carters' house in the hope that I'd show up, find it and take it home with me was preposterously small.

"Is it okay if I hold on to this Collective and do some research?" I nodded.

He sighed. "It's clearly a magical object. We werewolves get tingly around magic, and this makes me tingle a lot, but I couldn't guess as to its purpose. Still, I'd be worried to see it in the hands of unsuspecting humans, so I suggest you think twice before handing it to your client." He placed the statue back onto the bedside table. "Ivy, why don't you tell me what exactly happened? Was this anything to do with being a satyr?"

My gaze followed the line of the carpet to the hardwood floorboards. "No. It's nothing to do with that. This was Lathan's doing. He was there, in my head."

"You had a pretty rough time with him, didn't you?" His voice, like his aura, nudged the weight on my shoulders loose.

I glanced up. His smile was that of a man totally focused on doing the right thing. A noble smile. A comforting smile. A smile that squeezed the tears straight from my eyes. Dear God, not now.

Too late. My emotions liquefied, and my chest was unable to contain them. Gone was my desire to be dignified. I just wanted the pain to stop, and to be held, and to be told everything was going to be okay.

"He does this thing." I shook my head as if I could rid myself of the memories that way. "He gets into your head. Takes everything you treasure and destroys it over and over, until you no longer care. He revels in your pain, but his real goal…"

Parker went through a door and came back with toilet tissue.

"Thanks." Tears refracted the light, but I could just about make out his encouraging smile. A smile on which I pinned all my hope.

"His real goal is to break you. And he does. He..." I wiped my nose. "He fills your head with nightmares so real, you spend days awake believing they are your dreams." My body shook so hard my speech slurred.

Parker gathered me in his arms and stroked my hair. "Let it out. It's okay."

The tears streaked hot along my cheeks and chin. I rubbed my eyes, which only intensified the burn. "Because the agony is so real, I didn't..." I punched his shoulder, but he only drew me closer. "Lathan's obsession crushes you. The bastard pounds you into submission." I pressed my nose into his chest. "And in the end, you just...you just accept..." The hurt in my throat stole my words.

With stoic calm, Parker simply held me.

When I'd drained myself, I fell back into the pillows. The tension had left my limbs, which now lay by my side like rubber appendages. By all accounts, Lathan's mental assault should still have me quaking in my boots, but a powerful blanket of serenity, a total absence of emotional noise, covered my senses.

I curled toward Parker, drying my face on the bed sheet. He brushed a hand over my shoulder then held up another item. Or rather two. Joining the parts along their jagged lines would produce a polished oval, adorned with tens of tiny guards. I lifted my head. While it would take time to untangle the etched lines in the metal to discover their function, a cursory glimpse sufficed to understand their insidious nature.

In its original state it was sure to pack quite a punch. Mind magic of the highest power.

"I figured this was responsible for your...convulsions." He studied the broken object. "It was stuffed under your sink. Unlike your Collective, I recognized this one straight away. It's a Gallom. These buggers can boost the reach of magic. Especially the stuff that's meant to mess with your head. If I remember my history right, the seven kinlords used them to control people, both kin and human, outside their realms. That way, their range of influence extended into Oldworld. The Guardians put a stop to it. Destroyed the Galloms and told the Big Seven to stop playing with Oldworld."

"No prize for guessing who got hold of one anyway." I took the broken item in my hand, turning it over to study the incredible workmanship which had gone into creating the miniscule guards.

"What I can't figure out is how it had such an effect on you. It's only a kind of telephone." Parker shook his head.

"That's all Lathan needs, thanks to this." I showed him my mark.

He grimaced. "I'm so sorry."

I gave him the shrug of a girl too tired to do anything else. "I've never seen anything like it before. How did it get into my house?"

"You're asking me? I could have sworn that whoever tried to break into your house two nights ago had been unsuccessful. I mean, those guards of yours, they're strong, really strong. But now?" He shook his head.

"Well, *I* didn't put it behind the sink." I sat up against the headboard. Where was my life going? If the demons chasing the Collective didn't kill me, Lathan would find a way to snatch me. "This is your guest room?"

"My bedroom, actually." He studied the pattern on the blanket.

"It's nice." The décor reflected the simple, clean lines I'd noticed in his office. There were few personal touches. Rightly so. A room shouldn't replace the personality of the person occupying it, my dad had said, and only dull people tried.

Despite the tempting comfort of the bed, reality awaited. No sooner had I pulled back the blanket than I covered myself up again. "Please tell me you didn't see me twisting on the ground in *this*." I pointed at my shorts and cami pajama set under the cover. "Oh God. This is so embarrassing. Why do you always catch me when I'm making an idiot of myself?"

His grin was all teeth. "Just lucky, I reckon."

I forced the blanket up to my nose so most of my face was blocked from his view.

He rolled his eyes. "Don't be such a girl." He picked up the broken Gallom and rose. "I'd better get rid of this. You go clean yourself up. I'll see if I can rustle up clothes for you."

"Thanks, Parker," I whispered.

The werewolf had a knack for infuriating me, but once again he'd proven to be a better friend than I deserved. He nodded and left.

Two large fluffy towels on the end of the bed drew my gaze. An invitation to use the en-suite bathroom. I walked into a tiled room. The ginormous shower was enclosed between three solid walls, with a glass screen to cover the front. Four nozzles pointed toward the center of the shower, three from the sides and one from above.

The hard jets invigorated my skin, and their pulsing action relaxed me better than any massage. Tucked away on a shelf in an alcove, matching bottles of shower gel and shampoo beckoned. My first whiff of their fragrance conjured up images of Parker. I squirted it liberally over body and hair, allowing the citrus and spice combo to soak deep into my skin, replacing the immortal stench of Lathan's touch.

After rinsing I lathered up again, scrubbing and scouring my skin clean. Eventually my muscles unclenched, my thoughts occupied by nothing more strenuous than whether my hair deserved a third helping of shampoo or not. Any minute now the overprotective werewolf would charge in to check on me. If he found me naked, what would he do?

A quick cold rinse, and I stopped the flow of water. The towel slung around my body, I nudged open the door.

"There." Parker pointed one finger at some clothes draped over the arm of a chair.

My own T-shirt and pants. He must have run over to my house to get them.

I smiled my gratitude and tiptoed over to pick them up. His nostrils flared. Who could blame him? With my dripping-wet, unbrushed hair I was a real mess. He, meanwhile, was uncharacteristically taciturn. His gaze shot to a point on the wall behind me.

My vision swam and I stumbled. He caught my arm and righted me, his large hands gripping my bare, wet shoulders. His face hung somewhere between a need to be elsewhere and concern.

"Are you okay?" His voice was hoarse.

The dizziness subsided. "Yeah." I sounded like him.

"Good. You should probably get dressed."

I cradled the clothes to my chest and scampered back into the bathroom. Parker expelled a long puff of air. Then the door fell shut.

This had become awkward fast.

I emerged again in fresh clothes. The smile on my lips didn't need much of an effort. But before I uttered another word of gratitude, Parker rushed into the bathroom.

My gaze roamed around the room. Would it be rude to leave now? Even with my limited social skills I was pretty sure the answer was yes. In any case, I still hadn't gotten around to asking him which female members of his pack frequented Kelley's. As long as he was in a giving mood, I might as well take advantage. The armchair in the corner creaked under my weight, then cradled my butt as if it belonged. I folded my hands in my lap. By the sound of it, the shower was still spewing out water onto— Not a thought I should follow to its end, or else Parker stood a pretty good chance of becoming my next rebound. Instead, the shelf near the window drew my curiosity.

A black-and-white photo on the wall showed a couple dressed in old-fashioned clothes, with two children sitting by their feet. Was Parker's family as convoluted as my own?

A number of crime fiction books were neatly stacked on the left bedside table, from which I gathered that Parker preferred to sleep on that side of the bed. Mine was the right. Not that that mattered, of course. Otherwise the room gave no clues into the werewolf's life. Not unless I began opening drawers, but that would possibly stretch the limits of his hospitality too far.

A glance out the window offered a prime view of my home. A shudder slid down my back. How had I deluded myself into thinking I'd cleansed the house? The guards should have kept me safe from Lathan, but I'd come to know the kinlord better. He always found a way. My hand automatically sought his mark.

He may have been able to use the Gallom to manipulate my mind, but I was pretty sure my body hadn't been affected. Otherwise he'd have walked me out of my house and into the arms of one of his helpers. So there *were* some boundaries he couldn't yet cross, no matter what magic he used.

The bathroom door opened, and Parker emerged. His hair gleamed wet in the light, and he was clad in a pair of jeans, while the rest of his magnificent body was on display. I gulped down a gasp. My motive had taken notice.

CHAPTER NINETEEN

I WASN'T SURE IF MY MEMORY from our misunderstanding in the woods had been correct, but a second glance now confirmed it. There wasn't a hair on Parker's chest. Just a sharply defined torso with enough ridges I'd be happy to spend a lazy afternoon tracing. He was taciturn by nature, yet his eyes always seemed to invite a conversation. But what would I say? How could I describe my feelings about him or the recent upheaval if I couldn't even be certain of them? I clutched my necklace and wheeled around to the window. As if the view onto my house could hold my interest as much as Parker's defined body.

I clued him in on how my search for Fred had led me first to Ewan at Kelley's, then to the werewolf pack. By now, he'd put on a fresh T-shirt, but not even the humorous slogan 'I only answer rhetorical questions' made me forget the smooth strength lurking underneath. The strength that would enable him to sweep me up and carry me to safety, away from all the trappings of reality.

"So you really hired the vampire?" Parker raised shoulders and eyebrows.

Better wipe the mental drool off my filthy mind. "Sure."

"It wasn't a trick to convince me to do a spot of hacking for you? After all, a quadruple murder is a serious issue to investigate, and you knew I wouldn't help you if it put you in danger."

To be fair, two of those deaths he listed were down to Flo. Yet this snippet wouldn't ease his mind. No, the only way to make this protective wolf sit back on his hind legs was to set off the deflection cannon. "First off, it's Florian, not *the vampire*. Vampire is his race. Flo-ri-an." I counted off on my fingers. "Secondly, I don't do tricks. And before you go all huffy about danger again, I'm perfectly safe."

He inclined his head. "So this is why you hang out with fang-boy all the time?"

"No, I hang out with him because he's my best friend."

His brief smile grew grim. "We still haven't worked out who could have hidden the Gallom. Assuming your guards did keep the would-be burglars from entering your house, could it have been somebody else? One of your friends? Who's been to your house recently?"

"Let me think." I rubbed my nose. "Grand Central Station aka my house first opened just after my birthday." I pulled a face. "When Florian found out about me. Then I met you, you know, when my parents dropped off my present, and then there's Julia. Next came Waylon. My...dad's friend. Although he was only there for an hour or so."

"Anyone else?"

I bit my lip. "Greg. He's...a friend."

"What kind of friend?" Parker's eyes narrowed.

"I met him a few days ago." Uncalled-for warmth crawled up my neck. Wasn't I over this little-girl innocence by now? "The other night, we shared a cab home and he stayed for coffee. Twenty minutes. Besides, he has no reason to—"

"The euphemistic sort?"

"Excuse me?" I glared at him. Although, did I still have dibs on the moral high ground? Seeing who I'd become, Parker's question wasn't that far-fetched. "No, a real coffee, not that it's any of your business."

"There's your guy. A stranger. Makes much more sense than a couple of random criminals overcoming the power of those guards."

"I don't see it." I slowly shook my head. "The coincidental meet, my leaving my money behind so we had to share a cab, letting him into the house. He'd have to be clairvoyant to have planned this. Besides, he's human. This Gallom he's supposed to have hidden isn't, is it?"

"Perhaps not. Tell me more about this Waylon, then."

I blew a strand of hair out of my face. "Nothing to tell. Friend of the family. Breezed into town to crap all over my life, now he's hitching a ride out of Dodge."

"Is he the one who told you about your kin lineage?"

I bobbed my head. "He's genuine. I've seen the photos of him with my parents. Besides, he's the one who saved me when I nearly got abducted and—"

"Christ, Ivy. When did you get abducted?"

Uh oh. "A few days ago. Lathan was behind it, I think."

This line of conversation had taken an uncomfortable turn. Parker fell silent, his arms crossed in front of his chest.

I cleared my throat. "Not that I want to make the situation worse, but would it be okay to ask around about Heather? It's the only lead on my boss's whereabouts I have."

His mouth wriggled before settling into a smile. "Sure. Show her photo around. If anyone here knows anything, they'll let you know. All I ask is to be kept apprised."

"Seems fair." I bit my lip. Heather's photo was still back home. The place where Lathan had torn through my defenses.

Even though the Gallom was gone, there could be more. Parker had assured me it was unlikely for Lathan to have access to two of them, but *unlikely* seemed light years away from *certain*. When it came to the demon, there was no such thing as being overly cautious.

I gave Parker a weak smile. "Actually, I have another favor to ask. My file with the photo is in my living room and…" I coughed to play for time, hoping he'd jump in and offer to accompany me.

His expression remained the same. Blank and I suspected deliberately neutral. My gaze wandered to my foot which had begun kicking at an invisible object on the carpet. *Sheesh. Thanks for the save, buddy.*

I rubbed my neck. "Would you come over to the house with me? You know, just in case. I'm sure it's safe now. You checked, right? But I'm done underestimating Lathan." The sentences came out in a rush. Now he'd think I was a defenseless little girl again.

"Sure," he said with a triumphant grin. "Anything I can do to help."

Damn, I knew it!

Despite Parker's presence, I popped in and out in record time. My first unfettered breath came when I was tucked away safely inside his mansion again. Parker had trouble keeping up.

He was called away for a phone call, but a gesture was all the permission I needed to go exploring. The pack's abode appeared bigger than the Dupree mansion. White paint made such a difference. Sadly, the endless corridors held little myth, even though they twisted like the bowels of the Minotaur's labyrinth. Only the light brown doors which were spaced along the hallways disrupted the clinical monotony.

Parker's hand-sketched map helped me find my way around the wings of the building. Ewan mentioned he'd seen Heather in the company of a female, but a female wolf in a bar by herself struck me as unlikely. It wouldn't cost me anything to ask everyone in the building. Interestingly, most of the werewolves I encountered were male. At least they were chatty, giving me unprecedented insight into the life of a werewolf.

"Last April, Parker's sister moved away to marry into 'nother pack." A short but powerfully built man in his forties leaned, one arm high, against the doorframe to his room. "There's only eleven females now."

"And they all live here?"

"The only way to keep 'em safe. Some wolves go rogue and poach women, willing or not."

I frowned. "That's terrible."

"That's nature, hon. Cubs are a rare treat, and females even more. They're precious."

Finally some sort of explanation for Parker's mother hen act. He'd been conditioned this way.

I shifted to prevent my leg muscles from cramping. Once again my job was more hard work than excitement. "When you encounter a werewolf in Silverton, how do you know if he's rogue?"

He waved a scarred hand. "Some of us live in town. That's cool. Spreading out means covering more territory. Anyone that's not ours, and that didn't tell us they was coming to Silverton, they're rogue. And we'll deal with them rightly."

"Wow, thanks for sharing."

"Hey, the boss trusts ya. No reason I shouldn't, right?"

He gave me a firm handshake and disappeared back inside his room. With new food for thought, I picked up my trail.

With each new face came disappointment. Had Ewan lied to me when he'd pointed at Parker's pack? Perhaps he'd simply wanted to lift my mood before putting the moves on me. Or had he deliberately led me up the garden path?

I knocked on the next door. A stunning dark-haired girl ripped it open. "Come in." She beckoned with her hand. "Quick." She checked up and down the hall then closed the door. "Nosy neighbors, you know?"

I nodded. "I'm Ivy."

"Heidi." With darting eyes and a slight build she was more gazelle than wolf. Only her posture hinted at some spunk behind the fragile exterior. "I think I know the girl you're looking for."

My brows went up.

She grinned. "Gossip spreads faster than warm butter here. Can I see the photo?"

"Here."

She tapped onto the picture. "Yeah, I remember her. The chick from Kelley's. Bitch spilled her drink down my favorite shirt. A red-colored cocktail."

Probably a Silverton Mist. Cherry brandy and cranberry juice with a twist of lime. "You're sure it was her?"

"Not the kind of thing I'm likely to forget." Her eyelids lifted sharply. "She's your friend?"

"We're friendly. She's my boss's daughter. She disappeared."

"Right." Heidi pointed at a sturdy armchair stuffed beside heavily lined mauve curtains.

On the wall, a little boy and a little girl in fifties-style clothes snuck a kiss in a black-and-white poster. The kind I haven't admitted to liking since I was twenty. So Heidi was probably younger than the twenty-three, twenty-four I'd originally guessed.

I sank into the chair. "Thanks. Do you remember what day you ran into Heather?"

She flopped onto a large posted bed. "Not sure." She gripped her ankles and swayed back and forth. "It would have been a Friday or a Saturday maybe?"

"Did you talk to her?"

"Damn right I did." She leaned back onto her hands and glanced at her wiggling toes. "That sort of stain doesn't come out. She was all like 'whatever,' so I said see how she liked it. I tipped my drink over her. It was only beer, though, and that doesn't stain well. Stupid cow didn't react, just looked around as if I wasn't there and ran back to the guy she was with." Her features darkened.

I clutched my hand in my lap. The girl before me had no idea how important her clues were. "I get it." I nodded my encouragement. "This guy, you remember what he looked like?"

"Yeah, blond hair. Seen him before when…"

"When what?" I copied her glance to the door. "I'm not going to tell anyone."

"Crap. Yeah, all right, I've seen him a couple times before, at Abraxas. You know, the place near the new mall. Where I've absolutely never been."

"Gotcha." I bobbed my head. "Can you tell me anything else about him?"

"Don't know his name or anything, but he's a bit of a player." She curved her arm over her head to tuck a few stray hairs behind her ear. "He's never tried it with me though. I'd have given him a right earful."

No doubt about that. I rose and flexed the photo in my hand. "Thanks, Heidi. I appreciate it."

"Appreciate what?" Her grin returned for a flicker before her expression darkened. "Hey, in return, how about you tell me about you and Parker?"

My ears heated up in an instant. "What…" I laughed. "Uhm. What about me and Parker? We're friends."

"Friends?" She studied my face. "Because someone said you two are really tight."

"Tight like friends." I placed my hand on the door handle. "That's it. He's helped me. With work, you know."

Her mouth relaxed into a grin. "Oh, work. Good." She nodded. "Anyway, about Abraxas…"

I mimicked the locking of my mouth and waved her goodbye.

That had been awkward. Someone did have a crush on Parker, but it was quite clearly her. Still, her information had been invaluable. As it turns out, my suspicions about a man being involved in Heather's departure hadn't been entirely wrong.

After a little detective work, I tracked down Parker in his office. He tucked his fingers in the belt loops of his jeans and leaned against the edge of his desk. "Did you find what you were looking for?"

"I did." I slapped the rolled-up photo against my palm. "Heather was seen with a guy who's also known to frequent a place called Abraxas. A night club."

"Yeah, I know it. My boys go there now and again to let off steam. It's not the place for you." His eyes lit up. "Send Pretty Boy. He'll love it. I hear the women there are so easy, even he shouldn't have to strain."

My hand formed a claw and scratched the air. "Meow."

"Look, Ivy, I'm serious. Don't go there by yourself. At least let me send someone along."

Didn't he get how much his protection efforts encroached on my freedom? The freedom I'd taken such a risk to regain when I escaped Lathan's clutches?

I shot him a look. *That* look. The look that said *back off or else*. "I can take care of myself."

He grunted. Would he explode into one of his safety-first rants, or keep his admonishment to himself and implode instead?

I threw my hands in the air with a theatrical sigh. "I'll think about it, okay?"

"Where are you off to now?"

"Work. I'm not going back in there in a hurry." I pointed a thumb over my shoulder at my house.

"It's safe."

I swallowed past the knot that wouldn't leave my throat. "Yeah. The house might be ready for me, but I'm not yet ready for it. I'd rather put my nose into some research."

He led the way out of his office. The delicious smell of a hearty home-cooked stew rolled up the stairs. I patted my stomach. Before I went anywhere, I'd have to get some food in me.

At the front door, I stopped. I pulled Parker toward me by the fabric of his T-shirt and planted a peck on his cheek. "Thanks again."

His hand went up to his face. "Anytime. Just be careful, okay?"

"Always." I shouted the lie back over my shoulder.

For once he let me go without making a big deal. Yet I practically felt his gaze following me until I'd rounded the corner and got into my Mustang.

CHAPTER TWENTY

I SWUNG OPEN THE OFFICE DOOR and the chirpy tune died on my lips. My hand flew to my mouth. Florian, sitting cross-legged on the floor, smiled up at me. Folder after folder paved a path between the filing cabinet and his desk, and stacks of paper formed small mountains around him.

I knew I shouldn't have left him to his own devices.

"What do you think you're doing?" With a Herculean effort, I fought my way across the room and dropped my bag with a heavy *thump*. Dust tickled my nose, and I leaned over to open the window. "What is this mess?"

He shoved his pile of paper to one side and leafed through another. "I'm reading our files. You know, to get a better grasp of what's going on. What the business entails, that sort of thing." He nudged another stack around the desk leg and skimmed the next document. "I've nearly read half of them. You did warn me the life of a P.I. may not always be much fun, but most of these sound positively dreary."

I picked up a file and rolled it up. "These other folders aren't going to change your mind. And if they don't find their way back to the filing cabinets pronto, I'll find a new home for them myself. One that should prevent you from sitting for a few days. Now, get!" I thwacked the folder on his head.

He jerked. "Jeez, are you in a mood today."

I pressed my hands against my waist.

"Okay, okay." He got to his feet.

Amazing how quickly a vampire under duress filed. You'd think everyone would want to hire them. Twenty minutes later, the place was shipshape, except for the cloud of fine particles floating in a cone of sunlight.

"Now listen." I gave him the 101 about the Gallom that had found its way into my kitchen.

"Holy hell. What bastard would do that to you?" He hugged me tight. In fact, since I confided in him about the power of his touch, he never let me go without physical contact for long. "Parker? You can't trust him. And Waylon, he was a right cad." He squinted at me. "We're still angry at Waylon, aren't we?"

"Totally."

He pulled me close again. "Greg? Julia? Your stepdad? Ha. I know. Your mother."

I laughed despite myself. The way he played the blame game was a lot more fun than Parker's blind stabs at random people in my life.

He released me and sat on the edge of his desk. "No kidding, though. Until we figure out who it was, you shouldn't be alone. This is getting serious."

My life had been in danger since I escaped Lathan's clutches. So in that respect, not much had changed. I had little choice but to get on with the act of living.

I shrugged. "We'll see. My house is safe for now. Maybe we were wrong and the guys who'd tried to break in succeeded. Except they weren't there to steal the Collective, but to plant the Gallom."

"Unlikely." He squinted as if rethinking his conclusion. "But it's best not to rule anything out."

"Lathan is pretty powerful." My voice fell to a near hush. "If he can find a device that crosses the Rim, who's to say he can't also find a way to get through my guards?"

"I guess."

"Mind if we change the topic?" I gave my tone a cheerful lilt. "Have you heard anything new about God?"

"Like a new gospel?" Flo chuckled. "You were wrong. This isn't getting old at all."

My glare made it pretty clear we disagreed on that issue. "I meant God, our criminal mastermind and lord over Silverton's demons."

"Oh, him." His twitching lips morphed into a keen grin. "Why don't Eli and I go and look up a few of our old family contacts?" He fished his car keys from his pocket. "If God is any kind of player in Silverton, they'll know who he is."

"I don't know." I glanced at my hands. "Eli's not exactly a fan of my work."

"You leave him to me. He owes me a couple of favors."

I touched my fingers to my heart. "And you'd call one in for me?"

"For my best girl? Anytime." He gave an exaggerated wink.

I play-fanned myself with my folder. "Well, if you put it like that." I dropped the kidding gestures. "Be careful though. I'd hate having to train up someone else for this job."

"Sure thing. And you might want to stay with my sister tonight, because I don't think I can stand guard outside your house. This might be a whole-night kinda shakedown." His eager nods underlined his enthusiasm.

I pouted. "I don't need babysitting."

"No, but you might need a friendly shoulder."

"I'll give it some thought."

"That's all I'm asking." One final hug, and he breezed out the door, letting it slam shut behind him.

Just then, from my jeans pocket, the opening bars of the Hawaii 5-0 theme filled the silence. I reached for my cell. Parker had something for me, and he sounded excited.

Jumping into action on Parker's say-so grated, but he'd never shown that kind of keenness before. Perhaps he'd unearthed the Collective's secret.

Heidi greeted me with a cautious wave. "Go on up. The boss is waiting."

"Thanks."

Upstairs, the office lay in shadows, despite its abundance of windows. Parker got up from behind his desk.

"How can you see in the dark?" I switched on the lights.

He checked the weather. "I hadn't noticed the clouds pulling in. Here." He handed me an embossed leather tome, decorated with worn gold leaf. "It's the most comprehensive 'what's what' in the kinworld you'll find, and pretty rare. I'd forgotten I had it." He pointed to my left. "The sofa's yours for as long as you want it. I have work to be getting on with but holler if you have questions."

He'd called me over for a book? "Oh. Thank you." I glanced at the sofa. It was pretty comfortable, and with Parker's calming aura, hanging out here wasn't the worst way to spend an afternoon. Sure, I'd be better off drumming up more business for Fred, but everything considered, more business would at best lead to more problems. And I didn't need those.

He settled back behind his desk and typed on his computer. His brown casual top made his brown eyes appear lighter than usual. What would he say if I—?

"Ivy?"

I blinked. "Yeah?"

"Did you need anything?"

A lobotomy and intensive gene therapy, please. "No. Sorry." I tapped the leather cover. "Getting started now." I made myself comfortable and, careful not to rip the pages, opened the book on my lap.

The volume had been written by elves and gave an account of

their experiences with other kinfolk, listed alphabetically. Predictably, I looked up satyrs first.

"A satyr's powers are deeply embedded in their copulation-based culture. Their two main traits are MOTIVE, *a constant need to copulate, and* ALLURE, *the power to arouse another individual's sexual appetite. These are inextricably linked, and for this reason the satyr race is best avoided by the responsible elf. Satyrs are a polygamous people, and both traits can be managed only with frequent, satisfactory copulation. However, given that the satyr's interests and predilections are varied, it is extremely rare for this race to experience any copulation as unsatisfactory."*

The last of my good mood dissipated. Provided I find a horizontal outlet for my motive, I, too, could be a useful member of society. Stupid elves! I shot a glance at Parker. Had he read this? His eyes were locked on the screen in front of him. He chewed his lip, looking pensive. I remembered that lip and wouldn't mind a nibble on it right now.

Christ. Stop it already.

I flicked through the book for the section on werewolves.

You couldn't get much more opposite to a satyr. To them, deep spiritual bonds, an *intention* ceremony and, eventually, psychic connections brought about by a mating for life were paramount. I thumbed through the pages until I came to the section on brather demons. Courtesy of my maternal grandfather, brather genes were the second worst bane of my existence.

A single paragraph celebrated the brather's change from crime lords to practical sainthood when they took on Guardianship. Waylon's behavior had opened my mind to hundreds of ways of describing him, yet saint wasn't one of them.

So far, I wasn't too enamored with the book.

I leafed further through the volume to the next entry of interest. Go figure. The elves weren't fond of the sidhes either. Their one-size-fits-all approach belittled sidhes of any background, without bothering to list the individual subspecies. With one exception. Leanan sidhes.

"The leanans use the traits of their forefathers to good effect in order to blend in with their environment. They are spiritual creatures, whose charm, gentle nature and beauty are highly coveted. There are many advantages to pair bonding with a leanan, although such a union is not entirely without risk. Repeated or intense copulation will result in the leanan and her partner (or partners) developing a permanent state of blissful attraction and eventually love. Her chosen male (or female) will also gain her entire skill set, so he (or she or they) can successfully defend the leanan and their offspring against dangers."

I re-read the first sentence. Was the manner in which I used my motive and allure a choice? My attempt to twist my allure around Ewan had flopped at first. The only way I succeeded was by increasing my motive, which very nearly led to cheap sex in an alley. But perhaps practice would make all the difference.

A thought struck me. My dad had worked as a Guardian, despite lacking the brather genes. Union with my mother would have given him the power he needed. That was the upside. But why hadn't Waylon mentioned the downside of entering into a relationship with me? At least my mild obsession with him finally had an explanation. Blissful attraction and love? He must have known the deal. He was a freaking Guardian, for God's sake. Had he been hoping for 'repeated or intense copulation' to gain the traits of my forefathers? He might be brimming with demon and Guardian powers, yet my skillset would be quite the trophy in his cabinet. He himself had insisted on numerous occasions my satyr characteristics were just some of many I might have inherited.

One round of sex, and I was hung up on him. Good thing he was gone, because I didn't need any more headaches, especially when I should be focused on work or on staying alive.

"Parker?" I pushed the book aside and walked over to a window.

"Hmm?"

"The Gallom. Do you think it at all possible the intruders left it behind?"

He twisted his chair to face me. "Highly unlikely. But if we rule them out, we'll have to look at others who had access to your house. The newcomers in your circle of friends, and I'm excluding Waylon for his ties to your parents for the moment, are Greg and I. I know it wasn't me. That means Greg tops the list of suspects."

I rested my forehead against the window frame and stared at the trees that nearly touched the pane. The cool glass did little to help my thoughts along. Greg? Had I been so wrong about him?

"You said Lathan initially entered your head in your sleep." Parker's voice gently drew my mind. "Can you remember when your dreams…?"

"Got served with an extra dollop of crazy?" I tapped the window frame with my knuckles to attract the attention of a small bird huddled on a branch. "The night after Greg came into my house."

"Did he step into your kitchen?"

The larger tree, more branches than leaves now, danced to a mournful silence. And the stupid bird didn't pay me any attention. Parker's words wanted to cause chaos, wanted to hurt me, but my ego wouldn't let them. Greg liked me. I knew he did.

"Ivy?"

"I'm thinking." But I wasn't. Truth was, I didn't know. I'd made coffee. Had Greg joined me in the kitchen? Or had I taken the cup out to him? My shoulders slumped. "I don't remember."

Parker rolled his chair back.

I turned to him, my back flat against the glass pane. Time I zeroed in on the crux of my insecurities. "What if he went out with me so he could hide the Gallom in my house?"

Parker pressed the capped tip of his pen against his jaw. "If you can't tell if his interest is genuine, maybe it isn't." His mouth twisted as if in distaste. "How did the two of you meet?"

"First time was at a coffee shop. I spilled latte over him."

He gestured with his pen. "Go on. Did he bump into you or was it the other way around?"

I replayed the scene in my head. "I bumped into him. Only because he was standing at the wrong end of the line."

"And you met him again where?"

"Outside the Bankside Hotel. When I opened the exit door, Greg was…"

"Yes?"

My pulse drummed in my veins. Had I found the inconsistency that would prove Parker's theory? I trudged to his desk and slumped into the chair opposite him. "He'd told me he'd been at the bar with his friends, but he bumped into me walking *into* the lobby, not out of. Come to think of it, I didn't actually see him buy any coffee at the coffee shop either."

Hardly conclusive evidence. However, if you wanted to find a flaw in the halo I so desperately wanted to force onto Greg's head, this might be it. "Perhaps I'm making stuff up now." I let my arms flop by my sides. "I just want this to be over, you know?"

"You got his number?"

"Greg's? Yeah. Why?"

"Why don't you invite him over, then? Here, to my house. This way if he's solid, no sweat. On the other hand, if he does pose any danger to you, I can always lend a helping hand. In case we need to beat him to within an inch of his life or something."

Although my stomach tightened, I picked up my cell. "I'm not sure we have enough evidence. What am I going to say? How am I going to know if he's innocent or not?"

"You'll be all right." He reached across and put his hand on my arm. "I'll be right here next to you. I have an excellent nose for detecting lies."

No kidding.

Even without the influence of his dominating aura, I'd come to understand my life was easier if I did as he asked. Who was I trying to fool? I wanted him to take charge and sort out this mess. After days of running up a hill, was it so wrong to give in to the desire to let someone carry me for a while? I selected Greg's name on my phone and dialed.

"Hey Greg, it's Ivy." I stared at the ground, unable to converse like a normal person with Greg and look at Parker at the same time.

"Ivy, sweetheart, what a lovely surprise. Miss me already?" Greg's warm tone nearly brought out a smile.

"Sure. Erm. Do you have time to come over?"

"What did you have in mind?"

"I just wanted to see you." I inhaled to keep my voice steady. "Tonight'd be great, say six? Only I've had a bit of an accident in the kitchen. Nothing major, but my house is out of bounds for now. Do you remember there's a building up behind my house?"

"Yes, the great white thing."

"Mm hmm. That's where I'm staying till my place is habitable again. Can you meet me there?"

"For you, anything."

I hung up, grinning despite myself. Parker's cough reminded me of the stakes.

"It's done." I plodded back to the window.

"At least you'll know," Parker said.

Was I doing the right thing? If Greg had nothing to do with Lathan, I'd alienate him for nothing. Whatever happened, my dreams of cuddling up with him would probably be history now.

Sunshine filtered through the clouds, illuminating the red and yellow trees to the side of our homes. From this distance, my garden looked lush and green, not half dead.

Two figures materialized in my yard; simply popped into existence. I blinked. Was I imagining things again? One hulk of a man knelt beside the French door and fumbled with it.

A word sparked in my brain, like the heart-stopping shock I get when Flo blasts his stereo at full volume. 'Demons!'

No way. No freaking way.

CHAPTER TWENTY-ONE

I BOLTED OUT OF PARKER'S OFFICE. "Bastards." The incantation for the speed guard on my belt and the defensive guards I retrieved from my pocket came staccato through my jerky breaths. I flew down the stairs, two steps at a time.

Not again, you assholes.

Cold air stung my lungs. My shin-high fence was never designed to keep people out, yet I stumbled, flailed, and caught my balance.

The two demon burglars focused on their work and didn't react to my footfalls on the soft grass.

If only I'd taken up Parker's offer of martial arts. Coulda woulda shoulda.

"Stop that." My voice wasn't as intimidating as it was choppy. A lucky kick in the first man's groin sent him to his knees. An even luckier blow from my guards slammed his skull into the wall. He collapsed in a heap. His head lolled to the side, his movements sluggish.

His partner roared. A fist the size of a football snaked at me. I twisted and sliced the edge of my guard across his wrist. A trickle of blood appeared.

"How did you—?" His arm went flaccid.

Interesting. I didn't know my guard could do that.

With the demon's entire left half limp and useless, I focused my efforts on his belly. Blue sparks sprayed from my guards. The plump demon side-stepped before the burst of energy connected.

A blade glinted in his hand. Crap, where did that come from? He slashed the mean-looking five-inch knife at me with a proficient flick of the wrist.

I swerved out of its path, dodging the weapon by a hair's breadth. He shot a low punch into my waist. A hot clamp clawed into my flesh, crunching my kidneys. My vision blurred. I stumbled, right cheek first, into the brick wall of my house.

The metal tang of blood coated my throat and drops trickled onto my sleeve. I pushed away from the wall. The air shifted beside me, and I dropped flat. The demon's leg swept past me, and I rolled out of his way. Barely. With a grunt, I raised my guard, sending the last of the magic in his direction. The blast sent him sprawling back. He windmilled his arms, but couldn't fight the momentum. His ass hit the deck.

Parker leaped over the garden fence. Thank God. My assailant pushed himself to his feet with more agility than his figure suggested. Parker's hook punched his nose. The demon recoiled. *Wham.* Parker's fist struck again. The rotund man collapsed like a satchel of books.

Violent shakes ripped through my body. My hands pressed against the ground to steady me, my breaths fast and threatening to bring up more than just used-up oxygen. At least it was over. Parker was here. My face throbbed, and was definitely beginning to swell. Next time, I'd run *away* from the demons. Not stomach-first into their fists.

"We'll interrogate them later, guys." Parker glanced to his side at some moving shapes, presumably his pack. "I'll take her. You drag those two."

My tummy had other ideas. I crawled over to what would one day be my vegetable patch and fertilized it with gusto. My shoulders heaved, the strong taste of bile pushing up more until there was nothing left.

A few minutes later I sat alone in Parker's office, clad in a new top and with freshly brushed teeth. The stress and fear ebbed out of me into the yielding sofa cushions. It required no leap of imagination to assume the goons were God's men. Whoever he was, he sure liked to surround himself with demons. If my eyes hadn't played tricks on me, they'd appeared out of thin air. Not many were as skilled as me in the use of guards, but I was unfamiliar with this type of magic.

My heart still pumped full-force, the rush of my pulse like white noise in the quiet house. Moving with deliberation, I retrieved the touchstone from my pocket. I'd sworn I wouldn't make the first step, but if anyone could shed light on the demons' magic, it was Waylon.

The spell on the piece of paper was short. I was pretty sure I'd remember it even without the cheat sheet.

"Ivy?" An ethereal image of Waylon appeared above the stone, with the crisp clarity of a science-fiction hologram. As desperate as I was for answers, I allowed myself a little shudder. That mouth that did so much damage to my self-restraint pulled downward. "Sweet Hernando. What happened?"

I leaned to catch my reflection in the glazed cabinet on the other side of the office. My lip had split, and where the rest of my face used to be, an angry red blotch was ready to guide lost ships safely to harbor. "I'm fine. A bit bruised, is all. Nothing on the bastards who did this to me."

"Fuck, babe. Do you want me to come back? I'm in the middle of some deep shit, but if you need me..."

Don't break a nail on my behalf. "No. I'm calling for information. Two demons appeared out of nowhere in the middle of my yard. Have you heard of anything like that? Invisibility of some sort?"

Waylon gave an economic nod. "Try checking their wrists and ankles. This isn't the safe kind of magic you're used to, but skin magic. It's the only way. If the guards had to draw energy from outside their body, the shifting air would give away the wearer's location. This way, it drains the poor sod's own reserves. But it's highly effective for a short while."

"Okay, I'll check. Thanks."

"You'll need the incantation if you wanna use the guard yourself." Another spell that was easy to remember. Guess it had to be for knucklehead demons like them to use it.

He gave a ghost of a smile. "Was there anything else? Are you being careful, babe?"

He was in the middle of trouble himself, and yet he asked about me. So perhaps he wasn't a complete jackass. "I'm fine. Worry about yourself."

"Does that mean you're no longer angry at me?"

Hardly. "Why should I be angry? We had fun for a night. Let's not make a big deal out of it."

"You know it was more than that. I was there. We fucked like we were made for each other. Didn't you feel it?"

Even now, his breathy words soothed my frustration. I averted my head. "Don't do this."

"You're right. This ain't the time for that kinda talk. But I'll be back. Soon."

I terminated the image, yet his face remained burned onto my retina. The elves had been correct. Despite my better judgment, my attraction to him remained. If Waylon returned before my trust fund money arrived, I'd melt under his advances faster than a snow cone in Florida.

I hid the touchstone away again. Would Parker let me see the demons? I doubted it. Dammit. I hated sitting around feeling sorry for myself. A crumpled old napkin and a little spit cleared the worst of the blood from my face. I stuffed the tissue back into my pocket. Something sharp cut my finger. I put the injured finger in my mouth, then reached back in to find Parker's map of the building.

While the map didn't show the path to an 'Interrogation Chamber' in red pen, applying a little common sense to the problem might go a long way. The stairs at the back of the building led to a basement. Interesting.

Parker liked order and was anal about safety. He wouldn't stow away dangerous people like the two demons up here among his people's bedrooms. Unless he kept a shed in the small piece of wooded land behind his mansion, this basement was probably where the werewolves did their dirty work.

I slid open the door. Muffled music played in one of the rooms, the bullet exchange of a TV action thriller twanged from another. The back stairs appeared to be seldom used or else were meticulously cleaned, because there wasn't a stray piece of muck in sight. As I'd hoped, nobody stopped or questioned me. Voices jarred the air on my left. Two men argued about how intruders could have slipped past their cameras without triggering the alarm.

At the end of the hall, I found the door to the basement. I eased it open and made my way down a weakly lit set of stairs. A musty odor rose from the concrete floor and cinder block walls. The narrow corridor that opened in front of me tapered and terminated at a brown wooden door. In front of it, a guard stood straight like a toy soldier. I stifled a curse. Despite his lack of obvious weapons, his broad shoulders were evidence of a person who knew how to subdue a waif of a gal like me. At least his presence confirmed the demons were held inside the building.

The man's face snapped up. "Hey, you."

My instincts screamed at me to flee. I didn't. Parker had warned me never to run from a werewolf. Besides, the mystery of the invisibility guards nibbled at me. How were they made? How did they work?

As purposefully as I could muster, I strode toward the guard. "I'd like to see the prisoners."

"Do you have permission?"

"Would I be here otherwise?" Perhaps my firm belief I had *my* permission, coupled with the vagueness of my reply would get me past his lie-detecting nose.

"Well, show me."

So much for my cunning plan. I patted down my pockets while keeping the man at bay with a confident smile. And there it was. Not the permission slip, but the most evil thought I'd ever had. Could I be this devious? Perhaps. I needed to try.

Those demons were mine to question and to frisk before Parker discovered their invisibility guards. He'd probably withhold them from me in another misplaced attempt to keep me from harm.

I tore the necklace off my neck and deposited it inside my pocket, giving my allure the rope it needed to hang someone with.

"Are you the only guard here?" I touched his arm. "Look at this." I squeezed his biceps. "Guess you're strong enough to hold off any unwanted visitors by yourself, aren't you?"

The werewolf frowned. "Perhaps."

My allure hadn't yet triggered. With Ewan, it had sprung to life once my motive was up and revving. God, I hated my plan already. My full attention pressed onto the guy's broad shoulders. His chest plate lifted evenly. The muscles under his long tee promised quite a sight. A little bit of sweat, and my hands could have all sorts of fun exploring his valleys and peaks. His square jaw slackened. A pink, fleshy tongue poked out to wet his lips. Generous lips. Lips that slowly rearranged into a smile.

I swallowed. Oh yes, I could imagine these lips working their magic on my skin. Heat rose in me, tunneling my vision on him. I moved my hands up along his shoulder, grazing his neck and ears. His soft, thick hair was scrumptious enough to claw into and make him kiss me hard.

He didn't recoil at my touch. Hardly moved. His chest worked harder now. I blanked out the feeling in my panties, the involuntary tightening of my entrance. He flared his nostrils, his eyes dilated. I'd never dissected the physical indicators of a man in the thrall of attraction, but by God, he was feeling its full effect now.

"Just a glance inside?" I twirled a strand of his hair around my finger, focusing my thoughts. If this plan failed, I was nothing more than a prize fighter begging to get laid. "Those men hurt me, and I want to have a quick peek at them, all secured and tied up. Maybe you could come with me to keep me safe?" I caressed his cupid's bow with my fingertips. If Parker had taught me anything, it was that a werewolf's protective instinct was quick to respond.

The guard playfully snapped for my finger. "Well, one look won't hurt." He produced the keys from his pocket.

A rush of endorphins filled my head, part arousal, part triumph. Would I be applauding my arrival at the lowest rung on the ladder of morality later, or sink into the ground in shame?

"I'm Grant, by the way." His shoulder moved and the lock clicked.

"Ivy." I slid my palm down his spine.

He turned and caught my hand. "I know who you are. I've seen you around."

I sidestepped him and dragged him with me into the room. The demons were indeed tied to chairs. Their faces, as far as I could judge, looked worse than mine. Neither of them shifted, and their eyes were shut. Evidently my questions would have to wait.

I still needed to ditch the wolf to get to the guards, though.

Grant lifted my chin with his finger. "They the ones that hurt you? Did this to your pretty face? We'll just have to punch 'em some more later on then, won't we?"

My outward giggle seemed to be exactly what he wanted to hear. Inside my belly, a flame burst forth. He stroked my skin and I moaned.

Shit.

If he pushed me further, how much longer could I control my motive?

I took a quick step back, my smile deliberately coy. "You wouldn't happen to have a glass of water for me, would you? It's hot down here all of a sudden."

He shot me a knowing grin and disappeared, leaving me alone with my attackers.

A pain exploded in my head, not unexpected after another unfulfilling encounter with a potential mate. I rubbed my temples, but my grumbles about my genes would have to wait. I slid my hand under the first man's sleeves to check his wrists, then along his trouser legs. At close range, their blood and body odor combined into something hideous. I grimaced. As if I needed the incentive to get this done quickly.

A simple silver chain with a small copper bead hung clasped around his hairy right ankle. Minuscule carvings decorated the bead. No doubt, I'd found my guard. I removed the chain and slipped it into my pocket. The other guy wore his in the same place.

Heavy feet stomped down the stairs. "Where is she?" Parker's voice bounced off the walls.

Could I hide? My eyes darted around the room, evaluating the shadows for suitable spots.

But why bother? With Parker's approach, a now familiar peace spread inside me, and a contented smile stretched across my face. I was safe with him.

Parker entered the room. "What the hell do you think you're doing?"

Despite the pack's demands, he often singled me out. Soothed me. Looked out for me. Even now he showed interest in my activities.

He grabbed my shoulders. The fresh scent of citrus on his skin embraced me. I placed my ear against his chest and rubbed my mouth along the soft cloth of his T-shirt.

Grant cast his gaze onto the ground and hunched his shoulders.

Poor Grant. But he must have known he couldn't compete with our alpha.

"Christ." Parker's tone softened. "Grant. Guard the door. This time, don't let anyone in here except for me or Rollo."

The playful nudge of my nose against his neck made him gulp. I lifted my chin to meet his eyes. He shook his head and a crack of a smile peeked out. "What am I going to do with you?"

That was a perfectly valid question. I rubbed my eyes, dazed. My inner animal had taken over again. The shame that fizzed in my head quickly pooled into my cheeks. Wasn't there a way to protect myself against werewolf mojo?

The stillness of Parker's company had me back to relative clarity within less than an hour. The humiliation remained. I had my nose stuck in the elves' book of wisdom, hiding my face rather than actually taking in new information. Aside from my burning shame about my behavior in front of Parker, guilt gnawed on me too. No one knew better how rotten it was to be at the mercy of a satyr's thrall. I lived with the compulsion every hour. And yet I'd subjected Grant to it for my own end.

The eighties-style digital clock clicked to the next number. I fumbled the necklace now safe back around my neck. Exactly six o'clock. Perhaps it was time to give Flo a call and inquire about his progress.

"It's six." Parker got off his chair.

I looked up from my book and packed some punch into my scowl. "So?"

"So, your friend's due soon."

Ouch. I couldn't believe Greg had slipped my mind. This was Parker's fault, of course. The guy needed anger management. If he'd controlled his temper, I wouldn't have wolfed out. My mood wouldn't be in the dumpster, and I would have remembered Greg's promise to come over.

"Let's wait outside." Parker beckoned and headed toward the staircase. "Fresh air will do you good."

"Do you think in the future you could stop being angry when I'm around?" I barely kept up with him. But then, his legs were considerably longer.

At the door he turned. "Do you think you could stop doing stupid things that'll get me angry?"

Touché. I chewed my lip, searching the depths of my brain for a clever riposte. In the end, I settled for a shrug.

Outside, we sat on the steps leading up to the entrance. Parker relaxed back on his arms. The last rays of the sun brightened his face. Shame that his temper and intrusive personality tended to drown out his looks. But under this golden light, he was strikingly handsome. Not as solid as Waylon, as worldly as Greg, or as delicate as Florian, but his easy charm definitely made my insides go gooey. The sexy stubble, his gentleman-like behavior when he made an effort, and his brutish protectiveness when he didn't, and the way his true emotions came out in his eyes. Something about him touched a spot in me that neither Waylon nor Greg had reached.

His effect on me wasn't just immediate, but long-term. The more time I spent with him and his aura, the less my headaches came through.

No, I would *not* become attracted. He was a friend. No more.

Not staring at him made it easier to convince myself of the platonic nature of our relationship. And platonic it would have to stay. Werewolves were strictly one-species guys. Outsiders like me didn't get a look-in. Fact. Besides, he'd never made a move. I allowed myself a tiny smile. He was far too sensible to try it on with a walking disaster zone like me. And to think, my mother had brought us together. Crazy.

The drive leading past my house was bathed in sunlight and long shadows, and the breeze tickled my skin. The comfortable silence didn't separate us but connected us. Two friends chilling. Kinda nice.

"What was so important about those two burglars anyway?" Parker shielded his face with his hand. "Were they sent by Lathan? Or do you think they're anything to do with the case that Pretty Boy promised me you wouldn't get involved in?"

"Could be. It's complicated."

"You are involved and it's complicated? Now there's a surprise."

"Don't blame me. Fred asked me to pick the statue up, you know, the Collective. It turned out to be pretty popular. Sadly, and may I add, painfully, the statue's fans seem to be demons, including the guys in your basement, by the way, which suggests a connection between them and the Collective."

"I don't envy you your life."

"I don't blame you." Damn hair. I tucked another strand away. "In any case, the sooner I find out why anyone wants the hideous Collective, the sooner I can work out what to do about it."

A car's engine purred from behind the trees, and seconds later Greg's Corvette swung into the driveway.

"That him?" Parker cocked his chin.

"Be nice," I said. "We don't know anything for sure. Actually, maybe I'd better speak with him alone."

He rose and folded his arms. "Have I been talking to a wall? Over the last few days you've been getting mixed up in all sorts of crap. Obviously, you're incapable of staying out of trouble. I'm handling this."

I tipped my head side-to-side to roll the tension from my shoulders. There was no talking to that man. I positioned myself next to him, putting on a painful smile to cancel out the werewolf's frown.

Greg ambled across the driveway toward us. I moved one step, then Parker's hand hooked into my elbow to keep me in place.

"Hi. Greg Davies." Greg's hand stretched out toward Parker.

"Reeves." His arms didn't move.

Christ, this was embarrassing. "He's in a bad mood." I winked, hoping to lighten the atmosphere.

Greg wrinkled his forehead and shifted around the wolf. "Hell, Ivy. Are you okay? Your face." He looked at me with big blue eyes. "What happened to you?"

Maybe I'd overthought the whole thing. Why did I doubt him? I needed him. Parker wouldn't understand, and I wasn't sure I understood it myself, but Greg had to like me. If I wanted to get over my physical cravings for Waylon, I had to find something real, something tangible. The touch of a man I could learn to love.

Parker's witch-hunt was messing everything up.

"Hey." Greg's narrowed gaze flickered with concern. "Who hurt you, Ivy?"

My gaze fell on the sand-colored pebbles that someone's shoes had carried from the graveled drive onto the steps. "I'm okay. This is why I asked you over. You see, we've been having trouble in our neighborhood lately, and Parker here is trying to get to the bottom of it. So, um, did you notice anything odd, you know, out of place when you were at my house? Any shady characters?"

"I don't think so." He gripped my hand. "What happened?"

Parker's arm sliced through our connection and shifted his back into my line of sight. "Let's cut this short. Are you working for Lathan?" His super-clear enunciation carried the full force of his accusation.

"Shit, what's going on here?" Greg bent at his hips, but the alpha's broad frame allowed no eye contact with me.

Parker's hand tightened around my arm and kept me in position behind him. "Answer me. Do you work for Lathan?"

"No, I do *not* work for this Lathan." Greg raised his voice. "I've never even heard the name."

"Are you saying you never hid a Gallom in Ivy's house?"

"Stop it." Of all the ways I'd imagined this to play out, my versions had contained a lot less yelling and a lot more civility.

"The hell I did." Greg flung his arms to the side. "I don't know what that is."

"Hmm. Curious. I don't detect a lie." Parker sounded genuinely surprised.

"Of course not, seeing as I'm not fucking lying. Ivy, do you run all your friends past your guard or am I a special sort?"

I nearly let out a sob. This wasn't what I'd intended. "I'm sorry, Greg, I—"

Parker raised an arm. "You're free to leave now, Craig."

"No, he's not. *You* are." I shook my arm, but Parker held tight. "Greg, I'm sorry. This isn't how it was meant to go."

I finally pushed past Parker, but it was Greg's turn to retreat. Not even my math teacher used to look as disappointed in me as Greg did right now.

"I *am* sorry." My gaze fell onto the ground. Greg marched off down the drive. I glanced to my right. "What the hell was that, Parker?" Tears brimmed in my eyes. "You can't go around accusing people!"

"You signed off on the plan. I got results, didn't I?" His face showed surprise and a little hurt, like he genuinely thought he'd done a good thing. "At least we know it wasn't him."

"Sometimes you're a total psycho." I stormed off. "Greg. Wait up. I can explain."

Hand on the door handle, he stopped by his Corvette, but didn't get in.

Good. Now I simply had to think up the explanation I'd promised him.

CHAPTER TWENTY-TWO

THE PLASTICKY SLEEVE OF GREG'S windbreaker rustled under my pleading touch. "Can we go somewhere? I want to explain, but not here."

Greg's gaze shot from the mansion to me. Eventually, his frown relaxed. "I reckon it won't hurt to hear you out."

He left his car in Parker's drive and we strolled out onto the narrow sidewalk that ran along the main road. The woods behind the mansion were used by the pack, but a smaller patch of wooded land lay a short hop away. The temperatures fell quickly at this time of the day, and I turned up the collar of my padded jacket.

"I'm waiting." His words were sharp. The harshness was diffused by the elbow he offered me.

I hooked in my arm. "You're right. Parker was out of bounds. Like totally. No excuses."

"But?"

I bit my lip. How did he know there was a 'but?' "It came from a good place. Someone has been messing with my home. Tried to break in. We chased them off, but he's worried for my safety and his…family's."

"And he thinks this Mr. Lathan is behind this?"

Mister. Ha. If only he knew. "Yes. Parker thinks he's some gang leader harassing the neighborhood. I agreed to let him ask you if you'd spotted anything, anything at all, the other day. Didn't know he'd go ballistic on you."

Making out that Lathan was Parker's problem and not mine? Genius. Comparing the demon kinlord to a human small-time gangster? Priceless. Just imagining what Lathan would think about this assessment gave me a warm feeling of satisfaction.

We stepped off the sidewalk onto the soft grass leading into the woods. Darkness settled over us, but out here, next to my almost-boyfriend, little scared me.

I squeezed Greg's arm. "Parker was angry, and, well, you were the perfect punching bag. An outsider."

"And strong punches he packed." He ducked under a low-hanging branch. "Did the burglars steal anything?"

"No, I think we got there just in time."

He stopped walking and maneuvered me into the spot opposite him. His finger traced around the blotch on my cheek. "Did Parker do that to you? He has quite the temper."

"No." I averted my face. "I got too close to a burglar."

He pulled on my chin, but I held my face to the side. A bird swooped off the tree overhead, its flutter the only noise out here.

"Why won't you look at me?" His gentle tone made me want to bury my head against his chest.

"I-I don't want you to see me like this."

"Oh sweetheart. It's not that bad." He finally gathered me in his arms. "Even now you're the most beautiful woman I've ever come across."

I peered up at his sparkling eyes. "Liar."

"Sometimes. But not now."

I grinned. Thank God the swelling had gone down since this afternoon. "Skilled liar."

"I can prove it." He bowed his head and grazed my lips with his. "I wouldn't do that if I didn't mean it. Oh." He startled back. "Did that hurt?"

My pulse raced. "Not at all."

The corners of his pale blue eyes creased. "I'm so glad you said that." He landed another kiss, just as tender.

My pain, the stress, even my anger at Parker, melted away. I held still against Greg, probing his taste. His tongue teased me, inviting me in. I locked hands at the back of his neck and complied. He received me with a sigh, and my insides softened.

Our kiss gathered urgency. I clamped onto him, reluctant to part for a second. Under my enthusiasm, he stumbled back against the trunk of a tree. A branch snapped beneath his feet, sending another bird into flight.

With Greg pinned in place, my body molded itself against his broad chest. My breath became his breath, my heartbeat his heartbeat. God, I needed his touch. My spine shuddered, loosened, arched under his deepening kisses. He lifted my jacket and slid his hands under my top. His warmth on my naked skin spun my mind, occupied my senses.

Greg whirled me around. Wedged between his tall, strong body and the trunk, I grew impatient. My heart chugged like an engine, and I sighed his name. His soft fingertips, too soft for manual labor, clawed into my jeans and massaged the swell of my buttocks.

"Oh God," I whispered.

He grunted and moved his hand from my butt around to the front, trying to get purchase on my entrance. Too tight. Dammit.

He fumbled with the button of my jeans. "You drive me crazy." His usually melodious voice reached me as a smoky flame that fanned my desire. "I want you right now."

Finally. With my zipper undone, his hand found my panties. Christ, yes. If I didn't feel him inside me within seconds, who knew what I'd do?

No! I pushed him off, breathing hard. Startled by my own reaction, I covered my mouth with my hand.

His lips, full and glistening in the slivers of moonlight, quivered. His glazed eyes blinked in quick succession. "What's wrong?"

I couldn't be with him just yet. I wouldn't. Greg was supposed to be my Something Real. But once again, my motive was getting ahead of me.

I dug my head into his chest and screeched into his jacket. "This is ridiculous. I want to be with you. I want to be with you so badly."

"But?"

Frustration prickled inside me. "Not here. Not in the cold, against a tree."

"There's no audience." His tone, still rough and breathless, told me he was still under my spell. "It would be good. Real good. Primal." His lips found my neck. He bit.

I leaned back without stifling the shiver that gripped me. "I know." My fists curled into his windbreaker, lightly pounding his arms.

Crap. Why hadn't my morals kicked in earlier? The last thing I wanted was to play with the feelings of someone I genuinely cared about. He deserved so much better.

I gathered my nerves to calm my tone. "We'll be together, and it will be great. When I don't have tiny branches poking me in places I don't want to be poked."

His gaze cleared, sparkled even. "I wouldn't call my branch tiny. But sure. Whatever you say."

I laughed. Not the choppy sort induced by a decent joke, but a carefree one, brought on by sheer joy. Sure, my crotch puckered like crazy, my pulse urged me to reconnect, but my mind was lucid. Greg was the one. And he'd totally be worth the wait.

Whatever it took, I'd get control over my motive. I wouldn't hurt him.

He obediently buttoned up my jeans, took a deep breath, and groaned into the dark sky.

I slung my arms around him. "Am I forgiven then?"

"You have an interesting way of apologizing." He kissed my nose. "Yes, you're forgiven."

Thank the heavens for that. But next time, I'd be much more careful. It hadn't really occurred to me just how much I could hurt others with my unwanted powers.

I looked up from under my eyelashes. "And you're still taking me out this Saturday?"

"Wild horses couldn't stop me." His words came in a sexy, breathy tone that connected straight with my pelvis.

I held his face with both hands, my thumbs tracing its contours. His jaw showed early-onset stubble, adding a manly roughness to his otherwise buttersoft skin. "Good. By the way. You told me you don't make out on first dates. How do you feel about second dates?"

"I have no rules about that. You?"

I leaned in for another kiss, neither gentle nor wild. Merely a promise to the man who let me forget my troubles, if only for a short while.

Back at home, I threw myself into the welcoming embrace of my living room sofa. Once again I had denied myself sex when it counted. Him too. Somehow, I'd make it up to him. Even though my head pounded, it was a good headache. I'd *earned* that headache.

"You've got mail," the female voice I'd selected as my text alert on my cell phone said. I checked the message from Greg.

"Missing you already."

He really was the sweetest.

"Me too." I smiled and hit 'send.'

My relationship with him would be perfect. No premature intercourse was going to mar it.

Except I'd be leaving, wouldn't I? Crap. I was going to do to him that Waylon had done to me. When had I become such a horrible person? Perhaps I could somehow stay in touch with him. We could make it work, I was sure of it.

Neck cradled by my polka dot throw cushion, my gaze fell onto the guards on the wall. Would they continue to shield me from danger, or had they already let me down? With Greg cleared by Parker's lie-detector nose and off the list of suspects, perhaps it was time to face facts. My guard-making skills weren't as solid as I'd made myself believe.

I stood and walked to the glass doors. A patch of crushed grass served as a reminder of my fight with God's demons. Inside the house, my battle against Lathan had been reduced to a coffee stain in my light-brown carpet. A small blemish compared to the mountain of pain within me, where no amount of cleaning or sprucing could clear it away.

My hand curled around the invisibility guards in my pocket. The cold metal contained no spark of life. Not surprising, since without connection to the demon 'batteries,' the beads stored no magic. I removed them from their chains and twisted one onto the loops of my bracelet, the other onto my guard belt.

The doorbell rang, and I ran to open it. A bruised and bloody Florian leaned against the door frame for support, taking great gulps of air.

"My God, Flo. Come in." I stepped aside to let him enter. "What happened?"

The battered vampire collapsed over my threshold onto the ceramic tiles of the hall floor. He sighed, and my heart tightened. With my help he made it into the living room, where he fell onto the sofa like a dead fox. Fur still shiny, but dead to the nudge.

"Hang on, Flo." I dashed into the kitchen for a cloth and water to clean him up. He had to be okay. He had to. "There." I mopped most of the blood off him and attempted a thin smile. "At least now I can fully appreciate your bruises."

"I'm glad you find my poor aching body so amusing." His pitch was whiney and pained, but a twitch of his lips gave him up. He wasn't as badly hurt as he looked; most likely, his inherent magic was healing him as we spoke.

Perhaps I should have guessed he was playing up his injuries, since his tailored shirt and jacket didn't even look crumpled.

"You're okay." Not a question. I briefly closed my eyes to focus on loosening my neck muscles. "What happened? Is Eli okay?"

"Eli, Eli, what about me?" He raised his arms. "Yeah, he'll be fine."

"Do you need…blood?" I bit my lip.

"Are you offering?" The twinkle in his eyes was back.

"Wondering, is all, so don't get excited."

"No, we ate on the way here. Luckily, once under glamour, our food doesn't mind what we look like."

I relaxed. He appeared to have suffered no lasting damage. In hindsight, my worries about the wellbeing of a nearly immortal vampire struck me as silly, but with Flo, I wouldn't take any chances.

"You can't be feeling that bad if you and Eli had take-out." I carried the water and cloth back to the kitchen, making sure my posture showed no sign of my earlier concern.

"You're not your usual shining beauty yourself, you know," he shouted. "What did I miss?"

I filled him in on the burglar demons while I boiled the kettle. Those of us who didn't feed on body fluids needed the occasional assistance of caffeine to raise us back to our best. Although Florian looked like he could use a cup, too.

"So, what did your contacts tell you?" I yelled over the clanking of the spoon.

"You make it sound so easy. We were devilish and dashing and not prepared to take no for an answer."

I rolled my eyes, an action I usually reserved for moments when I was within Florian's line of sight. "Okay, what *did* you take for an answer?"

"A faceful of fists, as it turns out. Let me talk you through it. Eli was parking the car, so I went in ahead to meet my informants. I was a few feet from my fae contacts when two men jumped me from behind. Demons, judging by their strength, although who knows? Anyway, luckily enough, Eli got the car parked at last. He's not the fastest at that, but I can't do everything. So he came in and saw what's happening and did his Vulcan death grip on them."

"His what?" I took the mugs in from the kitchen and perched on the edge of the chair opposite Flo, who dangled half dead, half lazy over the arm rest of my sofa.

He greedily gulped the liquid refreshment. Tongue of steel that man had, because the coffee was still steaming.

He rolled his shoulders. "You know, the thing Eli does where one minute someone's alive and the next minute they're on the floor dead, and it looks like all he's done is tap 'em on the neck?"

I wasn't sure how I felt about adding another two deaths to my conscience, but I made sure my concern didn't color my voice. "So you don't know who sent your attackers?"

"Actually, I do. Once Carl and Hassan finished sniveling in a corner instead of helping us fight the demons off, they—"

I sat opposite him and pulled up my feet. "Carl and Hassan who?"

"The fae. My informants. The guys I was going to see. Don't you listen?"

"Oh, yeah, sure. Carl and Hassan." Words served with an extra dollop of sarcasm.

He scrunched his nose. "Yeah, them. After a little persuasion—if you know what I mean—they said the attackers worked for a major league crime boss. They didn't specifically mention God, but they meant him. I'm sure."

I straightened. "How major league?"

"Prostitution, trafficking, that sort of thing. They reckon he's got a pretty large number of demons following his orders." He placed his cup on the table.

I bobbed my head. "So, it's as we'd figured. God must be a pretty juiced-up demon."

Florian tapped his forehead. "I don't know. You want to be careful about jumping to conclusions. One thing I've learned over the years, demons aren't necessarily the worst of the kinfolk out there, or the most powerful. We haven't been doing too badly ourselves, have we?" He chuckled, and immediately grimaced.

One elbow in my lap, I cradled my head in my palm. "On the statue front I'm out of ideas. At least until Parker convinces the demons in his basement to cooperate. It gives us time to concentrate on Heather, though. We should pop into Abraxas to see if we can find Heather's friend. The guy she was seen with."

Flo looked at me over the rim of his cup. "I don't think we should spread ourselves too thin, but I guess we deserve a night on the town."

"Okay then." I shifted over and snuggled against his room-temp warmth. As I'd hoped, my headache was gone in an instant. "Parker offered to send muscle."

"He did?" He shrugged. "Why not?"

Holy cow. My little vampire friend had prospered into a chilled-out wolf fan.

"Fine. But if you want Parker's help, *you* call him." No way would I ask the crazy-ass werewolf any favors.

"Okay." He retrieved the phone from his pocket, dialed, and spoke politely to Parker, who readily agreed to his request.

What was it that scared me more? Parker and Flo's pervading peace, or the fact that Flo already had him on speed dial?

CHAPTER TWENTY-THREE

WHY DIDN'T EVERY MORNING START like this? The sun shone strong rays into my bedroom. The wind that whipped my windows overnight had calmed. I jumped out of bed, my mind fresh and disturbed by nothing more than old dreams of Lathan. So what if the demon had done bad things to me in Alethia? I was free of him now. His kidnap attempt had failed. His Gallom attempt had failed. After everything he'd thrown at me, I was still standing. Amazing what a bit of perspective did to raise your quality of life.

I checked my cell for missed messages. Bingo.

"Thinking of you. See you soon. Greg."

If he'd been here, I'd have given him a bear hug right now.

"Can't wait." I sent.

Humming a happy tune, I shuffled into the kitchen. It was ten thirty, a healthy time to get up. Gotta love being a P.I. An official-looking envelope had fallen through the mail slot onto the tiles in my hall. My pulse soared. I ripped it open, skimming the contents once, twice. Thank the heavens. The money was now mine. My attorneys had cut through the worst of the red tape with… Hang on. It looked like my stepfather had a hand in this. 'On his urging,' they'd chased some forms, which sped up the process. Go figure. Guess I should probably buy my stepfather some chocolates.

All I needed now was to figure out how to spend or invest what was left after buying my dream home.

I grinned so hard my cheeks ached.

At long last, true financial independence beckoned. I darted to my jacket hanging on the rack next to the dome-shaped mirror. My photo, as creased as it was, was about to become reality.

I froze. What about Fred? Crap. I couldn't leave him without making sure he was okay. My investigation was progressing. We'd made more headway than the police had made, and I wasn't yet done. The trip to Abraxas, the club Heidi had mentioned, could yield good clues on Heather, which in turn might lead me to my boss. I had to find him.

Postponing my departure didn't sting half as much as I thought it might. After all, what did a few days matter compared to a life without kin? Still, better not linger. Lathan wasn't going to give up, and Parker's confusing effect on me was beginning to piss me off. With the photo once more stowed away in its dark holding place, I trudged into the living room.

Out in the yard, Parker waved at me. What the hell was he so cheerful about?

I opened the French door and strode inside. "Come to scare off more of my friends?" Funny how the alpha wolf brought out my inner bitch.

"Oh, do you have any more friends?"

On balance, I probably deserved that.

He entered and leaned against my living room wall, one hand hidden behind his back. I peered, but his frame blocked my view. Well, it was unlikely he should have brought over chocolates by way of apology.

He crossed his feet. "Still on the warpath?"

"Not undeserved." I lifted my chin to underline my point.

"Totally undeserved."

I chewed my lip. "Let's split the blame in the middle and not mention the incident again."

"I don't—" He raised a hand. "Never mind. Did you…make up with Greg?"

Make up? Hell, we made *out*. Except, no way would Parker appreciate my word play. "I convinced him you weren't as deranged as you come across."

A cloud of light-headedness indicated his shifting mood. My vision darkened. He walked to my black sofa and sat. Within seconds, my mind was clear again.

He leaned back, one hand slung over his head. The other lifted the Collective. "Last night I contacted our Elders about this. They insist it's not the kind of thing you want to keep lying around."

I raised my eyebrows. "Hang on. You thought the split lip the demons gave me was because they secretly liked me?"

"Smart-ass. The Collective can be used to create a stable two-way gateway between here and Alethia."

I recoiled. "What?" Bad, so very, very, very bad. I treasured the distance between me and Lathan dearly. If anyone used the Collective for its purpose, nothing would stop him from getting his hands on me again. "Why would anybody want that?" I mumbled. "Can we, I don't know, smash it?"

"Something with enough magic to punch a hole through the

Rim? Maybe it's not a good idea to smash it and let that magic escape uncontrolled."

My insides collapsed and I slumped into the seat opposite Parker. "I guess."

"It used to be a simple figurine." He rolled the Collective in his hand. "A powerful demon duped an elf into telling him how to turn it into a gate-opener. The demon killed hundreds of kin and humans in Oldworld before the elf tracked him down. The Collective disappeared, and hasn't been heard from since."

"Until now." I glared at it through narrowed eyes.

"Look at it this way. Once it's drained, we'll give it to the guys who're after it. They'll assume the statue never had any power to begin with, and you'll be safe."

I nodded slowly. "It's a plan." A vague Hail-Mary plan.

He placed his elbows on his knees. "Now for the bad news. The Elders are unfamiliar with any spells that could safely destroy its magic, although they're sure such a ritual does exist. We just need to find it. I was hoping the vampires have books I don't."

"They might." Although nothing as old or informative as Parker's Elf Encyclopedia.

He placed the Collective on the table. Was that a sound? Sure enough, it whispered again. Quiet, but unmistakable. If I didn't figure out this spell, how long would I keep my sanity and my freedom?

Spurred on by renewed determination, I leaped to my feet. "I'll ask Waylon."

"And why would he know?"

Ah yes. Parker had no idea who Waylon was. "He knows stuff. You wait here. I'll be right back."

He stretched out his legs and placed both hands behind his head, signaling a level of comfort in my house that grated. I seized two pillows to lift the blasted statue and carried it into my bedroom.

I plopped onto my bed. My mattress bounced under my weight. Feet entangled in my bright orange blanket, I activated the touchstone.

Waylon's face popped up.

"Everything okay?" His even timbre teased nerve endings all over my skin.

These pesky satyr hormones still had sway over me.

I cleared my throat. "Well, not really. I need your help again. Remember the invisible guys I asked you about? This statue," I swiveled the touchstone so I didn't have to touch the Collective, "is what they were looking for, I think. I stumbled onto it at work, and now some people are desperate to get their hands on it. It's called a Collective."

"Collective?" His head gave a sharp jerk. "Shit, Ivy. This is fucked up. That statue can turn back the flow of magic that's holding up the Rim and funnel it into a portal between Alethia and Oldworld. Sweet Hernando. That's all I need."

"Couldn't you use it to cross the Rim? I mean, at least it would be safe if you had it, right?" And I'd have one less problem to deal with.

"What?" He brushed a hand through his hair, and almost immediately dragged his focus back to me. "No, that's not how Guardians build gateways. We manipulate the Rim. It was designed so it would let us through easily. To create a Collective, you make blood sacrifices. You know, rip out somebody's soul at the moment of their death, ideally under shitloads of screams, and channel the pain into opening a portal. Guardians stay away from that."

The blood drained from my face. The whispering, the faces, it all fell into place. "There are people trapped in here, aren't there?" I murmured. "Souls. Stored as energy."

He nodded. "Until they're released. Their suffering is a huge power source. If this gets in the wrong hands, Oldworld will be fucked."

My diaphragm tautened, producing short, shallow breaths. "I can hear them, you know. I see their faces and feel their pain. I thought I'd imagined it, but..."

He shook his head. "I'm sorry, babe. I wish I could change that for you. What you feel is their auras. Auras remain connected to the souls, like a shadow, long after the bodies are worm food." His eyes narrowed. "You gonna be all right?"

"How do I release them?"

"You? By Hernando. Don't go anywhere near this." His squint relaxed. "Fuck it. I'm coming back."

My heart thumped against my chest. If he returned, I'd melt again. I knew I would. "Just tell me what to do. I'll be fine."

"This isn't anything like weaving guards. Untrained as you are, you can't control it."

"What about the IEA?"

"I don't like the idea of that lot getting a whiff of your existence." He massaged his chin. "What a cluster of badness. But yeah. Honestly, I have my hands full here. People are dropping like flies around me, and I still haven't worked out who's responsible. If you ask me, they're all bastards, but I can't shank them all, now, can I?"

I frowned. No one would be able to stop him, so some moral imperative must hold him back. Glad to hear some lines even he won't cross. "So, the IEA?"

"If you say you're with me, they should leave you alone. Get some paper and a pen, and I'll tell you how it's done. Pass them the notes and then stay away from them *and* the Collective." He walked me through the instructions, then sighed. "I'm not liking this, babe. Not one bit."

"I'll be careful. Thank you." A few more seconds of soaking in his face, and I hung up.

For a while I sat on my bed, staring at my white, unadorned wall. Two people had proven themselves to be beyond reproach, and before I contacted the IEA and told them about the statue, I needed to discuss my next step with them. If the IEA's agenda and their loyalties were doubtful, I didn't want to trust them with a device as potentially powerful as the Collective.

With the statue clamped between the two pillows, I returned to Parker.

He studied my notes. "That's a lot of magic. But there may be a way."

Reinforcements came in the form of a tall wolf with Asian features and flawless dark skin. Within a few minutes of Parker's phone call, he stood in my yard, his black wavy hair flowing around his shoulders.

"Hi." I stuck my hand out through the door.

"I'm Ali." He shook. "And you're Ivy." His smile was disarming. His forearms looked strong and capable. The sort of arms that would keep me safe at night.

"Ivy?" Parker nudged me.

"What...what?" Damn, just when I thought I had it under control, up popped the motive.

Parker's eyebrows were way up. "Aren't you going to invite him in?"

"Sure, come in, Ali. I'll make us coffee." A little stretch in the kitchen and an extra helping of caffeine should bring me back in focus.

"We're four short," Parker said when I returned.

"Short of what?" I placed the tray of coffee on a side table and went back for sugar and cream. "Tools in the box? Ants of a picnic?"

"Of the number of wolves we need to perform the spell." Ali rubbed his eyebrows. "We don't have the manpower."

"Oh." I tried to keep the disappointment from showing. "It was just a thought. Waylon said the IEA might have someone who could help me."

"Absolutely not." Parker glared at me. "You won't go anywhere near the IEA. Besides, all I said was we couldn't do it four short, not that it can't be done at all."

My sigh of relief was audible, teasing a smile from both men. "Okay then. Let's think. You only need to find four more werewolves?"

"It's not like there's a steady supply." Parker walked over to the wide-open French doors and stared out into my yard, hands clasped behind his back. The late morning sun streamed around him, outlining his perfect body in a white halo. "There's my sister, Carmel. She could come back for a little while. She wouldn't even need a new initiation, since she's still tied to my pack through me. And her pup makes thirty-four."

He fell quiet, except for the occasional pensive grunt. Ali stuffed his hands in his pockets and leaned back into the sofa, his eyebrows knitted in thought.

"Does it have to be werewolves?" I sipped the last of my coffee. "Or could anybody with magic join your pack? Say, Florian for example." I glanced at Ali. "He's a vampire. Chock-full of magic. Good friend of Parker's."

The alpha narrowed his eyes.

"A vampire?" Ali shot his boss a bemused expression then tilted his head to the side. "Well, that could work. But to initiate him into the pack, he'd have to do the trials."

"There isn't time." Parker swatted away the suggestions. "The Elders were clear. The Collective needs to be dealt with now."

"Actually." Ali rubbed his chin. "There is one other way."

Parker turned his glare full-force on him. "I am not setting up the vampire with one of our females."

"It would only be for a short time. After a few months or so, they'd declare their trial period a bust, and no harm done."

"Are you crazy?" Parker broadened his stance, a flicker of power pulsing around him.

I closed my eyes for a moment, anxious to follow their conversation without submitting to his aura.

This time, Parker's second-in-command didn't flinch. "Desperate times, desperate measures. When that werewolf in Philly mated with a demon, the demon counted as a full member. It's the fastest and easiest way to gain new pack members."

Now there was some interesting information. I sat up. "A mating between a werewolf and demon? I thought you guys were against non-werewolf relationships?"

"Not at all. Interesting you should have given it some thought, though." Ali grinned and looked first at Parker, then at me.

I followed the sudden urge to fondle my hair and stare at my dancing toes.

"You know what?" Parker said. "Let's use the bloodsucker. But you'll be the one declaring your intention on him. It's your idea."

Intention? As in the first step to a mating? Like in a werewolf bonding?

"Eh, hello." I waved. "I didn't know Flo would have to get pretend-engaged to someone. And another guy? I don't think he's going to agree to that arrangement."

"Yeah." Parker shook his head. "Especially because there's nothing fake about this ritual. Magic will link the two, an intimacy of mind as it were, so they can decide whether they're ready to mate. Wolves bond for life, and you better be damn certain about your partner."

I swallowed hard. Mate for life? Yeah. No. Flo definitely wouldn't go for that.

"It's a shame it won't work with humans, otherwise you could be our thirty-sixth." Ali winked. "Humans simply don't have the magic to create the bond or to channel power into our alpha."

Parker and I exchanged glances. A grin wormed itself onto his face.

"Oh, no." I lifted my hands. "Waylon said I'm too new to magic and haven't got enough control."

"I'd be the one controlling the flow of magic, not you." Parker's eyes lit up. "Yes, I think this will work."

"You aren't human?" Ali said.

I shook my head. "Believe me. I'm more surprised about this than you. Still, I'm not the right person to do this. What about Julia or Eli? They're both pretty powerful vampires."

Ali shook his head. "We're going to have enough difficulty selling the idea of one vampire to the pack. Two would be impossible."

"Talking about me?" Florian leaned against the French doors. The wind blew into his dark shirt and black jacket, which ballooned around his slim waist. "I heard the words vampire and impossible in one sentence. Poor Ivy. I swung by to see if you wanted company. It appears you've already got more than most people should have to deal with."

"Funny." Parker turned his back on Flo.

Ali rose, adjusted his pants and walked up to my friend. "Ali." He extended his hand.

"Florian." The vampire gave a dazzling smile and reciprocated the gesture.

After Parker had explained the plan, Florian burst out laughing. "A vampire in a wolf pack. It's like the beginning of a bad joke."

"Would your family object?" Parker's shoulders and features tightened. "You know what such a ritual requires of you. You will become part of our pack. Obey our customs." His gaze focused. "Submit to my authority."

"You're serious, aren't you?" Flo brushed a palm across his face. "Yeah, my family would think I'd lost my mind. Still, I'm not stupid. If it needs doing, it needs doing. A portal between the worlds is a problem for everyone. Besides, we can dissolve the connection after the Collective has been destroyed." His face darkened for a millisecond. He turned to Ali. "I'd expect flowers, you know." He gave a flirtatious smile.

"I would expect sex."

The smile disappeared. "You're kidding, right?"

Parker gave a quick cough. "Now that that's settled, let's get the show on the road."

CHAPTER TWENTY-FOUR

GAWKING AT MY FRIEND-TURNED-TRAITOR WASN'T enough. "Are you tripping?" I couldn't even look at Florian, who sat between me and Ali, discussing the mental plan as if it was going to become a reality. I shook my head over and over. "I'm not declaring anything on anyone. Besides, angry werewolves and I don't mix, and the whole pack would definitely consider us little more than snacks, right?"

Ali nodded. "Safety. There you go, already thinking like a wolf. But as Parker's *intended*, you'll be fine." His eyes twinkled. "A challenge on you would be a challenge on him, and that's a fight nobody would risk."

"As your friend said. It needs to be done." Parker's mouth twitched. He enjoyed my discomfort way too much. He bobbed his chin at his second-in-command. "Ivy's quite a handful. I imagine Pretty Boy here won't be that easy to handle. Can you manage?"

The wolf ran his gaze along the vampire's body before bringing his eyes back up. "Sure."

"Hey." But Flo's protest was too weak to make a dent in Parker's newfound enthusiasm.

The alpha slapped his hands together. "Let's not hang about. I'll get Rollo and Flynn up to speed on the plan, but as far as the others are concerned, this is legit." He squinted. "I don't want to get into discussions about trampling over our ancient customs. Got it?"

Florian gave a lop-sided grin.

I closed my eyes. "And we'll dissolve this connection right after?"

"No, not *right* after. A few months, then we'll split up." Parker's gaze lost focus. "No one will be surprised if we don't make this a permanent bond."

My shoulders slumped. "Do I have a say in this?"

"You brought the Collective into our lives, Ivy. You have a responsibility." His firm voice left little wiggle room.

So what if he had a point? I pouted. "Jerk."

One glance from him, and I mumbled a half-assed apology.

Consensus was not to delay, and the guys scheduled the ceremony for later tonight. Parker and Ali left, inviting Flo to come along. Why was everyone so excited? They knew this was a bad idea, right?

I clamped my hands between my thighs. No way would this end well. My head was already so deep in kin-stuff, but joining a pack of werewolves wasn't the most ingenious of steps. As for Parker declaring his intention? I was firmly with Greg now, and my engagement to someone else wouldn't go down well with him. Not to mention how Parker would feel about my relationship with Greg.

Only, what choice did I have? The IEA were representatives of the kinlords, among them Lathan. Not to mention a bunch of demons were breathing down my neck. And who knew how long I'd be able to keep the Collective from them?

I was totally screwed.

Way too soon for my liking, it was time to get out the big guns. Large copper sheets on a pure steel base. Energy traversed my skin and spilled into the plates. My protection guards would create a safe area for Parker to perform the spell. The more my life descended into chaos, the more comfort weaving guards gave me. I shaped the lines. I molded the magic. No one interfered, because for once, no one's knowledge trumped mine.

The sun sent long shadows onto the soft ground of my yard, but no rain would get in our way tonight. The brunette on TV with the toothy smile was usually right about these things. I set up the heavy guards in a circle to cover a space of approximately twenty square yards.

Heidi stepped over my small fence, a toga-like robe draped over her arm. "This is for the ceremony."

I squinted at the fabric. "You want me to wear this?"

"You wanna join the pack, you gotta live by our rules." Her cold voice made me look up.

I tried out a smile. "How do I, I don't know, fasten it?"

Her glare remained hostile. "You're the special one. Work it out."

Ouch. She wheeled around and swayed her butt out of my yard. The backlash had started. Swell.

Bruises still shadowed my face. Parker's pack wouldn't get any more reason to point fingers at me, so I used the makeup Julia had left for me.

Around seven in the evening, everything was in place for the ceremony. I double-checked my guards, straightened the toga I'd donned over my regular clothes, and ran out of excuses.

All the wolves joined us for the 'happy' occasion in the spacious entrance hall. A couple of balloons hung from a picture frame, perhaps out of a sense of obligation to create a more festive atmosphere. Along the wall, a wooden table offered finger food and alcoholic refreshments.

Flo, Ali, Parker and I were the only ones clad in togas, or extra-large lab coats, each with a rope tied around our midsection. As much as I needed some Dutch courage, I wouldn't be the first to approach the buffet. My stomach clenched too hard anyway. To my right, Parker mumbled with Ali, his hands gesturing violently.

I nudged Heidi, dressed in a *Rock Hard* T-shirt and black pipe jeans. "So, what now?"

Her gaze remained fixed ahead. "We don't talk about what happens in the ceremonial chamber."

"But how am I supposed to know what to do?"

"Shush." She moved to the other side of Rollo, whose face was as unreadable as my near future.

Would Heidi's crush on Parker result in a huge relationship mess? Maybe I should confide in her how uncomfortable this whole situation made me. But Parker had been adamant. No spilling Collective secrets to his wolves.

If I came up with a plan, any plan, in the next ten seconds, I could blow this whole thing off. Predictably, my brain merely showed the loading circle. Ali led Florian into the chamber. My mouth didn't call to them to stop this ridiculousness. The door slammed shut. The stone had begun rolling.

More than thirty pairs of eyes stared at the wall behind which the ceremonial chamber lay. What was going through the wolves' heads? They didn't want me in their group. Certainly not engaged to their alpha. So why didn't anyone question the ceremony? Sure, Flo and I, in particular, had become regular visitors, but for a species that prided itself in taking love seriously, our party guests weren't that curious about our motivation.

Parker took my hand and went rigid. A bubble of aura expanded from him, an aura of terrifying power. I let out a moan, joy pulsing through my veins. My legs buckled and I fell to my knees. A fierce throb bulldozed up my thighs and spine and detonated in my head. I steadied my breathing, ground my teeth through the pain.

Parker stood tall, broad-shouldered by my side. A red plume surrounded him, with a scent so sweet it spun my mind. He surveyed his attending pack.

Each one of them was on their knees like me. At least one custom I got right, even if it had been by accident.

He lifted me to my feet. "You good?"

"Yeah." I rubbed my eyes. "I assume you're now the proud daddy of a vampire boy?"

The door opened, and Florian and Ali appeared, toga robes no longer as neat as they were when they'd gone in. The congregation rose and welcomed them with cautious applause. Ali led my friend out, hands clasped, and smiled. The slow clap quickly gathered pace. Florian shielded his eyes against the lights. He shot Parker a nervous glance and straightened. But where was his mischievous grin? His cocky gait?

He whispered into Ali's ear and stalked up to me. "Good luck." He patted my cheek. His tentative smile unsettled me further.

"Are you ready?" Parker's voice traveled into the corner in me where I liked to hide from my fears and paranoia. The red plume had disappeared, but the memory of the power that had brought me to my knees lingered.

My pulse raced. Why hadn't his influence over me bothered me before? He touched me like no one else. His aura flowed into me, twisting my mind any which way he wanted. He took my worries at a whim, soothed my headaches without lifting a finger.

As much as I *wanted* Waylon, and as much as I *needed* Greg, Parker, so innocent with his sweet smile, had the ability to devastate me. And I was about to give him the key to my heart?

"Come on. It's time." He dragged me through the solid wooden door. The intense fragrance of sage and blackberry wafted in white puffs from an assortment of incense sticks, probably to cleanse the air and soothe our nerves. Fingers crossed.

Statues surrounded a central pit in the dark room. Candlelight sparked against the glazed floor tiles and the poster-sized guards on the wall. Ancient guards, filled to the edge with magic I'd never encountered. A chill came over me. Another reminder I was out of my league.

"What now?" I crossed my arms and tucked my fists under, still hoping the sage's calming effect would kick in any second.

Parker positioned me inside the hollow. "I've never gone through the ritual. The ceremonial chamber is like Vegas. What happens in the ceremonial chamber..."

"...stays in the ceremonial chamber. Got it."

"But hang on, somewhere around here..." He twirled. "Ah, got it." He unrolled a scroll of yellowed paper. "Looks like these are the instructions." He angled the text so he could read in the flickering light. A window or two would have made the task easier, but I suspected in wolfland, dignified ceremony went hand in hand with the word *creepy*.

"I promise you, my beloved, respect and understanding."

Startled, I looked up. Parker's finger pointed to the next section on the scroll.

No way.

"Read it." His urgent tone made it clear backing out wasn't an option. This was happening.

I wet my lips. "I promise you, my beloved, respect and obedience." Obedience? This was seriously messed up.

"To complete the bond, we must light three candles." He picked up a large matchstick and mumbled the spell. The first candle, forming the upper point of a triangle that surrounded us, came to life. Its shadows danced across the wall like a puppet show.

My stomach somersaulted.

He lit candle number two. "Ready?"

Did it matter? I nodded, my lips glued together. The third flame popped into existence. I let out a gasp. A longing stirred inside me. The longing to be held and cherished. I glanced at the door, ready to sprint, but trembling knees bolted me to the spot. Parker's helping arm kept me from falling. He gathered me close, hands on my waist.

The red plume of power exploded once more from his chest. It grew high into a slim column, looped, and swooped down into my heart. I cried out. Shit. Nobody had mentioned I'd be in agony. The three candle flames, blurred dots through my tears, shot up and joined his aura. My jaw tautened, countering the razor-sharp teeth of their combined force.

A sharp sting pierced my throat where the pendant touched my skin. *God, no. Not my allure.*

Parker's eyes widened. "You're perfect." He grazed my cheek with his free hand.

He was under my satyr thrall. Perhaps I should have pushed him away, but in this room, both my allure and my motive were subject to the whims of magic. Neither was under my control.

His lips pressed onto mine, not slow or fast, just as if they belonged. My heart shuddered against my ribs. Electricity sparked in my hair, flicked my cheek, but it had lost the ability to hurt me. The magic fused us together. His past, each layer that made Parker who he was, opened up to me like the pages of a book. His fierce determination to protect those he loved. The first time he lay with a woman. The temper he hated so much. And a delicate heart so afraid of being hurt.

The scroll, the room, the entire universe fell away.

Our lips parted. A breeze nudged my hair, spiraled into a whirl that towered over our heads. The flames flickered and extinguished, plunging us into darkness. Parker stiffened. A spike retracted from my inner core, ripping me open. His aura, our magic, reversed direction and tunneled into his chest.

He doubled over, slapping the empty air for a hold. His face distorted, eyes bulged. His tan skin became ghostly white.

"What do I do?" I supported him best as I could. "Parker?"

He groaned, sweat pearling on his upper lip.

"Come down. Onto the ground." I kneeled by his side, cradling his head between my arms. Was I supposed to chant something or re-light the candles? "Tell me what to do."

He swiveled his head and gulped for air. I clutched him tight against my chest, stroking his neck until the rise and fall of his shoulders slowed. My lip quivered, and keeping him calm when I wanted to scream took all my willpower. But this wasn't about me. This was about making sure Parker was okay.

He whimpered.

Was he seeing my innermost secrets, the ones I didn't even admit to myself?

"Shh." I swayed with him in my arms. "It's going to be okay."

The three candles inside the pit lit up.

His brown eyes had morphed into solid gold spheres. "That was one hell of a ride."

Was it over? I wiped the sweat off his forehead, swept his moist, short hair out of the way. "I was worried about you."

"Well, you took me by surprise. There's definitely werewolf in your background, and something more powerful." He licked his lips. "Something *much* more powerful."

I snatched back my hands. I wasn't ready to go there yet with him. "Do you think you have enough juice to destroy the Collective now?"

His head tilted to one side, like a dog pricking its ears. "I do now. Carmel's just arrived with Lukas, her son. Wow. You have no idea how much energy is coursing through me right now." He gave a giddy laugh.

Better keep it together, buddy. No amount of power would do us any good if he couldn't focus.

He jerked his chin toward the door. "Let's go." We pulled each other up. He mumbled a few words, and the dancing lights snuffed out of existence.

I heaved open the bulky door, and bright lights bored into my eyes. I whipped my face away from the overhead lamps and surveyed the hall through a squint. The semi-circle of people shifted, and whispers whirled through the air. Parker took my hand.

A clap to my right infected another and another into enthusiastic applause. Go figure. A blonde woman pushed through the small crowd toward Parker, her cheeks flushed, and tears glistened in her eyes. Either a girlfriend he hadn't told me about, or more likely, his sister Carmel.

"I'm so happy for you." She kissed his forehead, smooshing his face between her palms. Then she looked at me. "You're her? Come here." She smooshed mine, too. "This was sudden." She prodded her brother's shoulder. "A day's warning. I didn't have time to buy a dress."

He shrugged. "You look fine." She struck his arm and he winced. "You look great, I mean."

"Better." She hugged me. "I'm Carmel. I'm so glad to meet the woman who wants to make an honest man out of my brother."

Parker nudged me back to him, presumably to remind me to watch my answer and to avoid any lies.

I sputtered a cough to suppress any feelings of guilt. "Right. Um. I'm Ivy."

"We should get to know one another." Carmel beamed. "You probably want to learn about his bad habits, don't you?"

Her open friendliness punched my heart. A sister who hated me would at least set my mind at ease.

But this situation wasn't her fault. I smiled. "Actually, I'd *love* to hear embarrassing childhood stories." *So* not a lie. Any ammunition I could get. "I want to speak to my friend real quick. Be right back." I gave Parker's hand a squeeze then wandered off to find Flo.

Ali embraced me. "Well done."

For what? "Er. You too."

He patted my back and left.

Flo's hands stuck deep in his toga's pockets. "Weird. Huh?"

I took a jagged breath, my icy fingertips rolled away in tight fists. "Still can't wrap my head around it. Have you experienced anything like it? So...intimate?"

"Definitely not." His foot traced a line on the ground. "And not something I'm likely to forget. Do you... Do you feel different?"

I listened to my body, the galloping pulse and the knot in my stomach that told me something had changed. "I guess. You?"

"Yes. But not just about me. Ali looks at me and I... Hell, this freaks me out. This ceremony messes with you." A tiny smirk lifted his features and he leaned in. "If I start to go gay on you, you'll tell me. Right?" he whispered.

I grinned. "Hardly on me."

"You aren't supposed to talk about the ceremony in front of others." Heidi's voice cut between us.

"Sorry," Flo and I mumbled.

"You will be." Her glare practically spat venom. "As soon as you step out of line, I'll be there."

"Enough, you two." Rollo pushed Heidi and me apart.

"Mine!" The gruff sound connected with an old, reawakening place in my pit. A place hidden so deep, I hadn't known it existed. I peered around. No one behind me. Had I imagined the voice?

"She started it." Heidi pointed at my nose.

Sheesh. I empathized. I really did. She was crushing hard on her alpha, but I'd had a hard day, so I built myself up and glared.

A growl erupted, and Parker's arms locked around me. "Apologize this instant, Heidi."

The excited mumble of the other wolves died down. Heidi shrunk, her skin at once stone gray. "I-I'm sorry. I didn't mean it."

I nodded. "Don't worry. We're good. Right?" Parker had no idea he'd just done more harm than good. I squirmed against his air-tight grip, but to no effect. His breath quickened, the muscles touching my back flexed.

She wheeled around and slunk out of sight. He released me, his nostrils flared. "If she gives you trouble, let me know."

His heightened protective instinct was the last thing my social and work life needed. High school had taught me how to handle moody girls. He, on the other hand, needed a crash course in sensitivity.

"Don't be so hard on her." I stepped back and placed my hand on his chest. "And shouldn't we get started on the statue? Your Elders told you to do it soon, right?"

The tenderness left his eyes. "Yes. You're right. And they don't issue warnings lightly. Let's get this over with then."

"I'll check if everything's ready." Glad of the excuse to get away, I stalked off to my yard.

The drive was peppered with yellow leaves, while the grassy mess outside my house had remained free. The last thing I needed was for a stray leaf to disrupt the spell. My setup looked good, but it needed to be perfect. Parker's life depended on it. I circled my arrangement three times. Each guard sparked with energy, a consistent prickle against my fingertips.

"Everything working?" Parker's tone was neutral.

He walked up, tall and strong, and my heart fluttered. I swallowed. My burgeoning affection for him wasn't a good start to our fake engagement.

The pack followed at a distance, Florian and Ali in the lead, their steps in sync.

"We're ready." Ali jigged his head at the pack and leaned in.

"I've told them we need their assistance in a ceremony to do with a vampire artifact. Like, Florian joins in our ceremony, and this is part of a vampire ceremony."

I scowled. "You lied to them? I didn't even know that was possible."

He grabbed Flo's hand. "Good thing this guy's such a skilled raconteur. He spun a confusing tale with enough truth to completely befuddle everyone. Not one lie." He smiled. "You have to teach me how to do that. Anyway, assuming this works, we can reveal the true meaning behind this spell later. I don't want to get their emotions involved right now."

Parker looped around my setup, his hands high above the guards as if warming them over a fire.

I sidled up to him. "Can you feel it?"

"The energy? I never understood guards, you know. I mean before. Don't get me wrong. I knew they were effective, but they were just plates. Decorations for the home. Now their power calls to me."

I studied him for a second. "Quite heady, isn't it?"

His eyes flashed. "This is your power. I'd know it anywhere. Yours and mine. It tugs on something inside me. Something it recognizes as kindred."

So he was feeling it too. I rubbed the tennis ball in my throat. "How long is this connection between us going to last?"

He dropped his arm. "Like I said, a couple of months. You're officially stuck with me until then."

Ali came up from behind and handed his alpha the Collective. I dislodged a guard to let Parker into the circle, but snatched his arm. "We don't know how safe this is."

"I'll be fine." Holding the statue away from me, he drew me in for a hug. His nose nudged my neck and he inhaled sharply.

A visceral fear for his wellbeing coiled around my lungs and stomach. If something went wrong, it would be my fault. I was the one who'd involved him in my dangerous affairs.

He entered the circle and smoothed a patch of grass with his foot. I replaced the guard in the ground, and joined Flo and Ali at a safe distance. At Parker's nod, the pack closed the circle to stand shoulder-by-shoulder. He placed the statue by his feet, arranged four lit candles around the Collective, and chanted the words Waylon had given me.

The firework I'd expected didn't happen.

I squinted through the darkness at the Collective. Maybe I should have asked Parker *before* the ceremony what to expect. Or had I got something wrong? A mistake could get him hurt. My stomach dropped. Not on my watch. I shot forward.

"Look." Flo yanked me back.

CHAPTER TWENTY-FIVE

The atmosphere sizzled. Parker's body rose into the air. He hovered three feet above the statue, his head tilted back, arms wide. *"Ephemera-shilami, hear me, spirits."*

His mouth didn't move, but his voice echoed inside my head, as clear as if he were speaking the words. A wisp of a cloud formed over the Collective, curling up like mist in the morning sun.

This wasn't mist, though. A chill penetrated my flesh and latched onto my bones. Screams sliced through our shocked silence. My heart galloped as if to get away. A smoky tendril arched from the statue's tip, lifting into the ether, and whisked into oblivion by a gust of wind. Another scream melded into the first. One, two, then tens and hundreds of auras, the last remnants of the victims' souls, floated into the sky. Their volume combined into a vortex, looming high with Parker hovering in its center.

I reached for Flo's hand. How many people had died for this tool? Their souls reduced to fuel so demons and other kin might open portals into Alethia.

My back snapped straight. At the same instant, the wolves opposite me tensed, paralyzed by some force. Parker's aura connected to my power source.

Not just mine.

The force he drew from us streamed into him. Auras of all colors twisted around his red plume, propelling it upward and outward. White lashings of energy shot from his eyes, guiding the souls to a place where they might find peace.

Their connection to us was a gift. Their lives and ours had never crossed, yet they handed us slivers of their souls to keep with us. A warning. A memory. A plea not to let them be forgotten.

My tongue stuck to the inside of my mouth, as if I'd been yelling, but the ache was locked up inside, impaled on a thousand spears whose tips pierced my guts.

With a *whoosh,* the vortex collapsed into an unnatural stillness. Even the leaves on the bulky tree in the corner of my yard no longer rustled. All the souls had left. The Collective was empty. I glanced at the faces in the circle.

Oh no. Apart from me, everyone kneeled, holding their stomachs.

My heart thumped. "Flo?" I placed my hand on his shoulder.

He blinked up through a curtain of tears. "Hell, that hurts."

I clutched him to my chest. Why wasn't I hurting? Or Parker?

My gaze scooted to my right and my lungs iced over. Parker! His face distorted, worse than it had in the ceremonial chamber. Why didn't I feel any pain?

I dashed forward, leaped over the guards, and instantly collapsed on the other side. My belly was on fire, my stomach acid was molten lava flowing into my limbs. I rolled on the floor, pushing my fists into my belly to quench the flames.

Sweat on his forehead, Parker leaned over me, mouthing something. "...to me. Can you hear me?" His voice shook with worry.

The pain was gone. Just gone. I reached up and wiped his frowning face. "I'm good. I think."

The lines on his forehead smoothed. "You shouldn't have come in here. I was trying to keep the pain from you."

I punched his shoulder playfully. "Stop protecting me. I'm not made of sugar and spice, you know?"

He pulled me up with one hand, and the momentum propelled me into his arms.

I hugged him. "As long as you're okay."

His breath skipped across my skin, releasing tiny tingles inside me. "I'm good."

I freed myself and turned to the others. Everyone was up and standing again. How would Florian and Ali explain away this strange ceremony to the other wolves?

"At least it's over, right?" Parker draped his arm over my shoulder. "One less thing to worry about."

"I guess. And honestly, right now I just want to..." A jagged breath. "I'm tired."

"You can't leave." His voice quaked.

Was he kidding? This had been a day of pain, and I needed a break. "Why not?"

"The party. We're meant to celebrate."

My shoulders sagged. Too tired to argue, I deposited the guards in my living room and joined him and the pack on their way to the mansion. The gravel crunched under thirty-five pairs of feet, excited voices discussing the spectacle we'd witnessed.

Ali nudged me. "I'll field their questions. You should have some food and take a break."

I smiled. "Thanks. I owe you."

Parker drew me close, his arm once again wrapped around me. "One hour. Then we're allowed to withdraw from the party. You know, to talk about couple stuff. They'll be well on their way to getting drunk by then anyway."

I placed my head against his shoulder, even though my grateful gesture made walking difficult. Yet his nearness soothed my grief for the tortured souls. "Don't expect sparkling conversation from me."

He chuckled. "I never do."

Well, the wolves knew how to party. Alcohol flowed, the delicious food tempted even me, and I didn't hate not being knee-deep in danger for a short while.

As Parker had promised, within an hour we got to sneak away to his office. As soon as the door closed, we slid out of the togas we'd worn over our regular clothing.

I sat on his sofa, and he rolled up his chair.

"How exactly does this work now?" I asked.

Every one of his breaths seared into my consciousness. Every shift of his head made my heart give an extra beat. His proximity had never had that kind of effect on me before. At least not while I wore my necklace.

"How does what work?" He raised his eyebrows.

"This. Us." I licked my lips. "Do we now pretend to have sex or something?"

He straightened. "Definitely not. We're not bonded yet, Ivy."

Relief and disappointment zapped through me. "Okay. Good." *I think.*

He lifted his feet onto the sofa, next to me. "Our time during intention is about getting to know each other. Sex can be part of it, but it's not a component of the tradition. Quite the opposite. The time right after the ceremony is typically a time to relax, talk, confide our secrets."

I glanced down. "I believe we aired most of our dirty laundry in the ceremonial chamber, didn't we?" Oh no. My gaze shot back up. "I'm sorry. I know we're not supposed to talk about it."

He chuckled. "Actually, you and I may. Just not with outsiders. I finally get why. If anyone had conveyed to me just how intense it would get in there, I'm not sure I'd have been so willing to go through with it."

"You had to." A bitter twang coated my voice. "To destroy the Collective."

"Yeah, right." But his eyes twinkled. "The Collective."

I woke in my own bed. I was engaged. Kind of. My stomach melted from confusion and the warm memories of the ceremony. After my chat with Parker, I'd gone home and dropped into bed, too exhausted to have nightmares. Even now I struggled to get back my energy. Instead, I watched TV, read a thriller Flo had lent me months ago, and did nothing else. Everybody gave me the space I needed, which I appreciated in a huffy sort of way.

In the afternoon, I drove out to the shops. My fridge was running out of stuff that wasn't past its use-by date, and I was running out of potato chips.

At eight in the evening, just as my headache returned with a vengeance, alone-time was up.

My doorbell rang. Florian, legs crossed and one arm resting against the house wall, stuck his wrist, or rather the watch on his wrist, into my face.

"Stop that." I swatted his arm away.

He only pulled out the big guns—his dark green shirt which set off his auburn hair perfectly, and low-rise slacks—on special occasions. His deceptively casual chic was a calculated first step to his seduction routine. In his mind, no woman would be safe from him in this getup. He'd probably spent a couple of hours in the bathroom, using more product in one session than I'd possessed in my life. Why he bothered was beyond me. He'd look yummy in a potato sack.

I gave him a quick hug, which also happened to soothe my throbbing head, then shot off into the living room, trusting him to follow.

He hawed. "That's what you're going to wear to the club?"

Work had been the last thing on my mind. But I had promised, or perhaps even initiated, a visit to Club Abraxas.

I looked down at myself. "Perhaps I'll get out of the sweatpants. But what's wrong with my T-shirt?" Despite my best attempt to sound confrontational, a smirk leaked through.

"Um, the stains? But you know what? Your call. Far be it from me to comment on the vagaries of female fashion."

"That would be a first." I heaved an exaggerated sigh. "Give me ten minutes." I trudged off to my closet, leaving him to get comfy on the sofa.

"Take fifteen," he shouted. "Trust me, it'll be time well spent."

The red dress I'd got from my mother was just as clingy as the black one I'd worn for my date with Waylon, and the right amount of slutty for a club. Who'd have thought I'd wear another dress so soon? I slipped on a pair of navy stilettos to go with the dress. The guard belt remained looped around my jeans. As clueless as I was, even I knew a narrow belt around a dress was a fashion no-no. Not that I was defenseless. The tiny guards on my charm bracelet packed more punch than their size would suggest.

A couple of minutes with Julia's foundation, concealer and a quick slash of red lipstick to draw the eye away from the bits I couldn't cover, and I was good to go.

I stepped into the living room and gave a twirl. "So?"

Florian looked me up and down. "I'd have you."

"Out of your league, buddy." But he'd coaxed a grin out of me. "Now stop ogling your boss and let's get going." I slapped my jacket pocket to double check I'd packed my camera. Yup. All set for a night of spying.

I locked the door and turned. Parker and two of his men had gathered by my car, somber expressions on their faces.

The road leading past my house was exceptionally quiet for a Thursday evening. Usually at this time, a steady flow of through-traffic filed past to avoid the sweeper trucks that made Silverton sparkle in preparation for a new influx of weekend visitors.

Parker smiled. "You look lovely."

My pulse jigged. "You mean despite my bruises, fat lip and puffy eyes?"

The twitch of his mouth was the only sign of his displeasure. "Can I talk to you?"

"Sure." Oh no. What had I done wrong now? With squared shoulders, I joined him around the corner. "What is it?"

"I didn't want to press it last night, but I need to know about what I felt in you yesterday. Your ancestry. Something tasted like siren or, I don't know, something…seductive. And I don't mean the satyr."

"Leanan sidhe," I whispered.

Parker bobbed his head. "Makes sense. God, what a treat. I mean, the races in your background zipped through my head too fast to keep count. Right at the core, though, this ball of raw essence slammed into me. A sphere of incredible, demonic power." He lifted my chin so my eyes locked with his. "Brather demon, right?"

I nodded slowly. He gave a toothy whistle.

I shifted. At least the truth was out. "My mother's father was a brather demon."

"So he was a Guardian." He picked a strand of hair from my

face. "And if he and then your parents were Guardians, I assume Waylon is one, too?"

I wet my lips. "Don't ask me questions about who or what my friends are."

A shadow flitted over his face. "Friend? He was more than that to you. He hurt you." He hooked his fingers into the nape of my neck. "And we should also talk about Greg."

I closed my eyes. "God, I hate that you saw that." I lifted my hands. "Hey. I know this is messed up, what with the ceremony and your pack and my relationship with Greg. And we'll have to come to some sort of arrangement. But don't forget Carmel was generous with the dirt on you. I know about that vanilla ice-cream obsession of yours. Plus, I caught a few of your memories during the ritual, too. There was that time when you hoped to lose your virgin—"

His hand clasped over my mouth. "Don't spoil our relationship so soon."

I laughed. "You fdarded id." I bit into his hand to free my head. "You started it."

He smirked. "Fair enough."

We rejoined his friends, the grin still etched into my cheeks. "You haven't by any chance managed to convince your houseguests to share their feelings yet?"

"As you may recall, yesterday was a busy day. Rollo's on it now."

"Rollo?" I furrowed my brows. "That's the blond surfer dude who grunts a lot, right?"

The three werewolves laughed. A sparkly-eyed, hulky black guy flicked something off his well-worn motorcycle jacket. "He's a boy of few words—at least not ones oldies like us are familiar with."

"Far be it for me to put my nose in your business." I made a point not to react to Parker's cough. "But is a teenager equipped for interrogation? The guy in the basement guarding them struck me more as the kind of person who'd relish a spot of violence. You should let him loose on them."

"Grant had good things to say about you, too." Parker's tone sharpened.

A fistful of guilt punched a right hook straight into my solar plexus. I scratched my bare leg with the toes of my shoe. Had he discovered exactly how I'd secured Grant's cooperation? That I'd taken advantage of a defenseless man for my own ends? No. If he had, he'd no longer speak to me. Hell, *I'd* no longer speak to me, if that were possible.

"Don't be fooled by Rollo's appearance." The dark-skinned man who looked more like a bear than a wolf waved a hand. "He's no teenager, and a lot tougher than he looks."

I eyed him cautiously, but he seemed totally serious. Guess we'd see soon enough.

"Are you going, Parker?" The innocence in my tone probably fooled no one.

"Did you want me to?" He crossed his arms.

I shook my head. "These two will be plenty of protection, thanks."

"That's what I figured." His voice hitched.

Flo and I took his Mercedes. Our backup, the black guy and his polar opposite, a pale, lanky man with light-colored hair, had their own rides. Despite our brief head start, their motorbikes overtook us after a few minutes.

"Should we talk about yesterday?" Flo kept his gaze peeled on the road. "About me and Ali. And about you and Parker."

"What about me and Parker?"

He hawed. "How are you coping with this link you share?"

Good question. If only I had a satisfactory answer. "*Coping* describes it perfectly. It's a temporary bond. I mean, we're not going to be linked forever. And you?"

"It's confusing." He chewed his lips.

I studied my friend carefully. This new, quiet Flo seriously wigged me out.

He pulled into a spot a short hop from the large neon sign that read 'Abraxas,' and we got out. For once, the wind wasn't strong enough to ruin my hair. At least not more than nature already had when it put those waves into it. My stilettos found good footing on the parking lot's concrete surface. This club's owner clearly wanted the club experience to be a smooth one, and had even installed plenty of lighting.

Clubbing wasn't something I wasted my time with, but Abraxas's rep had penetrated even to a recluse such as me. Among a certain group of women, like those I went to school with when I was still part of Silverton's in-clique, Abraxas had become a rite of passage. A sexy, slightly dirty place you visited *ironically*.

Our werewolf backup leaned against their tricked-out bikes. With their broad shoulders and icy stares, bodybuilders wouldn't want to mess with them, which was probably why Parker picked them.

"I'm Flynn, by the way." The dark-skinned man nodded, his black cropped hair reflecting the clear moonlight in flecks of purple.

I smiled. He was the kind of guy who eventually put you at ease. Confident manner, but not smug. A voice that could sell you vacuum cleaners for your linoleum carpeting.

"That's Jim." He cocked his chin.

Flynn's partner gave a twitch.

"We'll scope the place out. Give us five minutes." Flynn unfolded his arms and set off. They walked across the parking lot, their gait as wide as their shoulders.

I snuggled up to Florian. "Remember when I asked you to give me a lift to the Carter's home for a routine pickup? That favor has spiraled out of control, hasn't it?"

He chuckled. "Just a little. Ali says Parker thought you'd be trouble the first time he spotted you. Wish I had such a good nose for problem-makers."

"You regret becoming friends with me? 'cos that ship has sailed. You aren't getting rid of me quite so easily."

"Does that mean you're not moving?"

"Oh." A rush of heat flooded my body. I peered up. "How did you find out about that?"

"How did I find out about your not-so-furtive conversations with your attorneys? The crinkled photo of your dream house fell out of your pocket the other day. It actually says *dream house* on the back."

"You never mentioned it."

"No, *you* never mentioned it." He gathered me closer. "When are you leaving?"

"My trust fund just cleared." I stepped back and clawed into his sleeves. "I still need new ID and stuff. But you know I'm not trying to get away from you, don't you? I don't want Lathan to find me, that's all."

"I get it. I may not *like* it, but I get it." His voice was tinged with sadness. "What about us?"

I swallowed hard. "We'll see each other all the time. Don't worry. Let's talk about this later. I'm not going anywhere *today*. Besides. What I really want to talk about is you and Ali."

"Don't be silly."

"You two are getting on really well."

He shrugged. "Well, yes. He's a good guy. We have a lot in common. But he knows that nothing's going to happen."

I pursed my lip. Flo might have assured Ali that he wouldn't get involved with him, but something about my best friend told me there was something he was keeping even secret from himself. But Flo couldn't be forced. He'd talk when he was ready.

I gripped his wrist and checked his watch. "We should go."

He sighed. "Okay. We'll make it work."

The club's up-market image continued inside. The generously sized building was fitted with glass and mirrors from floor to ceiling. My heels clacked against the entrance landing, which overlooked a spiral of black and chrome tables and chairs facing the main stage. Spotlights focused on four women in various stages of undress who dangled from or writhed against metal poles, transfixed in artificial ecstasy.

The movements of the ladies on stage were too charged, their bodies too perfect, to be merely human. I blinked, but my kin-o-meter came up with the same result. What in the name of all that was holy were succubae doing here?

Mind buzzing, I followed Florian down the glass stairs into the large pit that served as the main floor.

Flynn and Jim passed us on the way. Flynn pretended to bump into me. During his long apology, he leaned in. "Everything's looking good."

"Or not." I subtly jerked my head to the stage. "Succubae."

He lifted his brows. "Crap."

Succubae fed off emotions and life force during climax, and stopping midway to Jollytown out of consideration for their partner simply didn't happen. You'd have more success telling a tree to stop making oxygen.

Dance music blared, putting a lilt even in my step. Florian led me to an empty table near the back. "Did you say succubae?"

"Good ears."

"Holy shit."

My lips twitched into a wry smile. "Well said."

"I thought they only existed in Alethia nowadays. What are they doing here?"

Since when had I become the go-to person on kin issues? "Perhaps they're doing an internship."

He rolled his eyes and pulled out a chair for me.

A shiny, black bar stretched along the side. Behind it, five human women in low-cut white dresses fixed drinks for thirsty patrons. Another four waitresses tended tables, their bras and panties visible under the black light. Sexy, not tawdry.

At first sight, Abraxas catered to men. However, a small number of women had accompanied their partners, or perhaps come for carnal reasons of their own, and nobody looked at me with suspicion.

Florian went off to get us our drinks, and I cast a more discerning eye over the clientele. Our location wasn't ideal. Not only was our table quite dark so far away from the stage, I also had to be discreet in how I held my camera. With any luck, Heidi could later pinpoint the man she'd seen with Heather, but that would only work if I didn't get chucked out of the bar.

My plan wasn't without its problems, admittedly.

I set the camera on *film* and pivoted it to capture the whole room, keeping it cupped by my hand.

Odds were, the additional services that were offered in the back rooms were enough to get the police interested. Would a manager prove cooperative if we threatened him with the cops? Or with the IEA? Because if the succubae also entertained human men, Abraxas was a dangerous place. Satyrs or demons might find a brief tryst with that particular species rewarding, but for humans, intercourse was most likely fatal.

Florian returned with the drinks.

"Thanks." I pressed the camera into his fidgety hands. "Take this. I have to go to the little girl's room."

The privacy of the toilets was perfect for striking up a conversation.

Unfortunately, the women who visited the bathroom didn't feel talkative. After fifteen minutes, I washed my hands and left. The poppy tune, perhaps the same as earlier, perhaps not, pulsed inside my head. A middle-aged fae counted cents and dollars out on the counter. The bar lady smiled at me.

My gaze slid to the door behind her. That *Private* sign was just begging for trouble. I waited for her and the man to finish their transaction and sashayed up to it. It wasn't locked. I slipped through the door into a wide corridor and tip-toed across the smooth floor. After I'd passed an assortment of paintings, I peeked around the corner into another corridor. Crap. A security camera.

So far, my visit to the club had been a bust, but what better opportunity to try out the invisibility guard I'd ripped off the demon's ankle? The spell came to me as if I'd been using it for years. As soon as the guard activated, my muscles tensed. Skin magic wasn't unlike giving blood. Within twenty minutes or so, the sucking and draining on my reserves would leave my legs wobbly, my emotions damped, and my head light. So I was on a clock.

The guard that converted my energy into magic tickled my skin. I crept up the corridor checking the names on the office doors.

My breath caught. Gregory Owen Davies. *My* Greg? He'd mentioned his work at a bar, but I hadn't expected it to be *this* bar. On second thought, this may not even be *my* Greg Davies. I traced the letters on the metal rectangle with my finger, from the G to the Owen. *Oh no.*

I crumpled against the wall. A biting chill uncoiled from my core and spread into my fingers and feet.

G. O. D.

I ran through our conversations, questioned every word and phrase. Parker and I had been so concerned Greg might be in league with Lathan, the idea *my* Greg could have sent the demons after the Collective never occurred to us. Why would it? Greg was human. Had I missed the signs? Was he kin after all?

The rumble of my invisibility guard snapped my attention back to the freezing corridor. Whatever happened, my emotions had better not run away from me. The guard would gobble them up in an instant. *Now, breathe.* I shook my limbs and the noise faded.

I'd suspected Greg once before and had to eat sour grapes. This time, I'd get my facts straight.

I listened at the door and let myself into a small office. The room was stuffed with paperwork, everything neatly filed and labeled. The correspondence in the in-tray provided no evidence one way or another. By all accounts, the Greg who worked here was a simple and honest businessman.

So far so good.

Footsteps approached, and I froze. They stopped outside the door, and the doorknob turned. I shot glances to my left and right, then ducked behind the desk, not quite accepting the fact I was invisible.

"When's the next shipment coming in?" Greg, *my* Greg, asked in that tuneful tone of his. He dropped a packet of papers onto his desk with a thud.

My heart jumped. If he caught me, my presence, let alone my invisibility, would be hard to explain. I sidled closer to the wall.

"Tonight," a much deeper voice said. "Two of our current succubae aren't working out. They don't understand their job description, so I recommend we…terminate their employment."

I clasped my hand to my mouth. If they knew the dancers were succubae, my opinion of my almost boyfriend was in dire need of an overhaul.

Greg sighed. "We assumed turnover was going to be high. The ladies can't help themselves." His warm laughter echoed through the room. "Keep the ones we have working. They understand the cost of draining my customers. And the other two, well, sacrifice them. But make sure you don't leave a mess. We don't need the IEA sniffing around."

I clutched my knees to my chest. Where was the funny, kind Greg I was ready to fall in love with? I closed my eyes, willing my stomach to settle.

Greg sat on the desk, his legs inches from my face. "Are the human girls ready?"

"Yes. Training them took months, but the first small batch shipped out last week. They're being distributed to our venues in Alethia as we speak. The rest are at the warehouse. It'd be a lot easier if we had the Collective, of course."

Oh no. Was this what had happened to Heather? My fingers and feet went numb, either from the magic exhausting me or from the revelation that the man I'd wanted to make my lover was nothing more than a dangerous psychopath. He needed the statue to transport succubae to Oldword so he could rent them out like pieces of furniture, and to send humans to Alethia for the same sick purpose.

I breathed through my nose. No need to panic yet. Assuming he'd taken my boss's daughter was too great a leap to take without evidence.

"Don't worry about the Collective." Greg's voice still clashed with his cruel words. "It's under control. The girl, Ivy, worked out to be more difficult than we figured. She's got the local pack of werewolves in her corner." He shifted position and nearly kicked me in the face. "But the alpha made a big mistake attacking me like that. After that, she almost begged to be taken to bed." His laughter slid down my insides like pure liquid evil.

My guard's hum climbed a pitch. Greg leaned down and twisted his head, his baby-blue gaze fixed on me.

CHAPTER TWENTY-SIX

W ITH EYES I ONCE THOUGHT capable of great kindness, Greg stared through me at his office wall. My shoulders relaxed. He couldn't see me.

My blood flooded with feel-good endorphins, quieting my heartbeat and the guard on my wrist. For once, skin magic had its benefits.

"What is it, boss?" the deep voice said.

"Nothing." Greg sat back up. "We thought we heard something."

I frowned. Who was *we*?

The other man walked to where I sat, his demon aura connecting with me through my invisibility cloak. "I can check it out, if you want. Maybe a faulty line running along there?"

"Leave it, Joe. We've got work to do. We're behind schedule already."

"We haven't been able to find a good work-around without the Collective. One dead succubae powers the transport of five or six human slaves to Alethia, but shipping magical species to Silverton takes more sacrifices than we have. One dead human only allows three, four parcels each. We've had to up the death count. The local paper's already talking about the rise in crime, and at some point, the IEA is going to get suspicious too."

"Once we have *her*, we'll have the Collective."

"Wouldn't it be easier to kill the girl and take the Collective from her?"

"We tried that once." Greg tapped his foot. "But how many demons have we sent to fetch the damn thing now? And after all our efforts, who still has the Collective?"

"The girl."

"That's right. We need to get her alone, without her backup. If our mind control hadn't rolled off her, we wouldn't have had to go through this charade. We're beginning to think there might be more to her than meets the eye. She has a certain appeal." Greg laughed quietly. "Once we're done with her, she'll probably fetch top dollar. I hear someone called Lathan might be interested in her."

My mouth went dry.

"You want to deal with the demon kinlord? He doesn't work with people he doesn't know."

"I don't care who he is. In the end, kinlords are just businessmen you told me, aren't they?" Greg lifted his arms in an off-hand gesture. "But hey, if he doesn't want her, there are plenty who will."

So that's why Parker hadn't discovered a lie when he'd interrogated Greg. Greg had genuinely never heard of Lathan. Perhaps we should have asked more questions.

Crap. If I hadn't stopped Parker, he would have. I was such an idiot.

"What about the old guy?" Joe asked.

A rush of ice flooded my veins. Not…not Fred? No. Once again I was jumping to conclusions. There was no evidence. I forced my pulse to slow.

"I don't care." For the first time, Greg's smooth tone slipped. "He still has a few years of labor in him, so ship him out with the girls."

"Teaches him to snoop, doesn't it?"

Both men laughed.

Greg had Fred. My insides spun. I'd thought I could spot a dangerous lunatic a mile off, but somewhere I'd failed.

I brushed at a fly. No, not a fly. The bead on my bracelet vibrated again. I blocked out the men's conversation. That damn guard was going to give me away.

How had a human set up this kind of business anyway, bossing strong, powerful demons about without breaking a sweat? Waylon hadn't mentioned humans could have superhuman strength. Or had he? Did Greg share his body with a djinn?

He *did* refer to himself as *we*. Plus, it would explain why I didn't get a kin vibe off him.

"Come on. We should inspect our goods." Greg got to his feet and headed out the office, followed by Joe. "Is it two or three new succubae today?"

Their voices trailed off. I leaned my head against the wall, ready to nod off. As much as the magic numbed my mind, it also numbed my flesh. I pushed through the fatigue and got up.

The empty corridor floated past me, the paintings mere dots of color now. I opened the door to the bar, and the swell of music slammed into me. My feet moved with the rhythm, but my will held strong. I wouldn't give in to skin magic's seduction.

The stalls in the ladies' bathroom were free. I slipped inside the one in the center and deactivated the invisibility guard. The walls contracted and expanded. My eyes' lines of vision crossed and uncrossed until, inch by inch, I became aware of my body again. What a bitch of a high. Shakes racked my body, sweat ran slick under my arms, my chest, even along the back of my knees.

I cleaned myself up with toilet paper and water. At least Julia's makeup hadn't smeared. Once I was happy with my composure, I returned to our table.

"Where have you been?" Flo's superficially innocent smile contradicted his panicked tone.

"Tell you later. We'd better go. Right now."

He had trouble keeping up with me. Heels or not, I needed air fast. Fresh air. Clean air. With as much dignity as I could muster, I stalked back to the car. My hands and arms trembled. How had Greg fooled me? Why hadn't I seen his rotten center?

"Well?" Florian crossed his arm. "What sort of trouble did you get yourself into this time?"

I peered into the eyes of my friend. My vampire friend who'd killed nearly as many men in a couple of weeks as Bruce Willis had in the course of his film career. My stomach pushed bile into my mouth. Now I'd puke all over my fancy shoes. Swell.

"Hey. You're pale." He placed his hand on my back.

His touch soothed me, but not enough.

He dropped his voice. "What happened?"

I rolled up, getting ready to empty my stomach, but only brought out heavy, raspy breaths. *No puke. Well, who said tonight was a complete disaster?* I straightened, and massaged my tummy. "Turns out, I've been dating God." My attempt to smile failed. My top lip simply trembled too damn much.

"What? Parker's God?" Florian's frown stood pale against the darkness. "That makes no sense."

"Parker? Why would you…? No, dumbo." I whacked his arm. "Greg."

"Are you sure? Isn't he human?"

"Heard it from his mouth. He was dating me to get to the Collective." My insides were at it again. I hummed into my whirling stomach to keep the acid down. "He also has Fred." I fell against his Mercedes. The alarm gave pulsating wails, and the car's headlights flashed.

Flo pressed the button on his fob to stop the noise.

"How could I be so blind?" I stared at my friend. "I mean it. Why didn't I see it?"

"I don't know." He came up beside me. "But it's no biggie. I mean, who among us hasn't accidentally dated a lunatic psychopath?"

"This isn't funny."

He tilted his head. "It's a little bit funny."

"Fred's about to be shipped off to Alethia, to be put to work like I was. Where exactly are the giggles?"

He raised his hands. "You're right. That bit isn't funny. I'm sorry."

The trample of heavy boots approached. Flynn and Jim's scowl suited their leather getup.

"Are you all right?" Flynn asked. "You left without telling us. Parker's not going to like that."

Since when were my actions anyone's business but my own? Was that the side-effect of my new relationship with Parker?

That couldn't happen. After Lathan, I resolved to never again give up my freedom, or the right to make my own decisions. Desperation clawed on my insides. I'd be no one's property, and I would not be treated like my opinion or wishes didn't matter.

"I'm fine." I tore open the car door and got in.

Once home, I slammed the front door shut behind me and rushed past my coat rack toward the kitchen. I needed…something. My pulse pumped through my veins as if trying to keep up with my mind. How could I rescue Fred? Trap Greg and beat him into submission?

Parker, Ali and another wolf sat in my living room, chatting. I held onto the wall. How had a stranger made it into my living room? I touched one of my guards, which hummed its protective tune, undisturbed.

Parker shot me an infuriating grin. "Turns out I can invite people into your house. It's like I own it."

The evening was getting better and better.

Flynn and Jim knocked on the open door to the yard. Flo's face peeked over their shoulders.

"Come in, guys." Parker waved. "How did it go?"

They looked at each other before their gazes drifted to me.

"What happened?" Parker's tone cut into the silence.

I set my jaw tight. Coffee. A big bucketful might shake me out of this nightmare. The last thing I was ready for tonight was his smug face when he learned of Greg's true identity. I wheeled around and disappeared into the kitchen.

"Well, it turns out there was another twist, in a manner of speaking." Florian sounded uncertain.

"Oh God, what did she do now?"

I stormed back in. "Stop it. I did nothing, and nothing about this is funny."

"What?" Parker's eyes widened. "I don't even know what this is about."

Why did I still want to throw myself into his arms? I clenched my fists and straightened my neck. "Greg's the guy who sent the demons. He needs the Collective to ship slaves to Alethia. Slaves like Fred."

"Greg? That guy?" Parker scratched his forehead. "A criminal mastermind? I don't know. We questioned him."

"We asked him if he knew Lathan or had placed the Gallom in my house. Turns out, he was innocent on both counts." I swallowed. "Just about the only things he wasn't responsible for."

"We couldn't have known to ask anything else."

I peered up and knew at once he was only trying to make me feel better. Because I was the one who'd stopped him from digging deeper.

"And Greg has somehow organized a bunch of demons?" He frowned. "How?"

"A djinn is riding him, I think. It's the only explanation for how he can control demons." I shook my head as if not believing my own explanation.

"Hell. I had no idea that was even possible." He held his chin in his palm. "A djinn, eh?" He scowled. "You're not going to do anything stupid, are you? If he has an organization that can pull off that kind of smuggling, he's far too big for you."

"Me? Yeah, this is not a battle I'll take on myself." The whirlwind inside calmed, and with it my voice. "As I said, he's possessed by a djinn. So you guys plan whatever it is you plan. I promise I won't step out of line."

He let out a deep breath. "Good. Glad to see you're learning."

I narrowed my eyes. "Don't patronize me."

"I'm not trying to. But you tend to be careless about your safety. Anyway. Now that the Collective's harmless, we'll make them steal it from somewhere we can control, and we can go back to our lives. I mean, if it turns out the statue isn't a working portal-opener, well, that's hardly your fault, is it?"

"Maybe." I studied his self-assured posture. "But what about Fred, and those girls they're smuggling?"

Flo raised his hand. "Eli works for the IEA. I'm sure they'll take care of it for us."

"Will they?" I smoothed my hands over my hair and clasped them on top of my head. "Nothing I've heard about them has given me the impression they'll be on our side. And since Greg's smuggling pliable human slaves into Alethia, the kinlords might not be happy if the IEA shut off their supply."

"Perhaps not," Parker said. "But we'll talk to them. It's not your problem anymore."

I snapped my hands to my side. "Greg *made* it my problem. And sending demons after Florian and me is not something I accept. If you know me at all you understand I can't just cool my heels. Is this how you'd react if he'd taken your sister instead of my boss? Would you act then, or run with your tail between your legs?"

He clamped his nose between steepled hands, his chest moving in a long exhalation. "Ivy, we're out of options. The safety of my pack comes first. Always. That now includes you and Florian. Besides, getting yourself killed won't help your friend."

"I hate to agree with him." Florian reached for my arm.

I snatched it away. "Then don't."

"Ivy." He raised his shoulders like a man out of ideas. "We'll gather information, keep an eye on Greg. We need to learn more about him first. Maybe we'll come up with a plan."

The wind that blew through the open doors clung to my bare legs, my neck, covering my skin in the kind of cold that penetrated into your blood. I slid down the wall as if in a trance and clawed my fingers into the short-loop carpet. "If Fred can't work, they'll kill him. In any event, he'll be in Alethia, out of my reach."

My friend crouched by my side and rubbed my shoulders, but the chill refused to leave my bones. "I'm sorry." He cocked his jaw, giving the wolves the signal to leave.

Parker growled. "Listen. If we think of something, I'll let you know. Okay? But you're going to stay put. I'm not kidding."

They filed out the door. He glanced over his shoulder.

I whipped my face away. Not to be ungrateful for what he'd done for me, but his support had always been on his terms. Maybe this was my own fault. I'd assumed he was a good guy, but good guys didn't leave old men and young women to be tortured and enslaved in Alethia. Hell, what made me think a werewolf, any kin, would give a crap about anyone?

"Do you want me to stay?" Flo asked.

I peered into his dark eyes. My best friend, and he let the wolf bulldoze over me. If he'd stood by my side, demanded Parker's intervention, we could have convinced him.

I swallowed the biting remark on my tongue. "No. I want to be alone."

"Okay then." He patted my arm. "But if you need anything, I'm only a phone call away."

He walked off as if the adventure was over.

My time in Alethia haunted me. But while I'd been safe since my return, other girls had been plunged into a similar situation. All those months, I hadn't lifted a finger to help Fred find his daughter. If I'd investigated sooner, we could have uncovered a way to find her. Busted open Greg's smuggling operation. And Fred wouldn't have had a reason to go off snooping, and he wouldn't now be facing slavery.

So fuck Parker, fuck Florian, and fuck everyone who thought this wasn't my business.

I bit my lip. For all Waylon's faults, he didn't coddle me. And helping others was his job, his vocation. But I was under no illusions. Asking a demon, especially this demon, for help would come at a cost. Was I ready to pay the price he'd demand?

I pulled the crumpled photo from my jacket pocket.

Up on the balcony overlooking the sea, I would kick back with a bottle of wine, watch the ocean waves crash against the shore. My house, my freedom, had been my dream for many years. A hopeful light on my darkest days. But like all dreams, it didn't stand the test of reality. My throat tightened as I crawled to the fireplace. One click of the lighter, and a hungry heat blackened the photo's edges. Pixel by pixel, the flame devoured my dream and melted it into a heap of ash.

Fred's life came first.

CHAPTER TWENTY-SEVEN

I SWITCHED ON THE BEDROOM LIGHTS, my heart heavy and close to crumbling. The alarm clock on my nightstand said it was nearly ten. Not that late, but the last two days had drained me to within an inch of my life. My orange blanket invited my limbs to rest, but if I lay down now, I'd drift off. Who knew if my nerves would hold into the morning? I reached for the touchstone and spoke the incantation.

Waylon's face hid in shadows. Only his green eyes shone through with any kind of intensity. I shuddered.

Typical. First his presence drove me insane, now his absence did pretty much the same.

I gave a casual wave. "Am I interrupting?"

"Catching some z's." He yanked something off to his side, and the lights popped on.

God, his bed hair was so sexy. Never mind that. I gave him the lowdown.

"I've only been gone a couple of days, and you're already so deep in shit you could fertilize the whole of Nebraska." He screwed his face into a grimace.

"You do say the nicest things."

"You let an alpha declare his intention on you? Have you lost your fucking mind? I told you I'd come to help. You didn't have to do that."

Was this hurt in his voice? "Not that it's any of your business, but Parker and I will be dissolving the connection in a few months' time."

"Why not now?"

"I think he doesn't want the pack to know the ceremony was staged for the sole purpose of deactivating the Collective."

His lips twitched. "As long as he hasn't developed feelings for you. If he has, this is going to get messy."

"No need to worry about that." I flicked my hand. If anyone was in danger of developing inappropriate feelings, it was me. Parker knew better. My stomach fluttered. Or did he? "Anyways, not that

I don't enjoy this jealousy of yours, but I called because I have a proposition for you."

"You do?" That kissable mouth morphed into a smiling kissable mouth. "Tell me more."

A lungful of oxygen cemented my resolve. "Do you still want me to become a Guardian?"

"Hell, yes."

"Then help me get my boss back. You do that for me, I'll let you train me." I lowered my voice. "You no longer have to be alone."

He licked his lips. "Are we talking about the training, or have you forgiven me?"

"For dumping me?"

He frowned. "Hang on. I did the opposite. I asked you to come away with me. How is that dumping you?"

As if rationality had ever won arguments. Besides, that's not how it had sounded at the time. I primmed my lips. "To save us a fight, let's agree you did dump me. And yes, I might forgive you." Because the moment he'd come near me, my satyr hormones would sabotage my efforts to stay clear anyway.

His face went through a hundred emotions and then settled on something akin to resignation. "You got yourself a deal."

I rolled my shoulders to release the tension in my neck. Waylon had my back. "How soon can you get here?"

"This group I've tracked to New Orleans is gearing up to a mass sacrifice to break their friends out of Alethia. But I'm close to a location, so I should be able to wrap up my shit here in a couple of weeks."

My lungs trembled. "A couple of weeks? I need you now."

"I get that, babe. But the world only has one Guardian. What do you want me to do?"

As unreasonable as it was, I didn't care about the rest of the world. Only one person mattered. Fred. I pushed all my emotion into my gaze. "Help me."

"Ivy." He closed his eyes.

Okay, so I knew his work was important. But so was my boss. "What if I took on Greg? You said yourself, I have Guardian genes."

"You?" He shook his head. "You're not there yet."

"I'm *good* with guards. Just tell me. How do I counter a djinn's magic?"

"That's the easy part. By themselves, djinn-ridden people are just people, but they use mind magic. They will inflict unspeakable pain on their minions, usually kin who are powerful in their own right, until they have no choice but to obey. As a Guardian, you're immune to the mind magic, but not against their minions."

My posture relaxed. "If he's a normal guy, how hard can it be?"

He bunched his mouth. "Were you not listening? His crew can kill you sixty different ways."

"Waylon, I would never forgive myself if Fred dies."

His gaze flicked to the side and back to me. "Shit. Okay." He rolled his eyes up. "The things you make me do, Ivy, I swear." His jaw set hard. "Give me a couple of days to prepare things over here, and I'll be with you."

A smidgen of guilt nudged my stomach. Perhaps my demands were too high, but right now, Fred's safety was paramount. And a couple of days might be soon enough. By destroying the Collective, we'd cut off Greg's shipping method. For now, Fred would stay put. My lungs expanded for a deep inhalation. "Thank you."

"You're welcome, babe." His gentle tone startled me. I peered up, but his face was back to being blank. "There are some things you can do to prepare." His instructions didn't faze me. "Just sit tight."

"Well, I'm not going to do anything stupid."

"If only I could believe that." He rubbed his temple. "You run into these things blindly."

I shot him a buck-up smile. "I'll be good."

The spray from my shower pelted my skin, drumming new life into me.

My entire relationship with Greg had been a setup from the get-go, every kiss and touch a lie. He made me spill the coffee over him, then he crushed my confidence by blowing me off. When he finally showed an interest, I lapped up his attention like a love-starved puppy.

Shame he never met Lathan. Kindred spirits through and through.

Everything would work out, though. Waylon would be back in time. He had to be. Because if not, I'd probably do exactly the stupid thing Parker always feared I'd do.

I tossed the towel into the corner of my bedroom. Waylon had shown more support than Parker and Flo combined, at least in this respect. When it was someone else's skin on the line, they were nowhere to be seen. Although a tad rough around the edges, Waylon at least understood priorities. He'd shown his trust by tasking me with preparing the guard we were going to use to ship Greg off to Alethia.

I picked up a cool piece of metal from my supply, about the size of a coin, and got to work. Twenty minutes later, I was done. Child's play. The finished plate took an empty spot on my belt. For good measure, I made a second one for my bracelet. A third one ended up in my drawer. Waylon made one hell of a teacher. With the right instructions, weaving guards was a cinch.

Once done, my inner ant was on the move again. Idling wasn't in my repertoire.

My years as a private investigator had equipped me with certain skills. For example, I knew how to find people who didn't want to be found. Today I was looking for properties, but the principles were the same. If Fred was held in a warehouse, chances were the building was in Greg's name.

George Davies, Grimbold Davies... No ownership in the name of Greg or Gregory Davies.

Owen Davies, on the other hand, was the registered owner of several plots of land in and around Silverton. I compared the details with a map. No luck in the warehouse district, but he did own three large estates on opposite sides of town. No way was I going to hurl myself into danger. I mean, I hadn't suddenly turned bimbo. That said, it wouldn't hurt to drive by to determine which of these, if any, was where they kept Fred.

A warm sweater and my camera, and I was ready to go. The dark orange of dusk settled across the sky, and a breeze fluffed my hair. I dropped by Florian's to see if he was up for a spy mission. My knock got no answer, and I called his cell. Nada. Here I was being open-book about my plans, and he'd disappeared without telling me. Chances were, he was with Parker and Ali. I pouted. If Flo preferred hanging out with his new friends to hanging with me, good luck to him.

For the first address, the GPS directed me from the smooth surface of the main road onto a bumpy dirt lane. Pinkish-brown dust swirled in my headlights, and the silhouette of a building rose at the end. If I got too close, the sound of my engine might attract attention, so I parked off-road and covered the remaining distance on foot. Something fluttered above me, a bat or an owl, perhaps. I scowled into the sky. *You'd better not give away my position.*

Across the field of stubby wheat stalks lay an old farmhouse built entirely from wood. I hid behind the wide trunk of a tree and scouted the area.

When I was sure no one was around, I scooted from the tree to an old army-style truck. Behind the farmhouse, a barn stretched a good way into the darkness. Light scattered through the grimy windows, attracting moths and other flying critters. Now might be a good time to have Florian by my side. But even if I got hold of him, he'd probably tattle to Parker, and Parker would shout at me again. Besides, I didn't need anyone's permission. Soon, I was going to be a Guardian, helping Waylon go up against The Circle. Time to grow a pair.

Yet my feet didn't move. Maybe I should place an anonymous tip to the police department, and have them check it out.

I shook my head. Telling the cops would be too premature. I didn't even know if Fred was here. Besides, evil supernatural crime lords weren't really on their agenda.

And if I was going to help Waylon defeat Greg, I needed a definite location, and for that I needed proof. I took one last deep breath, put up my hood, and climbed onto one of six barrels deposited below the window for a view inside.

The rear third of the barn was obscured by a plastic sheet. Metal guards on tripods circled an area in the center of the sand-dusted stone slabs, not unlike the setup I'd used for the spell that destroyed the Collective. It took no expert to determine the guards in the barn were of inferior quality. Mass produced by some fae in Oldworld hoping to make a quick buck. Not suitable for whatever they had in mind here.

The white sheet stirred, and Greg stepped into the light. No doubt. This was the right place. He gestured at Joe, who followed at his heels. In his hand, he carried—

No way. I squinted. Yup, he was holding the Collective. Parker had intended to get the blasted thing to the demons one way or the other, but I hadn't expected him to do it quite so soon. Joe entered the circle of guards and placed the statue on the ground.

Good thing the Collective was inactive, because those lame plates wouldn't hold a fly, let alone a two-way portal to Alethia. Joe closed his eyes and mumbled something. A spell. Or the lyrics to 'It's Raining Men,' for all the good it did.

Greg shouted at his demon minion, who hunched over, his face distorted in pain.

Joe tried again. He raised his hands in theatrical fashion as if conjuring Satan himself. Again, no portal. Served them right. No one who lied to me would get away with it.

Now where were those slaves? If I was an evil djinn-ridden human, I'd keep them in the back, behind the plastic cover. I hopped off the barrel and sneaked around the building's perimeter. Planks, tools and rusty vehicle frames made up a dangerous obstacle path. Without a flashlight, keeping my footing wasn't easy. At the other end of the barn, where the smell of horse was still strong, no barrels or crates offered easy access to the windows. I collected some of the disused materials I'd avoided and stacked them into a pile. Dammit. Too unstable. Maybe I could cart one of those barrels around.

I turned the corner. The outline of a tree moved and grabbed my hair. I cried out. Not a tree. Joe had slipped close to me, and I hadn't heard a thing.

"*Ivy.*" A voice sounded from far away, and my heart jerked. Parker was here.

But it was Joe who clamped his arms around me. My gaze darted, but Parker didn't interfere.

Stupid Ivy. Of course he hadn't followed me, and wishful thinking wouldn't get me out of this mess.

"Let me go." I bucked against Joe's iron grip.

"But why? My master will be pleased to see you." His words lacked strength, as if he didn't care about his master's feelings one way or the other.

My heart thudded in my ears. "Th-the cops are on their way. If you leave now you could escape." I wiggled against his grip. "Not get caught with the others."

If I *had* called the police. What was I thinking coming here without backup?

"That's not how this works." On the other side of the barn, he shoved me through the open door.

I fell onto my knees and glanced up at the face that went with a pair of highly polished shoes.

"Ivy, sweetheart. What a lovely surprise." Nothing about Greg's tone indicated he was pleased to see me.

Old planks on the ground and rusty tack were leftovers from the horse stabling that once took up half the space. Cracked lanterns hung from thin beams holding up the roof. I crawled to the nearest pole and used it to haul myself up to near standing. A polished shoe kicked my kneecap, and I dropped back onto all fours. Hundreds of jackhammers attacked my leg at once, driving the air from my lungs. I rolled onto my butt and cupped my knee.

"We thought we'd found the wrong statue." Greg scoffed. "We should have suspected something was up when it fell so easily into our lap today. Your presence here tells us you have something to do with it." He crouched before me and lifted my chin with his fingers. "Who are you?"

I spat at him. He hit my face. *Whack.* His slap didn't so much hurt as cleave my skull in two. My vision swam for a moment, then I turned my gaze back at him, nose up. "Ivy Bell."

"No. No, you're something else." His eyes narrowed. He ripped the necklace from my neck and dropped it immediately as if it was on fire. "A guard." He stepped back. "Search her."

Joe turned me this way and that, and retrieved the rest of my guards, including the ones on my belt.

"Check her pants and her sweater."

"Don't." I rolled into a ball. "You've found them all."

The demon bastard pulled on my trouser legs, never mind my throbbing knee, and yanked the sweater over my head. While I sat shivering on the dirt floor, my arms clasped to cover my bra, the demon checked my pockets and seams. Nothing.

"I told you." I glowered at both men.

Greg grimaced at the pile of metal plates on a small table by the door. "Quite the collection. What are you? Fae?"

"Wouldn't you like to know?" I peered at the open entrance and the fields of wheat behind them in the dark. I could hide among the stalks, but the fields were too far to run with a busted knee. Especially with a demon around. "I told your lapdog here. The cops are on their way."

"No, they're not." Greg shook his head. "And it's sad you haven't figured out we have spies inside the police department. And inside the IEA, in case you're wondering. But they sure don't have a record of you. So, again. What are you?"

Half naked, I didn't have anything left to withhold but my secrets.

"It doesn't matter. You know, ever since my friend Bertrams hired your boss to track the Collective to that couple of humans, we've been having nothing but trouble. But not because of Bertrams. Sure, his sudden death was a problem, but we could deal. The humans were halfwits and didn't know what they had. And your boss? Despite his snooping, he knew nothing about the statue's real worth. But you?" He pointed at me. "You're trouble squared, missy. You very nearly derailed us. The question is, what are we going to do with you?" He cracked his fingers. "Should we kill you or make a profit?"

"Not in Alethia, you won't." I jutted my chin at the abandoned statue in the center of the guarded circle.

He tilted his head. "The Collective would have made our life easier, but don't think for a moment it's the only means we have at our disposal. We'll think of something."

"Sir." Joe's meek voice barely covered the distance to his master. "Our contacts on the other side are waiting. We're already overdue."

Greg raised his eyebrows. "Excuse me?" A flicker, no more than a vibration in the air, shot from his hand.

Joe dropped onto the ground, screaming. "I'm sorry. I'm sorry."

"Stop whining. You know the rules. You behave, we pay you well. You question us, you get hurt." Greg lifted his shoulders. "I really thought you'd get that by now." He looked at me. "He's right, of course. We used our network of contacts all over the country to train our girls. They're well-behaved. No longer capable of thinking for themselves. And our Alethian clients expect their wares." He frowned. "Joe, tell Ben to get the succubae here. If we use them, we should be able to fulfil at least part of our contract."

Joe scurried away, head bowed.

My stomach dropped. The destruction of the Collective had been for nothing. A gust of wind blew some straw through the open door, and I shivered.

"Where are our manners? You're cold." Greg picked up my clothes and dragged me across the barn by a clump of my hair. I grabbed his hand to ease the pull, but between his determined stride and my injured knee, my feet didn't keep up. I stumbled and slapped with my soles for traction, scraping my heels and the sides of my thighs on the unforgiving ground.

The plastic sheet slapped my bare skin, a metal door creaked, then Greg shoved me head first onto the dirt-covered slabs. My jeans and top landed on my head, followed by my sneakers. "I'll come for you later, sweetheart."

He fastened a latch on the door and walked off. The light struggled to make it into this part of the barn. Pieces of straw mixed with dust and tiny stones that clung to my hands like sticky tape. I slipped back into my clothes, careful not to aggravate my knee, and laced up my sneakers.

"Ivy?" a weak voice drifted toward me from beyond my field of view. I knew that voice anywhere.

"Fred?" I lifted up onto my arms.

Fred moved away from the wall. His hunched posture aged him twenty years, his hair thinner than ever, his eyes clouded. Streaks of dirt stained his face and his grimy and crumpled clothing. An angry welt flashed on his cheek.

I drew him into a hug, cautious not to squeeze too hard. "I'm so glad you're alive."

Over his shoulder, about ten, fifteen girls, perhaps more in the shadows, lay crumpled against the wall. Their blank faces didn't react to my presence. Some sported bruises on their bare arms or black eyes. The missing daughters and sisters of terrified families. Discarded puppets to someone like Greg. I gripped my neck, startled by the icy touch of my fingers.

"Ivy." Fred leaned on me. "What are you doing here?"

Typical Fred. Always worried about me. Didn't he realize I'd come to save him?

"Never mind me." I put on a brave face, ignored the glistening tears in my vision. "How did you get here?"

"A tip led me to this barn." He averted his face. "I got careless."

"Is Heather here?" I tested my leg. At least the thudding inside my knee was fading.

"She's…in the back." The girl he pointed at looked nothing like the vivacious student I remembered. Heather's greasy hair stuck together in clumps. Her arms were thinner, and her top might originally have been white before dirt and dried-on blood had sullied it.

"She won't talk to me. Doesn't recognize me." His voice caught.

My chest tightened, and it took a few tries to fill my lungs with oxygen. "What happened?"

"The girls are trained in stages. The first is cleaning and cooking and ironing. But when it came to stage two, the…" He inhaled sharply. "The sex. My little girl refused, the crazy man said. They forced her, but no matter how much they hurt her, she wouldn't." A sob.

My heart liquefied as if draining out of me. I'd never thought I'd witness my proud boss weep. "Take your time."

He shook his head and sobered. "They beat me. Humiliated me. Tortured me. Right in front of her. When my baby girl saw what they were doing to me, she gave up. She went with them, willingly. And when she came back... She hasn't been the same since." He buried his head in his hands. "I'm supposed to protect her. Not be the reason she..."

I placed my hand on his shoulder, wanted to comfort him, but all warmth had left me. Even if we got out of this situation, how much of Heather would we recover? My shoulders tensed with each breath. Who was I kidding? We wouldn't get out of this mess. Waylon might find me in a few days, but a few days would be too late. By then, I'd be a mere shell like Heather.

I frowned. Greg had my guards, but still didn't know what I was or that I had a secret weapon. My allure. I struggled through the pain to pull myself up on the rusty iron bars that surrounded our prison cell. Goosebumps ran up my arm. The plastic sheet kept in little warmth, and a draft shook a dilapidated door that hung askew on its hinges. Maybe I *could* get us out of here.

"Fred, are you up for an escape attempt?" I whispered.

He ran his hand through his wispy hair. "I've tried. The bars are thick, and these men are strong. I don't think they're human." He pointed his chin at Joe, who paced in front of the cage.

I bit my lip. "I'll deal with him first. Just be ready."

I waved to Joe and shot him a broad smile. Behind him, the plastic sheet billowed, letting slivers of light into our dark corner. He frowned and took up guard position, his body angled away from me. Fine. So a smile didn't cut it. When I'd used my allure against Grant, I'd needed to build up my motive. Of course Grant had been much more pleasing to the eye than Joe was.

From this perspective, the demon had a pretty decent build. More wide than muscled. Compact.

Crap. This was harder than I thought.

Aside from an unusually small pair of eyes, his face was attractive enough, in a boy-next-door kind of way. His arms looked capable of lifting me. At some point in my past, Joe might have been a firm Maybe. Even now he possessed an intensity that, if channeled into passion, promised an eventful night. Something shifted below my stomach. The longing for a touch, for a connection. Would Joe make love generously or take his fill first?

A warm shiver ran across the small of my back. Oh yes, where nature was average, my imagination filled in the gaps. His head gave a tiny tilt before swiveling toward me. His eyes darkened and he licked his lips.

"Do you think I'm attractive?" My voice softened, now almost sultry.

Joe came over, not yet ready to give himself to me.

I reached through the iron bars to press my hand against his chest. Oh my. I'd been wrong. Plenty of strength lurking in those muscles.

"W-what are you doing?" His eyes widened.

"Do you want me to stop?"

"No." His reply came like a bullet. "No. Don't stop."

I shifted my hand across the wide expanse up to his neck, grazing his ear. He trembled. Inch by inch, I drew him nearer. Next to me, Fred moved, but my attention belonged to Joe.

The fingers of my other hand traced his moist lips. "I want to kiss you."

"You-you do?"

"Very, very much." I tugged him toward me.

He hesitated at first. His tongue probed my mouth, then his confidence grew. Sparks danced from nerve to nerve, lighting fire after fire in my pelvis. His hands surveyed my butt, yanked me closer, but the bars got in the way. We sashayed along them and met at the door.

"Come in and get me," I purred.

Joe fumbled with the keys at his belt and opened the door. We melted into each other's arms. Perhaps this man was no more experienced than I was, but he was not afraid to explore. He sucked in my yips of arousal, hands crawling under my sweater. The bulge in his pants twitched, and I lifted my leg to feel every jolt.

The air shifted, and Joe dropped to his knees. He tumbled sideways onto the ground, and his eyes rolled up.

Behind him, Fred held up a shovel. "Am I interrupting?"

I shut my eyes and pushed my motive deep back inside. "Good timing."

"I can't believe you wrapped him so easily around your finger."

"It's a new skill." I patted his sunken cheek. "I'll tell you later. Right now, you're going to get the girls out while I take care of Greg. But be quiet. We can't have him hear a peep. The plastic sheet is not exactly soundproof."

His eyes twitched. "You can't take him out on your own." I twirled my finger and he smiled. "Oh, right. Well, be careful."

"I will. Wait until you hear me with Greg, then go out through the back." I pointed to the wooden back door next to our cell. "There's a truck outside. Don't go to the police. They'd put the girls in some hospital. What they have, doctors can't fix." I peered at the girls' lifeless bodies. "The house opposite mine, the one with creeper all over it. Ask for Julia and explain what happened. She might be able to help them."

Glamour was the strongest mind magic I knew. If anyone could guide the women to recovery, it was my friend.

Fred's attempts to coax the girls into coming with him failed. Not one of them budged.

"They have been trained to obey commands, so command them to move," I said.

He pulled back his shoulders. "Get up." His tone more general than mouse. "Now."

The girls stirred and scrambled to their feet. He bobbed his head at me.

Time for me to do *my* job.

Greg stood with his back to the room, talking on his cell. I inched to the table holding my guards and picked up the plates. Just holding them topped up my confidence. A little.

Greg spun. His phone clattered to the barn's stone floor. "How did you get out?"

"Magic." I opened my palm and focused on my newest guard. Perhaps I'd get the chance to use it.

Greg's lips pulled into a snarl and he ran toward me. His hard head slammed the air from my ribs and we landed on the ground. His hands circled my neck and squeezed. Panic flailed in my stomach. I gripped a chunk of his hair and pulled his head close. His grip loosened, his rapid breath beat against my cheek.

I bit his ear. His scream startled an owl under the roof into flight. He snatched his wounded organ and glared. I smashed my fist against his throat to shove him off. He fell onto his ass, still cupping his ear.

Pulse hammering in my veins, I scrambled up and tightened my fist around my guards.

He sprang up. "You'll pay for that, you little bitch."

CHAPTER TWENTY-EIGHT

DAMMIT. I DUCKED FROM UNDER Greg's arms, into the guarded circle. He leaped after me, but stopped short of the guards.

I eyed the plates that fizzed with the weakest of magic, and gathered confidence from the fear in his face. "Seriously? Scared of a few guards? Who's the damsel in your relationship? The djinn or the human?"

I fumbled with my guards and separated out the most important one, the one I'd made from Waylon's instructions. If Greg couldn't enter the circle, and Joe was still out for the count, I might just stand a chance to rid myself, and the world, of his nasty façade.

His scowl was marred by uncertainty. "We're one and the same."

"Ri-ight." So far, our scrap had been more catfight than a serious brawl. Of course, neither of us was a fighter. Not like Flo or Parker.

Greg straightened. "You're not human yourself, are you? Are you...a Guardian?"

My gaze darted to make sure nobody surprised me from behind. "What if I were?"

"No. Can't be." He licked his lips. "The Guardians are dead."

I scoffed. "You're one to talk. I thought your kind had left our realm for good."

"When we heard the Guardians were gone, we came back."

"Should have stayed where you were." I leaned forward, channeling Christopher Walken's essence, albeit not speech, in 'True Romance.' "We are many. We're gathering strength every day. And we're going to find your kind and destroy you, one bastard djinn after another."

As memorable as my performance was, Greg didn't cower. The fire still burned in his eyes. "You can't hide in that circle forever." He wheeled around. "Joe?" His voice boomed through the barn.

"He's having pleasant dreams." I eyed the circle of mediocre magic. As long as it kept out Greg, I'd be fine. I lifted the guard and spoke the spell Waylon had entrusted me with. Nothing happened.

My stomach dropped. What had I done wrong? I repeated the

words, yet the magic that was supposed to flow into me stayed out of my reach.

I glanced up at a grinning Greg.

"Time to give up, now." He shook his head in mock sympathy. "Or I can wait you out."

Sweat collected on my brows. Why wasn't the damn thing working? My gaze darted around the barn, assessing my chances of simply outrunning him. Fred and the girls should be in the vehicle by now.

"As you like." Greg crossed his arms. "How about I tell you what I'm going to do to you when I get hold of you?"

A cold shiver skidded across my spine. I didn't doubt his threat. Once again, the feeble circle protecting me drew my focus.

Hang on. Just because the guards were weak, didn't mean they didn't work. Perhaps they blocked out the energy. After all, containing magic and protecting it had been their purpose.

I swallowed. I'd have to leap out. And be fast. If my plan didn't work...

"I'll take you hard, my dear. My human half has needs, and my djinn half has the tools to make the experience extremely unpleasant for you." His words struck my chest like arrows.

I couldn't wait. My gaze scooted to the door. "Are those your precious slaves escaping?"

His startled face turned away from me.

I stepped aside, out of the circle, and spoke the incantation. Fast. No time for breaths.

A tremor raced up my arm and my guard grew heavy. Greg whipped back to face me, his skin pale, almost gray. From the sharp edge of my plate, a cone of blue light shot out. Thanks to Waylon's lesson, I knew the purpose of each line on my guard. How it shaped my words into energy that built portals. And how it could destroy anyone in its path.

Greg took two steps around the circle. I retreated, but kept my arm aloft.

Rumbling, the blue jet split into two streams that flowed past Greg and met behind him, clamping his body tight. His mouth moved, but a guttural roar of powerful magic swallowed his words. A ball of energy collected behind him, heating up into a pulsing red sphere that exploded into a large window. From the portal's depth, the deep howl of the lycae clawed its way out and mingled with the magic's grumble. Greg checked behind him, strained to break free, but I held the guard in place.

This time, no sweat formed on my back, my muscles didn't tire.

The only force that powered the glittering portal came from him. For once, a flavor of skin magic I liked.

Greg shook, and his body shrank before my eyes as his life drained into the portal. The humane thing would have been to push him through before he was too weak to defend himself against the lycae. But he'd hurt me. Hurt the ones I loved. Used innocents for his sick games. Why shouldn't I empty him? Kill him?

Joe stormed in, tearing the plastic sheet to the ground. "What are you doing?"

I glared at Greg, my lips trembling. My revenge on him wasn't complete. He hadn't suffered enough to be allowed to go, but I could no longer wait. A double-flick of my wrist shoved my former almost-boyfriend into the portal and into Alethia.

The window swished shut, and its howl cut off, the one sign it had existed evident in a handful of stray sparks fizzing through the air.

"Where'd he go?" Joe's head rotated from left to right.

I stared at the plate in my hand. Heat had melted it into a rough mess, and its grooves had been destroyed. This guard had fulfilled its destiny. Why was I feeling sick?

I pulled my shoulders back. "To hell."

Joe stepped back, his arms raised high. "Don't hurt me."

A wry laugh bubbled up inside me. "We'll see." Joe being scared was good. But I was no fool. He was a demon, and my portal builder was dead. Instead, I filled the defensive guards on my bracelet to the brim with energy. Just in case.

A black man, at least seven feet tall, scurried into the barn, trailing dust in his wake. "The slaves are fleeing." He skidded to a stop. "Where's the master?"

"Gone." I fake-beamed, keeping my palms stiff by my side. "And he's no longer your master."

The men gaped at each other then scrambled out of the barn. An ignition started, followed by squealing tires. I took one last look around, then ambled out the door with a swagger on my hips and my heart in my mouth.

How the hell was I still alive? Perhaps I was a Guardian after all.

⎯⎯⎯⎯ •◆• ⎯⎯⎯⎯

Back at Julia's, I moved up a chair for Fred so he could sit next to his daughter, and positioned myself by the long, velvety curtains blocking the moonlight. A small table lamp illuminated the glass beside it. Its light held Heather's unmoving face in shadows.

Julia carried in a tray and put it by Fred's feet. She was perfectly turned out as ever in her long flowing dress, her hair piled up on top of her head, with strategically loosened strands framing her face.

Fred stroked his daughter's head, muttering quiet words.

I pushed myself off the wall. "You've got to eat, Fred."

He looked at me, his forehead pleated in a deep frown.

"You're skin and bones, both of you. Don't let her starve to death. Not now that she's safe."

"You're right." He put his arm around her to helped her up.

"Do you think it might be a good idea to erase their memories?" I shot Julia a tentative smile, not sure my suggestion was wise.

She nodded. "Perhaps, but the process does carry risks. We're talking about the equivalent of brain surgery."

I swallowed hard. "What do you think, boss?"

He stepped over the untouched tray to join us. "If you'd asked me this a month ago, I would have thought you crazy. But after what I've seen, I believe anything. Even that you can erase experiences." He bowed his head. "So if you do have the power to make my girl forget, I'd be grateful."

She bowed her head.

Funny how not too long ago, I'd chewed Waylon a new one because he'd helped reshape my mother's memories. But without Julia's intervention, Heather might be lost forever.

"I'll get the supplies. And I promise, I'll start with her before I work on the other girls." Her hand pressed on my shoulder like an anvil. "Have you seen my brother?"

"No."

"You saved these people by yourself?"

"I had a plan." I scoffed. "When that fell through, I had no choice but to free them there and then."

"I wish you'd taken Florian."

"It worked out okay. We're alive."

"I suppose so." She patted my arm and silently closed the door behind her.

"Thank you." Fred grasped my hand. "I'm sorry I didn't say it before."

I flung my arms around him. "It's good to have you back, boss."

"Good to be back." A bit of color flushed his cheeks.

"Now, eat something."

His grin was slight, but a welcome sight.

I backed out of the room and headed over the road. Everyone was safe. Their ordeal wasn't yet over, but I'd done what I could. My door creaked open into an unlit corridor, but I didn't cross the threshold. No sounds. A smile crept across my lips. For once, I had my house to myself.

Two arms slipped around my waist and a set of teeth plucked the flesh just under my ear. My heart responded with a thump. Only one man knew what drove me wild with minimum effort.

"Miss me?" Waylon's breath warmed more than my skin.

I turned in his arms. His face should no longer steal the air from my lungs, nor should his eyes still melt my core. Yet no one had told him that.

"You bet." My tone was uncharacteristically tender.

Our kiss was at once familiar and new. His hands worked their magic on my butt, his tongue caused sparks in my mouth. How I'd missed his taste. His touch.

The tiniest voice told me I shouldn't be doing this. That Waylon hadn't done anything to deserve me. That I'd promised myself to another. But that was crazy talk. The ceremony with Parker had been a practical matter, not a romantic one. As for deserving me, well, he was here, wasn't he?

Good thing Waylon knew how to keep my mind on him.

He arched his back to lift me off the ground and carried me inside. I giggled, trying hard not to let go off his lips. He found the bedroom and dropped us onto the mattress. His head wandered to my shoulders, and I got a chance to catch my breath.

"You're early." I grazed the back of his neck, one of his most sensitive spots.

"Mhm?"

"I didn't expect you back until later in the week."

He lifted his head. "You needed me."

Oops. "Um, about that. Change of plan."

He narrowed his eyes. "What did you do?"

I scrambled out from under him and sat up against my padded headboard. "Why does everyone always assume everything is my fault?"

"You need to ask?" He slid his arm around my shoulder.

Fair point. I nestled against him. "I tracked down Greg's warehouse with the computer, so you'd have somewhere to go and fight evil."

"That's a good move." He rested his palm on my stomach, where it continued to supply me with wonderful warmth. "What's the problem?"

"No problem. I didn't want to send you to the wrong place, so naturally I drove past."

"And?"

I swallowed. "I got caught."

He snapped straight. "What happened?"

"Badness."

"Don't piss me off." His deep voice dropped a few notes. "Specifics?"

I lifted my shoulders to assure him nothing was my fault. "Greg put me in a cell with Fred and the missing girls. Since he took my guards off me, I couldn't do anything. At first. But after I seduced Greg's pet demon, Fred—"

"You did what?"

"I kissed him." I coughed. "Well, I had to distract him somehow."

He took his hand off my tummy. "Next time, sing or juggle flaming torches."

I replaced his hand and snuggled back into his shoulder. His displays of jealousy did wonders for my ego. "Anyway. Fred sneaked up on Joe, the demon, and took him out with a shovel."

"That must have been a hell of a kiss."

I scrunched my face. "I'd like to think so. And while Fred got the girls out of there, I dispatched Greg to Alethia."

He curled his hands into fists. "That was totally idiotic, babe. I told you not to do anything stupid. Do you ever listen?"

I pouted. "I didn't plan on dealing with Greg right then, but I saw my chance. What's wrong with that?"

"Sorry. You're right. You did good." He squeezed me toward him. "What about his pet demon?"

"That portal took it out of me. And I didn't fancy getting into another battle, so I let him go. I think he was grateful."

"You did?"

I shrugged. "In the end, whatever they did, the demons had little choice. Greg made them do it. At least I have to assume that." I poked his chest. "If I thought all demons were bad, I'd not be here right now with you, would I?"

"Good point." He raked a hand through my hair. "Not sure if I'm pissed at you for taking such risks, or proud."

"Oh, you're definitely proud." I shoved a bucketful of conviction into my voice.

"You think?" He kissed my forehead.

"I can tell." I lifted my face for more.

He smiled the smile of a man who knew he was beaten and liked it. "You might be right. Why don't you let me show you my appreciation?" He edged down my body, using both hands and his mouth to attend to as much of me as he could. My sweater practically fell off me, so swift was his motion, although he needed help with my jeans. My hand rested on his head, lost in his thick, soft hair.

He placed his mouth on my panties and flicked his tongue. I gave a yip. No one had done that before. He pulled the fabric past my butt, down my leg, but the warming air from his mouth remained in place, hovering over the spot that pulsed for his touch.

He brushed his fingers up my inner thighs and gently pulled my folds apart. I didn't dare breathe. Didn't dare move for fear he'd change his mind. His lips deposited gentle kisses on my skin, while his thumbs teased my opening. The softest wetness covered my clit. His tongue took its first, firm stroke, and my brain exploded into mush. He ran up his tongue again, like a cat licking up milk. I spread my legs for him, and the ball of longing released the moisture that told him I was ready for more.

His thumbs entered me, while his mouth didn't miss a beat. I moaned, and nearly bit my arm.

"Touch yourself." He peered up. "Slip up your bra. Now."

I had no choice but to obey. He rewarded me with another flick. I bucked my hips, my palms now hugging my breasts.

"Rub your nipples, babe. Do everything I'd do to you if I had two mouths." Another stroke. "Do it."

My fingers tightened around my stiff nipples, tweaking and rolling them in step with his tongue. Wells of crackling electricity collected under his mouth. And the pounding between my legs grew.

"You taste like raspberries." He drew his tongue along my folds and clamped his lips around my clit.

My hands tightened around my breasts. He sucked in my wetness, my tender swelling, like a starving lion. My moans grew into a multitude of "yes's" and "oh Gods," and my fingers resumed their jobs on my nipples.

The sensation in my breasts, combined with the nerves firing under Waylon's attention, built into a pressure like no other. His tongue licked fast and prodded deep. Each contact with my sensitive nub set off an explosion in my brain. My feet slid up at his sides, heels dug deep into the mattress, knees wide apart.

Release came in colors and a scream and in strong thuds that wouldn't stop. Waylon remained in place, breathing hard, although not as hard as me. My breasts puckered, too, where my nails had cut the flesh.

Another shudder gripped my body.

Waylon laughed and glided up my sweaty skin. His lips pressed on top of mine, making me taste what he'd tasted.

"Okay." My lungs still worked overtime. "Way to show your appreciation."

He ravaged my mouth again, then withdrew. "I'm not done. Not by a long shot."

He kept his word. All night, and once more in the morning. After another near-blinding orgasm, I fell back into my pillows.

"We rock in bed." His voice reeled from the exertion.

"Yeah."

"I mean, we seriously rock. When we fuck, it's like we could power the world with our energy."

I caressed his cheek. "Is this all this is? Sex? Don't get me wrong. It's good, but I don't know if it's enough for me."

He shifted up against the wall. "We're having another one of those talks I don't like, right?"

I moved up beside him. "Looks like." I pulled the blanket up to cover my breasts. "I'm not asking for marriage, but I read this book written by elves. They said that after sex, we will find ourselves in a state of attraction and bliss. And if that leads to further sex, my powers, whatever they are, will be copied over onto you." I squinted at him. "You could have told me about that."

His Adam's apple bobbed as he fixed his gaze on the wall opposite us. "I didn't know."

My spine snapped straight. "How could you not know? You're a Guardian." My pitch was now an octave higher.

"I don't..." He swallowed again. "Josie and I were trained by your grandfather, but she was so much more experienced than I. When she died..." He rubbed his face. "Fuck, babe. There's all that stuff that you don't know."

"Like what?"

"Shit." He banged the back of his head against the wall. "You really wanna know? Jeez, I'm hanging on by a thread. Half the time I don't know what I'm doing. I have these powers, magic comes easy, but the knowledge... I just don't have the knowledge."

My heart contracted. "I'd just assumed you had all the answers. I'm sorry."

"I don't want pity." His tone was harsh.

"Not pity. But I'm sorry you have to do this alone."

He scoffed. "And now I have to train you in a superb act of the blind leading the blind. But I have no choice."

That much had dawned on me. I'd seen what Greg had done to Fred and those girls. Remembered in full surround-sound my time as a slave in Alethia. The world needed Guardians. Plural 's.'

"I know." I traced my finger over his chin and felt it relax under my touch.

He pulled up one leg and scooted his butt closer to me. "I hoped that by sleeping with me, you'd have more of a reason to come with me. Perhaps leaving this world would be easier."

He might as well have punched me in the gut. I snapped back my hand. "That's why you slept with me? So nothing about this was real?"

"That's not what I'm saying. Being together is better than being alone, right? If what you say is true, and our relationship gets more intense, fantastic, but it also means I'm deep in the shit. I hate seeing you throw yourself into harm's way *now*. A year down the line, I'll be a nervous wreck."

I gave a dry laugh. "You, a nervous wreck? I'd pay to see that. But seriously, I… Is sex enough?"

He frowned. "What are you saying?"

What was I saying? My pulse beat stronger in my veins. Was I ready to let him go? I threw back the cover, picked up my T-shirt off the floor, and put it on.

"Hey." He sounded annoyed. "Talk to me."

I stepped into my jeans and buttoned them. "How do we know if anything you or I feel is real or a result of some magic?"

His jaw set. "I'd be okay with it either way. We'd still feel this attraction, wouldn't we? This is a good thing. And it worked great for your parents."

My throat closed, and I dragged in shallow breaths. Why was this so hard? "My mother and Dad might have really been in love. We don't know, do we?"

He huffed and got up, showing me the naked wonder that sent my hormones shooting straight for my crotch.

"You're seeing problems where there aren't any." Waylon stuffed his legs into his pants and zipped up his boots. "I'll be back next week to pick you up." He walked over and fixed me with an intense stare. "Perhaps by then you'll have come to your senses. We're good together. Don't spoil it."

His proximity and his familiar smell combined into a devastating goodbye present. I swallowed. He headed into the corridor and out the front door.

I ran after him. "I don't want you angry." On the driveway, I stopped him by clutching the sleeve of his jacket. "It's just something to think about."

He turned around. The wind had swept his short hair into an assortment of angles. "I understand, Ivy. And I'm not forcing you to do anything." He pressed a hard kiss onto my mouth. "Just don't expect me to give up on you, because we fit."

With those words he left. I stayed to watch his car bullet past my drive. My lips quivered. My stomach pulsated in protest. What had I done? I should run to the road. Tell him I was sorry.

But my feet didn't move.

Still, questioning our physical relationship wasn't the only lightbulb moment I'd had. The insight Waylon had allowed me into his life as a Guardian made me more determined than ever to accept his training. This wasn't about keeping my promise to him anymore. This was about me stepping into my parents' footsteps and fulfilling their legacy.

Not a minute later, Flo darted across the road, impeccably turned-out as always. "So, you and Waylon, eh?" His clipped words lacked warmth. "Good night?"

Why wasn't he grinning? My smile faded. "What's wrong?"

"Nothing." He crossed his arms. "It would have been nice if you two hadn't kissed in front of the werewolves' security cameras. You're meant to be engaged to their alpha, remember?"

My ears warmed. "I'd forgotten about the cameras. Do you think I'm in trouble?"

"More than you know. Parker was convinced you were in danger. And boy, is he pissed. As am I, by the way. Julia told me about your one-woman rescue mission. What were you thinking, going by yourself?"

My face fell. I'd expected praise, not to be told off like a misbehaved child. "I'm a grown woman, in case it's escaped your notice. I can do and act as I please."

His beautiful features crumpled into a scowl. "What else is new?"

My glum mood hit rock bottom. "What does that mean?" I held up a hand. "You know what? I don't want to know." I dashed into my bedroom. Inside of me, everything shook and shivered. Flo never argued with me.

I lifted my overnight bag onto my bed and threw some of my clothes into it.

He scowled. "Where are you going?"

"My mother's." I stuffed my feet into my sneakers and laced up. "Why?"

A spot of anger darkened my vision. I'd been captured, faced the threat of being returned to Lathan, battled a djinn and a demon, had challenged Waylon, and now my best friend was making a scene? "With you acting like this? You're surprised?"

"What, just because for once I don't treat you like the sun's shining out of your ass, you bolt?" His arms flew wide. "Why is everything always about you? You do what you like, and the rest of us can go to hell, is that it?"

My cheeks sank under my quivering lips. "You know I don't think like that."

"You act like it. Do you even know what's going on in *my* life?" He beat his chest.

"Yes, you spend it with the wolves. Not with me. What more's there to know?" I could feel the venom leaving my mouth and wished I could suck it back in. But the angry flame in my belly wouldn't let me apologize.

He slumped his shoulders. "You should at least go speak to Parker."

I slammed the bag onto the floor and jammed my arms into my jacket. "Leave me alone. And how about the next time I see you, I get to speak to my friend, and not to Silverton's werewolf spokesperson?" Bag in hand, I stormed out onto the driveway.

He leaned against the door frame, his face grim. I limped across to my Mustang and climbed in, started the engine, and reversed out onto the road.

He didn't wave.

Jackass. Right? Perhaps my actions had put Parker in a difficult spot, but what had I done to Flo? I'd tried to talk to him about his issues before, but he was so damn secretive. This wasn't my fault. My Mustang skidded around the corner. After its prolonged repairs, the car purred like a kitten and responded like a dog. Why wasn't Flo like that, instead of making such a drama when he didn't like my attitude?

Waylon had given me one week to say goodbye to my friends and family. I'd originally planned a couple of nights with my mother, followed by a chick-flick bonanza with Florian, curled up on the sofa. Then, we'd see. As long as I spent my remaining time with him, I was okay. That was all I wanted. Flo time.

Hard to see that happening now. The Collective and Fred's disappearance had brought us closer together, I'd thought. Had that been an illusion?

Something niggled at me. Guilt. But why should I feel guilty? When Florian and Parker turned their backs, I did something amazing. I stopped a preternatural crime lord and lived. Fred was safe. Was a little *well done* too much to ask?

I approached my mother's estate and drove up the driveway. Once again Alan's car wasn't in its spot. Although perhaps he wasn't the ogre I used to think he was, spending two nights just with my mother was important to me. The maid showed me through to the small parlor, where my mom busied herself with her correspondence. Physical letters. Not e-mails.

"To what do I owe this honor?" Mom glanced up from her desk. "Are you ill? You're white as a sheet. And your hair. You must take better care of yourself, Felicity. Has anything happened?"

Her concern soothed my mood, and I put on a reassuring smile. "I busted my knee, and I've been working hard. I just felt like a change of scenery, so I thought I'd spend the night. Is that okay?"

She rose and embraced me. Instead of asking her if *she* was okay, I pressed my face against her neck. The new mother-daughter bond we'd built last time I was here would take some getting used to, but I was game.

"As long as you're not sick." She patted my back. "Now go, shower and get changed. By the time you've washed and made yourself presentable, dinner will be ready."

I did as I was told, like a good girl.

During dinner my mother stole glances at me, brief, curious ones. No doubt she puzzled over why I'd turned up out of the blue. By dessert she dropped the covert observation and ramped it up to a full-blown stare.

"What's wrong?" I frowned.

"How would you feel about a round of cards?"

Her question took me by surprise. "You mean that?"

She tittered, with a little snort at the end.

A deck of cards was a ghost of the past, of happier times. Before I'd soured our relationship by moving out on the misguided notion that distance from my parents would be good and healthy. When my dad was still around.

"Canasta?" She tilted her head in innocence.

As if I'd forgotten she killed anyone in canasta. "Yeah, okay." I set up the folding table in the living room.

The maid cleared the dinner plates, and my mother sent her home for the night.

I took my seat and twirled a piece of hair around my finger. "Are you coming?" I rapped on the tabletop.

Mom entered with a smile and a couple of bottles under her arm. She handed me a cola and poured a glass of Bordeaux for herself. My gaze drifted to the empty chair to my right. No matter how hard I tried, the image of Dad wouldn't sharpen in my head.

"I miss him, too." She squinted at the same empty spot. "I wish ..." She took a sip of her wine, then cleared her throat. "You know, if he were here now, he'd wonder why you're staring into space when you should be shuffling the deck." She shot me a shy smile that warmed me to my toes.

I dealt and pulled a foot up under me. "No cheating."

For a brief moment our eyes met and we understood. Perhaps our relationship wasn't dead. Perhaps it was possible to build a new one from the ruins of the past.

Predictably, I went to sleep late. When I woke, the first shimmer of sun pierced through the lined curtains in my bedroom. I stretched out across the huge, super-soft bed and let out a loud yawn. The evening had been perfect. Only my argument with Florian and a possibly well-deserved guilt trip over Parker spoiled my mood. That, and the return of my Lathan nightmares. I'd slept just fine in Waylon's arms.

I checked the clock. Nearly ten a.m. My stomach rumbled. Mom would have been up since six. A grin swept over my face. I must have looked incredibly pathetic yesterday, otherwise she'd never have allowed me to sleep past seven.

With a bounce in my step I padded into the kitchen and peeked out the hall window to check the driveway for cars. Maybe Mom had gone out and forgotten to ask the maid to wake me. Nope, her car was here, and so was Alan's.

"Ivy?"

The voice sounded muffled. I checked the kitchen and the hall. Both were empty.

"Ivy? Can you hear me?"

I knew that voice.

"Ivy, come on. I know you can hear me."

"Parker?" I twirled on my heels, yet saw no one.

"Where the hell are you?"

"In my mother's kitchen. Where the hell are *you?*" I bent at the hips to peer under the table. Had he used an invisibility guard?

"At home. I was worried about you. I know you and Florian had words. There are things we need to talk about."

"Hang on. Are you saying you are in my mind? How the—" If Alan walked in on me speaking to myself, he'd think I was more of a fruit loop than he already did.

"Oh that. This new connection surprised me, too." And yet Parker's mind voice sounded pleased with this development. *"This form of mental communication doesn't usually come about unless you're well and truly bonded to someone."*

My blood ran cold. *"How did this happen?"*

"It wasn't supposed to. Believe me, our shamans are all over this. It started last night. First I thought you called for me. But that seemed insane. Then early

this morning, your scream woke me. Next, you asked me about old sweaters and if I knew if Lathan was going to kill you. You sounded upset. About the dying, not the sweaters. I think you were dreaming."

"Oh, that's wonderful. How do I turn this off?"

"We stop talking. You can contact me any time you want. Just think my name."

Why was nothing simple? Damn it. The moment I'd got rid of the statue's whispers in my head, here was another voice crowding in on my thoughts. Perhaps I should cover my head in tin foil from now on.

I locked my jaw. *"We can talk when I get back. Just leave me alone until then, okay?"*

"I can do that."

The reprieve was all my mood needed to lift. After a few more hours of human company, more specifically my mother's company, I was sure to feel myself again. A breakfast of eggs and bacon filled my belly. I left the dishes on the table, unwashed. As much as I disliked my mother's pomp, having a maid was neat.

The roads outside the estate were quiet and too far away to carry their rattles and clanks into the house. But I'd become accustomed to the bustle of my neighbors in and around my home, and the stillness was intrusive. I checked the drawing room and the dining room, but no sign of my mother or Alan. Were they upstairs acting out a second wind in their romance? I grimaced. *Gross.* I trudged along the corridor, when a stack of magazines on the coffee table drew my attention. I walked into the small sitting room and picked up a copy. Smiling faces of celebrities I'd never heard of. Perfect garden reading. I turned, and almost yelped. Mom napped on a powder blue recliner. So much for my dirty thoughts about her and Alan.

My smile for the woman in front of me came from a place of pure tenderness. With her delicate features smoothed out and relaxed, she looked at peace. Perfect as a doll. She'd even thought to match her choice of furniture to her shoes, an elegant pair, hand-stitched with a cornflower thread on a baby blue base. I blew her a kiss and tiptoed out the room.

The sun shone as if no one had told it it was fall. The garden's sweeping lawn vibrated in lush greens. My knee had healed overnight, and I was safe. At last, I had peace.

I inhaled the earthy scents carried by the breeze and settled in on a white, wrought-iron lounger in the shade of a tree.

Clomping footfalls approached, and I lifted my magazine against the glare.

"Lemonade?" Alan poured me a drink. Typical. Even in his home he didn't move a muscle without his suit and his shiny shoes. Still, it was a nice gesture.

"Thank you." I smiled. "And I also wanted to thank you for helping me with my trust fund. Sorry I didn't say it earlier."

He shrugged. "You're welcome."

"Is Mom up?"

"She's still napping. I hear you two were a little rowdy last night."

I grinned. "I guess we were."

"Let her rest for a while, okay?" He took the carafe back into the house.

I swigged the icy liquid in a few gulps, savoring the bitter tang. What a glorious day. Lounging outside in the middle of October. Only in California. I yawned and turned my attention to the gossip the magazine reporters found newsworthy.

* * *

A noise woke me. A deep roar like water rushing down a cliff face, drowning out the songs of birds. A gust of wind whipped my face and raised goosebumps on my flesh. Ten yards from me, a column of smoke and dust larger than an oak rose from the lawn.

Shit. A tornado, so close to the house. I leaped up from my chair to sprint inside, but froze. The twister wasn't moving.

Alan hunched beside it, tears rolling down his face. A dark liquid flowed down a blade in his hand and spilled onto his arm.

I rammed my feet into my sneakers. "Alan?" I made to run toward him, but bounced off an invisible wall. Pain exploded in my nose. Through a curtain of tears, I held out my hand. Whatever kept me from helping my stepdad, it was as solid as glass. Yet the wind blew through it, tousling my hair.

Alan stared at his knife. His mouth moved, and more dark fog billowed to the heavens. Fifty feet in the air, the column kinked and disappeared in the ether. My pulse skipped and skidded through my veins. Some kind of magic had taken hold, and I had to get out of here. I felt for a way out, but the wall curved around me. My fingers detected neither a crack, nor unevenness, although its sponginess confirmed the thing wasn't made of glass. I traced its smoothness to the grass. No way. More than six powerful guards encircled me. My stomach lunged for my throat.

"What's going on, Alan? Are you all right?" I clawed the ground, but the guards were located outside the magic shield.

His face twisted into a grim caricature, his eyes red and hollow. No sign he'd even heard me. Instead, he broke into laughter and fell to his knees. "We're ready, master."

My skin tautened, and the mark on my shoulder prickled.

Everything sprang into focus, as if my mind were a camera, zooming in on the images like details in a pop video. The vortex. Blood on a knife. Guards to keep me confined.

Most of all, baby blue shoes. The ones worn earlier by… Against my better judgment, my gaze slid to the mules in the grass. The twister spiraled up from them, obscuring the rest of the body. My lungs turned to water, the weight pressing against my heart. Waylon's words about how the pain of a dying person could power a portal swam through my brain.

But no. It wasn't true. Couldn't be true.

"Mom?" My voice was hushed.

Why wasn't she moving?

I scratched at the wall, finding no traction, then pounded and punched for a way out. I had to get to her, save her, tell her everything was going to be okay. "Alan." I let out a scream. "Oh God. What have you done?"

His features tightened. "Not me. You, Felicity. It's always been about you, hasn't it? You should have taken your money and run. But you're too stupid to even get that right." He shook his head. "Two women I've had to sacrifice for you, two wonderful women. You stupid little girl."

My knees buckled and struck the bumpy ground, the impact bruising my bones. "You bastard! You fucking son of a bitch." My palms slapped the barrier, the bangs reverberating as pain in my wrists. "Let me out."

He turned his back on me and set up a black cube adorned with swirling silver guards.

From far away, the wisp of a voice barely grazed me. Then it was gone.

"Please, don't do this. Alan! Are you listening?" My words trembled, out of control.

He opened the lid of the box and placed a hand inside. "We all serve a master, Felicity. Mine is more powerful than most, and generously shares his gift." His red-rimmed eyes bulged like golf balls without pupils.

"You're mad." I kicked the wall and grimaced at the twinge in my ankle. My guts were about ready to dissolve.

"I'm sorry about your mother, you know?" He hoisted a telescopic pipe from the cube and twisted it into position. "Such a good heart underneath the self-restraint."

The wind whipped my hair in all directions. My skin, my flesh, my nerves went numb. Even my heart thudded against my ribs through layers of cotton wool. Nothing made sense.

Alan bowed deep before the box. "As always, your loyal servant, master." The air around the pipe end sparked and flickered. Pixel by pixel, a hologram coalesced into the face that made my bones crumble and my blood turn to ice.

CHAPTER TWENTY-NINE

S PARKLING RIBBONS OF DARK AIR whooshed from the portal into Alan's chest. So that was the prize for his betrayal. The reward for his crime.

"Well done, human." Lathan's oily cadence crackled through the air, tearing fresh gashes into my heart. "Drink my power. You've earned it."

Alan arched his back, his arms wide to welcome the skin magic with all of its addictive and giddying properties. He collapsed into a heap, a serene smile giving him an air of insanity. Lathan could send his power through the Rim, but at least he could not cross over. I could, though. My Guardian genes would make sure of that. Still, if Alan was Lathan's only tool, my future might not be as bleak as they would like me to think.

Lathan turned his attention to me. He'd swept his blond, long hair out of his face and tightened it into a queue. "Didn't I promise we'd be together? This time you're ready for my advances." His soft laughter sent a burn down my spine. "You can feel it, can't you? This need to consummate our relationship? What is this urge like?"

Such a beautiful face. Such a horrid, dark mind. I leaned my head against the barrier, too drained to keep from crumpling without support.

"The weakness will pass, Felicity. You're still suffering the effects of the sedative the human gave you."

My gaze pivoted to the now empty glass of lemonade.

"And don't think of appealing to the human's inner goodness. He's mine, body and soul."

I rocked back and forth, as if the regular motion held comfort. None of this could be true. This wasn't how my life was supposed to go. I didn't deserve this.

"My sweet Felicity." His tone took on that charming, dulcet quality that haunted my dreams. "If you'd come back to me of your own accord, the death of your human mother could have been avoided."

I peered up at him then scowled. My blaming me was one thing.

But Lathan pointing his finger? I don't think so. The hollow of my stomach filled with something solid. Hatred. Disgust. Spunk.

I lifted my chin. "It was Alan who smuggled the Gallom into my house?"

My stepfather lifted a thumb and swayed, a lopsided grin on his face.

That smug bastard. I got to my feet and glared. If Lathan wanted me with him, Alan would have to let me out eventually.

Lathan shook his holographic head. "In case you're getting any ideas of a last minute reprieve, I'm sending old friends of yours. I trust they've learned their lesson and won't allow you to slip away this time."

My gaze flicked from his virtual image to the vortex stacked high into the air. A growl fanned out from its depth. The growl from my nightmares. My cold breaths iced up my lungs. The bottom part of the dusty column smoothed into a glittering surface that reflected shards of light. The window resembled the one that had swallowed Greg. A portal to lead me straight to hell.

The first spindly leg breached the horizon. I shrank away. Two furry, muscular creatures emerged, hunched on their hind legs. Their protruding snouts revealed deadly canines dripping with saliva. I'd witnessed first-hand the damage the lycae's teeth could do. Stumpy front legs swung awkwardly from their shoulders. Occasionally a claw touched the ground to coordinate a step.

Blood pumped hard through my eardrums. A crackle. *"Ivy? You're in trouble, aren't you?"*

"Parker?" My mind, turtle-like, played catch-up. "Where are you?" My eyes darted right and left, searching. He was nowhere. Elsewhere. In-between my wintry lungs and quivering guts, a familiar sensation flared.

"Hold out, okay? Whatever is happening, you'll survive it. You always do."

Renewed strength trickled into the corners of my being, fortified by his faith in me. He was right. I wasn't lost yet. No matter how ruthless the lycae, Lathan did not want me killed. I could use that to my advantage.

The demon must have read the thought from my face. "You cannot escape me. Not today."

I shoved my hands in my pockets. Empty. Alan pointed to the table outside the force field, where my guards glistened in the waning sunlight. My necklace lay coiled next to it. Where had he put...? I reached for my wrist. The son of a bitch had overlooked my bracelet. Was his carelessness my lucky break? My defensive guards had worked well against Florian when he'd been gripped by his blood frenzy, but taking on two lycae might be suicide. Despite their awkward physiology, those beasts were fast.

The wind flagged and faded. The gleaming portal smoothed into a silvery reflective surface. It was nearly time. The vortex's slurps now sucked in the other direction. Its vacuum tugged on me, intensifying the barbing of my mark, ready to spit me out at Lathan's feet.

Alan removed a guard, and the force field fell. He stepped aside and gestured for me to take the lead. The lycae flanked me on either side. I scanned the path leading up to the vortex and mapped out the entire playing field. Too close to the portal, and it would be game over. But before I could collapse the vortex and deny Lathan his prize, I had to deal with his lackeys.

My hopes rested on an old classic combined with the small bead on my guard bracelet. I pretended to trip. My arms flailed through the air, slapping for something to hold on to. The lycae growled. One skipped to the side so I wouldn't flatten it with my fall. The last word of my incantation slipped out and I leaped forward to disappear into thin air.

"Find her!" Lathan's command thundered through the portal.

But my invisibility was absolute. The lycae fell into a yapping frenzy. Their search had them crossing each other's paths, blocking Alan's advance. Luckily, their sense of smell was no better than a human's. I danced past them, avoiding their claws and drooling snouts by the breadth of their whiskers.

I headed away from the portal and slammed into another force field. A shock jolted through my face, driving tears to my eyes. Alan had placed more guards, well-hidden in the grass. One lycae probed too close to me, pricking its ears. I teetered between my desire to find the concealed plates that imprisoned me, and the primal need not to let the beast get too close. With a last desperate glance at the ground, I darted off in the other direction.

Lathan yelled at his minions, threatening them with punishments too evil for a human mind to imagine. Alan stalked, arms outstretched like a zombie. Probably still dizzy from the skin magic. Any other time, this image would have been funny.

I dodged the melee of searching limbs and climbed onto the garden table where Alan had laid out my guards. I folded in my legs and rolled up in its center. So far, so safe. How did I get to the box? If I destroyed it, Lathan would no longer be able to shout instructions.

With a vigilant eye on my enemies, I charged the plates.

Not two minutes later, I got my first opportunity. One lycae's eagerness to find me had sent it into the zone of the vortex. Quietly, quietly. One tiptoe in front of the other. The creature's dirt-clumped fur reeked of rotting flesh, its spit dangled from its mouth in long strings.

"*Fintero.*" My magic burst forth in a blue jet, burying itself in the lycae's chest. It tilted over backward, toward the portal. I supplied another helping jolt from my guard. The vacuum did the rest and sucked the lycae into its bowels.

"No!" Lathan screamed as if to shatter my bones.

One down, two to go. The sparkling jet of magic had given away my position, and I hightailed it outside the portal's reach.

Lathan's lips pulled back into a snarl. My mark flared, and with it tentacles inside my brain sprang into being.

"*Mine!*" Parker's voice.

A ball of searing heat flashed inside, warming my head and my body. It spread fast to soothe my fears and cocoon my mind. The demon's influence shrunk and dissolved. Lathan lost his hold just as Parker claimed his stake in me.

The demon's pale green eyes darkened. "How is that possible? What magic is that?"

I gave a half-smile. That was Parker-magic.

I took two great leaps and flung the box powering Lathan's image into the gateway. His words of protest didn't make it past the first syllable. The magic that had powered his holographic presence cut off, and his face disappeared.

I allowed myself a deep breath. But I wasn't done yet.

Without its master's guidance, the last lycae zigzagged across the lawn, circling its tracks, sniffing the air. Pathetic.

Not so Alan. His movements were methodical. Guess his skin magic had worn off. He covered the area inch by inch, feeling for my form, listening for my breath. If the lycae wasn't so panicked, the two could trap me between them and the remaining force field.

Alan's solo-technique proved ineffective, though. I could out-duck him for hours, provided the lycae didn't come to its senses.

"*Ivy. We're here.*"

"*Here where?*" I glanced up. Parker and Flo circled the force field, pounding against it. For a second I feared my mind was playing tricks on me, but they were real. My friends had come for me. A rolling sob climbed into my throat, but I didn't give in. Not until I was safe. "*I'm by the small table. I'm invisible.*"

"*How do we help you?*"

Alan's strides quickened. He cast panicked gazes at my friends, without dropping his arms.

I made myself small to avoid his fingertips. *"Can you find the guards that power the field?"*

"No, we've checked. They're inside the field."

Dammit. *"Then I'm on my own."*

"Don't give up on us. We'll think of something."

Parker dragged Flo with him onto the grass, hands aloft as if they were praying. Or doing magic.

The transparency of the shield turned into a translucent blue, highlighting the ripples that propagated upward from the hidden guards. If I followed the undulations, maybe I'd find them and bring down the barrier.

"Now, Ivy." The strain in Parker's words was considerable.

I glanced over my shoulder—and understood. Their spell had had one purpose; to distract Lathan's minions.

Not a bad plan. Hunched low, the remaining lycae growled at the undulating wall.

"Stop it." Alan shooed it by waving his hands, but stayed three feet behind it, not an inch nearer.

I couldn't blame him. Those creatures were lethal.

"Idiot." My stepfather wheeled around to resume his search.

I sneaked closer. The lycae's sulfuric breath blew into my face. I placed my palm in front of my nose, took a lungful of air, and kicked. The lycae's rump lifted off the ground. It snapped its teeth into emptiness. A shove with my guard, aimed at the beast's shoulder, deposited it into the portal. Its high-pitched shriek cut off.

"Are you still with me?" Parker shouted in my mind.

I swallowed. *"I'm here. Don't yell."*

More sweat rolled down my neck, my hands shaking. The vortex's continuous glugging dragged on. I'd glimpsed its heart, and it was hungry. Two steps took me outside its gravitational well, but the strain of the invisibility guard now became my greatest problem. Soon, I'd have to turn it off.

Only Alan left. A human. I could take him. If vampires and demons had no answer to my guards, he wouldn't either.

Why didn't I make my move?

His long and even strides carried him from one corner to the other. Occasionally he broke out left or right, but never close enough to touch me. He was sick in the head from skin magic, incapable of rational thought. An addict. But he must have had sober moments. His help with my trust fund to save me was proof there was still humanity in him. And my mother had been happy with him, hadn't she?

Her mules lay untouched at the base of the portal. The rest of her was shielded from view by the mirror-like window. She shouldn't be dead. This wasn't…real. A silent cry hooked into my chest and ate the energy powering my invisibility. Her smile, her rare but infectious laughter crushed my brain, thwacked it like a lump of Play-Doh, until the scream tore from my throat.

Alan whipped around.

No, that bastard deserved worse than my wrath. He deserved Lathan's.

I circled him then approached. The spell I had planned needed proximity to work. His lips pressed together, his eyes blood-shot. I whispered Waylon's incantation. *Snap.* A crack against my shoulder. Alan whipped his hand to his neck.

Lathan's mark was now on him. I didn't even have to check.

For one glorious instant nothing else mattered. My heart danced in my chest, untethered. Ever since Waylon had taught me the words, I'd clung to them in my mind, in the desperate hope I'd one day be free. Now I was. If only Alan saw my smile right now. The fate he'd designed for me would be his.

The portal glugged and bubbled. *Nearly* free.

No more Miss Nice Gal. As my opening salvo, I kneed him straight in the balls. A combo of kicks and magic from my guard herded Alan toward the gateway. He stumbled and blocked the fall with his hands, then pushed himself up off the grass. His fists covered his face like a boxer. He was bigger than me, certainly stronger, but invisibility had its perks, not the least of which was the dulling of my pain.

I aimed a kick sharp into his groin. Whoa. What a beauty. He doubled over and grimaced. *"Parker, you'd better be watching this. You might learn something."*

My knee cracked into Alan's chin, whipping his face to the side. His hands had nothing to defend against. My fist slugged his fleshy nose, and he yowled. One intense burst from my guard catapulted him back. A few steps too far.

"That's my girl." Parker's voice danced with pride.

Alan's eyes widened, his mouth shaped into an angry 'O.' He slanted back, wind-milled his arms. The portal had its meal and didn't let go. His tall frame elongated like a rubber band, which snapped back onto itself and yanked him into the glistening window. My dry throat rattled with every satisfied inhalation.

I wiped an arm across my forehead to mop up the sweat. Nearly done. The portal crackled, but it did not close. Mindful to keep a careful distance, I circled in from the rear, safe from the pull, and kicked at the guard at its base, next to the outstretched arm of my—

I crouched and prodded the carving on the metal plate with my trembling fingers. Each line told a story. I traced the rippling energy to where it connected to the vortex. All it took was my thumb in a groove, and the flow of magic was blocked. The portal collapsed into the guard in less than the flicker of a flame.

Silence.

My gaze drifted to the outstretched arm limp in the grass.

safe, breathing, breathe deep. look. dead, dead body, dead mother. my dead mother.

Fragments of something insubstantial wriggled through my brain. Thoughts. Memories. I let them run their course, waited for the words to form notions, concepts, then sentences.

I swayed.

"Ivy?" The two syllables shrilled through my brain. Over and over. Colors came back into focus, shapes. I deactivated the invisibility guard. This time, no happy feeling caught my low, no buzz to counter the pain. Just brain-twisting vertigo.

"Thank God. Are you okay?"

Parker and Florian stared at me through the bluish shield with slumped shoulders. My gaze swiveled back to my mother's body, laid out like a doll. Her hand frozen mid-wave. Waving, not drowning. Waving goodbye?

My knees touched the ground and I collapsed beside her. A fist compressed my lungs, converting my breaths into wild snaps for air. Had Alan told her I was the reason she had to die? Did she spend the last seconds of her life hating me? "Come back to me," I whispered. "I'm sorry, Mom. Don't leave me."

Only silence escaped her gray lips. Her muscles didn't move. Wouldn't ever move again.

I stretched out beside her and placed my head on her blood-stained shoulder. With trembling fingers I stroked her cold face. So soft, so flawless. So perfectly beautiful.

She was smiling now. I was with her, and everything would be okay.

When I came to, darkness had settled over the estate. The cold grass hugged my frame, moist against bare skin where my top had ridden up. Not a bird chirped. The crickets didn't sing. I rubbed my burning eyes, stretched sore limbs. My leg kicked out, a reflex.

I was alive.

My hands grazed the coolness of my mother's body, caressed her stiff cheek. Then I sat up and glanced around.

The furniture was still in perfect arrangement on the lawn, my glass in its original position on the table by the lounger. It had been a tidy fight. The one thing out of place—the dark stain on my mother's sun dress.

Across the blue-tinged wall, Parker and Florian crouched on the grass not twenty feet from me. Vertebra by vertebra I dragged my tired bones off the ground.

Parker got to his feet. *"Talk to me."*

I nodded, but no words came. Jerky steps carried me along the shield, gaze locked onto the ground. A flicker among the grass. The guard, hidden underneath, was a masterpiece. A nasty masterpiece. I knelt and blocked the magic powering the wall.

Florian and Parker's voices cut through the silence like a knife. Their words merged into a meaningless, monotonous drone.

Parker picked me up and cradled me in his arms. Carried me away. Away from my old life, from the place where my innocence died. I stared out, past his shoulder, and my tears flowed silently as I said good-bye to the only mother I'd ever known.

It took two weeks to finalize the arrangements for my mom's funeral. Following an anonymous tip, the police had found her body and the knife that had been used to kill her. It was covered in Alan's fingerprints, and the police were now searching for him. Since Lathan didn't forgive failure, my guess was their prime suspect was already as dead as Monty Python's parrot.

Nearly fifty people had said their goodbyes at my mother's funeral. That she'd been well liked wasn't a surprise, but made me smile. The funeral parlor organized the wake, and it was what people would consider 'tasteful.' My mother would have been pleased with their effort. I only put in a brief appearance to thank the well-wishers. More than anything, I preferred to remember the person she used to be; the way she was when I last saw her alive. The happy, smiling version of her.

I lay curled up on the sofa, watching the most light-hearted chick flick Saturday afternoon cable had to offer, my head in Florian's lap.

"It's a relief to come over here and get peace and quiet." He held his mug of steaming hot coffee perilously close above my head. "Have you ever experienced the wonder of a grown man who's learned that every fairy-tale creature he's read about is real?"

Fred and his daughter had moved in with the Duprees for the foreseeable future, while Julia worked with Heather to sort through her memories. The remaining girls had been sent to other vampire families who'd offered to help.

I shook my head. "I'm guessing Fred's excited about it?"

"And then some. Eli's in his element, of course, answering every single one of Fred's thirty billion questions in ear-aching detail. He and Fred have developed this strange bromance."

Eli did have a penchant for existential philosophy.

"So how are the other two men in *your* life?" Florian asked, a smirk evident in his inflection.

"You know you're the only man in my life, don't you?" I turned onto my back and fluttered my eyelashes up, glad for the distraction from my grief.

"That's gratifying to hear. Only right, too. I've yet to experience your sexually-charged satyr traits." He leaned back with a mischievous wink, his free hand combing through my hair.

I sat up. "Listen, Flo. You have forgiven me, haven't you? You know, from when I was…"

"A bit of a cow?" His expression was more serious than I liked.

I hung my head. "Yes. I was selfish. Just…" I inhaled. "I couldn't understand why nobody took my concern for Fred seriously. I was so used to Parker and you helping me out with all my problems, the fact you didn't jump at the chance to help me with that hurt."

"You've said it many times." His voice quaked. "I didn't think we could go up against Greg, and I was still dealing with the after-effects of the ceremony. Besides, Parker is responsible for more lives than just yours or mine. You were asking him to go up against a pretty powerful dude."

I nodded. "I know. I wasn't fair."

"What do you want me to say?"

My lips trembled. "I don't know. That you forgive me."

"I told you that I do." A slow smile spread across his face. "I honestly and completely and totally and absolutely do."

I hugged him and lay back down, all in all quite content.

"What about the wolf and the demon?" Flo's sly voice proved his words weren't as innocent as they appeared.

I reached up and flicked his nose. "The wolf, I mean Parker, has been good. He's more careful with his temper. And busy taking care of my mother's estate for me. All that paperwork." I shuddered.

"What are you doing with the place? Moving in?"

"Are you kidding? I'll be away most of the time, but when I come home, I want to see these adorable cheeks." I smooshed his face. "Besides, Parker has plans, and since I have little use for the estate, I thought, why not. Let him do something good with it."

"That's generous. Any further psychic connection?"

"A few, but mostly in my sleep, apparently. He mentioned you and Ali experience it, too. It's a head cruncher, isn't it?"

He shrugged. "It was at first. The other day, two werewolf scientists did these tests on us. They left you alone because, well, Parker wouldn't let them anywhere near you, but, oh, were they excited. I haven't yet told Julia about any of it. In truth, I'm beginning to enjoy this new bond. Ali's an alright guy. For a wolf, I mean." He tucked another strand of hair behind my ear.

"Aha." I wagged my eyebrows.

"What *aha*? Why do you say it like that?"

I smirked. "Nothing. Forget it."

A frown wrinkled his nose. "You're making it worse."

I prodded his arm. "Listen, you wanted to talk to me about this before, but, well, you didn't. What's going on with you two?"

He gave a long resigned sigh. "With Ali and me? I don't know. I'm not gay." He scowled at me. "I'm not." His gaze drifted. "But there's that connection, and he's kind and funny and I like hanging with him. True, I do sense he wants more, but..."

I nudged again. "But?"

Flo leaned back his head. "I'm not ready. Maybe I'll never be. Physically, I'm less attracted to him."

I bit my lip. "Perhaps you haven't tried yet. I mean, you have this connection of the heart." Like I had with Parker. I swallowed. So not the moment to think about that. "But you're fighting it. Maybe you should let things happen the way they happen." I shrugged. "Just sayin'."

He scrunched his face. "You're fighting your bond with Parker too, aren't you?"

"That's different." I sent him my shut-up glance. "And honestly, I'd been looking forward to no more head mojo. Lathan's kind of taken the fun out of it for me. I'd prefer to be alone inside my thoughts for a while, thank you very much."

"Poor baby." He patted my head in mock sympathy. "But it is odd. How, with the bond and your hormones, you and Parker have never...bumped uglies. What's that about?"

I set my jaw against a jumble of emotions. Longing, determination, resolve. "Don't be silly. We just don't feel that way about each other."

The poor boy was seized by a coughing fit. "Right. Sure. I'm just saying it's odd that he's the one guy..." He shot me a sheepish smile. "Anyway, I wonder how lover boy's gonna react to this psychic development between you and Parker. Can I be there when you tell him?"

"Please don't call Waylon lover boy."

"No?"

"It's complicated, I told you." I half pouted. "Because of my being a leanan and the sex, we have this physical connection. I'm under no illusion that it's going to be easy, but going away with him will do me good. Since my mother..." My voice broke.

"Yes, but your mother's death isn't the only reason you're going away with him, is it?"

Damn. Flo knew me far too well.

"My biological mother died for a cause she believed in." I swallowed hard. "No one knows more than me just how terrible some kin can be. The IEA is in the kinlords' pockets. Who will stand up to the Lathans? No." I shook my head. "Waylon can't do this alone."

"That sucks, but I get it. Doesn't hurt he's hot, though, right?"

I stretched to grab a bag of chips off the table and placed my head back on Florian's legs. "Actually, right now that totally blows. Life would be a lot easier if he was ugly." I chuckled. "He's dealt The Circle a serious blow, so he's giddy as all hell about that. Worried about me, too, apparently. Gave me strict instructions not to get into any more trouble."

"You took pretty good care of yourself. I should have said that earlier. Sorry." Flo rewound the Blue-ray to a particularly sappy scene which had caught his interest, and shifted the box of tissues closer.

The doorbell rang. Already? I swung my legs over and got up.

"Ivy, can I talk to you?" Parker's head popped through the open door to my yard.

Hovering between speaking to Parker and answering the door bell, I did a two-step shuffle.

"I'll get the front. You two talk." Flo ambled into the corridor.

Dammit. I'd been putting this conversation off. Parker knew I was leaving soon, of course, but I hadn't given him a date. Each time I was about to mention it, my heart got one step closer to bursting.

"Hi." I gave a small wave. "Come in, Parker."

"Flo said you're leaving today."

"Oh, is it Flo now?" I mellowed my smart-ass reply with a smile. "Yes. I told you about my deal with Waylon. He got to pick the date."

"I see," he said. No anger, no joy. His emotions were suddenly as guarded as his face.

I licked my lips. "You know, I'm sorry for every stupid thing I've done, and grateful for all the wonderful things you've done."

"I know." His nose flared. "But you understand that when the pack find out you left me, you could be jeopardizing my position as alpha."

As if I didn't guilt out over this enough. "Why? It's like I'm away for work."

He led me to the sofa. "These rituals are important to us. To the pack it looks as if we're stomping all over tradition."

My gaze on the ground, I swallowed. "This is something I have to do. What my parents wanted me to do. I didn't mean to cause trouble." My finger traced an invisible line along his cheek. Shit. I snapped my hand back and curled it into a ball. "You can tell them we're having a long-distance relationship."

His emotions rolled into me, something bitter and… I couldn't put my finger on it.

"Maybe it's for the best," he said.

My mouth went dry. "Yeah. And maybe," I breathed through the sudden pain in my chest, "you should spend some time with Heidi. I think she likes you."

His expression darkened.

"Ivy?" Flo's amped-up voice galloped into the living room. "Waylon's getting antsy."

I took Parker's hand between mine. "Take care of Flo for me, will you?"

He nodded solemnly. "Of course."

I jerked up off the sofa and grabbed my packed suitcase. "I'll call sometimes, if that's okay."

"Sure."

We inched toward the door, neither of us in a hurry. I coughed. "I'm taking my cell. So you could call me, too."

"I will." His voice hitched.

Waylon waited in his car, probably to let me say my goodbyes in peace. When did he become Mr. Tact? I smiled at him then turned back to Parker.

"Most of all, take care of yourself." I flung my arms around his neck, drew his scent into me. The pressure in my lungs forced itself into my head, threatening tears.

"Ivy." His tone sent shivers down my spine.

I brushed my finger over his lip to stop him from saying any more. Yet a whole different conversation took place in the fleeting moment our eyes met.

Flo tapped my shoulder and gathered me into a hug. "Write to me," he mumbled into my hair. "All the time, okay? And bring me back some goodies from your travels. And don't forget Julia's birthday party. And don't worry about the business. Fred and I will take care of it. And Ivy?"

I glanced up.

"I'll miss you."

"I'll miss you, too, you goof."

I tossed my suitcase onto the back seat and joined Waylon in the front.

"Hey, babe." His grin was way too sexy for my mood.

I clenched my jaw. "Just drive."

He started the car, put the gear into reverse and pulled out onto the road. I hunched in silence, dealing with the growing distance from my home and friends. We left the woodlands far behind, where the roads widened and the family homes turned into farms. I wiped at my eye to soothe the burn.

"I might have the perfect plan," Waylon said. "First we'll fuck for three days, then have a hearty breakfast, and finally catch ourselves some bad guys."

He did *not* just say that. A renewed flame blazed in my belly. I slapped the door panel and straightened. "Stop the car."

"What?"

"Stop the car."

The Honda skidded and screeched to a halt. He frowned. "What's wrong? Did you forget something?"

I turned to him and cursed my quickening pulse. God, I liked him. But did I have a future with him? My thoughts, almost by default, shot to a pair of gold-flecked eyes that had a completely different hold on me. As long as my connection to Parker was this strong, I didn't know if I was able to have a relationship with Waylon, even if I could overlook his manipulations.

I balled my fists. "I can't do this."

"What?"

"I can't go with you." I raised my arm. "Let me finish. I can't leave my friends. You can train me, and I want you to, but here in Silverton."

His hands tightened around the steering wheel. "That's crazy. Trouble doesn't concentrate in Silverton, you know."

I swallowed. "I get we'll have to travel, but for now, I'm staying." I straightened. "Please turn around."

"The hell I will." He bit his lip, but his hunched shoulders told me he was tense to bursting. "You're having cold feet. That will settle."

I opened the door and stepped out. "No, it won't. And I'm not going to have sex with you again. If you want to train me, you'll know where I am." I grabbed my bag from the rear seat and stalked off.

Parker was the man I wanted. No point fooling myself any longer. He was my antidote to Waylon.

Of course I had no clue if he was even remotely interested in me. My behavior hadn't always endeared me to him. Crap, I wasn't even sure if *I* could be with anyone as obstinate and overprotective as a werewolf. But the idea of not being around him, not letting his aura soothe me, not gazing into those eyes again, hammered my heart into tiny pieces.

Behind me, Waylon's car stayed in its spot. Was he going to come to his senses and drive me home? It hardly mattered. I'd walk the entire way if I had to.

Around the bend, the road home stretched on forever. A few cars whooshed by too close to where I was walking, but the fire inside me drove me on. Would Parker be angry at me for leaving? Glad I'd come back? No point wondering how Heidi would greet me, although her crush didn't strike me as an insurmountable obstacle. I stopped in my tracks. Still, I'd put Parker through so much.

My bag slipped from my quivering fingers, and I bent to pick it up. Was I making an idiot out of myself?

An engine whirred. A car veered toward me and came to a halt, wheels spinning on the asphalt. What a jerk. I straightened and glared.

My chest tightened around my lungs. I knew that BMW.

Parker threw open the door and got out. His determined chin and quick, powerful gait stole my breath. Oh God. He was here. He'd come after me. Something inside me lifted and fluttered. Perhaps my heart.

He stepped close, his eyes glistening. "Ivy."

I shook my head. No words were necessary.

He squeezed his mouth onto mine. His electric touch infused my spine with tremor after tremor. My whole being came alive. His hands roamed my body and lit small fires everywhere.

This was right. I belonged in his arms. He growled, his hot breath filling my lungs. My hands, quivering with need, forced him nearer. He whispered my name, rolled it in his throat, before delivering it in a low, rumbling voice. A voice that drove me wild. My lungs couldn't keep up. Sipping for air, I dislodged myself from his arms.

Parker held my face between both hands. "What about Greg? And Waylon? Because I couldn't stand it if—"

"History."

"Are you certain about this?"

I gave a resolved nod. "Absolutely." I turned my gaze back onto the road behind. Waylon hadn't followed. Soon enough he'd change his mind and train me. He had no choice. Neither had I. I glanced up at Parker's moist lips, which were caught in a wide smile. A smile so tender, it extinguished all doubt.

Being a Guardian was my future. But Parker was my now.

THE END

AUTHOR BIO

CARMEN LIVES IN THE SOUTH of England with her beloved tea maker and a stuffed sheep called Fergus. An avid reader since childhood, she caught the writing bug when her Nana asked her to write a story for her. She spends what little spare time her social media accounts allow on various niches of geekdom, among them tabletop games, fantasy books, comics and physics. You can find her at www.carmen-fox.com.

BOOKS

Her urban fantasy, *Divide and Conquer*, is available now. Interested? Here comes the blurb.

Two women. One prophecy. Zero places to hide.

FLUNG FROM HER MUNDANE SEATTLE existence into a world of magic, scientist Lea struggles to make sense of a destiny she doesn't want. The moment she finds comfort in the arms of a man who appreciates her inner nerd, a new magic sweeps the realms.

Nieve, Lea's instructor, may be seasoned in the art of war, but she's clueless when it comes to romance. To save her world, she allies herself with her enemy, a kindred warrior soul, who leaves no doubt he's after more than her cooperation.

As each tick of the clock swallows another person's memory, Lea and Nieve will do anything to hang on to theirs, but betrayal drives a wedge in their friendship. Can they reconcile and rally the troops before the magic wipes out their pasts?